Emily Slapper grew up in Northampton before studying Cinema and Photography at the University of Leeds.

After graduating she moved to London to work in advertising whilst hoping to one day become a screenwriter. But wanting to write films turned into wanting to write books and so she started a Creative Writing MA at Royal Holloway.

In her spare time she loves walking around South East London with her dog, Tina.

Also by Emily Slapper
Everyone I Know is Dying

IT MIGHT NEVER HAPPEN

EMILY SLAPPER

ONE PLACE. MANY STORIES

HQ
An imprint of HarperCollins*Publishers* Ltd
1 London Bridge Street
London SE1 9GF

www.harpercollins.co.uk

HarperCollins*Publishers*
Macken House, 39/40 Mayor Street Upper
Dublin 1, D01 C9W8, Ireland

This edition 2025

1
First published in Great Britain by HQ,
an imprint of HarperCollins*Publishers* Ltd 2025

ISBN (HB): 9780008629175
ISBN (TPB): 9780008629182

Set in Bembo by HarperCollins*Publishers* India

Printed and bound in the UK using 100% Renewable
Electricity at CPI Group (UK) Ltd

This book contains FSC™ certified paper and other controlled sources to ensure responsible forest management.

For more information visit: www.harpercollins.co.uk/green

For my mum, Suzanne, and my dad, Gary.

★

(Look at these two.

Embracing in the navy light of an unknown room, as the person they know best slips away. Aware of what is happening and so, in a way, party to it. And yet. Yet. It is not something they want. They are only just finding out that what we want and what we need aren't always the same thing. They have been sure that their fate is in their own hands – they have been desperate to believe this – and now they are learning it is not.

They are teetering on the edge, close to finding the release that comes from falling off it. Into the chaos. Accepting the fact that good and bad things will happen. That things will go to plan and things will fall apart. Because now they know it's not always advisable to err on the side of caution. To plan for the worst. It is tiring to carry an open umbrella the whole time, and it makes us believe getting wet is the worst thing that could happen. Because otherwise why would we take the precaution?

This ending is a pivotal moment in Noa and Elliot's story. They are learning that tolerating our fear of the unknown is what gives our lives momentum. That struggling against uncertainty does more harm than good. That the world becomes difficult and scary when we shy away from risk. But how can that be? The opposite is true, surely!

Let's see, shall we. Let's watch with compassion and interest. How did they get here? Where will they go?)

1

Twenty-five years old

(Throughout her youth Noa looked sighingly, jealously at couples that seemed head-over-heels in love with each other. She wanted that so desperately she felt it physically in her heart. It seemed equally unlikely and likely that she would get to be in this type of relationship one day. But living without knowing which of the two possibilities would win out often felt unmanageable. For Noa, the process of turning uncertainty into hope – the best flavour of uncertainty – was how she coped with this. Unfortunately, to an untrained palate, hope and delusion are difficult to differentiate.)

Noa first met Louis on an app that Noa told people she'd deleted. And she had deleted it. Until she went to a boozy brunch with her friends and got the nicest photo of herself she'd ever seen. It was taken side-on. A candid. She was smiling at someone else, her brown hair looked unusually straight and uniform and it was tucked behind her ear so you could see the cool piercings she'd recently added in an attempt to seem more like the 'I'm not like other girls' girls. Her teeth looked straighter than they were and her vintage blazer made her seem fashionable in a way that she wasn't. Her jaw didn't even look doughy. She knew as soon as she saw it that it was the type of photo she'd been waiting for. Noa already had the one that shows you have friends, the one that shows you're down to earth, the one that shows you have a sense of humour, and now she had a royal flush: the one where you look good.

At first she told herself she was only on the app for the fleeting ego boost of a 'match', but then she saw Louis. His profile looked rushed, not thought through, like he'd made it at the pub one night for a laugh. Every photo showcasing an array of enticing traits: blonde pushed-back hair, square jawline, body like Ryan Gosling, bomber jacket, attractive friends. She swiped right and wasn't surprised when the 'You've got a match!' graphic didn't pop up. So when, two weeks later, it finally came up on her phone, she was already infatuated with him.

They started speaking and seeing each other and meeting up (when he was free). Full of anticipation and infatuation, she found herself eating less and a few weeks into seeing him her jeans were leaving less of a red mark on her waist at the end of the day. She put more effort into her appearance even when she wasn't seeing him: straightening her hair, painting her nails, wearing things other than a T-shirt and jeans. (Not one to usually care about how she looked to this extent, Noa always put time and effort into things that would best please and seduce each individual man.) After a while she was even finding it easier to be happy for her friends who posted photos of themselves in a European bar, holding champagne, the sun setting, left hand held delicately up to the camera, faces turned, beaming, towards the love of their life.

What Noa got from being with Louis was a notion of herself which she felt proud of. Louis seemed unattainable and had high and particular standards. He told Noa on their second date, 'I usually get with really skinny girls. My last girlfriend had an eating disorder.' Noa, filled with a confusing mixture of jealousy and compassion for the girl, responded eventually by looking down and saying, 'I'm so sorry.'

'No need to be sorry. I'm saying I liked it.' He tipped back his glass to finish off the dregs of his pint and then gestured to hers. 'Another?'

That night Noa had furiously bitched about him to her flatmate Elza.

'How weird, right? Who says something like that? Seems like she dodged a bullet there.'

'That's more than weird, Noa, that's psychopathic. Who the fuck would be glad their girlfriend has an eating disorder.' Elza had a way of asking questions without them ever being actual questions.

'Probably all men,' Noa said, rolling her eyes. Elza squinted at her, like she was trying to gauge something.

Over the years, Noa had watched her friends become (less discreetly) disapproving of her relationships. Of the men she chose, how she acted around them and how long the relationship dragged on. She hated it, she wanted to please her friends, she longed for the respect they had for each other. But it was impossible. Every man she dated seemed worse than the one before. It was only ever on reflection that Noa could see the problems with the man or the relationship or the things she'd put up with. She struggled to let go of this idea that The One was out there, waiting for her, as long as she tried hard enough to find him. (Searching for The One was what gave Noa hope, purpose, drive. It was what she hung on to in the dark. It protected her from the question that terrified her: *what if I end up alone?*) Every time something ended with a man, she looked at her broken self in the mirror and vowed not to be with someone like that again. She'd snottily cry to Elza and promise to choose more wisely next time.

But as the night after her second date with Louis wore on, and Noa's phone screen remained black, she felt something familiar happening in her brain. She felt herself deciding that she needed Louis and must do anything in her power to make him hers. When Elza offered her half a KitKat with her tea, she said no, and determination swelled in her chest.

She managed not to text him after that date, so when he messaged her eight days later (not that she was counting) Noa already felt like she was becoming the woman he wanted. She was aloof. And two pounds lighter. From then on they saw each other three times a week, which was shocking to her. Tangible proof that she was worth something.

Noa bought new, matching, lacy underwear and took photos to send to him. He would screenshot them and she would keep going back to look at the photos, zooming in on parts of her body trying to guess what bits he liked and didn't. The curve of her hip? Or was it despite that? Did he think her legs were womanly or stubby? Did he notice that she was on tiptoes trying to elongate herself? Did he like her face or should she have cropped it out?

Their relationship was consistently the same. Which meant that it was quite intense for the start of a relationship, but quite superficial for a more serious one. A few months in – and by her suggestion now 'unofficially exclusive' – they were still only meeting at the pub, going back to his to have sex, and then parting ways the next morning.

One evening Noa felt particularly impatient to do something about this and take it to the next level. It was cold and dark and Noa was pulling some straighteners slowly down the underneath layer of her hair when Elza walked in.

'Hey No, good day?'

'Yeah thanks, I'm going to see Louis. What about you?' Noa said, going over the same piece of hair again.

'No, I'm not going to see Louis tonight actually.' She gave Noa a funny little smile and got a laugh back.

Noa could feel Elza's eyes on her. 'What's up? Do I look weird or something?'

'Don't get me wrong, you look beautiful with your hair straightened. . .'

Noa immediately caught Elza's eyes through the mirror (not hiding her intense concern terribly well). 'But what?'

'I didn't say "but".'

'Yeah, come on, there's no "don't get me wrong" without a "but".'

'Okay, you're right, there is a but. . . A big one.' Elza walked over and slapped Noa on the bum and they both laughed. Although Noa couldn't help a quick look down to reassess the size of it.

Elza ran her fingers through Noa's hot hair as if analysing it. 'I guess it would be nice to have it natural for once.' She looked at Noa through the mirror again but this time her expression was serious.

'Yeah, so, that's a nice idea in theory. But in reality my hair comes out to here.' Noa gestured the width of her shoulders.

'It's only in the harmful ideology that's pushed upon us from a young age that the Eurocentric style of long, straight, blonde hair is superior to anything else.' Elza rolled her eyes and walked away as if to give up. But Noa followed her into the kitchen.

'So what then? Just wear it all puffy and frizzy?'

'No babe, wear it how you like.' Elza started unpacking the food from her string shopping bag.

7

'Okay, yeah, obviously. But how would you wear it? Or like, can you expand a bit?' Noa squeezed sections of her hair nervously.

After Elza put the last thing away she turned to face Noa again. 'My beautiful friend Maureen has super curly hair and she has this specific routine for it.'

'I don't have curly hair.'

'Oh yeah? Well I'm not exactly an expert,' Elza said ruffling her short, black, shiny hair. 'But I'll see what I can remember.'

Elza took Noa into the bathroom and started washing her hair in the sink, carrying out some kind of routine using the random products they owned between them.

Noa, feeling giddy in the firm but careful hands of Elza, started chatting excitedly. 'So you know how you asked me the other day what I like about Louis? I've been thinking and I realised that I love how he's so driven. Like, at work right, he's been promoted twice in two years because he works these insane hours. And I told him he needs to take care of himself, and all he said was, "No matter how hard you work, someone else is always working harder." He says that to himself in the mirror every day, apparently.'

'Flip your head over.' Elza put conditioner through Noa's hair and dipped it back into the water in the sink, scrunching sections upwards with her hands.

Noa continued, 'I think that's so inspiring. I can't relate at all. I just watch the clock, waiting for the day to end, y'know what I mean?'

Elza squeezed Noa's hair with an old T-shirt and then twirled sections around her finger. 'Yeah that is impressive in a certain way I guess, but I didn't know you cared about anything like that.'

'I didn't think I did either but seeing how much *he* cares about everything. Like, he goes to the gym five days a week even when he has the flu.'

'That doesn't sound healthy to—'

'It's not really about health though. It's about perseverance.'

Elza led Noa into her bedroom, ran out and came back in holding a sieve.

'What's that for?'

'I'm improvising.'

Elza proceeded to put parts of Noa's hair into the sieve, raised it towards her roots and then gently used a hairdryer underneath it.

Noa spoke loudly over the top of the noise: 'It's so motivating to me. Like the other day right, I wanted to get some M&Ms and he told me that looking healthy is much more satisfying in the long run than putting empty calories' – Elza turned off the hairdryer and Noa accidentally shouted the end of her sentence – 'into your body.'

There was a lull while Elza found some coconut oil and rubbed a tiny bit between her palms to work into Noa's hair. Elza's voice was soft when she finally spoke.

'I'm not even going to unpack what "looking healthy" means, but I have to ask: are these things even important to you? Before you met Louis all I heard you whine about was wanting someone to go to Paris and eat pastries with.'

'Yeah but that's—'

'I'm just saying it kinda sounds like you're retrospectively deciding Louis' personality is exactly everything you want in a man. If someone had described these traits to you before you'd met him, would you have found them so desirable?'

Noa felt her mood dropping fast. But before she could think of what to say, Elza passed her a make-up mirror. Soft, shiny chestnut curls framed Noa's face. She whipped around to look at Elza. 'What did you do?'

'Well, I mean. . . you were there? I just worked with your hair rather than against it.'

Noa gazed in the mirror again, twirling the ringlets around her finger. She felt emotional but before her mind could try to work out what kind of emotion that was, she was wondering what Louis would think.

Unfortunately for Noa, he did not mention the new hair either way. She sat there at the pub, listening to him chat about Paleo, flicking her hair around and zoning out. She felt awful and that quickly turned into a kind of desperation to feel something good. To hear him say she was pretty or perfect or everything he ever wanted. They went back to his flat – as usual – and after having sex they lay facing each other in his low, wide bed. Noa's sense of emptiness was growing.

But then Louis said, 'Did you curl your hair?'

Noa perked up. Ready to absorb and store away the whole conversation. 'Well, no, it turns out it's naturally curly.'

He stroked her hair and she closed her eyes automatically to intensify the feeling of his touch.

'It's not naturally curly though, is it? I've never seen it curly.'

'That's cause I straighten it.'

'Yeah but when you're here in the morning it's natural, right? And it's more like. . . poofy.' He flicked her hair.

'It's hard to explain but you have to do this whole routine and then it goes curly.'

'Well it's not natural then, is it?'

Noa pulled her chin back to look at her hair lying on the pillow. She considered the statement. 'I guess you're right.'

'I'm always right,' he said, pushing himself out of bed. He walked into his en suite calling out, 'I prefer it when it's straight.'

Noa jumped out of bed and followed him into the bathroom. Hugging his torso while he washed his face.

'Why?'

'I just like it better that way. People have preferences.'

'What if I said I would prefer it if you had a shaved head?' Noa spoke in a playful tone and reached up to ruffle his hair, semi-solid from the V05 Matt Clay.

He flattened it back down. 'Well, I don't shave my hair so I would tell you to do one.'

Noa waited until he rinsed his face and then turned him to face her. She wanted to say, *You've made me feel like I have to straighten my hair for you to find me attractive* but instead she said, 'I guess I won't wear it curly again then.' She did her best puppy-dog eyes.

'Noa, come on, don't be like this.' He flattened her hair between his palms and tried to press the curls out. 'What I'm saying is you're perfect as is. My type is brunette, tanned, short girls, straight hair, big brown eyes. That kind of thing.'

'Quite specific then,' she said, making a mental note of the words he'd said. Especially 'perfect' and 'my type'.

'That's a normal amount of specificity, I'd say. And if they've got all that, I don't even mind a bigger nose.' He tapped the end of Noa's nose, kissed her on the forehead, picked her up by the waist, spun her around and placed her down behind him. Her body and mind felt unsteady, in a good way, she decided.

★

It was the next day and Noa was standing in Louis' hallway inspecting her nails to see if there was anywhere left she could bite. The sound of a key in the front door made her jump and suddenly she worried she had done a bad thing. She lunged for the door and opened it before he could get there himself. Louis' keys hung, jangling, from the outside lock. Noa removed them and held her hands out in the air.

'Surprise!'

Louis stared at the keys as it they would explain something to him.

'What's the surprise?'

'Surprise – I'm still here! I didn't leave!'

Louis looked down at nothing, considering something. 'What's that to do with the keys?'

'The keys?' Noa looked at them in her hand. 'Nothing?' She moved to the side and he walked past her and into his bedroom. He came out a few minutes later wearing Nike joggers and a vest and walked straight into the kitchen leaving Noa – again – standing alone in the hallway playing with the keys mindlessly.

'Shall I leave?' she called eventually. Louis came out of the kitchen as far as the doorway and leaned against its frame.

'You don't have to leave.'

(Some people's hearts would have sunk at this, reading into it all kinds of passive meanings but. . .) Noa's shoulders dropped and her face relaxed into a smile. She put the keys down and walked over to him and pulled his hips towards hers, whispering in his ear, 'I knew you had that stressful meeting today and I thought I could help.'

He pushed her shoulders gently back so he could look at her face. 'It wasn't a stressful meeting, Noa, it was a meeting I have every Friday with my team.'

'But you said you were exhausted?' Her eyes turned big and soft and she squeezed past him and guided them both into the kitchen. Laid out on his faux-granite worktop was some mince, chopped tomatoes, various vegetables, a pre-made chilli spice pack, guacamole, sour cream, cheddar, microwave rice, Doritos and salsa. 'I bought ingredients for chilli!'

Louis picked up the crisps and put them down again. 'Looks like you bought dinner for five.'

Noa had started with just the basics in her basket. But she kept picturing handing the bowl of chilli to Louis and wasn't satisfied until the imaginary dish had all the trimmings. It put her over her weekly budget, but she didn't mind. She loved doing things for the people she cared about. And besides, she imagined (optimistically) that maybe next week she'd only want to eat a plain chicken breast and broccoli every night. And maybe Louis would make her dinner in return. That was the kind of thing she wanted more than anything in the world.

'Well, yeah, I thought you could freeze some?'

'That's very sweet of you.' He kissed her on the head and poured himself a glass of water. After downing it and filling it back up again he said, 'But I've got people coming round tonight.' Noa felt herself turning red.

'That's cool,' she said in a chirpy voice. 'You can use the ingredients another time anyway.' She spun around and walked into the bedroom to collect herself, hoping he would follow her. But he didn't. She packed her bag, slowly, just in case.

Once she had gathered everything she stood in the little laminate hallway and smiled sweetly at Louis. All she wanted was to be his official girlfriend, to cook him dinner, to attend and host parties with him, to wait for him at home after a long day. But no. Not yet,

13

she told herself. She stood on her tiptoes and kissed his little mouth. He kissed her back and then she kissed him and he kept kissing her. Noa's tote bag dropped off her shoulder and she tried to catch it unnoticeably in the crook of her arm, desperately not wanting the moment to end.

And it didn't. He picked her up and she wrapped her legs around his waist. She worried for a moment that he would find her heavy but then pushed the thought away, focusing instead on the fact she was basically living in a romcom (rom is generous, com is ludicrous).

Even after the three months they'd been together, Noa was still surprised she could give such an attractive man an erection. Seeing it there, defined under his joggers felt like someone was calling her beautiful. He put his hand down her tights and touched her through her pants. This gave Noa a thrill. She liked the idea of the slowness, of taking time to get to the main event. But before she could relax into the feeling he moved the material to the side and mashed his finger around looking for the magic spot. She realised, with a pang of guilt, that she had done nothing more than place a limp hand on his covered penis. Horrified, she progressed them onto taking their clothes off. Trying to do it as sensually as she could, she trailed her fingers up his body while removing his vest but he took it as incompetence and pulled it off it himself.

Both naked, he tried again to prepare her by doing something she could only guess he'd learned simply by hearing the phrase 'flicking the bean'. Trying to work out for a second where that phrase had come from – considering the fact that this made her want to squeeze her legs together – she realised she'd left the moment and told herself to refocus. But it was fine because he was already reaching for some lube.

Once he was inside her she tried to work out the sexiest way a woman could act in missionary. She tried grabbing his back but she couldn't get this image out of her head: a clip from a sitcom where a man tells a woman that having sex with her is like having sex with a 'dead horse'. Noa tried to thrust her hips a bit but Louis stopped and looked confused. She put that memory in a box she'd try not to open ever again (but would in fact open many, many more times).

Noa tried to manoeuvre Louis underneath her without them separating. It didn't work out so she pulled herself together and straddled him, guiding him inside her. Louis moved his hands over her hips and she boxed up that memory in order to revisit any time she worried he wished she was less curvy. (Unfortunately though, the recollection would never reassure her.)

Once she got into the swing of things, he spoke: 'Tell me you like it.'

Thrilled for some direction, she – accidentally – cleared her throat and said, 'I like it?'

'What do you like?'

'I like. . . your hard dick. . . inside me?'

Noa closed her eyes, replaying the inquiring tone of her voice. But Louis groaned. She opened her eyes and tried again. 'It feels so good. . . your dick.' He groaned again and she felt a small pleasurable contraction inside her. She did a porn-y imitation moan to communicate this but Louis didn't seem to notice that it was feigned. He made a lower, longer noise this time which trailed off into an exhale. He was back in the room.

Louis popped Noa off him, and cupping his penis, walked into the en suite. Noa listened to the shower turn on and flopped onto her back. A smile crept across her face.

After a minute she got up, cleaned herself in the main bathroom and re-dressed. By the time she was back in his bedroom he was climbing into some fresh Calvin Kleins.

'You can stay for the thing tonight if you like.'

Noa wished she was looking into his eyes when he said it, rather than at his pert little butt, so she could gauge his sincerity. But it didn't matter, a glow of happiness was warming her already pink cheeks.

'Okay, thanks.' She grabbed her make-up bag and hopped back into the bathroom.

Something inside Noa told her not to ask anything about the event but to take it as it comes. So by the time fifteen people had arrived she was feeling surprised and a bit put out. There didn't seem to be a particular event being celebrated and there was certainly no limit on guests. She told herself it didn't matter, he had invited her now and that was the main thing. Her nervous energy propelled her to flit around, washing up glasses and asking people if they wanted another drink. She could feel Louis watching her sometimes and decided it was because he felt so grateful for everything she was doing.

She didn't dwell too much on the fact he was introducing her simply as 'Noa' until Sandrine arrived. Sandrine was a beautiful French girl who Louis mentioned in his anecdotes sometimes. She arrived holding a bottle of 'natural' wine with a cool illustrated label. At least three people tried to speak to her as she went to the kitchen to put it down. Even in her big trench coat she looked slim and chic. Noa took in her plain outfit: mid-wash blue jeans, little black boots, navy woollen jumper. She pictured herself in it and decided she would look plain and outdated. Sandrine, on the other hand, looked like an off-duty model. If models could be five foot four.

Louis went to stand behind Sandrine and squeezed her. She turned around and slapped him. 'Louis! Please.' Her French accent was like treacle. Noa took a deep breath in and went to stand next to Louis.

'Hey!' Noa said to both of them.

Louis moved next to Sandrine and put his arm around her shoulder.

'Noa, this is my greatest friend – Sandrine.' He squeezed her towards him. 'Sandrine, this is Noa.' He pointed to Noa.

Sandrine wriggled free and kissed Noa on both cheeks and then the original cheek again. Her silky, straight brown hair smelt like apples. 'It is lovely to meet you, Noa.'

'It's nice to meet you too. I've heard loads about you.' Noa waited for Sandrine to say the same back but she didn't. Instead, Louis guided her away by the small of her back and Noa collapsed to the floor crying, internally. Externally, she went to sit on the toilet and picked at her nails. She just needed Louis to remember how well they went together and then he would forget about the pretty, sweet French girl.

She'd made him like her before and she could do it again. She thought back to their first date at a pub in Islington. It was so lovely, he'd explained Management Consultancy to her and laughed when she'd said, 'But can't they just work out all that stuff themselves for free?' He'd also laughed when she'd explained that the reason she didn't go to the gym was because, 'I'm severely allergic to moving my body around at fast speeds.' Louis had put his hand on her knee and told her she should try weights. She also remembered, after they'd had sex that night, how she couldn't help staring into his eyes, brown and earnest, and telling him he should consider part-time modelling. He'd rolled his eyes but she could see that he loved it.

Noa knew what she had to do. As she was leaving the bathroom she saw his deodorant on the side and sprayed a little 'pfft' under her T-shirt in case it would subconsciously alert people to her and Louis' togetherness.

Noa headed straight over to the kitchen where Louis was chatting to his friends Scott, Johnno and of course, Sandrine. She poured herself a large cup of the fancy wine. Delicious, naturally.

Noa laughed along with a joke she didn't hear. 'What are you guys talking about?'

Sandrine touched Noa's forearm and explained, 'We were saying how the English view cooking as chores, so then of course you will end up making pasta from a tin sauce!' She removed her hand and Noa felt like Sandrine was the most attractive person she'd ever met.

Johnno joined in. 'You can't go wrong with a Dolmio, sorry not sorry.'

'Dolmio? What's this?' Sandrine asked, pushing her perfectly arched eyebrows together.

'It's like an Italian pre-made pasta sauce we have,' Louis explained.

Sandrine chuckled. 'Italians don't use that. They use fresh. Every day.'

Noa jumped in: 'Once I tried to make pasta sauce from scratch and it was so bad, like inedible bad. I couldn't have told you what I'd done wrong. Until about a week later, when my flatmate asked where the ketchup was and I said I'd used it all up in pasta the other day. Turns out ketchup isn't a substitute for passata.' Noa shrugged her shoulders. '*That's* why we need Dolmio.'

Everyone laughed and Noa could see Louis noticing and laughing more himself. She felt her best self. 'I've seen what you cook though, Louis, and you must be the exception to the rule.

You might as well be European. Everything's always so fresh and healthy and tasty.'

She kept going like this, making self-deprecating jokes, and then finding a way to compliment Louis or ask him to explain something to her. Within an hour he was standing next to her and even said something which made it clear they were seeing each other.

'Noa here,' he said with his hand on her head, 'wanted to cook for me tonight. She went and bought enough to feed a small family and then surprised me when I got home. Luckily I've heard that pasta story now, before anything actually happened.'

Sandrine beamed at them. 'Aw, Louis. It is lovely to see. So you've both given keys, it's serious, no?'

Louis turned to look Noa in the eyes, lowering his eyebrows, 'Well, no. . . actually. I haven't. How did you go shopping and come back without keys?'

'Oh. Well. I just. . . left the door on the latch and then when I got back I waited outside the building until someone else was going in.'

There was a pause and Noa's whole body tensed. The conversation moved on but Noa knew she was in trouble. She kept smiling but could barely speak. She could feel Louis' anger burning next to her.

After excusing herself, Noa went to sit on Louis' bed and racked her brains on what to do. But it wasn't long until he silently joined her.

She opened her mouth but he spoke over her, 'Never. Ever. Put my property in jeopardy like that again.'

Noa's eyes welled up and she tried to speak but he spoke over her again. 'Ever.'

Louis stood up and re-joined the party and Noa cried silently into her hands. Her mind quivered, terrified that she might end up alone again and she bit her lip vowing not to let that happen. (Anxiety often choosing the wrong thing to protect us from.)

Noa and Louis didn't break up then. Or after the next argument. Or the one after that. But anytime things were going well and he said, for instance, 'You look nice today', Noa would take this to mean, 'You look like Sandrine today.' Anytime they would argue and he said, for instance, 'I don't like it that you cry so often', Noa would take this to mean, 'Sandrine would never cry so much.' It goes without saying how Noa would take it when Louis said, 'Sorry I can't, I'm busy tonight.'

There was never a moment so bittersweet as the moment when Noa had proof something was wrong. It was standard procedure with the men she dated. It was a devastating relief to find out her concerns had been right. But it gave her something to present to the man, to use as leverage to recover power, receive sympathy. And most importantly, to get reassurance that she was The One. *Please forgive me!* she imagined them saying. *I will never do it again, you're the one that I want!* It was an escape from the hell which was the not knowing, the suspecting, the feeling like he was slipping away. It was sad, yes, but it was also the only thing that gave her control.

Their relationship dragged on (with neither of them particularly enjoying it) for another four months until Noa popped her AirPods into Louis' jacket pocket, tracked their location on her laptop and confirmed what she expected. He was lying to her.

The moment Louis confessed he had been going to Sandrine's flat, Noa felt the biggest rush of relief and anguish. The fact that she was right all along, the fact that the pain of the unknown was over, the fact that she could make him fight for her now, prove to her that the relationship meant something. These all felt like a corset being cut open. But then came the emptiness. The fact that this had happened again, the fact that she wasn't good enough for him, the fact that maybe if she'd tried even harder. . . (The real fact is she wasn't totally right, Sandrine was too content in her life to get with a man like Louis – an insecure man who wanted power over the women he was with – but that wasn't stopping him from trying.)

After she confronted him they argued for a while until Louis told Noa that he needed to go to sleep. She climbed in beside him, full of regret, too worried to cry, her brain buzzing with ways to make this all blow over. But a few minutes later she heard a bodiless voice.

'I think it would be best for you to leave.'

A few weeks later Noa lay on her side alone in the dark. Her face brightly illuminated by the phone she held barely 30 centimetres in front of her. She was waiting to see the date change to the one that had been creeping up on her. The date that she'd recently noticed food in her fridge went off after. The date she turned twenty-six. She knew it wasn't old and yet somehow it seemed more significant than her eighteenth or twenty-first. It felt like she had run out of excuses for being so disconnected from everything. Like she was floating above the world trying desperately to attach to something before it was too late. But she hadn't attached to anything or anyone. She'd frantically moved through university, jobs, relationships, trying to put things in place that would build a happy future. But now she had turned twenty-six, no one cared and she felt no further towards her dream life than when she was seventeen.

Her mum had sent her a voucher that could be spent at seemingly any shop in the UK – *Get something you want xx* – which took the impersonal nature of giving a voucher to new extremes. Elza had asked if Noa wanted to do anything, and when Noa told her that no, she didn't want to do anything, Elza had disappointingly taken that at face value.

She plopped her phone down on her bedside table and turned onto her back. An image appeared out of nowhere of her mum lying on her stomach in bed, her head turned out to face the blank wall, her hair limp and fallen across her face, her eyes glazed and only one of them blinking. Noa walking in with a cup of tea singing happy birthday. Her mum's gaze never leaving the blank wall. Noa sitting on the bed, moving the hair off her mother's face, seeing that some of it was in her open mouth.

'Happy birthday, Mum.'

'It's not your birthday if no one knows it is.'

'I know it's your birthday.'

'You don't count.'

And now, Noa, in her bed, alone, so alone, squirmed as if this was a premonition of her own life. The thought was hard to bear, she tried to look away from it but it only became stronger. Her mind developed the idea until it was less of a thought and more of a vision, fleshed out with details and feelings. Her heart cramped and she decided she wouldn't let things turn out like that. *Your life is in your own hands*, she told herself. It wouldn't be the first time she had put her mind to something and got what she wanted. Twenty-eight seemed like a good age to have found The One. She had two years to find someone who loved her. (It was the wrong thing to aim for, but she didn't know that yet.)

2

Twenty-five years old

Elliot sat on his bed, his body throbbing with fatigue and fear. He needed to work up the courage, psych himself up, but was reluctant to let his mind touch the thoughts and feelings he was always so careful to ignore. So instead, without attaching words to the image, he pictured his younger self, clammy with sweat, counting his numbers, and then, his more recent self from a few days before, walking fifty minutes to ScrewFix, practising normal expressions and excuses for needing to buy the rope he was holding.

Elliot always felt lucky that he didn't have time for thinking. He woke up, got himself and Willie ready for the day, and then went to work at the call centre, and by the time he'd come home and cooked dinner and done the day's chores, his mind was so achingly tired that he struggled not to fall asleep as he cleaned his teeth.

He felt lucky that he had managed to secure a Monday to Friday 9 to 5 schedule, when other people who worked at the call centre got unpredictable shift patterns given to them at the start of each month.

He felt lucky that instead of standing up all day behind a till he got to sit down and speak to people on the phone about TV aerials and satellites and CCTV systems, trying to sell them products (but often failing due to an overriding preference to not pressure strangers into parting with their money when they quite clearly didn't want to).

He felt lucky to have this job because for the first six years after sixth form he had drifted from retail job to retail job, struggling to help his brother feel safe in a routine when he didn't have one himself. Struggling to help his mum feel financially stable when he didn't himself. But this job at the call centre, that he felt lucky to have, offered him structure, the chance to earn up to £30,000 a year through commission (he never earned more than £18,000), and the opportunity to work in a fast-paced environment with a sociable group of young people.

As the main elements in Elliot's life started to feel less meandering and more permanent, a thought had been keeping him up at night: would he be able to get through the days if they were like this forever? Looking at the lives of those around him it seemed that the way people coped with this endlessness was by implementing weekly rituals. Pub trips and nights outs and more pub trips. So he tagged along. But that gradually made him feel worse. He didn't know how to act, he didn't know how to enjoy it. And the pretending was exhausting. The forcing himself to stay in his body, to listen to the things that people were saying and not become overwhelmed by the feeling of being alive in a room full of loud music and hard-to-hear conversations and strong tasting drinks and sticky floors and people's eyes slowly becoming unfocused or laser-focused on those around them.

He began struggling to get to sleep but waking up at 5 a.m. He found himself counting down the time in little increments *If I can just get through this. . .* crossing off each part of his day as if it were a to-do list. (But after a while, when your whole life is nothing but a to-do list, even the supposedly enjoyable parts, it becomes something you want to get to the end of.)

And suddenly (it wasn't suddenly) it became too much. In the small amount of free time he had, he lay in bed, his brain aching, trying to think of a way out. But he could only think of one way. Elliot considered telling someone, but what would he say? His life was no harder than anyone else's; in fact, he could mentally go through all the ways in which he was lucky. And so it was because of all this luck that he had decided to give himself one last shot at being alive.

His plan was to go out, act normal and try to have fun with the bubbly people he worked with. He would physically force himself to drink alcohol and talk to guys about sports and talk to girls about whatever you talk to girls about and laugh in group conversations and dance with the right amount of smile on his face. He would try as hard as he could to be like everyone else and then maybe he would feel like everyone else. And if that didn't work then he could be sure there was nothing left to try.

The night had gone as expected. It felt, uncomfortably, like the alcohol was absorbing into his bones, like it was poisoning his blood. The conversations had been exhausting and stilted, he hadn't known how to form facial expressions or which questions to ask and when they got to the club, huge and packed with people, he felt untethered, unable to move his feet up and down and up and down and up and down in the dance that everyone did, because his feet weren't on the ground. They were lifting, inch by inch, until finally he was above everyone's heads. He looked down at them all, now hovering under the two-storey high ceiling, watching everyone writhing and jerking and he felt like there was no one else in the world who felt this unable to integrate themselves. (Oh, Elliot. If only he knew.)

He blinked and was back on the dance floor. He needed to get out of there.

The next day Elliot sat hunched and motionless on his bed, trying to keep a blank mind while simultaneously trying to access the pain needed to go through with such a thing. He jumped at an unexpected chime from his laptop. Elliot (happy for a postponement) placed the rope he was loosely holding in both hands onto the floor, sat at his small desk, and clicked the button to light up the screen. It was a Facebook message. Dom.

> hi mate
> so random
> but do you work at teleforce?
> my mate said he works with an elliot wood

Elliot had watched the screen waiting for the next message to pop through but it didn't. That was it.

Elliot, shrugging, typed out a reply.

> yeah
> I do

He didn't know what else to say but his eyes were bulging with the fear that the conversation would end. He watched the screen desperately, a shard of hope inside him cracking as time passed. Then more messages popped up.

> sick
> It was Smithy btw
> Josh Smith?

we're going pub tonight
wanna come?

Elliot hadn't spoken to Dom since he was sixteen and he barely knew Josh. He couldn't get his head around this invitation. He clicked on Dom's profile and saw how rarely he was tagged in any pictures. And the few on there were unfussy, bright, unplanned, photos where you could see his faintly yellow teeth or acne-scarred skin. They made Elliot smile and he read the messages again. (What had always drawn Elliot towards Dom was the simplicity of him. It felt straightforward, like there was nothing to read between the lines or communicate subtly himself.) His throat scratched with emotional relief as he accepted the invitation, deciding *this* would be the last chance.

And so he went to the pub. Elliot was early but Dom was already sitting there with a pint when he arrived. Dom looked like the most neutral person Elliot could imagine. Clothes: not too trendy, not too outdated. Hair: strawberry blonde and short but not styled. Expression: neither contemplative nor gormless. Elliot swelled with gratitude for his company.

'Elliot, mate. Good t'see you again.' Dom grabbed Elliot's hand and slapped his back with the other.

'Cheers, mate. You too.' And he meant it, almost grinning at hearing Dom's strong Stokie accent.

When Elliot came back with his pint, Dom said, 'So you still live in Stoke then? Never moved out?'

'Nah, always been here.'

'I'd thought you'd leave, to be honest. You happy here then?'

Elliot was taken aback by the probing. He'd barely taken a sip of his pint. He said the only thing that he could think of: 'Yeah.'

There was a pause and Elliot wondered if the conversation would flow or if they would struggle to find stuff to talk about. He remembered one of the things he'd planned on the walk over to say if there was a silence.

'So what have you been up to? Since I last saw you.'

Dom's pale eyes lit up and he started laughing.

'Mate, I haven't seen you in ten years. Where d'you want me to begin?' Dom was cracking himself up. 'I guess if we're looking at this from a "what have I spent *most time* doing" angle then probably: brushing my teeth, cooking tea, taking a dump. That kind of thing.'

Elliot was smiling but not laughing. 'Is that right? Well, you'll be happy to find out we've still got a lot in common then.'

'What have *you* been up to these ten years then? Cos it certainly ain't going through puberty.'

They both laughed (the teasing based on nothing and therefore easy to take) and finally relaxed into things. They spoke about football. Elliot showed him his ankle, blue and swollen from when he twisted it on a night out. Dom said it must have been a 'mad one.' Elliot said yes, because it was mad, in a way, but Dom didn't need to know he sprained it frenziedly sprinting the half an hour walk home. Dom showed him on Facebook that Joe from school had become some kind of professional bodybuilder and they laughed at his fake tan and tiny pants (but as two waifs they couldn't help having a secret envious wave of admiration).

And then Smithy came. They'd met a couple of times when Elliot had been called into the main office to talk about the quality of his phone calls (too 'half-hearted', not 'sticking to the script enough'). And so Elliot wasn't thrilled to see him again, but as the three of them got into the swing of things he found himself laughing

28

for the first time in months without having to pretend. There was still the sore, tender coating to his brain. But his feet felt solid on the ground. His thighs heavy on the squeaky pub banquette. The conversation easy and clunky. The windows steaming with the heat of the pub.

Eventually, when they were playing pool and the conversation lulled, Smithy said, 'You like it in Sales then?'

Elliot exhaled. 'I'm shit at it. I constantly want to tell people they don't have to buy it if they don't want to. I hate it.' It was thrilling to say something true.

'You should apply for a job in back office then. There's something going in Logistics. Your breaks aren't timed and you've got no targets, so in my mind it's a lot better.'

Dom broke in, 'Honestly though, forget sales a sec. What do you actually want to *do*?'

Elliot's body tensed, 'What d'you mean?'

'Just like, we all hate our jobs. That's standard. But right now I'm saving to visit my half-brother in Australia. It's gonna be class. That's the important shit.'

Elliot pretended to line up a shot to give himself time to think. Once he'd potted a red he tried to say as casually as possible, 'Ah, y'know. Just staying here helping my mum out and that.'

'Nice, nice.' Dom scratched his head and looked off into the distance for a second and then said, 'But like, not real-life stuff. What's your *dream*?'

Smithy was busy walking around the pool table so Elliot couldn't deflect the question to him. 'I dunno, I've got too much on, to be honest.'

Dom shrugged. 'Aw c'mon, dreams are free. You might as well have one.'

Elliot was angry that the light feeling he had recently acquired was being replaced by a heavier one. He couldn't think of anything to say so he shrugged and lined up another shot.

Dom's voice turned slightly earnest. 'It's easy to end up pissing your life away is all. I've seen it happen plenty of times.'

Elliot potted two more reds before he spoke. 'So is that what I'm doing? Pissing my life away?'

'Well, you already told me you spend a good amount of time on the toilet.' Elliot could see Dom smiling and trying to catch his eye. He couldn't help the sides of his mouth pushing up but the lightness had gone.

Elliot won the game of pool, mainly through pure desperation for it to end, and then rushed off.

Elliot thought frustratedly about what Dom had said as he strode home through the sharply cold air. He wished he'd stood up for himself. Told him that life wasn't so simple. He had to look after his brother, and anyway, trying to do something else was futile and selfish. He knew that one day he would have to be Willie's full-time carer. And so what was the point in setting up a life that didn't account for that? He had to choose this life. It was a comforting thought.

When Elliot got into his room that night he felt embarrassed at the sight of the rope on his floor. He sat on his bed and looked up at the single bulb light and the otherwise empty ceiling and he felt like a fraud. What was his plan? Who was he performing this for? He heard Willie moving around downstairs and kicked the rope under his bed. He would never have left Willie like that. His eyes burned with shame.

★

On Saturdays Elliot had a lot to do. It was a day to reset the house and prepare for the upcoming week. His mum worked on the weekends because that's when Elliot didn't work, so the house was his territory. In between helping Willie through his routines he stuck in his headphones and cleaned and wrote lists and prepared meals. Not an extraneous thought passed through his brain.

By 5 p.m. fatigue kicked in strong. He took himself up to bed to have a break. As thoughts threatened to sneak into consciousness, Elliot found himself fidgeting. Turning on his side, jigging his leg, turning on his back, clicking the joints in his fingers, turning on his other side, chewing on his nail. Eventually, restless, he got up and sat at his desk instead. Without thinking he rolled back on the wheelie chair over to his chest of drawers and reached his hand underneath. Muscle memory let him find the exact place of the notebook and pull it out and throw it on his desk. It was dusty and made him uneasy to look at. Before he could bring himself to open the book, it dawned on him that he was still feeling defensive at what Dom had implied (a relief – because who among us doesn't find defensiveness a more comfortable state than hopelessness?). What was wrong with looking after your family anyway? Why was that pissing your life away?

Elliot's phone alarm went off, got up, slid the book back under, and went downstairs. It was time to get Willie his tea.

He took the brown-and-yellow floral plate out of the fridge, over to the kitchen worktop and took the clingfilm off the pre-made sandwich. But instead of taking it straight in, he took out the large chunks of cheese and cut them into flatter pieces, making sure they covered the whole bread right up to the crust. He went to the fridge to find some Branston Pickle but it was out of date by two years. So instead he found a reasonably firm tomato and sliced it up, trying a bit first to make sure it was all right, before layering it on top of the cheese. He wanted to sprinkle on a bit of salt and pepper but he could only find a solidified pot of Lo Salt.

In the living room Willie was watching a YouTube video about wildlife.

'Is that my tea?' Willie said, glancing rapidly at the plate and pointing at it.

'It sure is.' Elliot looked at his older brother and pushed down the unfurling guilt in his chest. He spent a second looking at Willie, noticing how much weight he'd put on in only a couple of years and – more importantly – how his trademark fizzing energy and passion seemed replaced by a stillness and rigidity.

Elliot sat down on the wine-coloured sofa next to Willie, fitting neatly into the completely flattened part of the cushion where people had sat on it for many years. He passed the plate over.

'What is this? Where is my sandwich?' Willie's hands linked above his head and his eyes darted around the room.

'That *is* your sandwich, Will.'

'No no no no no. This is not my sandwich. No no no no no.'

Willie screwed up his face and started humming. 'Hmm. Hmm. Hmm. Hmm. Hmm. Hmm.' Tapping his hands on his knees and rocking back and forth.

Elliot's stomach contracted one belt notch further and he froze for a second before kicking back into action. 'Shit, sorry. I don't know what I was thinking. I guess I just wanted to. . .' He stopped speaking because he had no words to finish the sentence with. 'I'll go make it again now.'

He walked back into the kitchen. He'd known that Willie wouldn't like this sandwich so why had he made it like that? (If you do the same nice things every single day – things you should be proud of, things that are having huge impacts on other people's lives – then it is hard to find the same sparkling pride you get from doing something out of the ordinary. But Elliot could never do a spontaneously nice thing for Willie, so fulfilment was hard to come by.)

Instead of answering this thought, he ground his teeth and unfolded the sandwich. Seeing it was soggy and beyond repair he threw it into the bin with as much force as he could, but a tomato slice got awry and sludged its way down the side of the bin. Elliot took another long breath in, and tried to recall if he was even breathing in the time between these deep inhales. He pressed his fingertips hard into his closed eyes and swallowed and then remade the sandwich like it was originally.

For the rest of the day Elliot worked at being the best son and brother he could. He decided that he would never let those melancholy feelings get out of control again. He'd lost sight of what was important in life. There was no reason to feel sorry for himself. He was lucky. Lucky to have a family, a stable job, a roof over his head, a purpose in life and maybe even a new friend.

When Elliot eventually heard his mum's car mount the kerb outside he took himself upstairs.

Before his mind could think anything he sat at his desk, rolled back, reached for the notebook and placed it before him again. Looking at it gave him a deep and awful feeling that he didn't want to unpack. But nostalgic curiosity made him open it. The red biro scrawl – *Please make Fraser my friend. Please make Fraser my friend. Please make Fraser my friend. Please make Fraser my friend* – covering the page was so shocking that his eyes widened. He closed the book as softly as he'd opened it and held it in his hands, not quite sure what to do.

Just then his mum's shrill voice called up: 'Elliot, what were you thinking with poor Willie's sandwich?'

The feeling from earlier flooded into his chest again. Elliot placed the book back down and opened it to an empty page, grabbed a pen without even having to look for the mug which held them. In the same spiky handwriting as all those years ago he began: *Please keep Willie safe. Please keep Willie safe. Please keep Willie safe.* He wrote it five times, fifteen times, and then once more. Embarrassed, he went to rip it out. But a thought unsettled him. What if ripping it out would somehow cause the opposite of what he'd written to happen? He shuddered and returned the book to its place.

Elliot managed to get on with things as the days and weeks and months repeated themselves. It wasn't just that he now had a friend in Dom (it was) but also he felt a sense of acceptance. There was no alternate life out there for him, this was it and he wouldn't resist it any longer.

3

The sun brought out the worst in people, Elliot thought. And he always felt like more was expected of him. Things that he couldn't give people: spontaneity, enthusiasm, constant socialising.

He was sitting at the end of a long table that the logistics team had booked for their summer party because he didn't feel like joining in the cheery conversations about people's various summer plans. But he began to wonder if he should have sat right in the middle of the table and nodded along at the relevant moments. It might have been easier to be invisible that way, rather than drawing attention to his stillness, his quietness, his weariness.

He silently went to the toilet, trying to work out how long he could stay in there without it looking weird. Elliot let the water run over his hands for a long time, relishing the feeling without the accompanying fear of the water bill his mother had instilled in him. He glanced in the mirror and immediately looked away, the same way he'd always done. But even in that brief moment he noticed how vacant he looked, how pale, and how much older than when he'd first joined TeleForce. There were no spots, no fringe, no anxious beady eyes. Just a plain, dull looking adult face.

He wondered whether he should go home. Since getting the new job, Elliot had managed to alleviate some of the heavier feelings he'd been carrying around. He focused on helping Willie, he met up with Dom, and he went to his new job where he vowed never to pretend to be someone else, noticing (correctly) that this was the thing which made him feel worst of all. The only consequence of being himself was that he made little connection with other people. He didn't feel like saying anything – as they chirped away about the things they'd seen online or as they bitched about each other – so he didn't.

He'd given the summer party a good go, he decided, but he was beginning to get that familiar pressure around the circumference of his head. And besides, he needed to ring the dentist to find out if there were any adjustments they could make for Willie.

As he walked back to the table a girl, Beth, waved him over, pointing to a chair next to her. She gestured to a translucent drink on the table. 'I got you a drink. I just guessed.' She blushed a bit.

'Cheers.' He took a sip of the dry tasting drink and tried to think of something to say without pretending to be someone else. This inability to instantly ignite a conversation was something Elliot hated about himself. He thought everyone found him awkward and boring. (And, yes, no one had ever called him the life and soul of the party, but what he didn't realise was that people were often intimidated by this quietness. Beth found it almost overwhelmingly enchanting, wondering what he was thinking in these moments. These enigmatic silences when in fact he was just trying to think of something to say. Since Elliot had joined the logistics team four months ago, she had been drawn to him. The constant pensive expression his thick straight eyebrows gave him, his intriguing pessimism, the way he stared into space biting his nails.)

'Going anywhere this summer then?' Beth shifted in her seat a bit and chewed on her lip.

'Not really.' Elliot swallowed, wondering how he could move the conversation on without seeming rude.

'Do you still hang with the people from the call centre? That's where you've come from, isn't it?'

'Urm, no not really. Have you got any summer plans?'

'Yeah, so, me and my mum were planning on going Turkey. But we haven't got anything booked in yet. Yeah, just that really. And y'know, the usual. I'm not a big tanner myself but, yeah, I do love the sunshine. . .'

Elliot lost focus a second, his brain letting go of her voice and settling instead on the two men speaking at the table next to them. They were talking about trains or something, a journey of some sort. Elliot didn't care about that either; he returned to Beth.

'But yeah, I know it's a bit obvious really isn't it. Everyone loves summer.' Beth took a breath and sucked on the straw in her fizzing drink.

'I hate summer.' Elliot looked at Beth and realised that there was being himself and then there was being too real. 'I'm not good in the heat.'

Beth separated her burgundy hair at the back and pulled half over each shoulder. 'Yeah so true. You can always warm up but you can't cool down. Well unless. . .' She held up her drink and stirred the ice around, smiling.

Elliot laughed politely and then excused himself without reason. He walked through the pub and out the front.

He took his phone out of his pocket and called Dom. It rang for a while and he was about to give up when there was the light click of someone answering and then a loud voice with a strong Stokie accent.

'Ay up. Go on then, what's wrong with yer?'

'What? What do you mean? I'm fine.'

'Christ, you had me worried there, Wood.'

Even after all this time it pleased Elliot to have his very own nickname, regardless of the fact it was only his last name.

'Why?' He took his phone from his ear and glanced at it as if it would enlighten him in some way and then put it back to his face. 'I don't get it.'

'Because yer rang? Yer dunna ring someone unless it's an emergency. This ent 1995.'

Elliot sputtered out a laugh and started pacing back and forth. 'Ah, right, sorry.'

'It's no problem. Just don't do it again.' Elliot could hear Dom's smile.

'Right, so, I'm down The Cow with people from work and it's pretty bleak. Can you come?'

He listened to the silence and prepared himself to persuade Dom. 'Dom, look. . .' (Elliot's 'Look' sounding slightly more like 'Luke' whenever he spoke to Dom) 'I know—'

'What's that, matey?'

Elliot held his forehead in his clammy hand, gutted at his plan falling apart, and considered whether he should push further. But then there was some rustling and then some jangling and Dom spoke:

'Right, see yer in ten.'

Elliot waltzed back through the pub and into the garden. He never felt pressured to perform around Dom and yet was still liked by him.

Maybe having him there would help Elliot stay true to himself, but a more likeable, confident version. He sat down, smiled at the early-evening sunless sky and then at Beth. Hopeful.

'Right, what'd I miss?'

Beth's eyes lit up (happy and confused at the change in tone and even, partially, in strength of accent).

'Well, not much, people were saying—'

'Doesn't sound like much. Shots?' He gestured back inside.

Beth shrugged happily, 'Yeah, why not.'

Beth laughed under her breath while Elliot, repressing a smile, talked her through the notes of the Apple Sourz shot he was sipping on. He cringed inside a little, wondering if this was something that the real him would be doing, or if he was pretending again? But a worse feeling grew inside him. A voice that said, *if not this then what? Maybe you don't know how to be yourself because that person doesn't exist?* (But it was easy enough to push down along with all his other authentic feelings.)

Elliot put his jacket back on and looked at Beth, taking her in. Her dark red hair, pale grey eyes with spidery mascara, piercing below the lip. He struggled to form an opinion.

'Cold?' she asked, nodding at his jacket.

'Yeah, well, a bit. Cold and burnt, if that's possible.'

'Ya nose is all pink.' She tapped his nose with the tip of her finger and flushed red. Genuinely taken aback by someone else's touch, Elliot smiled, embarrassed too.

'It's my own fault really. I don't know why I don't wear suncream when my skin is the colour of paper.'

He looked at Beth, waiting for her response but she didn't reply. She just smiled at him. So they sat there, smiling at each other for a few seconds, before she carried on.

'I like your jacket.'

For a moment it seemed as if she were going to reach out and touch that as well but instead she tapped her own chest where the Fred Perry emblem would be if she was wearing it. 'I like that logo.'

Elliot looked down and smiled. The alcohol was starting to warm him from the inside and his thoughts were softening, like they were being gently folded away for later.

'Cheers.'

'You always dress nice.' Beth's gaze was slightly losing focus and her compliments were becoming less disguisable as normal conversation.

He spoke while finishing the syrupy remains of his shot. 'Yeah? I dunno.'

(A trait of Elliot's that didn't sit neatly alongside the others was that he was very particular about the way he dressed. He liked clothes and he had some mixture of pride and attachment to his own collection. The rest of his personality was based around blending in and being generally indifferent to the ever-changing trends of the zeitgeist. And so he struggled to explicitly talk, or even think, about this anomaly.)

'Yeah, like, you always look kind of smart but cool. I dunno.' Beth went to drink her drink but realised she only had an empty shot glass. Luckily, just as Elliot's mood wavered, Dom strode into the pub garden.

'Ay up.'

Within minutes they were all sipping new drinks and laughing at Dom's anecdotes. The words *best friend* went through Elliot's mind.

'And I tell yer, her fart sounded like an actual question.' Dom blew a sound out which went higher at the end. 'I canna explain to yer what it smelt like. It hit the nostrils quicker than that smell does when yer walk past a Subway.'

Beth was almost shaking with laughter and Elliot, watching her, got a wave of pride for his friend. He looked at Beth again, ready to think something nice about her too, but the first thing that came into his mind was that she had a powdery face. His stomach tensed with guilt at the judgement, and so he thought instead what someone else might say was nice about her. *She has a cute little nose.* That's what people would say so that's what he thought. He took another swig of his pint and wondered if he was having fun.

It was an hour later and Elliot was somehow talking to Susan about her once in a lifetime trip to Disneyland with the kids. An unprompted electric shock of uncomfortableness brought him back into his body. He was drunk and he hated being drunk. It made him feel out of control. He quickly traced back over the conversation he'd been having to check he hadn't said anything weird. He wondered if he should leave. He looked around for his friends and saw Dom and Beth at the bar talking. Elliot watched as Beth whispered something in Dom's ear. He told Susan to 'hold that thought while I get a drink', and then stood up, leaving his half-full drink on the table, to re-join his friends.

The more Dom told funny stories the less able Elliot felt to find a gap in the fast-paced conversation in which to enter it, and so the quieter he got. It became hard to watch; every minute that passed Elliot saw a version of reality he did not want to believe existed; one where him and Dom didn't have a particularly close friendship, but where Dom liked everyone and everyone liked Dom.

Dom was directing his speech purely to Beth now: 'And so me and my mates were taking communion at Midnight Mass and the priest was giving out the little bread stuff and nodding, all the usual crap, and then it got to my turn and he pressed his palm on my head and was like' – Dom placed his hand on Beth's head and did an impression of a low, holy voice – '"May the devil be released from your soul."'

Elliot felt the moment that Dom touched Beth in his jaw. He never related to those testosterone bursts of violent energy he'd seen so often in guys he knew, but just then, for a second, he squeezed his thumb under his fingers hard until they turned white.

Dom asked Elliot to come outside while he had a ciggy and told Beth to stay inside as it'd gotten too cold for a lady in summer clothes.

Elliot sat moodily on the pub wall with his arms tightly crossed over his chest. Dom took a drag on his cigarette and then a sharp breath in. Once he finally let out the smoke he filled the silence.

'You alreet then or what?'

'Yeah, fine. Why'dya keep asking? I've not rang you again.'

'Why'd you ask us here then?'

'Sorry I wanted to see a mate. I won't trouble you again.' Elliot knew he sounded like a snarky teenager but he couldn't help himself.

'Are you seeing her?'

'Seeing who?'

'Reet, I'm off wom then if yer gonna be like that.' Dom dropped his cigarette and paced off into the pitch black. Elliot tried to force himself to call out for Dom to stop but he didn't feel able to say anything. Or do anything. He just sat there, getting more worked up and picking at the skin on his dry fingers. He started looking at the corners of the dimly illuminated pub door. Starting with the top right, then bottom right, bottom left, top left, top right. But he didn't count them. He made sure not to.

He was so enraptured with it that he jumped when the door actually opened and Beth poked her head out.

'You guys all good out here?'

'Yeah. Dom's gone home.'

'Aw, that's a shame. He was well nice.'

'Yeah he's a good'un.'

Beth tentatively moved over to sit next to Elliot on the wall. She was only wearing a black strap T-shirt and tiny denim shorts and it didn't take long for her to start shivering (even if it was partially for show).

Elliot turned to look at her, and she looked back at him.

Beth jiggled her legs up and down a bit as if to keep warm. 'I'm dead glad you joined TeleForce, by the way. It was so boring before you.'

Elliot's eyes were drawn back to looking at the door's corners.

(Beth looked at Elliot's active eyes and wondered what was going on behind them. Was he thinking about her? Was he too shy to kiss her?)

'Okay, well, I'm probs going back in. It's pretty chilly.'

'Ah, sorry, I was miles away.'

'It's all right.' Beth paused.

He looked at her and wondered if they would kiss. It seemed like the moment, and she did look pretty in a way he couldn't put his finger on. But he wasn't sure that she wanted to and didn't think that anything good could come of it regardless, so he smiled and said, 'I'm gonna stay out here a bit.'

Beth told him she'd see him inside and he gave her a big smile (with such blank, sad eyes, that she fell in love with him right there).

★

As soon as she went inside he left, sulking slowly and kicking an empty bottle down the road, a bubbling pessimism in the back of his throat. But when he sat on the concrete stoop outside his house, sobering up before he saw Willie, he realised he'd got caught up in something he didn't care about. His life worked as it was, nothing needed to change. (Oh, but it would. It always does.) He texted Dom, apologising, thanking him for coming, suggesting they go for a fry-up soon, and then heavily implied that he didn't care about Beth.

4

Eight years old

Noa walked around saying goodbye to each room in the flat. She ran her fingers over the embossed wallpaper of her bedroom and whispered, 'I am going to miss you. You have been such a good room to me.' She walked into the coral pink bathroom, looked into the floor-length mirror and whispered, 'I'm going to miss you, bathroom. I liked having baths in you.' When she'd done the five rooms that the flat consisted of she returned to her empty bedroom, sat down with her back against the faux-woodgrain door and tried to cry into her knees. She wasn't sad to leave her London home and move four hours up the country to a place where she knew no one. But crying felt like the right thing to do at this part of her story. She was a princess, being taken far, far away from her kingdom. Noa was prepared to feel lonely and frightened at first, and then slowly find herself adoring and being adored in return by the townsfolk. Her parents and their loud, barking argument coming through her open window was just part of the strife which would soon be overcome in the next part of their family's story.

The first days in Stoke passed in a muggy haze. Boxes, arguments, sandwiches for dinner, chaos, silence. Finally Noa couldn't handle it anymore. She burst into (genuine) tears. Pushing the top of her head into her mum's torso she breathlessly let it all out.

'I want to go home now, Mummy. I'm cold and really quite tired. I think we should go home.'

'This is our home now, sunshine.' Her mum stroked the top of her head until her crying subsided. She bent in half to get face to face with Noa. 'This is where we live now. And I know it might be scary but I promise you it will be worth it.'

Noa burst into fresh tears, 'It won't be worth it. I promise you.'

Noa's mum picked her up and placed her to sit on the kitchen worktop.

'Look, I'll let you in on a little secret. The reason we moved here is that there's a lot more space. And right now it might not seem like a good enough reason to leave everything behind just for a bigger house.' Her mum lowered her voice a little, 'But maybe there's a reason we need a bigger house. . . So we can have a bigger family!'

Noa's mind flashed with images of the next chapter in her story. She would be a new character: the older sister who shows her little sister the way of things, guiding her through the complexities of life. It was very appealing. It made this new, scary life sound comfortable.

It was only a few months later when Noa's mum asked her to sit down in the living room. She told Noa they had to wait for 'Don' to join them so she sat quietly on the black leather sofa with her hands in her lap waiting for some life-changing news. Her mum didn't usually call her dad by his first name and her mum's face was quite stern and she certainly wasn't being chatty but Noa decided that this all must be down to the fact that her mum was taking the announcement seriously.

As time passed, and Noa started to become uncomfortable, she decided to pretend that they were both waiting patiently for their butler to come pick them up and take them to their mansion in the country where she would meet her little sister. It was fun for a while but after twenty minutes Noa's mind kept wandering, prodding her with the question of what was really happening. To make sure it didn't land at some distressing conclusion, she started picking at the skin around her nails, focusing on the sharp feeling of her nail digging into skin and the satisfaction as bits of it peeled away.

Noa jumped when her mum eventually spoke. 'Right, well, I was going to make him tell you himself, but he clearly doesn't give two shits. Noa, your dad's left us for a little fucking child and he's not coming back.' Noa had never heard her mum swear before and was preoccupied with that until she noticed her shuddering and crying. Before she could think of anything to say her mum ran upstairs.

She wanted to cry like her mum but the tears wouldn't come. She couldn't believe the news that her dad was so fed up he'd gotten her a little sister or brother but wasn't bringing them home.

It took her weeks to understand that by 'a little child' her mum had meant a younger woman. Or as her mum subsequently referred to her as, 'a pubescent Barbie bitch'. Her dad moved back to London to be with his new girlfriend. The hardest thing was the loss of hope that this new life could be something fun, comfortable, fulfilling. With no baby sister on the horizon life felt endless and scary. Noa was left spending night after night lying behind her sobbing mother, playing with her mum's hair until she fell asleep and then drifting off herself.

★

It was hard for Noa to watch her mum fade away. It was like a bad mood or an illness or fatigue that seemed to linger indefinitely. Long gone were the days of fiery arguments and bubbly happiness. Instead her mum moved through the days as if they were nothing but a checklist.

What was hardest of all were the times when she would cry breathlessly, talking to Noa as if she were a confidante rather than a daughter. She would swing wildly from seething anger to self-hatred.

'Your father is dirt. I trusted him. I gave him everything and he left me with nothing' or 'What will I do without him? What is wrong with me? What will I do all alone?' or 'Noa, you watch and learn from all this. Your mother is ruined. Don't do what I did.'

Noa didn't know what her mum 'did' but she vehemently promised not to let the same happen to her. And she didn't need much persuading. It was terrifying.

It wasn't all bad though. Noa found pleasure in looking after her mum. It was instinctual. And more importantly it was somewhere to direct her energy. She brought her tea and toast on those weekend mornings which so easily turned into afternoons without movement. She knew to wait patiently for the spark of a good mood and then to nourish it into a full flame, offering 'makeover' days. She would rub moisturiser into her mum's hands or help reorganise a crumb-filled kitchen drawer. She liked finding the right thing. When it seemed impossible that her mum would smile that day, she would try different ways to cheer her up until she finally saw the reluctant faint widening of her lips. And that is where she found her grains of happiness. But it never stopped being painful that her mum wasn't returning these small acts of kindness. She longed to be cheered up or entertained herself but she was always the instigator of these things.

Her dad, on the other hand, was full of love but completely out of reach. From his new house in London he sent funny postcards and little gifts, diaries and children's toys that were slightly too young for her. She treasured them all, trying to picture him picking them out and wanted to ask him why he chose them. But she couldn't ask him. They barely saw each other and when they did it was stilted and overly organised. Trips to the cinema with brief, quiet drives to and from her mum's. Noa tried desperately to form some kind of common ground, a language that they could both speak, names or references or things to check in with each other about. She wanted to ask him what he did and know his opinion on things and bring joy to his life. But all these trips out and presents felt too removed to experience as a kind of connection. Noa wished she could combine her parents into one person. Someone to love and be loved by.

In spring Noa got invited to Lauren's ninth birthday party. She wasn't expecting to get invited, she never got invited to anything, so when she received the little card she knew things were on the up. She didn't have any proper friends yet, only people she stood near or was made to sit next to. But this felt like an opportunity for that to change. Friendships, she had seen from watching other people's, were a place to find a requited connection. Someone to think about as much as they'd be thinking of you.

Her mum said she would take her out shopping for some new clothes. Noa was more than ready for her makeover scene. She stood on her tiptoes to look in the bathroom mirror before they left and pictured the transformation – how sparkly and glossy she would look. She already knew what she wanted: lilac combat trousers, lilac vest, shiny lips, blonde highlights, elastic choker, boobs.

Noa begged her mum to go to Tammy Girl but she wouldn't even consider it. It was Debenhams or Next or nothing. Her mum picked up a few boring things and Noa dragged her feet along the floor and into the changing room. She eventually came out and walked around in a little circle exhibiting a white T-shirt with long red sleeves that she didn't like. She stood with her hands on her hips waiting for her mum to tell her that it was smart. But she didn't. She stood up from the stool and said, 'Ooo I didn't notice you'd grown little boobies.' Noa looked down at the small puffs that had appeared recently. She hated them and wished they were big and circular like the ladies in the Spice Girls or the young teaching assistant in her class. She wrapped her arms around her chest and this time waited for her mum to say that her type of boobs were classy, how she was better than those other girls with big ones. But again, she didn't. She pinched Noa's waist and laughed saying, 'Let's hope they get bigger and your nose gets smaller, eh?' Noa felt her cheeks heat up.

Lauren was standing, hand on hip, showing her friends the faux-wood hi-fi system that she got for her birthday. Noa strolled over and held out the wrapped present she had brought. But Lauren ignored her and continued showing the crowd how the CD holder electronically came in and out of the machine. Noa slowly lowered her hand, which was holding the present out, back down by her side and tried to nod along with the conversation. After Lauren had finished the demonstration and settled on N-SYNC to play, she turned to Noa. 'Hiya, Noa.'

'Hi Lauren. Happy birthday.' She coyly held the present out again.

Lauren gestured to the coffee table with a pile of presents on it. 'You can put it there please.'

Noa walked over using the time to rack her brains on how to integrate better. When she reached the table she realised someone was standing beside her. It was Becky, golden from year-round playing football outside, a short blonde bob and little button nose covered in freckles, she was different to other girls. Sporty like the boys were. Friends with everyone but best friends with no one. And so in need of one? Becky gave her a quick smile and re-joined the group. Noa's tummy fluttered.

Lauren stood with her plastic cup of pop, gossiping with her friends (in the same way that her mum, Elaine, did with her own friends and a glass of wine two metres behind her. When they finally all sat down for some organised fun, Elaine was drunk. She squinted at the children and imagined them as co-workers.)

'Right then, let's all go around and say a fun fact about oursens.'

(Lauren knew not to let a moment pass when someone could have time to judge the situation badly.) 'I guess a fact about me is that I'm nine today' – she cheers-ed her glass to the air – 'and that I like pink aaaand' – she pushed her shoulder forwards and pouted her lips – 'it's my birthday.'

Mainly the children's facts were their age, favourite colour or dog's name. Becky said her fun fact was that she had no fun facts and Noa shook with giggles. She already knew what she was going to say herself and was excited for it.

'My fun fact is that I am from London. It's really cool there.' She didn't know why but she was aware that this gave her a certain kind of status. That it was the coolest thing about her. She beamed after

51

saying it as if there were gasps in the room (not noticing Elaine and her friends rolling their eyes at each other).

After a few more (awkward, corporate) party-games they went into the kitchen for Lauren's party spread. Noa loaded her paper plate up with Party Rings, Jammie Dodgers, cocktail sausages, cheese and pineapple skewers and some crisps. She looked up to see Lauren and her mum eating one sausage each, without plates, and wondered if they were saving themselves for cake. As she teethed the cheese chunk off her first skewer she felt Becky by her side again. She swallowed the food down in a painful gulp.

'I've been to London. For my eighth birthday we went on the bus that drives you around and shows you everything. It was cool as shite.'

Noa couldn't help her eyes widening in shock and delight. 'Yeah, I've been on that bus all the time. It took me to school.'

'That's cool.'

'Yeah.'

'Yeah.'

It was going amazingly. This was the first time someone had started a conversation with her. But then Lauren's mum walked over. 'You sure you've got enough there, love?'

Noa looked down at her plate and said, 'Yes, thank you,' but as the words left her mouth she saw Elaine was laughing.

'Save some for the rest, darling!' One of Elaine's friends cackled from across the room.

'It don't surprise me that *she's* being greedy,' another woman added, in a serious tone at first, and then after the briefest pause, nudged the other one and burst into nose-pinching giggles.

★

When it was time to go, Noa's mum and Elaine gave each other (curt, fake) smiles and Lauren said goodbye to everyone except Noa.

Walking to their rectangular car, Noa decided that she was going to keep this heavy feeling to herself, be a brave girl, not give her sad mum anything more to worry about. But that was easier thought than done and as soon as she slid into the puckered leather seat she put her face in her hands and let a whiny (barely tearful) cry out.

Her words were long and dragged out. 'Mummy, I like this girl and I thought she wanted to be my friend but she didn't. I think she likes Lauren because she's prettier than me.'

Her mum started the car and with a few jolts began driving. Noa stopped her cries and took her face out of her palms to look at her mum, she already knew what she would say and was wondering why she was taking so long to respond. 'If you're going to rely on other people for happiness then don't expect to be very happy' or, 'You can give a man everything and he'll give you nothing in return', sometimes even a, 'Relationships are ticking-time-bombs and eventually they all blow up leaving you in ruins.' Noa's mum always had little quips like this to say when the credits rolled on *Cinderella* or if she overheard Noa playing with her Barbies; and usually Noa hated it. Every time it felt like something inside of her deflated a little. But right now, she was ready for it. She wanted to hear how she was better off without Becky, how she would have made her sad, how she had steered clear of something dangerous.

(Instead, Deborah parallel parked on a space along their road, switched off the engine and looked at her child's pink face. She thought back to when she'd first moved to Stoke and overheard – plainly heard – Elaine describing her as 'swarthy' to another mum in the playground. She dreaded to think what had happened to her daughter at that awful woman's party.)

'Noa, sunshine, look at me. The magic of friendship is having someone like you for who you are. If someone isn't friendly to you then that's their loss. You're perfect as is. I promise you, it won't be long until you make some friends, you need to hold out a tiny bit longer. Keep smiling. Keep being yourself. They'll come to you.'

Noa's mum tapped her thighs and opened the door. 'Come on, let's watch a video.'

She hadn't seen her mum so animated in ages. Before she got out the car she closed her eyes, wishing that if she could only see her future friend for one second then she would wait patiently for them.

5

Eight years old

Willie was screaming and crying, hands balled up next to his red face. Elliot was standing there with a bar of Dairy Milk, sucking it like a lolly.

'Elly, look what you've done. How would you like it if he ate *your* chocolate?'

Elliot took the chocolate out of his mouth and held out the wet, smooth end of it to his brother. He hated being told off more than anything in the world. He wanted his mum's angry face and voice to be gone as quickly as possible and would do almost anything to get there. This meant that although there were often upsets in the Wood household, they were more like emotional outbursts which ended with hugs and don't worrys. Elliot's mum brought them both new chocolate bars and he sat close to her on the settee, grateful for her quick forgiveness and hoping to himself that would be the last time he would ever upset her. (Oh, Elliot. If only that were true.)

Elliot's family life was stressful (and sheltered, although he wouldn't consciously realise this until later). But it was also full of joy. For Elliot it all came from finding the right ways to entertain Willie. They didn't play together per se but rather Elliot would organise activities: lay out dinosaurs for Willie to sort out and line up, gather things for Willie to stack and knock over, create piles of paper for Willie to throw in the air. He called it 'Teacher Time' and when he said those words Willie would scrunch up his face and move his wrists in circles with excitement.

One day Elliot was told that Willie had been taken out of school early and that he had to stay at after-school club. When he got home his stomach started to hurt. The atmosphere was strange and quiet. Usually his parent's arguments were loud and Willie was louder. Elliot wanted to know what was wrong but decided if he didn't ask then maybe the bad thing didn't happen, so he put a football video on that him and Willie loved to watch.

It didn't take long for Elliot's mum to join them in the front room. Elliot could see she had been crying in a sad rather than angry way, her face loose and pale rather than tight and red. They watched the video together for a while and then his mum asked to talk to him in the hall for a second. He went with her, racking his brains for what he'd done wrong, his stomach churning. She spoke softly, almost whispering, which put Elliot on edge.

'Today was a big day, Elly. We have found out why Willie is a little different to other children. He got told by a doctor that he has autism. Now, what—'

Elliot's dad strode into the hall from the kitchen, his voice low and loud.

'We will not be using that word in this house. What did I tell you, Ruth? What did I just tell you?'

He was speaking through gritted teeth. Elliot tried to tune in to the video from the other room. If he closed his eyes he could nearly focus on it entirely.

A heavy hand on his shoulder made him jump.

'Elliot, son. We will not be using that word.' He didn't take his hand off Elliot's shoulder but spoke to his mum again. 'There is no need for a label when he's only a child. That'll do more harm than good. These so-called experts—'

Elliot felt trapped underneath the hand and he was desperate to leave but was worried that leaving would make things worse. So he stood there, straining his ears to focus on Willie's concentrating murmuring.

At junior school Elliot was friendly with everyone but good friends with no one. He was used to playing with Willie and couldn't work out the rules and dynamics of the other children's games. So when his mum asked him who he wanted to invite to his eighth birthday party – his first ever – he felt embarrassed. But the pressure propelled him into action. This was his opportunity for friendship. He spent the endless wait until the party (a week) trying to interact with people at school. He made an effort to go outside his comfort zone, speaking up more at break times and walking home with two boys, Dom and Lee, instead of lagging a few steps behind. It went well, Dom liked football and Elliot found that easy to talk about. One day Dom and Elliot were so wrapped up in kicking a can down the road that they walked home without Lee. Elliot pretended not to notice, to be engrossed in the game, but the whole time he was fizzing with the feeling that for once, he was the first choice. He hadn't realised the longing for a friend was so large inside of him until the possibility of having one was close. (But children can be both fickle and stubborn and so the chances of getting an established friend in time for his party were about the same as calling heads on a coin flip.)

By the Saturday morning he was so nervous he could barely

enjoy opening his presents and was manically considering both the possibility that he could have the best day of his life, becoming full-fledged friends with everyone, or that something could go disastrously wrong and any hope of integration would be lost. When they arrived at the village hall, his parents started setting up and talking to each other in a sharp, hushed way that worried Elliot. He tried to run around with Willie but he seemed edgy and upset. (Elliot was a perceptive child and in his subconscious he knew what all this was leading to. Not that he had words to describe it or had any explanation for it. His brain had learned the warning signs without realising.)

His stomach started to hurt and he wanted to beg his parents to take him home and cancel everything but even more than that he didn't want to be a disappointment. So he focused his energy on looking at each corner of the ceiling and counted as he went. *One two three four.* And again. And again. Trying not to focus on his parents' argument or Willie's repetitive whines.

Guests started to arrive and Elliot had to stop mid-count. It felt very wrong. His mum made him stand there and take the other children's presents and say thank you, but Elliot could hardly get a word out. His shoes felt tight and he kept visualising pulling at the toes of his socks to loosen them and how relieving that would be.

It wasn't long until the party was in full swing. The turnout was good but Elliot stayed leaning against the wall, head down, shoulders hunched. His mum encouraged him to join in kicking a balloon around with the boys and he tried for a bit, hoping for a sign from Dom that he was special in some way. But he couldn't stop picturing his tight socks constraining his toes, and so he mainly stood still, grinding one of his scuffed trainers on top of the other.

Out the corner of his eyes he could see Willie pacing around and flinching at all the echoey sounds. The thought that maybe this party wasn't going well was life-shattering. This was his last chance to become part of the world and it didn't bear thinking about what would become of him if things didn't go to plan.

Elliot noticed his mum was guiding Willie towards him and knew he needed to keep his distance. He sped around the room, kicking the balloons with force and shooting them down with his hand-gun, sliding around on his knees. For a second he felt like he was playing with everyone else but soon realised he was actually playing on his own. Willie started to jump up and down, hands over his ears, repeating something but Elliot couldn't hear what it was. He turned towards Willie and machine-gunned him down (sound effects unfortunately spot on).

Willie collapsed to the floor, his mouth fully open in a constant scream. Everyone stopped and gawped. ('When the Going Gets Tough' by Boyzone played encouragingly in the background.)

Elliot watched his parents take Willie outside to the car. Their faces wore a horrible, crumpled expression and he was desperate to know what exact type of sadness it was or who they were sad at. He wished one of them would stay behind but they didn't even turn back.

He noticed everyone's eyes had moved to him in what felt like the first time that day. The parents stood around the edge of the hall muttering to each other, looking sad in a different way to his parents. A way that made Elliot feel angry and protective of his family. He felt like he should be explaining something to them all but there were no words in his head.

Soon parents kicked back into gear. Finding their children's coats, picking up a party-bag, flashing a squinted eye smile at Elliot and mournfully leaving.

The final mother walked up to Elliot.

'I'll wait with you in here, duck.'

She was smiling and Elliot realised his own mum had been doing that less often recently.

'It's okay,' Elliot said quietly, noticing that the boy standing with her was Lee. He looked down at his own trainers and focused on the frayed Velcro, picturing ripping it off and starting afresh with new, neat Velcro.

They stood there in silence for a while. Elliot saw something out the corner of his vision. Lee was pulling on his mum's coat and whispering pleas to leave. They caught eye contact. Lee looked at Elliot side-on, widened his eyes and pushed his lips to one side. Elliot knew that the look meant he was being judged as strange, different. He thought of Dom. His stomach clenched.

'Right, love. I'll go get your mum and tell her you're in here, all right?'

They walked out and Elliot stood there for what felt like a lifetime wondering if this would have happened if he'd been able to get to the end of his counting earlier. After a while he spun around the empty room until he felt sick and then lay down doing snow angels on the chipped parquet floor. Eventually his mum came back in, her face was pale with red blotches. They cleared up the hall together in silence. Elliot felt jittery, wanting to ask what she was feeling but didn't know how to word it. He counted down from ten, telling himself she would speak when he got to zero. And when she didn't he would start from ten again. But she didn't speak, not then, not in the car, not when they got home.

They ate tea with barely a word between them. Elliot counted the peas on his plate, desperate to pass the time. For it all to be over.

But it started to dawn on Elliot that he might be in trouble when his dad asked to speak to him before he went to bed. He hoped it would be happy and birthday-related, but something told him that because he had hoped for it, now it would not happen.

Elliot sat right on the edge of the maroon settee; his stomach tensed.

'Don't worry, you've done nowt wrong,' his dad said, smiling, but he didn't look happy. Elliot started gripping the tip of his thumb hard, so it turned a bright red, and realised it was imperative he didn't let go until the conversation finished.

'Look, Elliot, I know today weren't the perfect birthday and all that. But how you acted was disappointing.'

'I know, Daddy. I'm sorry.' The guilt was already gnawing a hole in Elliot's stomach.

'You don't need to be sorry. Look, son, I know Will is your older brother, but I'm afraid, in a way, you're gonna to have to be the older brother now.'

Elliot didn't speak because he didn't understand. He gripped tighter on his thumb.

'Don't be sad about it, mind. It's fun being the older brother. But the job of an older brother is to take care of the younger one, right? You look out for Will at school and help him out with stuff at home. That kind of thing. Always be thinking of him.'

'But what about my friends? What if I have to play with them?'

His dad smoothed his stubble downwards and then cleared his throat. 'Friends are not the priority right now. Do you understand me? You need to be protecting Will. Make sure he's safe and happy.'

'Yes, Daddy.'

'And don't be calling me Daddy anymore. It's "Dad". Not long till you're a man now, don't forget it.' His dad stood up and tapped

61

Elliot's shoulder twice, said 'Good lad' and left the room. Elliot kept squeezing his thumb and the tip went from red, to a red-blue. Eventually he started to get pins and needles in his hand and let go.

In bed that night he cried big, frustrated tears. Wishing his brother was different. Wishing his brother was dead. Wishing he was in a different family where everything was happy and he had friends and a football birthday party with no screaming.

The change to Elliot's life happened overnight but also gradually. Elliot's parents tried to explain it to him as Willie having 'good days' and 'bad days'. But labelling them only made it worse because the 'good days' always seemed slightly out of reach. Elliot took his new, secret role as older brother very seriously. All the big, hopeless feelings that had been in his stomach since the party, he channelled into protecting Willie and trying to solve the problem. But he felt awful at it, like he was failing at something which would be simple if he only tried hard enough. He stuck by Willie's side in a state of constant apprehension. His senses were always alert, like a character creeping through the house in a scary film. Looking out for any changes in Willie's behaviour that could be a warning. Trying to make sense of these fluctuations. Waiting for the day he would finally understand and be able to explain to his family what they needed to do to help Willie get better (he didn't want Willie to change, only to take away his pain). If he could just save his family from any more sadness, then maybe his own sadness would go away too.

One Sunday, while Willie was taken for an appointment, Elliot was given to his grandparents who took him to church.

On the walk home his nan told him about The Lord. 'You can

talk to him when you're sad or worried, see.' Elliot said yes but only in the same way as he said yes to everything his nan said. 'He will be there for you in times of need. He will love and protect you. He will answer your prayers.'

'Prayers?'

'Yes, duck. If you ask God for help, He will help.'

'What can He help with?'

'Everything.'

When they got back home Elliot's nan explained to him that prayer is simply asking God for the support you need and thanking Him for what He does. Elliot pretended to have a neutral reaction but inside, his mind was whirring. Could it really be so simple to solve a problem that seemed unsolvable? He excused himself and went upstairs. He found some pencils and an old colouring book and started writing on the inside of the back cover.

hello god. Plese help me and my family. mum and dad and brother Willie. we need your help becos things are not good. Please help my brother Willie with his bad days and give us good days onley. Thank you for helping nan and granddad and thank you for helping us and Willie. From Elliot Wood

Elliot read it back and felt good. He wasn't sure what to do next but slept with it under his pillow as he imagined that's probably where God would look.

Elliot's gut told him not to tell his mum and dad about his praying in case it stopped them being answered, like a birthday wish. After his original one didn't seem to work he compromised by praying for things to at least stay the same (but it will come as no surprise to find out that in fact things did change, constantly, substantially). His parents would have screaming rows. His dad spent less time at home. His mum became fiery. Throwing his toys in the bin one by one if he hadn't tidied them away. Starting an argument from out of nowhere if he looked or responded to her in a way she didn't like. Leaving for hours at a time if she felt 'unappreciated' or 'ganged-up on' or like 'she'd had enough'.

Elliot's own responsibilities increased. Astronomically. He helped with pretty much everything around the house, cleaning, cooking, organising, and most importantly ensuring Willie had what he needed when he needed it.

As the priority was keeping Willie calm and in a routine, Elliot's desires became secondary, even in his downtime. The only video that got played was *Small Soldiers* and it was played constantly. Willie eventually learned the entire script and when they watched it he would recite it over the top. When Elliot got told he was allowed to choose a video as a treat, he knew by the feeling in his stomach that if he chose a different one it could push Willie into what his mum now called a 'fit' and what his dad called a 'tantrum'. So it didn't take long for Elliot to understand that getting to pick something himself wasn't worth the hope and excitement, and it certainly wasn't worth what it did to his brother. Because that was the hardest thing of all. The shame and frustration he felt every time he failed to do his job as an older brother, to protect Willie from what looked like some kind of unimaginable pain. Screaming and rocking and slamming his hand into his forehead.

And then there were the beautiful moments with Willie. The kicking of a football in their small living room back and forth and back and forth and back and forth. Elliot's mind could focus solely on the positioning of his foot – because Willie's aim was a little unreliable – and an hour could pass without a single thought. Or they would put on a CD and dance around the room ('dancing' for Elliot meant jumping and for Willie meant spinning). Elliot loved to make Willie laugh. His laugh – little sharp bubbles – rarely came out with anyone else and felt like a special language. He was truly his best friend. And sometimes, on the sadder days when he saw other children chatting away, he told himself that he preferred his and Willie's way of playing anyway; words seemed unnecessary and laborious compared to their energetic bursts of action.

Elliot tried to establish himself as his own person. He'd noticed – after analysing other people's lives – that praise and love were usually given to someone being or doing something. So he understood what needed to be done. If he could somehow make an identity for himself, maybe someone would like him for it. He tried getting really into drawing, he tried being silly, he tried getting high marks in all his schoolwork, he tried feeling poorly, he tried being quieter, louder, he even tried asking to be called Liam. The best he would get from his parents would be a forced smile and the worst would be a frustrated wave of the hand. It was fresh humiliation every time he put himself out there and got nothing in return. The small amount of gratitude he got for helping his family started to have a bitter aftertaste. It seemed as if he was only appreciated and loved if he did good things rather than – like Willie seemed to get – a more consistent, unwavering type of love. Not attached to what he could offer but there regardless.

But still, he didn't have any more luck at making friends. By the time Elliot started middle school he struggled to see himself as anything other than an extension of his brother. He would watch the boys and girls, with an angry type of feeling, as they formed their identities as sporty, clever, cheeky, rich, naughty, whatever little thing defined them. He wanted to cry and say it wasn't fair but he didn't know who he could say that to. (Crying always ended with him being scolded by his dad.)

At junior school it felt upsetting not to have a friend but at middle school it felt embarrassing. At some point he realised that once you get labelled as friendless it's almost impossible to get unlabelled. Elliot hung out with Willie at break time from loneliness as much as from duty. They would sit together in the library talking (mostly Elliot) repetitively about obscure football players and 'swapping' their small selection of football cards with each other. It didn't take long for other children to notice Willie enjoying himself in his particular way – the distinctive sounds and movements he used to communicate – and feel the need to put a stop to it. At first it was the side glances from snickering groups across the lunch hall. And then it grew into mumbled comments as other children pushed their way past them in the corridor. The group eventually realised their behaviour could directly cause Willie's emotional explosions. And so they would purposely find him. Shouting and jabbing. Doing impressions of his walk and his staccato way of speaking. Elliot was out of his comfort zone. He wanted to stand up for Willie but was shocked into stillness (his subconscious and desperate hope for a friend told him to protect any semblance of a neutral reputation he had left). And so he backed off, spending his break times watching over Willie from the safety of a few metres away. He learned to become invisible. Jumping at every nudge and shriek. He would constantly analyse Willie's behaviour, the specific words he was repeating, or watching for signs like his hands going over his ears. He would wait for as long as possible. And then act a second before he knew it would be too late. He would take Willie by the arm and lead him into the toilet so he could meltdown in private. Elliot manically switching between soothing him and begging him to stop.

By the end of Willie's time at middle school, Elliot was getting bullied for being the 'retard's brother'. Even when he was hated, it wasn't for being himself. On their last lunchtime together before Wille went to a new, special school, Elliot watched Willie sitting alone, muttering to himself about Stoke City, flicking each finger with his thumb. Elliot thought about the year to come and felt so relieved and so lost that he couldn't eat.

After a few arguments and endless lists of chores, the summer holidays were turning out to be as stressful and upsetting as school. And so when they managed to form a new routine and there had been a few 'good days' in a row, Elliot asked to speak to his mum before bed. He didn't want to, he hated going to her with things when she was so stressed, but this was his last attempt.

She looked him in the eyes as if to say, 'go on then', and sat on the arm of the big corduroy chair. He tried to work out what she was thinking but she just looked back blankly.

He swallowed, breathed in, and spoke, 'Mum?'

She raised her eyebrows but didn't nod or say a word.

'Sometimes I... hate my life.' He didn't plan to, because he knew it would frustrate his mum, but he couldn't help bursting into tears. Her expression remained fixed so he tried to carry on, gulping in breaths where he could. 'I... I... hate it so much. I want Willie to be normal again and don't want to look after him anymore. I don't like it. I don't want to do it anymore.'

She still didn't say anything. His crying eventually subsided and so he tried again. 'I don't think I can help him, Mum. I think he needs to get better himself.'

Elliot watched as his mum looked at her lap and ran her fingers through the roots of her hair again and again. He didn't know whether she was angry or felt sorry for him. The uncertainty was worse than anything. He felt like he'd rather have her scream at him than not know what she was feeling. And so to distract himself he squeezed the top of each finger, counting in his head, *One two three four five*. The tension inside him eased a little.

Finally she spoke quietly in a way which was scarier than shouting. 'Elliot. Look around you. We are all trying our absolute best to get by here. Think about what it's like to be poor Willie. Think about what it's like to be me or your dad.'

Elliot did what she said and thought about what it was like to be them. He realised that he'd done something awful by complaining.

She continued, 'I'm not even going to give all that crap you said about your poor brother the time of day. He knows when you think these cruel things about him, y'know? And what do you think that does to him, hm? If you truly wanted him to be better, you wouldn't think things like that.'

Elliot started to cry again, but this time he bit his lip and tried not to. He managed to stay completely still and make no sound, but the tears were streaming from his eyes.

His mum sat next to him on the settee but didn't touch him. 'You need to think about how lucky you are. Imagine what Willie would give to be like you? You should be grateful for your life. Okay?' Elliot nodded. He desperately didn't want her to leave without giving him a hug and felt like he was radiating the plea from his body, but all she offered was a quick squeeze of his shoulder, told him to get himself to bed and walked out the room muttering, 'Believe me, things are about to get a lot worse.'

Elliot swallowed, bit the inside of his cheek and squeezed his fists until he stopped crying. (He wouldn't cry again for twenty years.)

He felt like a zombie, walking upstairs, like his brain and body had become detached. And he had this deep fear that they would grow further and further apart until his mind was drifting around in space, never able to reattach to his empty body. The helplessness he felt was verging on terrifying.

Scrabbling around in his mind for something to take the fear away, it became clear to him that there was only one thing left he could do. To take the responsibility for Willie seriously. Even more seriously than he already did. Focus on it entirely. Use it to fill his days with purpose. Let it become him. Learn how to help his family. And only then would everything be fine.

Praying to God didn't seem right anymore but he still believed there must be a larger power out there, something that controlled things, and so he decided to give it a name. Without thinking he found an old schoolbook and a pen and sat at his little desk, writing.

dear The One,
please help me keep my brother Willie safe and okay. I will do what you say and want in return. give me a sign of what you would like and I will do it. to show you that I'm being serius I will throw a 1 pound coin from my savings in the bin if you will give Willie and my family a good day tomorrow. I will chek back with you then to see if it has worked. thank you
From Elliot

(Speaking to The One let Elliot share the burden of his responsibilities, it gave him safety and certainty. It protected him from the idea that terrified him: *what if I have no control over what happens to me and my family?*)

As he lay in bed that night, Elliot redirected any pangs of stress to the comforting image of the pound coin he'd snuck into the kitchen bin. For a soothing moment Elliot felt in control of the situation. Things were going to be okay now, he told himself. And then he fell into a deep sleep.

6

Twenty-six years old

(Because of what happened to Noa when she was a teenager, she was forced to accept that everything her mum had told her was right. And so, exactly as her mum advised, she didn't expect anything from men. But she couldn't give them up. She wanted love, she wanted romance, she wanted a boyfriend, a husband, a life together, she wanted it all. So she lowered her expectations to the ground. And then, when that wasn't low enough, she dug a hole.)

Christopher was the total opposite of Louis, and that's what Noa liked about him. Since Louis, Noa had decided she needed a more purposeful plan if she were to find what she wanted. And so the obvious solution was to become a different woman in the hopes that it would attract a different kind of man.

She was doing well. She hadn't (on the whole) obsessed over men in a month, and she was filling her time seeing everyone she knew: her uni girls, her flatmate Elza and her friends from work. Everyone she knew was less romantic than her and yet everyone she knew had partners. She decided this couldn't be a coincidence. The independent lifestyle she saw other women lead became the main criteria for the 'new her': stop being so immature, stop being so romantic, start taking life seriously. Or in short – What Would

Elza Do? WWED? That was the mantra by which she would live her life now.

On one particular evening in October Noa had accepted an invitation to go to a lecture at SOAS University with Elza on how capitalism creates hunger and obesity. It was not something she was particularly excited about, since she knew it would be a downer, but she was accepting any invitation that the 'new her' would enjoy.

Noa sat down in the small, modern lecture theatre and wished it was acceptable to take Minstrels into events like this. There was a short, dry introduction but as Noa braced herself to be bored, a good-looking man walked up to the front. He was much younger than any lecturer Noa had at university and that alone made him attractive, but Noa pulled herself together. He wasn't attractive, he was just young and she was desperate for a crush. He introduced himself as Professor Fitzgerald and his voice surprised her. It had a posh undertone to it that she didn't expect considering his appearance. His dark hair was cut very short and he was wearing a well-worn looking suit and scuffed shoes. But he was tall and stood up straight in a way which made his outfit and haircut look cool. Noa (genuinely) managed to keep this positive reaction to his appearance from turning into the beginning of a fantasy. But it was once she started listening to the lecture that she couldn't help herself any longer. One minute he would speak passionately, giving the whole audience eye contact, and the next minute he would speak almost to himself, looking down and scratching his cheek or shaking his head at the bleak statistics he was reeling off. At one point he spoke about something so terrible he paused as if he were taking it in for the first time himself, which Noa felt was pretentious but hot. Sometimes it seemed like he was speaking directly to her, but Noa reminded herself that she once thought

72

Robbie Williams looked at her as if he was falling in love, when she was ten years old. Noa could interpret the briefest of glances as a romantic invitation if she wanted to.

By the end of the lecture Noa felt like he was a rock star. She couldn't help but see him as a celebrity after sitting there and watching him for an hour along with a crowd of a hundred other people. So when Elza suggested they go to the post-lecture drinks which were being held in another room, Noa's stomach fluttered with nerves. But she tensed her stomach and refocused on the conversation her group was having.

People drank red wine out of plastic cups and didn't mingle. Elza had friends there so that's who they stood with. The lecturer was behind Noa and she could hear strangers introducing themselves to him. Usually she would bug Elza to go and speak to him or position herself as near as possible to encourage a potential romantic meet-cute. But in the end she decided she wasn't going to be like that anymore. She was the 'new her' now. Mature and unromantic. WWED? She walked in the opposite direction and went to fill up her wine. When it was time, The One would present himself to her, she didn't need to force it.

'Is there any wine left in that bottle?'

His voice was smooth and made the hair on her neck stand up. She turned around and looked up; he was very tall.

'Oh. . . no. Sorry, here, have mine.' Noa said holding her cup out to him.

He laughed a short, breathy laugh. 'You don't need to do that. Thank you though.'

'Yeah, fair enough, who knows what I've put in here.' Noa raised her eyebrows and could feel herself going redder with every word she said, the wine flush not helping mask her embarrassment.

His eyes went temporarily larger, like he was shocked by her comment and he turned to leave.

'I . . . uh. I loved the lecture, by the way.'

He fully turned towards her again. 'Thank you. That's very kind.'

'I've never thought about a lot of the stuff you were saying.'

'Well, in a way, I'm glad that's the case. Otherwise I might have bored you. Then again, I would never want to deny someone knowledge simply for my own ego.'

'Are you a lecturer here then?'

'Yes, that's right. I'm a professor of Political Science.'

'I thought politics was the opposite of science?' Noa hoped she wasn't coming across as stupid, it was instinctual in her by this point in her life to make herself seem a little less clever than she was in front of men, but she knew this man was different. And more importantly, she was different now.

He did the breathy laugh again. 'I can see why you think that, but the beauty of Social Sciences is that by using the tools of the earlier established Natural Sciences we can hope to understand society in a substantially more precise way. Or at least that's what we try to do. I'm Christopher.' His hand was large and rough and she wanted to hold her hand inside it for longer than the one second it took to shake.

'I'm Noa.'

'Noa. That's a lovely name. Are you Jewish?'

'Depends who's asking.' Noa laughed nervously but realised by his lowered eyebrows it probably wasn't a funny joke.

His voice was serious. 'I'm sorry, I didn't mean to make you uncomfortable.'

'No, no. Not at all. It's nice that you know that. Most people just say "like the boy's name?"'

'Most people are stupid.'

Christopher smiled at her and she melted into the ground.

He continued, 'I love your accent, Noa. Where are you from?'

'Oh, really? I'm from Stoke but most people up there say I don't have an accent.'

'Well, as we've established, "most people" are wrong,' he said, smiling wryly. 'Everyone has an accent.'

'Yeah. . . I think they meant—'

'I think that they meant your accent is closer to Received Pronunciation than theirs. But I hate to think we're still suggesting that some people are accent-less. All that does is perpetuate the notion that some voices are more "normal" or "correct" than others. The beauty of our isle is in the vast array of accents we have in such a small geographical space. I think that should be celebrated.'

'Oh, definitely. What's your accent then?'

But Christopher was already smiling at Noa in a way that suggested the conversation was going to move on to something else.

'Noa, would you like to come out for a drink with me sometime? Or to dinner? Whatever you prefer. I'm massively enjoying speaking to you.'

'Yeah, I'd love to! Either's perfect.' Noa was fumbling for her phone, already coming to terms with the waiting, the wondering, the texting him first.

'Don't worry about that. Put your number into this and I'll be in contact.' He reached into his inside blazer pocket and pulled out a Nokia.

'Oh, wow. I miss these. That's so cool that you don't have a proper phone. . . I mean a smartphone, or whatever.'

'I don't know about cool but I certainly prefer smart *choices* instead of smart *phones*.'

Noa entered her number and handed it back.

'I'll contact you soon then. It was lovely to meet you, Noa.' Christopher leaned in and kissed Noa on one cheek. She took a deep breath in. She could have sworn he smelt like books, in a good way (of course).

Everything was perfect. Elza approved of them going on a date and was even excited for Noa. Christopher rang her less than twenty-four hours later. When she saw the number light up her screen she knew it would be him. She hadn't spoken to someone she knew on the phone for so long and part of her wondered if she shouldn't pick up, worrying it would be awkward. But it wasn't awkward at all. They spoke for an hour about their days and systems of power. It turned out he'd already planned their date. Drinks at his, then to an Indian restaurant around the corner.

'I know it seems a little forward to suggest going to my flat first, but why pay for expensive drinks when I can make them for you?'

Noa was a little worried that the version of him she'd painted in her head was going to fall apart. She'd experienced this type of thing many times before. Innocent reasons to go to someone's house and then the next thing she'd know they were kneading her boob like it was dough. But she wasn't going to say no. Everything else was too good for her to be thrown off by this little detail. It would probably be fine, great even. Because Christopher was great.

And she was right. His flat, in Bloomsbury, was the top floor of an impressive grey-bricked Victorian house. It was beautiful inside but very bare. His office was a full-sized room but aside from a small desk, a chair and a few bookcases filled with books, it was empty. His living room had a dining table with one chair and a small leather sofa. No TV, no rug, no knick-knacks or anything really. Nothing on the walls except another bookcase. His kitchen worktops were empty and when he opened his cupboard to get glasses to make their drinks, she noticed he had two plates, one bowl, two glasses and two mugs. There was something romantic about him, like he lived in the past. He wasn't anything like the other men she'd dated. He was original and intriguing and mature. For the first time in a long time things were headed to a good place, the plan had worked.

Christopher poured wine into the two glasses and led Noa into the living room. The sofa was small and she worried that this would be the start of the transition into something sexual, but he pulled over the dining chair and sat on that gesturing for her to sit on the sofa. Respectfulness radiated out of him.

'I love your flat.'

'Thank you.'

'How old are you, if you don't mind me asking?'

'I'm thirty, and you are?'

'Twenty-six. How did you get such a cool flat by thirty then?'

'It's not cool, it's practical.' He shrugged and held his glass up. 'To a lovely evening.'

They drank one glass of wine each and then headed to the restaurant. It was a vegetarian Indian buffet near Euston that cost £9 for all you can eat. Noa loved how unpretentious he was.

They did a bit of chit-chatting but as soon as they sat down with the food Christopher looked at her as if the date had properly started. 'So, Noa, tell me about yourself.'

'Oh, well, I'm from Stoke, as you know. Moved here after uni in Manchester, I work in recruitment. Urm, live with my friend Elza, who took me to your lecture, actually.'

'What did you read?'

'Urm, I guess I like a rom-com for the beach, love a scandi thriller, I do enjoy reading Austen and the Brontë sisters, but mainly I'll only read fancy writers if there's an element of yearning.'

Christopher was chuckling to himself. 'I mean at university! What did you read... what did you study?'

'Oh.' Noa felt herself turn red and her tongue was tingling with heat from the curry. 'Art History with Italian?' She wasn't sure why she said it as a question.

'Wonderful! I think everyone should pair a language with their studies. How can we truly understand something through only one lens? It's so restrictive.'

'Yeah, definitely. My dad's Italian. Well, actually, no, he's from London but his family are like Jewish-Italian. So I thought it'd be nice.'

He seemed impassioned. 'Yes, yes. That's exactly what we should all be doing. It's so stuffy in academia, people claim to have global perspectives but it's all for show. It's really important that you channel the knowledge of your ancestors through your studies. That's what they would want.'

Noa had to lean back, the food was too spicy and her mood was switching wildly between embarrassment and pride. She was out of her depth in the conversation but for once she felt proud of being Jewish.

'What about you? What did you study?'

Christopher put his knife and fork together on the plate even though he'd not eaten much. 'My thesis was on the global politics of food security and consumerism.'

'Oh, yeah, makes sense. Really interesting.' Noa was still hungry but put her knife and fork together and Christopher smiled.

He got out a shabby brown leather wallet and Noa reached for hers wondering if he would stop her. He signed a cheque in the air at the waiter to ask for the bill and then looked at Noa.

'You want to pay half and half, yes? I assume you're a feminist?'

'Of course! I would never expect a man to pay for me.'

'You should never *want* a man to pay for you either. It creates an uneasy power dynamic that modern women shouldn't have to be subjected to anymore.'

Noa remembered Elza saying that until there's income equality then maybe it's not such a bad idea for men to pick up the bill sometimes but decided not to say anything.

Christopher accompanied Noa all the way home but did not go inside when she invited him up. He put his hand on her shoulder and she looked up at him. She had been relieved when she saw he was wearing the suit again, not because she particularly liked it but because she was worried it was going to feel like one of those 'seeing a teacher on a school trip in their normal clothes' uncomfortable moments. And he looked good in the suit, with his strange short hair and masculine features. She was ready to kiss him but Christopher opted for her cheek again and said goodnight. Noa was practically drowning in green flags.

He called her the next evening and they spoke about their days at work. She felt a little embarrassed talking about her silly job compared to his proper grown-up one, but it didn't matter. She steered the conversation back to him and listened to what happened in his seminars. She always felt more comfortable talking about other people as she knew that was one of her most attractive traits – giving people her undivided attention. And anyway, there was something about the performance aspect of his job that was so sexy to Noa. She was obsessed with the idea of his students watching and lusting after Christopher but then him coming home and ringing her.

The next time they met he cooked her dinner at his. Vegetable goulash. She was leaning against his worktop watching him serve it onto a plate for him and into the bowl for her.

'Are you a vegetarian?' she asked him.

'Yes, aren't you?'

Noa couldn't help laughing. 'No, what made you think that?'

The tablespoon he was dishing the stew out with was lowered down onto the table, but still in his hand, while he thought for a second.

'I suppose I thought you were too clever to eat meat.'

Noa's stomach contracted. 'Well. . . Uh. . . I didn't realise it was an intelligence test. I guess I just like the protein. . . and the taste.'

'Of course it's an intelligence test. Why do you think Plato and Einstein and Pythagoras were all vegetarians?'

'Oh, well, I didn't know they were to be honest. I'm mainly familiar with their work on philosophy, science and maths rather than their diets.' She felt proud of her quick response.

He handed her the bowl. 'Well, they're linked. You should be vegetarian.'

Noa started to walk out the kitchen but he stopped her. 'Let's eat in here, there's nowhere to sit in there.'

'There's nowhere to sit in here?'

'So we'll stand?'

Noa was finding this all a bit weird. She was worried that she wasn't a polite eater at the best of times but this was going to be impossible. Plus, she didn't like how he was making her feel. Elza surely wouldn't approve. But then she realised Elza was vegetarian and wondered if she was in the wrong. She felt guilty for thinking badly of him. And reminded herself that if she wanted him to like her then she needed to be more like the 'new her'. WWED?

'I guess I could try and be more vegetarian.'

Christopher was struggling to eat the stew off the plate, he held it off the worktop and tried to scoop up bits of veg with his spoon.

'You can't be "more" vegetarian. You can be vegetarian or not vegetarian. That's like saying you could be "less" Jewish if you tried. You're either Jewish or you're not.'

'Well, I know one person who would agree with you there.' Noa laughed.

Christopher put his plate down on the side. 'That's not funny.'

Noa was taken aback. 'Sorry. I know it's a serious subject, but sometimes I joke about serious things because, well, I think that's a good way to get through life.'

'I think you joke about things like that as a defence mechanism. You don't feel you have the right to be upset about the Holocaust because it's so far in the past. You're worried about being a burden, being a "downer", making people feel uncomfortable. Well they *should* feel uncomfortable. It's not your fault that something deeply awful happened to your people.'

Noa smiled at his use of 'your people', only because she always felt like an imposter to the Jewish community. She'd barely been to synagogue, she hadn't had a bat mitzvah, she didn't speak Hebrew or believe in God. She just had Jewish parents.

'Noa' – he took the bowl out of her hand and put it on the side, then he put his hands on her shoulders and looked into her eyes – 'be proud of who you are and where you've come from and respect your ancestors.'

She felt tears come into her eyes. He was right. Christopher leaned in and kissed her. She was still feeling very overwhelmed by

81

the conversation and her emotions got all mixed up. By the time he pulled away she nearly told him she loved him. But before she could he held her hand and led her to the small sofa. They kissed again but Noa couldn't help feeling tense the whole time. Like she wanted to get the sex over and done with so they could move on to the next stage of their relationship. She drifted her hand up his thigh and then over to find his crotch, but before she could get there he stopped her hand and held it instead. She was absolutely mortified.

'Sorry. Sorry.'

He didn't let go of her hand. 'No need to be sorry. However I do think we should talk first.'

'Of course, sorry.' Noa was ashamed of herself and couldn't look him in the eye.

With his free hand he pushed her chin up so they were looking at each other. 'I really like you, Noa.'

She smiled but couldn't bring herself to reply. It felt way too early to say something like that, and she knew that it wasn't acceptable behaviour.

He continued. 'What kind of relationship are you looking for?'

She looked at his kind, dark eyes and wondered if she should say the truth. That she wanted big, true, long-lasting love. A husband, a house, children. But no, it was never good to say the truth. 'I'm not sure yet, I don't know. . .' She trailed off.

Christopher let go of her hand. 'Right. I see.'

'Why, what do you want?'

'If I like someone, I want to be with them. Properly. I don't understand why people do otherwise. The only valid explanation is that people don't truly like the people they are choosing to spend their time with.'

Noa's heart was racing. She was out of her depth. She didn't understand what he was saying. Did he want to be boyfriend and girlfriend? Was this the love that she'd always dreamed of? Was this how real, happy, mature relationships started? Was this the beginning of the end of solitude? One becoming two?

She stuttered, 'Well. . . I like you too.'

'And?'

'Want to be with you?'

'You don't sound too sure. I don't want to pressure you. I would hate that.' He turned to face his bare wall.

'I'm sorry, I'm just not used to this.'

'What are you used to?' He looked at her, concerned.

'I guess, I'm used to people *not* wanting to be with me.' She choked out a nervous laugh.

'Don't laugh at things that aren't funny, Noa.'

'Sorry.' She started biting her nails. She knew it was probably unattractive but she didn't have the luxury of pretending anymore. She was verging on frenzied. This wasn't the game she was used to playing. Maybe because it wasn't a game.

'What are you used to?' he asked again.

And so Noa told him all about Louis. But he didn't speak, he barely moved, he didn't even look at her. So she continued and told him about other mean men she'd been with. The more he sat in silence the more she filled it with words, and she told him about every horrible experience she'd had. Even what had happened with Elliot and Fraser, the boys from her school.

When there was no more to fill the silence with, they sat in it together. Noa knew she had ruined it. He probably saw her as some desperate slut or something now. She felt ashamed for how many men she'd been with, how many men she'd let treat her badly. But she also felt a tiny relief, getting that of her chest, being that open with someone else.

Eventually he reached out and took her hand again. His face was deadly serious. He even looked a bit angry.

'Noa, you sweet girl. I'm so sorry that happened to you. You didn't deserve any of that.'

Tears filled her eyes and started to fall out as he continued. 'I think those men are disgusting, depraved, deviant' – he was seething now – 'abhorrent plagues upon this earth. They didn't deserve a moment of your attention. I can tell by the way you described them that they were witless nobodies.' Noa was looking down, trying to wipe away the tears, but Christopher was making her look at him.

'Noa, I would never *ever* do that to you. Only low-life idiots would do such a thing to anyone, let alone to someone as lovely as you. If you would like to be my girlfriend I would treat you with all the respect you deserve.' He stroked her face and she buried herself into his chest to cry more.

Noa stayed round that night but they didn't have sex. She thought it might be awkward to sleep in a bed with someone you'd only kissed, but it wasn't. He stroked her hair until she pretended to fall asleep and then he fell asleep. But she couldn't. She was starving. She was overwhelmed. She felt deeply guilty for not thinking about her Jewish ancestors more. She felt heartbroken about the ways men had treated her. She felt giddy and excited and lucky to be with Christopher but also out of her depth. She still felt like they were strangers and she worried he would realise she wasn't interesting or clever enough and break up with her. She worried that he was lying, that he was a master manipulator and he would actually cheat on her like everyone else. (She was wrong.)

★

But over time that worry subsided. One day, when he was writing at the dining table he asked her to check something for him in a message on his phone.

'Are you sure?'

'Am I sure of what?'

'I just. . . isn't it private?'

He did a breathy laugh. 'What on earth would I have on there that's private?'

She found the message section on his phone and clicked through them until she got to the one he was referring to. With every 'Mother' and 'John Phone' and 'McKinsey Home' she scrolled past, another layer of distrust melted away.

But it didn't stop there. He met Noa outside her office after a day she was dreading. He introduced her as his girlfriend to his colleagues. He wanted to see her all the time. Noa was so happy. She had a boyfriend who was clever, attractive, respectful, kind, moral. They didn't have sex much but she didn't particularly mind. Sometimes when she was masturbating she wondered if it mattered she was doing that rather than having sex with her boyfriend. The main reason it worried her was because she started to notice he didn't really compliment her appearance. He said she was amazing and lovely but that was about it. It was always the beginning of the end when a man stopped finding her attractive, so she decided to take matters into her own hands. She was determined to make this work. To keep them on the right track.

Watching the sexual side of her relationship with Christopher peter out felt, to Noa, like a loss of control. Something that needed to be rectified. (Noa had spent her early twenties watching as other girls seamlessly transitioned from one night stands to relationships and it led her to view sex as a gateway to love. She only understood sex as a tool to use rather than an experience to enjoy. Every positive sensation she felt stemming from witnessing the pleasure of the man and anticipating what that could get her.) So Noa bought some sexy lingerie and wore it next time she went to Christopher's.

Noa was trying to kiss Christopher but he was reading a book and would only kiss her for a second or two before returning to it. She didn't want to pressure him so she sat back into the sofa and wondered what to do. But then he put his book aside and turned to her. They started kissing and, despite her nerves, she forced herself to be confident. Once he slipped the dress over her head he looked her up and down and she felt herself go cold. She couldn't tell what he was thinking and it was torturous. Eventually he looked away. Noa grabbed her dress, put it on and started crying. She was too embarrassed to speak. She gathered her things and went to leave but he broke the silence.

'Wait. Why are you leaving?'

'Because I'm embarrassed.'

'You don't need to do that.'

She turned, hopeful that he would beg her to stay. But he just gestured to her body with his head. 'Things like that. You're better than that.'

'Well, clearly not.'

He guided her back to the sofa and she went with him, desperate to feel better about herself somehow. To shake off the shame.

He stroked her hair and spoke softly. 'You're too intelligent to be doing things like that.'

'I'm not even intelligent. I don't know why you always say that.'

'Of course you are. My Italian art historian.' He tweaked her nose.

'Yeah, I studied that at university but I work in recruitment now. I don't even remember any of my degree.'

'But you're going back, no?'

'Back? To Manchester?'

'To study.'

'To study? No. I'm not. I'm done studying. I like working, having money. I like my job. I'm not good academically.'

'Of course you are. You said you were going to continue your studies to honour your Jewish ancestors?'

'What? When did I say that? No, no. I never said that. I don't even know what that means.'

He looked a mixture of furious and disgusted. Noa left crying.

The worst thing about the relationship was that it felt so close to being perfect. For once she felt able to love someone openly. He wasn't like the other men, repulsed by her affections. But she struggled to feel the warmth of someone enjoying her for who she was. It was as if he'd decided to love her and then that was that. The project was ended and now she was another bookcase in the room: needed but ignored. She decided this was her fault, she had lured him under false pretences after all. It *was* the perfect relationship, she just wasn't the perfect person.

That fortnight without hearing from him felt like hell. She couldn't complain to anyone because they all loved Christopher. Noa's mum had said she was proud that she'd found such a smart young man, Elza looked up to him, all her friends had said she'd finally landed herself a catch. This was her chance to leave the playing field and take what she had wanted for as long as she could remember. For once it didn't seem unrealistic that marriage and children would be on the horizon. The worst voice in her head was the quietest but it always made itself heard. It said: *If this plan fails, what do I have left?*

So in the end she had no choice. She would do whatever it took to stay with him. Exactly fourteen days later she went to his flat to say sorry.

He hugged her tight. 'Don't do that to me again, okay?'

'Okay.' She was so happy to be in his book-smelling company again.

'I'm giving this 100 per cent and I'm worried you're not.'

She looked up at him. 'I am! I am!'

'Good.' He held her close, moved her hair away from her ear and spoke softly into it, 'No more arguments.'

And there weren't any more arguments, really. But there could have been. Like the time Noa bought him another dining chair as a gift so they could eat sitting down and he dismantled it in front of her, explaining that she was propelling a consumerist world that was killing thousands of people every day. Or when Noa had chicken for lunch and he told her that she should stay at hers that night because he could smell the meat on her. Or when he didn't buy or plan or do anything for her birthday because he thought it would be more romantic to 'save the money for something important'. Or when he told her she was a 'loose woman' for getting drunk with her friends. Or when he told her she was greedy for eating big portions when people were out there starving and she clearly didn't need the calories. Or when he told her that he thought having a Jewish girlfriend would be culturally interesting but he could tell now that she wasn't properly Jewish.

Noa barely said anything when these things happened. The idea of breaking up terrified her. If she couldn't make this relationship work, this relationship that everyone approved of, this relationship with the perfect man who was so good to her, then surely she was destined to be alone. And to Noa there was no worse fate in this world than being alone. Yes, she might find someone a little nicer than Christopher but she might not. And it was never worth the risk, someone was always better than no one.

(Luckily) Christopher got scouted for a visiting professorship at Leiden University in the Netherlands and broke up with Noa. She cried into his moth-eaten wool coat for an hour begging him not to go but he said it was for the best.

'You're not right for me.' Was one of the last things he said to her. She felt a stabbing pain when he said it. She was so ashamed of herself. She was teeming with self-disgust. What a pathetic idiot she was, to lose someone great like him. She had tried everything, given him all she had and it still wasn't good enough. With every other break-up she still carried with her the private faith that one day things would work out and she would find The One. But now it was gone.

Noa's work gave everyone a week off for Christmas and so, using the holiday she'd saved up, she added an extra two and went back to her mum's. Even though it would mean someone telling her it was a shame she couldn't make it work with such a special man, the idea of being home was alluring. Her mum was the only person who would understand the grief that comes with accepting a future alone.

So she travelled back to Stoke desperately trying to picture a life the exact opposite of what she'd spent so long yearning for. And that's when she saw Elliot.

7

Twenty-six years old

Dom got a girlfriend. And every time Elliot met up with him, she was there. They weren't big into public displays of affection, and they did everything they could to include Elliot without making him feel like a third wheel, but that just made the whole thing worse. Elliot was attuned to every minute interaction Dom and Sarah had. A little hand-touch under the table, them both smelling of her perfume, Dom buying a different flavour of crisps than usual at the pub, the way Dom was keen to quickly wrap up their Saturday fry-ups. He even looked a little more filled out and Elliot could picture them cooking hearty meals together.

Elliot started to feel deeply uncomfortable and despondent. It was obvious that something was wrong with him, and so he made it his mission to find out what. He stopped seeing Dom so much and instead, in the little free time he had, lay on his bed to sieve through memories, thoughts, feelings. Looking for a clue as to what was his problem and what he needed to do to fix it.

He thought about Noa and wondered if everything that had happened back at school had fucked him up. He played the memories from that time again and found that they were still sore.

He thought back to when he worked at the call centre. He seemed to be popular enough with girls (and he was, they pined after his mysterious eyes, waiting to be texted back, desperate to find out what he was thinking, grateful for any nugget of attention from this attractive, deep, complex boy) but he never found a connection with any of them. He'd finally lost his virginity but it was as unsatisfying and stressful as he thought it would be. He always felt exhausted after being with a girl. When he was in the company of one he spent the whole time imagining how someone else, a more naturally confident boy, would act and attempted to replicate it. If he ever tried to be himself he would freeze, not knowing who that was or how to be him, and then would spend days afterwards feeling dirty with shame, going over and over the moments of silence that he'd let hang between them.

Since he'd started his new job in Logistics his mind had been all over the place so for a while he'd let himself stop thinking about relationships, he was settling back into things after all. But time had crept on and it had almost been a year. He was twenty-six. And now Dom had a girlfriend. He could see so clearly that the aim of life was to get into a relationship. All around him single people spent their time and effort working towards this goal, and once it was achieved, life was complete and happiness would follow.

Elliot was aware that Beth was pursuing him but there was always something holding him back. He lay in bed night after night trying to work out what he felt towards her. He did feel a certain tension in his stomach when she looked directly at him or when she found a way to touch him but he also felt a kind of repulsion when she spoke about reality TV or he saw the powdery creases around her nose or when she used her tongue to move around her lip piercing. And then the guilt from these thoughts made him avoid her for days.

Elliot tried to experiment with these feelings when he was masturbating. Picturing Beth he searched his body for physical clues; was that desire? Or was he faking it? Was that horniness for her or just in general? In the end every feeling drained away and he couldn't finish himself off.

He started to wonder if he was gay. He had no problem with the idea, if anything it would be cause to celebrate, finally he would feel like a normal person with normal desires. He remembered being obsessed with Fraser at school. Was that because he fancied him? Did he think he was cool or attractive? He tried to dream up an adult version of Fraser, or other men he knew as he touched himself but felt nothing. It was getting to the point where he could barely get himself off at all, even looking at porn, because he was so consumed with working out what it all meant.

He started to wonder if he was asexual. Maybe this all came down to a lack of attraction to anything. Asking himself, had he ever enjoyed masturbating? Did he like sex or did he only pretend to?

He spent hours googling all of this, trawling forums, psychology websites and blogs. Doing online tests and watching videos.

'When is too old to have first relationship'
'How to get over teenage romance as an adult'
'How to know if you fancy someone'
'Can you start liking someone after you get in a relationship with them'
'How to know if you're gay'
'If I don't mind being gay then why am I repressing it'
'How to know if asexual'
'Are asexual people lonely'

'What should sex feel like'
'Why does masturbation not feel good'
'Are some people incapable of love'
'How do you know if you're a psychopath'
'What to do if you're very shallow'
'Am I a bad person for noticing other people's flaws'
'What does attraction feel like'
'Are some people better off alone'
'How to know what is wrong with you'

He would go over all the romantic or relationship-based stories he heard from Dom or people at work or things he'd seen on TV or noticed in song lyrics. Wondering if he could see himself doing things like that. Wondering if he would like that or if he would only be pretending to like it. Wondering if he should be trying for these things or carrying on without them. He felt like he was going insane. His nails were bitten down so low they bled. He could barely sleep. He was desperate for answers.

Elliot and Beth had started eating lunch together. And it was good. Much like when he was with Dom, he didn't have to pretend to be someone else around Beth. He didn't find *himself* particularly likeable or knowable, but that had started to matter less. As long as she liked the shy, awkward authentic him, who was he to push her away?

It wasn't hard to segue the relationship into a non-platonic one. Elliot found it surprisingly easy to begin dating a girl. Much easier than befriending one. Every time he'd asked a girl if they fancied 'doing something' the whole dynamic changed. Silences became flirtatious rather than awkward. Physicality didn't require conversation. Inability to maintain a connection became playing hard to get. And at the very least, it felt a relief not to have to pretend he didn't notice her advances.

By the time Elliot's phone told him he'd arrived at his destination he realised he hadn't gone over the night ahead. He hadn't imagined all eventualities and planned for them. He hadn't decided what he wanted and what he didn't want from the night. He hadn't made notes on his phone about things he could say if there were awkward silences. But it was too late, Beth was waving to him from her upstairs window.

The house had a classic 'rented' feel to it. Worn faux-leather sofa, basic new-ish kitchen filled with mis-matching kitchenware, generic artwork on the walls that looked like something you'd get in a hospital, bedrooms filled with everything that someone owns. Beth cooked them pre-made tortellini and they ate it on the sofa talking about their days. But of course Elliot couldn't really talk about his day, explain how it was the same as every other day, describe the heaviness that hung in the air at home. And what did she have to say?

'Not much, not much. I've been tidying, for you.'

Elliot smiled but he couldn't look at her.

'And, urm, I like watching documentaries at the moment. I know it's mad but I love true crime ones. It's probably weird but I like watching things about murder!'

Elliot wanted to say that he didn't think it was weird to like something with an entertaining shock factor that most people liked. But he didn't. He just nodded and said, 'Ah, right, cool.' The thought passed through his mind that he would never be able to connect with anyone again and his life would drag on, empty of feeling, full of mundanity.

They went up to her bedroom and as he walked behind her up the stairs he took the opportunity to close his eyes and breathe in and out trying to curb the nervous nausea that he felt.

There was nowhere to sit except her bed and so when she sat on the edge of it, he stayed standing and looked around her room.

'I like your room,' he said, to say something.

'Thanks. I know it's a bit early to have Christmas decorations up but I love Christmas. I want it to last as long as possible.'

He went over to where tinsel lined the back of her desk and touched it.

She filled the silence. 'Do you like Christmas? Are you a Christmassy kind of person or. . .?'

Elliot wondered if other twenty-six-year-olds had conversations like this. 'Urm. Not massively.'

'I know it's kind of basic or whatever, but I do love it. Like, I'm listening to Mariah in November, let's put it that way.'

Elliot looked at the plastic Father Christmas and Snowman on her windowsill and felt sad. There wasn't much more to look at so he looked at her instead and realised he had to sit down next to her now. It gave him a sharp memory of sitting on Noa's bed, relishing the opportunity to look at her as she sat on her desk chair. It made his bones feel sad.

'Yeah, you're right. Put some cheery music on so we can forget how cold and dark everything is.'

She let out a little laugh and reached to get her laptop from her bedside table and put on a Christmas playlist. It was so depressing to Elliot he almost laughed. But then he did laugh, and she laughed too. Her little innocent laugh where she covered her mouth with her hand was endearing enough that it flipped a switch in Elliot. Love and lust were just frames of mind, he decided. They were always there, within him, he just needed to allow himself to feel them. And so he pushed himself further onto the bed so his back was against the wall and his legs were stretched across it. She joined him. He took a deep breath and tried to be himself.

'I don't want to rain on your parade but Christmas is surely hell? Like, that is what I imagine hell to be.'

She was still giggling and looking at him, but he stayed facing forward.

'If that's hell then what's heaven?'

'I guess heaven is being allowed to be fully dead. Like the opposite of an endless existence.'

'Heaven is not that! Heaven is being with all your friends and family that have passed away and watching over those who are left.'

'And what about when those "who are left" are in heaven too? Who are you watching then?'

'You're not watching anyone. You're spending time with the people you knew.'

'So when your children eventually die you won't get to hang out with them straight away? Because they'd be watching over the people *they* knew?'

'Well...Yeah... you wait for them, I guess.'

'Right. Yeah. Makes sense. They're a bit busy for a while.' Elliot was actually having fun. He felt a little more relaxed and kept reminding himself that he was enjoying the conversation.

'Why is Christmas hell then? Go on.'

'It's like a torture. Because you know it's coming but you can't stop it. And you know exactly what's going to happen, in the exact way it's going to happen. And there's something so horrifying about having to do the same thing again and again and again with no end in sight.'

'Okay.' She drew out the word like she was finding him a little strange. 'That does sound bad when you put it like that, but also is something bad just because it happens again and again?'

'Yes.' Was all Elliot could bring himself to say. He swallowed a feeling down. 'So, it's your turn now. Why is Christmas so good?'

'I'm surprised I even need to explain! It's full of delicious food and prezzies and family and friends and good songs.' Beth gestured to her laptop, which was playing Wham tinnily. 'It's a nice time. I don't know what else to say.' She shrugged and gave him a sympathetic smile.

For a brief second he pictured himself with Beth's family, paper crowns on, Monopoly ready on the table, Celebrations wrappers on the floor, and wondered if this was his chance. He could like Christmas too, he just needed a Beth. He turned towards her and looked at her mouth that she was pushing nervously to one side, wondering if he should kiss it. He leaned in and she leaned in and he was about to bridge the final gap when he wondered if he could get even more excited for what could be, before they kissed, so he would enjoy it more.

He leaned his head back and closed his eyes. 'Tell me about your Christmases then. I want to know. I want to picture it.'

'Well, there isn't much to say really. It's your standard Christmas.'

He looked at her, frustrated. 'Yeah, I know, but tell me like, who's there? What do you play? Eat? What's the little traditions? The good stuff.'

She shrugged and he felt the mood in the room change. 'These days it's only me and my nan. Dad's in prison and Mum. . . Mum does come sometimes, but not recently. I've got a little sister who's got a little baby but she's been with her man's fam the last few years.'

'What about you and your housemates? Do you do stuff together?' Elliot offered.

'Not really. I don't know them that well. I just rent the room.'

Elliot felt out of his depth. He didn't know whether to press or change the subject. He was always awful at making calls like that. And so, as usual, he froze and didn't say anything.

Beth carried on in a slightly forced chirpy voice. 'But it doesn't mean I think Christmas is hell! When I'm running the show I'm gonna make loads of traditions and it'll be well good. So. . .' She trailed off awkwardly. Elliot wanted to put his face onto his knees and pull on the roots of his hair, and so he pictured himself doing that. And because he was busy picturing that he didn't have time to think of anything else to say.

Beth closed her laptop and pushed herself off the bed. 'I hope you don't mind, I've got a few things to do tonight. Silly admin things, you know how it is.'

'Yeah, yeah, of course. Cheers for tea and all that.' Elliot was up and out of there in a flash. Beth didn't even come to the door but stood and waved to him from the top step.

Walking home, Elliot focused on biting the inside of his cheek every time he passed a lamppost. As soon as he was home he ran to his room, got out his old notebook and started writing.

Two people get together to stave off their own loneliness – good or bad?

If people are lonely does that mean they're desperate or does it mean they're picky?

Why does it feel like lonely person + lonely person still = loneliness?

Why does it feel like we would be using each other? Isn't that what all relationships are? People using each other as warmth in the room?

Well then why do I feel lonelier when I'm with her than when I'm alone?

Over the next few weeks Beth returned his smiles and questions but she did not instigate. She did not message him or ask to go on break with him or make him a tea. And at first he felt a relief, to eat his sandwiches in peace and to spend time with his thoughts, but after a while he started to look at her from across the office and wondered if he'd ruined his only shot at a happy, normal future. Now when he looked at her she seemed fragile and kind and pretty. He liked watching the slow way she typed and the giggle she gave away to people so easily. He re-read their texts and saw humour in them that he hadn't seen before. He saw it as endearing the amount she wore her selection of Fair Isle jumpers. He missed her.

By the 23rd of December Elliot's mind felt still. And he felt happy. He was excited to speak about the silly things he'd seen at work and the funny thing he'd thought about something in the news. He even spent slightly more time than usual planning his outfit for that day. He wore one of his coolest shirts – but not *the* coolest one because he didn't think Beth would 'get' it – and the Fred Perry jacket that she'd liked earlier in the year. At lunch time he sent her an email.

subject: long time no sandwich
body: Xmas Lunch?

She didn't reply even though he could see she was on her computer and he felt a type of desperate regret. It was clear, he had liked her all along. Why would he be feeling like this otherwise? This nervous tension coursing through his body. He struggled not to stare at her and instead stared at his inbox waiting to see a (1). It got to 1.45 p.m. and he realised it would be embarrassing not to go to lunch at this point, since he was an early eater and it was obvious he was waiting for her. He sat in the canteen pulsing his teeth together and wondering why he always fucked things up. He had to squeeze his eyes shut thinking about all the chances he'd missed.

Elliot startled at a pinch on his shoulders and let out a scared 'ah'. It was Beth. She sat opposite him.

'Sorry. I had loads to do. Ham?' she said, pointing at his sandwich.

'Always,' he said, looking purposefully at her eyes, her face. 'Cheese and pickle?'

'Always.' She smiled broadly back and he noticed she had a double dimple on one side.

'Pub tonight?'

'Well.' She pulled off a bit of sandwich and chewed it before replying. 'I'm not sure. I've decided to buy a last-minute tree.'

Elliot looked up thinking for a second. 'That's quite late for a Christmas keeno like you, isn't it?'

Beth shrugged and they both ate in silence for a moment before he carried on. 'Can I come then? I know I'm not a big Christmas guy—'

'—No, that's Santa!'

Beth laughed and then Elliot laughed and then whenever one stopped the other one started again.

'Yeah, you can come. If you say Christmas is hell one more time though. . .'

'I promise.' He held his palms up, 'No talk of hell or any post-life realms.'

It was fun, walking around the parking lot looking at tree after tree pretending they were noticeably different in any way. He was having fun.

'This one's a little *too* green.'

Beth was laughing every time he surveyed a tree and made a faux-serious comment.

'And this one's needles are close together in a way that's making me uncomfortable.'

'Okay, so where's a good one then? You're being Mr Positive tonight, remember?'

'Right. Yeah. Of course.' He tried then, his very best, to find one he thought was good. He'd never bought a real tree before but he took a second to picture a perfect one, in a film or something, and observe its characteristics. Eventually he found one that matched the image.

'I think this one.'

'Because the trunk is the *perfect* size?'

'No, genuinely. It's small but looks dense and it's, y'know. . . tiers. There's no gaps in the tiers. And it's a nice green.'

Beth looked at it and her face melted. 'You're right. It's perfect. Thank you.'

She pulled him in for a tight hug and his body felt warm and tingly. He didn't want to let go but he knew it would be weird not to.

They were lugging it back to Beth's, laughing as she taught him the lyrics to basic Christmas songs, when he suggested they stop at the pub. 'We can leave the tree outside, no one's going to nab it.'

And so they went to tuck it around the corner. After steadying it against the wall, they were left close together and facing each other.

In her big knitted jumper and tight jeans Beth looked cute to Elliot. She smiled up to him, so obviously feeling amorous that it made him nervous, in a kind of good way. He knew this was the time to kiss her so he breathed in and leaned down, but the timing was all wrong and she had started saying something to him. He straightened up again and apologised, hoping that the dark hid his blushing. But Beth said, 'Don't be sorry' and stood on her tiptoes linking her hands around his neck and pressing her mouth to his. He tried to focus on the kiss, but then he worried he wasn't enjoying it, and then he was so concerned about the thought he wasn't enjoying it that he had to squeeze his eyes shut. But then Beth stopped kissing him, took her hands off his neck and slid one into his hand instead. Elliot exhaled and felt his ribs expand. Beth started to lead him inside but the release of tension filled Elliot with a wave of desire and confidence. He pulled Beth back and kissed her again. This time focusing on the fact that things were finally going well.

After he pulled away Beth leaned in and pressed her head into his chest. She muttered something and so he leaned back and looked at her laughing.

'Huh?'

'I like you. A lot.'

Elliot squeezed her hand. 'I like you a lot too.'

'I like you, *a lot* a lot.'

Elliot, still holding her hand, started to walk inside. 'I like *you* a lot, a lot. But also I like being warm.'

And so they went inside, rosy-cheeked. Elliot welcomed the warmth of the pub and it seemed to him like things were going well. He felt normal.

'I'm actually feeling Christmassy now. In a non-hell way,' Elliot said, bringing them both back some mulled wine.

'You're the only person that would have to explain that,' Beth said, laughing into her palm.

Elliot turned in his seat to face her more.

'Thanks for showing me it can be fun. That's going to make a quarter of my year nicer from now on. Over a lifetime those quarters add up, y'know.'

Beth shrugged but looked very pleased. 'I'm not the first person to like Christmas.'

'No, but you're the first person to make me like it.'

'That's nice,' she said, smiling into her wine.

Elliot watched her face, pearly even in the warm light, and thought she looked lovely.

She looked up at him and he wanted to kiss her again. But not only to kiss her. To sleep with her. To be her boyfriend. To start a relationship. A proper life.

Beth filled the gap.

'One day I want to give up my job and move to the country, get a little cottage that I could make super-Christmassy every year. Basically I want a doer-upper, although I won't be able to do much of it myself so I'd need help with that! But yeah, I'd make it proper nice and cosy and make it somewhere you'd want to live forever. I know it sounds silly but I want a bit of stability. Everything to stay the same for a while, y'know? A nice family who wants to spend their time together and. . . I don't know what I'm saying. Sorry. That was so random.'

Beth was bright red now but Elliot was frozen. He knew he should respond or at least smile but he saw it so clearly. How seamlessly he would transition from being a helpful, stable son to a helpful, stable husband. She didn't want *him*. His reliability was useful to her. Which made sense, 'useful' being the only thing he ever was to anyone. He realised she probably wouldn't be able to name one thing she liked about him in particular, because he *was* no one in particular. What she wanted was a monotonous person who could give her the monotonous life she'd already planned out. In the same way he wanted someone to tell his silly little funny thoughts to. And now they had each other. But he felt more alone than ever. Overwhelmingly alone in fact. The music had become quiet and everything seemed further away somehow and he had the thought that hell would actually be this, being surrounded by people forever without any of them knowing who you are.

'I'm sorry, no, not random at all. It's. . . I get migraines and I think. . . I can feel it y'know, behind my eye.'

Elliot pulsed with a desire to turn off his consciousness, just for a bit, a year or so. He pushed his chair backwards and was mumbling something about having to get home before it kicked in when he bashed into someone.

'Shit. I'm so sorry.'

'No, no, that was me, sorry.'

Elliot looked at who he'd hit and saw a woman in an almost spherical puffer coat. Her smile and nose and eyes and hair were all big. Her olive skin and her gold jewellery added to the richness of her appearance. He itched the ridge of his nose to hide his smile.

'Noa?'

'What! Elliot!'

She pulled him straight into a hug. She smelt expensive, a delicate, floral smell. Emotion caught at the back of his throat. He stopped breathing, moving, thinking.

She kept her hand on his arm for a moment after the hug. 'What are you up to?'

'Just some bullshit job that means nothing—'

'I mean now!'

'Ah, right, I'm. . .' He turned to Beth who looked both shy and put out. Thousands of synapses burst in his brain at once resulting in too much information and so he spoke on a kind of instinct, saying what felt appropriate. 'I'm with my girlfriend.'

'Oh, yes. Hello. Nice to meet you, I'm Noa!'

Beth, smiling broadly, lifted her hand in a wave. 'I'm Beth.'

'I was leaving, actually, I've got. . .' He felt silly saying it now. 'I'm getting a migraine.'

'Ugh. I *hate* migraines. Get straight in a dark room, paracetamol, and something cool, like ice or a wet towel to put on your temples. Then I try to go to sleep and when I wake up I have a tea or coffee. I know caffeine is supposed to be bad for migraines but I think people say that to be preachy.'

Elliot wanted her to never stop speaking. She had the loveliest, formal voice that sounded like she was doing a speech or something. And she was effervescing with energy, her hands dancing in front of her as she spoke.

'That's great advice. I will 100 per cent do all that. Cheers.'

'Amazing. Well, it was so nice to bump into you! And nice to meet you, Beth.'

'You too.' Beth raised her hand again and Elliot's mind shivered with frustration. He wanted to make their interaction last longer, or get her phone number or arrange to meet up, but he couldn't walk out with Noa, leaving Beth on her own. And he wasn't confident enough anyway. So he smiled and sat down, the dread of existence creeping back into his limbs.

After he walked Beth and her Christmas tree home, he let his mind wander back to Noa. He kept laughing but he didn't know why. Desperately trying to hold on to what she was like

105

now, remember all the details. But the knowledge that he wouldn't be able to see her again tainted everything. He tried to reassure himself that it didn't matter because he was clearly never able to connect with anyone anyway. But it didn't help, because he knew things were different with her. A twinge in his chest reminded him it didn't work out for a reason. His jacket was not thick enough for winter but the cold hurt in a good way and he dug his fingers into his palms wishing he had nails to press into the skin.

8

Fourteen years old

Noa didn't set out to make friends with the most popular girl in the year. In fact, the bar was so low that she was originally prepared to make friends with anyone that would have her. In the first few years of senior school she drifted through a few different friendship groups. But at the beginning of Year 10 Nick Flannery moved schools, and so in the stricter lessons that required the class to sit alphabetically, Noa Farina and Verity Finn were thrown together. Noa didn't see Verity as an untouchable, even though she was the most popular girl in her class, Noa saw her as simply another person that would never be friends with her. (And it was this clear lack of intimidation that granted Noa an unexpected level of respect from Verity.)

One day, noticing Noa drawing funny caricatures of people in their class, Verity started asking for requests. After a particularly bad attempt at drawing their form teacher Verity giggled so much she rested her head on Noa's arm to calm down. Noa tingled with excitement. Not only was she funny but she was making a friend. She was already brainstorming the next drawing and imagining what it would be like to go round Verity's house when the bell rang and Verity stood up and left without so much as a goodbye. Life carried on like this, specific lessons full of laughter and silliness which ended as abruptly as they started. Verity didn't so much as smile at Noa walking through the corridors or in the canteen. She looked through her like everyone else. That was until the bag.

Noa was being allowed to visit her dad in London more since he'd had a new baby, Mia. Her dream had come true, eventually. A little sister. Someone to pour her love into. And she did. The baby cried a lot but Noa didn't care. Having a sister, crying or not, was as special as she thought it would be. But she couldn't help a small amount of disappointment underlying their interactions. Noa was fourteen now and their age difference meant that, like it was with everyone in her life, the relationship was completely one-sided.

Watching her dad's girlfriend, Frankie, grin into the small, soft thing in her arms made Noa's heart melt. She knew she was too young but she already wanted one of her own. A bond so close with someone that being separated would be life or death. (And one day, she would get it. It would be exactly what she wanted and yet completely different than she'd imagined.)

It was hard not to be in awe of Frankie. She was only thirty-three and to Noa she was like a celebrity. Her hair was long and creamy blonde and her body was visibly toned. She wore fashionable clothes that looked better than the coolest girls in her year at school. Her outfits always seemed planned, like she hadn't thrown on a top and jeans but had chosen a *specific* top to go with *specific* jeans. Everything she wore appeared crisper and thicker than her mum's soft, badly fitting clothes.

Noa was ultra-aware of her dad and Frankie's relationship. At home all she saw was suffering. Her mum, sad and alone, telling her how sad and alone she was. But at her dad's there seemed a joyfulness, a feeling that life was worth living, growing out of the centre of his relationship with Frankie. It was connection, it was making another person happy, it was the opposite of being a burden, it was what she wanted.

Frankie had an ethereal lightness to the way she navigated the world. Like she was simultaneously very present and not there at all.

'Frank, baby?'

'Yes, baby?'

Noa watched as Frankie stopped putting Mia's toys away and took to her dad's side on the sofa, stroking his cheek with the back of her index finger. He didn't take his eyes off the TV.

He spoke with a wry tone, 'Are you sure those toys go in that box?'

'Yeah, I mean, that's where I decided to keep them. Why, do you not want them stored there?'

Her dad broke eye contact with the TV and looked at Noa, who was sitting on the perpendicular, cream, leather sofa.

'It's just that I've never seen them in there before.' He burst out laughing and Frankie got up and returned to putting them away without saying anything back. Noa nervously laughed along, not wanting to upset her dad or Frankie.

'Seriously though, Frankie, you've got to keep on top of stuff like that otherwise we'll end up living in a pigsty.'

'Dad, come on, it's like, so clean in here!'

He scoffed. 'You would think that. Your mother couldn't keep a nice house even if her marriage depended on it.'

Frankie finished putting the toys away and stood up gesturing. 'Look, all done. Didn't take long.'

Her dad nodded in Frankie's direction. 'Exactly.' He did a double take at her expression and by the time he looked back at her his eyebrows were raised. 'If I knew having a baby was gonna make you into such a miser I would've said no!'

Frankie broke into a smile. 'You're right, you're right. I'm probably being a misery guts because I'm tired but it's not an excuse.'

Frankie kept her smile and looked at Noa.

'Noa, why don't you come upstairs? I've got some clothes you might like. Stuff that doesn't fit me after the pregnancy.'

Her dad's eyebrows were raised in a comedic way. 'Well you better keep that stuff, Frank. Y'know, as motivation to get back into it.' He looked back at the TV, his face completely serious again. 'Don't want to let yourself go just because you're a mum now.'

Noa noticed Frankie's hands were hovering over her already small-again stomach.

'Well, I thought Noa might want a few things anyway.'

He blew out a laugh. 'She'd be lucky to fit into anything of yours.'

Noa couldn't get herself to laugh politely at that. Her mood had deflated.

Frankie's wardrobe was built into one whole wall of their bedroom. Its mirrored doors made the room look large and impressive and Noa was in awe of what was behind it. Rails of brightly coloured clothes and boxes of shoes piled high. Frankie ran her fingers across the clothes and then turned to look at Noa.

'Okay, so what are we talking, a ten?'

Noa's hands went to her waist, which was the smallest part of her body. 'Maybe like an eight on top, ten on the bottom, I guess.' Even though she didn't feel ashamed of her body she was aware other people didn't think it was thin enough.

'Okay, okay.' Frankie looked down, thinking. 'And what about shoes?'

'A size eight. Although they're pretty wide. . . so it's sometimes better to get a nine.'

Frankie couldn't help laughing. 'Well you won't be getting any nine's here I'm afraid!'

Noa flushed. 'Yeah, sorry, I was only explaining. I know they're massive.'

'I bet there's some really flattering shoes out there though that would make them look a lot smaller?'

'Yeah, maybe.' Noa realised she was standing with one foot over the other like a child. She sat down on the bed, already fed up with thinking about her appearance.

'Your dad's probably right about us being different sizes,' Frankie said, looking kindly down at Noa. 'But that doesn't mean we can't find you something!'

Within an hour Noa had a thin floral bag, called a 'tote bag', filled with goodies. A beaded necklace, big round sunglasses, a brown belt made up of connecting circles that were studded with jewels, a selection of bangles, elasticated gemstone bracelets, dangly earrings and a neon pink and green Maybelline mascara. It was probably the best day of her entire life. She couldn't help wishing her mum was as cool as Frankie but then felt guilty for the thought.

As they said their goodbyes the next day Frankie whispered to Noa. 'Now go get yourself a boyfriend!'

Noa laughed nervously, 'Thanks, Frankie. I will!' But boys weren't on her mind right now. All she wanted was a friend. She wanted to be somebody's 'best friend'. That was what she wanted to be called more than anything, more than 'girlfriend'.

Frankie squeezed a bunch of Noa's hair. 'Do you have straighteners?'

'No. Not yet.'

Frankie looked concerned and then took her coat off. 'Here. Have this. See it as an early Christmas present.'

Through the car window she handed Noa the nicest jacket she'd ever seen. It was a navy bomber with a fur-lined hood. When Noa usually went shopping, she felt overwhelmed, it was like she was fashion-blind. As soon as she saw someone fashionable she could tell and was in awe of them. But when it was her turn to buy something she couldn't work out what was cool and what was average. The things that felt a bit 'out there' to her always tended to be the things everyone popular ended up wearing and the things that she felt sure were cool always turned out to be boring and slightly outdated. (But this selection of clothes from Frankie helped Noa to look one of the trendiest she would ever end up looking in her life.)

When term started again Noa walked into class with her head held high. She had layered on some mascara and was wearing the bomber and carrying the satiny tote bag, trying to act like she wasn't excited by how cool everything was. Being herself hadn't worked, trying to copy other people hadn't worked, but what about imitating someone that no one else knew? Noa was excited to try it.

Verity came in late and slunk into her chair without a second glance at Noa. The day felt long and pointless after that. The dreariness of the upcoming term stretched out in front of her. At lunch she read her book in an empty classroom because she couldn't bring herself to latch onto some group or other that didn't want her to be there. The stress ended up giving her a nosebleed and so by the time she'd sorted herself out, Noa was the one late to the afternoon lesson. She hurriedly sat down and got out her notepad to begin doodling away the time.

Verity leaned over (as if she could smell the indifference). 'I love your bag, Noa. Where's it from?' Verity rubbed the bag's material between her fingers and Noa's heart broke into light.

She quickly tried to remember where Frankie had said it was from.

'Oh. Urm. It's from Topshop. From the London one, on Oxford Street.'

Noa hadn't been there but was confident with her answer.

Verity's mouth changed into a little 'o' and she looked more directly at Noa than she ever had before. 'Oh my God.' She put extra emphasis on the 'd'. 'I've always wanted to go there.'

'You should go.' Noa imitated Verity's flat, unemotional voice and tried to think what Verity would say in this situation. 'It's well cool there.'

'How come you went?'

'I'm from London. So my dad and sister still live there and I go down there all the time. It's well good. There's so many shops.'

'Lush. What's the Topshop like then?'

Noa could feel Verity looking at her mascara. 'It's well good. It's got well nicer clothes in it and stuff than shops round here. And sometimes you see celebs or models.'

'For real? Like who?'

'Urm. . .' Noa racked her brain for names but drew a blank. 'I think I saw Natasha Bedingfield last time.'

Verity did a wide-eyed expression that said, 'Okay then' and got some gum out from her Jane Norman PE bag, offering some to Noa.

Their friendship was taken to the next level on a non-school-uniform day when Noa got to wear her new accessories. None of them were explicitly mentioned by Verity but she was invited – 'are you coming?' – to eat lunch with the cool girls. It was amazing but also disappointing. Yes, she was hanging out with the most popular girls in her year but that wasn't particularly satisfying to Noa. She was still the one on the outside who either barely spoke or got weird looks for the things she said. As they walked back to class the girls paired off in conversations and Noa walked on her own, playing with the beads on her new bracelet. Manically fantasizing about Verity calling Noa her best friend, about Verity inviting her to her house, about Verity showing any kind of particular interest in her. Singling her out as someone special. But as usual she felt tolerated, not treasured.

Life went on like this. Hope mixed with disappointment. The torture of semi-acceptance. Sometimes Verity seemed to love Noa and other times she barely spoke to her. One night Noa looked in her scratched bedroom mirror and asked herself if it was worth it. The yo-yoing. The heartbreak. The reflection answered: yes.

Alice was the second least popular in the group after Noa. The popularity hierarchy was positively correlated with how well-off the girls' families were. The more money = the better things = the cooler the reputation. The only exception being Erin whose family had very little but was stunning and often had a free house. Alice wasn't rich, wasn't stick-thin, didn't have boobs or a particularly impressive personality and like Noa, she didn't get invited to the parties. But she made it into the group because she was confident and sexual. She rolled her skirt up higher than anyone and bought the smallest polo shirt to showcase everything her push-up bra gave her. She hung out with older boys from outside school and only was part of the group because she talked about thongs and shaving her fanny and said she'd given a blow job to a boy from a different school.

And so, although they couldn't have been more different, Noa and Alice were in similar positions. But then it all changed. Alice got a boyfriend in their school. His name was Mike and he was the second most popular boy in the class after Fraser Bell. After this change Alice's social status shot up. Verity often spent her time chatting alone with Alice because Verity was desperate to be with Mike's best friend; tall, broad, loud, cheeky, Fraser. Verity even started wearing her skirt one waistband-roll shorter.

By the time it was halfway through the academic year it became clear that Verity's fifteenth birthday party, in April, was going to be a huge event. The girls didn't usually mind talking about parties that Noa wasn't invited to in front of her, but this was different because Noa was brought into the group by Verity. Noa noticed Verity shut down conversations in her presence from awkwardness. It was strange to Noa, sometimes she would look at how much she would be making Verity laugh and feel almost certain she got on with her best of everyone (it was true, she did find Noa funny and less boring than the other girls, but unfortunately getting on with someone was only a small part of how she chose her friends). But it seemed to have minimal impact on how close she could get with her. It didn't take long until Noa felt like she was on her way out of the group.

One night she felt a surge of determination to get invited. How could she sit idly by as her life slipped away from her? If she wanted life to be a certain way then she needed to guide it to that place. Lying on her bed, listening to music, Noa realised she was already equipped with the instructions and made a plan. First step: get Verity to speak to her about Fraser. Second step: get invited to the party. Third step: get a boyfriend. Fourth step: get to be Verity's best friend. For once, something was clear to Noa, boys were the key to her happiness.

It wasn't hard to get Verity to talk about Fraser. They hadn't spoken about him before because Noa didn't know what to say (and Verity could feel that). But it turned out all Noa needed to do was ask questions. Verity was desperate to talk about him, all the time.

When Noa got invited it was like everything else good she experienced in school, an anticlimax. Verity casually asked Noa what she was wearing to the party. No invite. No 'You should definitely come'. No excitement. But Noa could turn an anticlimax into the best thing that had ever happened just by reframing it. That night, as she lay in bed, she went over and over the fact that Verity had *chosen* her to come to her party.

She wasn't ready for the third step. She could barely get attention from girls let alone boys. She didn't understand them, what they wanted, what they talked about. And on the rare occasion when they interacted they looked through her as if she were a steamed up window they needed to see on the other side of. She was almost certain that this was where the plan would fall apart. But Noa was an optimist and so, donning her mascara and jewellery, she decided to first learn from Verity how to appeal to boys.

One day Noa mentioned that she had to go shopping for something to wear to the party.

'I'll come with,' Verity said, not looking up from her phone.

That weekend was magical to Noa. Walking around Hanley arm

in arm with Verity felt unreal. Like she was actually living in one of her daydreams. Verity looked amazing. She wore a short denim skirt and real Ugg boots folded down so the sheepskin was visible. She was covered in jewellery and her face was so (self) bronzed it made her blonde hair pop. Noa tried to take it all in like a lesson, watching the way Verity swung her hips as she walked and stuck her chest out and put all her weight on one leg while she stopped to look at clothes.

They went to TK Maxx, Primark and H&M and ended at Millie's Cookies. Noa spent all her £35 life savings on whatever Verity told her to and wondered if this was what it was like to be an adult (unfortunately, no). It felt like the world had opened up and it was full of endless possibilities. And when Noa assumed they would split ways and walk to their separate homes, Verity said, 'Come mine? We can practise your full outfit.'

Verity's house was a bus ride away. It was detached and inside it reminded Noa of her dad's except it was less plain. The plates were black squares and the carpet was thick and green. Her sofa was big and leather with the fluffiest, softest pillows Noa had ever touched and there was a bowl full of decorative sapphire gems on the coffee table. But it was Verity's room which was the pièce de résistance. Three walls were painted light grey and one was painted dark purple. Against the purple wall was a double bed, the headboard made of black metal swirls, and propped against it were a selection of cushions. The floor was covered in a white, furry rug that Noa couldn't resist stroking.

'Come here.' Verity guided Noa over to a small white table that was covered in make-up and products. She bent down and plugged something in.

'Are those straighteners?'

'They're GHDs, babes. Now sit there and let me sort this out.' Verity took down Noa's ponytail and assessed what she was working with. The feel of Verity's hands on her hair made Noa close her eyes for a second. Having Verity's full attention on her was almost too much to bear. The skin on her scalp and shoulders tingled. This was it. This was everything she had ever dreamed of.

Verity bent down and unplugged the straighteners. 'I've got a better idea.'

Noa found out that Verity's mum, Sandy, was a mobile hairdresser a few minutes later while sitting in their utility room having her appearance diagnosed.

Sandy had short asymmetrical bleached hair and heavy blue eyeshadow. 'You've got very frizzy hair haven't you?'

'Yeah.'

Sandy knelt down to look at Noa's face. 'So where are you from then? Originally?'

'I'm from London.'

'London, is it,' Sandy muttered to herself. 'You've got a nice tan, haven't you?'

'Thank you. I'm just naturally tanned, really.'

'But the rest takes away from it a bit, doesn't it?' Sandy gestured to Noa's face and body. 'If you were blonde it would look more like a tan, know what I mean?'

Sandy stood up and started parting Noa's hair into different sections. 'It's very thick, isn't it?'

'Yeah.'

'Aw. No bother.' Sandy rubbed Noa's hair between her fingers. 'Let's see what we can do, shall we?'

Noa had already changed so many things about herself, warped her interests and opinions into the same ones as the girls around her (secretly continuing to nurture her love for the things she *truly* liked in the background). So what was one more thing to change?

Verity kept leaving the room to make a snack or speak to someone on the landline or watch TV and Noa squirmed in her seat as Sandy pulled sharply at bits of her hair. After Sandy was done Verity waved over from her sofa and Noa had to leave. Her scalp was warm but her spirit was cooling.

When Noa got home that night her mum looked at her in shock.

'What have you done with yourself now?'

'I got highlights.'

'You look like a right slapper. No matter how hard you try, you're never going to be a Barbie type, Noa.' Her mum looked back at the TV, shaking her head and pursing her lips into a line.

Noa's heart broke. The truth is when Sandy showed Noa her straightened semi-blonde hair in the mirror she thought it looked kind of stripy and she didn't feel like herself. What she wanted was for someone to tell her she was beautiful. Just once.

Her voice broke, half frustrated, half devastated. 'But you constantly say that boys don't like girls that look like me. They like "skinny blondes". What am I supposed to do? It's a lose lose.'

Her mum's voice became soft and condescending. 'Of course it's a lose lose, Noa. Men don't want women like us. Everyone wants a Hollywood bimbo now. But it doesn't mean you should try and become one. Stop messing around with yourself and maybe one day you'll be lucky enough to find a man that will actually stick around.' She flicked her a smile and then muttered to herself, 'Don't hold your breath though.'

Noa stomped upstairs, parted her hair in different places and threw make-up on her face attempting to find some kind of 'look'.

It wasn't awful, she concluded. Verity wouldn't have suggested this if it was awful.

On the day of Verity's party Noa was invited to get ready at her house with the rest of the group. Looking at the girls dotted around the bedroom, rubbing in their mousse foundations, spraying their body sprays, fake-tanning, layering on mascara, dabbing concealer onto their lips, bronzing, straightening, singing to the R&B tunes blaring out, Noa's heart radiated with joy. Having friends was everything she thought it would be. Maybe she didn't even need to go through with part three of the plan because she'd already won the prize. She had a group of girl friends, who did fun things and included her in their plans. People were asking her to pass things or straighten the backs of their hair like she was an equal to them. There was no one she could pick out in that room who saw her as particularly important though, the thing she wanted so keenly, but she looked at Verity whispering something to Alice and wondered if that was about to change. In her new cami, denim skirt, dolly shoes and her trusty beads Noa felt as good as anyone else there and the anticipation of what was to come was exhilarating.

Once people started to arrive Noa realised that she was going to be fully interacting with boys all night. It wasn't like school where people shouted things across the classroom or went off to chat in pairs. People were standing around in mixed-sex groups talking, drinking and laughing. Noa took a deep breath in and told herself, this was it. This was going to change everything. She was on the precipice of having a best friend, she could feel it.

Every moment of the party felt overwhelming. She was

constantly having to think what to say or how to act and cringing painfully every time she made the wrong choice. Putting out her feelers, Noa tried to work out which of the boys would be a good target. He couldn't be anyone that her friends currently or had previously fancied, he couldn't be out of her league and he should probably be a bit desperate. Shane was the only one who met the criteria. She had no idea how to instigate speaking to a boy so instead she kept smiling at him and looking away, hoping that he would come over and speak to her. Shane would smile back, sometimes, but mostly he was duct-taping empty beer cans he'd finished onto the bottom of the current one that he was drinking until it made what the boys were calling a 'wizard staff'. Noa didn't know what time parties ended but she was getting nervous that she wouldn't have even one conversation with Shane and her chance to become serious in the eyes of Verity was slipping away. She decided not to leave this up to fate.

Noa took her warm can of beer and left the room. They were clearly never going to interact in front of everyone else, but maybe if she was on her own he would feel more comfortable. She walked around the ground floor of Verity's stylish house. The only room that was empty was the dining room and so she slipped inside, turned on the light, left the door open and then sat down, slightly around the corner so people walking past wouldn't notice. But it wasn't too long until someone strolled in.

'Ah, sorry.'

It was a boy from her class that she didn't really know. His name was Elliot and he used to be pretty geeky but had somehow made his way into the popular group. Still, she'd never really heard anyone talk about him.

'It's okay.'

Noa was about to ask him if he was all right but he blurted out, 'Are you staying in here?' He looked worried.

'Urm, probs for a bit.' Noa nervously pressed her fingertips into the soft metal of her can wondering if she should get up and leave. Elliot was staring at the ground. He was small and cute and nervous and Noa had the thought that they were the same person. The new, slightly uncool one who was hanging on to this lifestyle by a thread.

'You can sit down if you want.' Noa smiled at him and he looked up at her but didn't say anything or smile back. His leg moved as if he were about to move into the room when Fraser turned the corner and jumped on his back. Elliot looked like he was about to have a heart attack and collapsed to the floor but when they stood up Fraser was cackling and Elliot laughed too.

'I've been looking for you, fuck face,' Fraser said, pulling Elliot out of the room.

Noa got up. It was too intense to be sitting facing the door. So she moved to the opposite side of the table. Feeling positive, she sipped on her frothy tangy drink and waited. Her cheeks tingling with warmth. A few minutes went by until someone came in.

'What the fuck, Farina?'

Noa didn't turn around. She thought it would be mysterious to stay facing away and that it would encourage Shane to sit down next to her. A second later she felt the chair to her right being pulled out. She looked up and physically jumped.

'Oh.'

'Caught you in the act?' Fraser's sapphire eyes sparkled with confidence.

'What do you mean?' she managed to stutter out. They had never said a word to each other before.

'I *mean* what the fuck are you doing in here, Farina?'

No one had called her that before and her body grew hot at the realisation a boy was calling her by her surname. She'd seen it happen to other boys and girls as a kind of cheeky endearment but no one had ever called her anything except Noa.

'I. . .I was just having a think.'

Fraser blew out a 'pfft' of laughter, pushed off the chair and sat on the table instead, looking so directly at Noa she had to look away.

'What the fuck do you need to think about?'

She stole another glance at him. It was exhilarating, getting to see up close what Verity was so obsessed with. His blemish-free skin, broad shoulders, straight teeth, ultra-confidence. She wanted to carry on dissecting him but realised she had to reply.

'Nothing really. I thought I needed to think but. . .I don't.'

'Alreet, you weirdo.'

Noa took another sip and waited for him to leave. She wanted the humiliation to be over. But he didn't leave. As she brought the beer can to her mouth to take another sip Fraser pushed the bottom of it up so it spilled over her face. Her stomach flipped and she jerked around towards the door to see if she'd been pranked but there was no one there. Fraser was half lying on the table almost crying with laughter, so Noa relaxed slightly. It was just a joke. And actually, it was a joke that they were sharing together. So she started laughing too. He sat up and wiped some beer off her cheek and then said, 'You shoulda seen the fucking look on your face, Farina. You were scared shitless.'

They both started laughing again and Noa felt her mind wander. For the first time she imagined what it would be like if Fraser chose her. She pictured them at school: her sitting in his lap, her squealing as he did the fireman's lift to take her from her table to his, her texting him under the desk, her staring at him from across the classroom, her kissing him up against the B–Block walls. Basically her doing anything she'd seen other girls do with their boyfriends. But then she felt confused. Did she want to be Verity's friend or Fraser's girlfriend?

Noa opened her mouth to ask him if he was enjoying the party but someone must have walked past because Fraser bolted out shouting, 'Oi, retard!'

She took a deep breath in and out. She was starting to feel slightly fizzy from the alcohol and wondered if she should take herself to bed but as she stood up to leave, Shane entered.

They both looked at each other without smiling or saying anything. Noa didn't feel like speaking to him right now but was also aware that everything she wished for was happening. She took another step forward to leave but he moved in her way.

'Look how gnarly this is.' Shane held up his sellotaped stack of beer cans.

'Yeah, that's awesome,' Noa said enthusiastically, even though she didn't know why it was good.

'You can hold it if you like.' He thrust it into her hand. 'Try and take a sip from it. It's hard.'

He was vaguely shifting his weight on and off his heels and his words were slightly gargled.

Noa took a sip, pretending it was harder than it was to make him feel like it was impressive.

While she was still holding the 'wizard staff' Shane stumbled closer and pressed his warm, wet mouth onto Noa's.

It was not like she thought it was going to be. Their faces didn't lean opposite ways like people's seemed to in films and their hands were down by their sides. It felt like he was moving his mouth around on hers and making it wet. His breath smelt like Marmite and metal. He pulled away and she gulped in a breath. He took back his staff and she moved out the way so he could tip it up for a drink.

'Are you Jewish?' He looked at her with glazed eyes.

Noa felt uncomfortable. She felt like she should say no but didn't know why and didn't want to lie. She wondered how he knew. She worried if it mattered. 'Yeah. I mean, well, yeah I guess I am.' She mumbled.

'You can't tell.' He gave her a lopsided smile. 'You're pretty.'

When Noa got home on Sunday morning she lay on her bed, staring at the ceiling, emotions muddled inside of her. She had been to her first party, had her first kiss, but Verity didn't seem to care. She'd had barely any reaction when Noa giddily whispered it in her ear a few minutes after it had happened. Verity gave a slight shrug and that was it. The next morning the reaction had been worse, a bored-looking smile and a, 'Yeah, you said,' then joining Alice on the sofa, their heads knocking together as she leaned in to show her something on her phone.

Noa rubbed the heels of her hands into her eyes. How had she been so stupid? Why would Verity care about the fact she'd kissed Shane when he had barely any connection to Fraser. She racked her brain for other plans or fantasies, anything that felt hopeful. But all that came to mind was a picture of Alice sitting on Mike's lap. Then Verity on Fraser's. Her breath caught as she imagined herself in their position. Being picked out by a boy in front of everyone. Maybe there was a reason so many girls craved this. The attention of a boy could be equally good, if not better than a friend. Because what is a boyfriend if not the ultimate best friend? A whole new world opened up to her.

Noa reached over to her desk and grabbed a black gel pen. She wanted to remember this forever. She turned onto her belly and started writing – carving – into the wood of her headboard. 'You're pretty.'

9

Fourteen years old

(Anxiety is the mind's attempt to predict future threats and possible negative outcomes and protect us from them. What it does not protect you from is the impact of the anxiety itself. The physical and mental consequences of fear. That is a necessary by-product, anxiety tells us. But you protect your future self at the detriment of the present self. The day-to-day self. The one that is alive.)

Elliot sat there, on the toilet seat lid, waiting for lunch to be over. But it had only just begun. His body jumped at any small noise – a door swinging open, shrieks in the hallway, boys entering the cubicle next to him. He didn't know what he was scared of but he was scared. The same as he'd been every lunchtime for years.

He pulled his knees up and pressed his closed eyes into them, trying to think of nothing, but he couldn't manage. Images popped into his brain. Of his mum, her body limp, dead on the settee. Of Willie, left alone screaming and hyperventilating. They were so clear and sudden, like knives through his eyes. They made him squirm. It was the worst thing he could imagine happening.

He didn't spend his lunchtimes divided between a cubicle and the old cloakroom because he was hiding from anyone or anything in particular. But he needed somewhere to neutralise these bad images that popped up out of nowhere and made his body turn cold and then hot. He didn't know what was wrong with him, thinking weird things like that, but he had accepted this fate. As long as he kept his family safe by talking to The One and doing what he was guided to do, then these bad things were definitely not going to happen. His duty was to protect them.

On this day he neutralised these thoughts with a muttered phrase, *Keep my family safe, keep my family safe, keep my family safe, keep my family safe, keep my family safe.* The horror left his body and was replaced by a relieving vacuum. Elliot, his work done for now, sat there clammy and empty. His stomach ached with loneliness. He found himself straining his ears to hear snippets of other boys' conversations. Willie was Elliot's favourite person in the world, but a lot of their communication and interaction was non-verbal. They could have a whole conversation in meows or watch five hours of TV in blissful near-silence but sometimes he badly wanted to speak to someone else or make them laugh.

On this particular lunchtime Elliot overheard a silly thing another boy said and had to press his nostrils closed so they wouldn't hear him laughing along. The tingly joy that spread over his skin made him realise he couldn't remember the last time he'd laughed. Sitting on that toilet, chuckling to himself, he felt like he would rather take a risk and leave the cubicle than spend one more second alone. He stood up and, as quietly as possible, slid the lock *open closed open closed open closed open closed open* thinking, repetitively, at the same time that things would be fine. He washed his hands and then switched the tap *on off on off on off on off on off* to give himself the best chance at keeping his family out of harm's way while he risked not being easily able to neutralise any bad thoughts that came in.

The canteen was buzzing with people and smelt strongly of hot cheese and chips. He walked through the room and stood by the glass doors that led onto the playing field, and looked out of them as if he were waiting for someone. Not that anyone would notice. Unlike the Willies of the world, who are bullied for being too much, Elliot was like a walking void. Keeping to himself was a habit he'd gotten into at middle school. Back then he'd learned that bad things happened when people caught sight of him and Willie. And so they retreated, sitting together in the corner of the library chatting about Stoke City. When Elliot no longer had Willie, he would sneak to the toilets, keen to continue keeping any attention to a minimum. It was only once he'd started spending time in there that he started getting the bad thoughts regularly, and so it worked out perfectly. (What a coincidence.) It was a safe space and somewhere he could neutralise the thoughts. And that's how Elliot became the kind of unpopular that made him invisible. Living his life on the outskirts. Hoping to pass through the years unnoticed.

In the canteen the popular group of boys sat at the table opposite the door where he was standing. He leaned against the wall and watched them in glances. They were so animated. Pushing into each other, cracking up, laughing, leaning over each other's phones. It was mesmerising to him, how effortlessly and happily they interacted. It felt like watching a talented pianist as someone who could only bash on the keys randomly. Listening to their conversations the gnawing emptiness in his stomach started to soften. In fact he became too relaxed. He noticed that he was looking at them directly, smiling and even faintly nodding along like he was in the conversation. That was the kind of weird thing he did which made him hide away in fear.

★

That afternoon in English Elliot sat nearer the back than usual. Mrs Sands asked Fraser to read out a page from *A View from the Bridge*. He read out every line going up at the end, as if it were a question.

Elliot glanced behind to see Fraser's friends working themselves up into almost breathless laughter. The whole class was laughing so he felt free to let it out too. For the rest of the lesson he couldn't help smiling to himself remembering Fraser's ultra-serious face when he was performing for his friends like that. For the remaining hours of the day he let his mind drift, imagining being able to laugh out loud with that group of boys. Picturing the feeling of the class's eyes on him as he chatted over the teacher to his friends.

Unexpectedly (as it always was) a feeling that something awful, something unknown but dangerous was going to happen soaked through him. He promptly squeezed his left bum cheek *one two three*, and then the right cheek *four five*, and then the right again *one two three*, and then the left again *four five* and then he moved onto lifting his big toe so it pushed out of the hole that was forming in his shoe, *one two three four five*, and then the other big toe *one two three four five*. The bell rang as soon as he got to five and it felt amazing, like The One was telling him that he'd done something right. But that afternoon, instead of using the luck to wish for the safety of his family, Elliot wished for friends.

When he got home he found his mum standing frazzled in the kitchen. She thrust over a scribbled list of things he needed to do and told him to get on with it.

Throw out-of-date things in fridge away, take the bins out, take mine and Willie's bedding off, put it on to wash, put new bedding on, tidy Willie's room, hoover.

The image came into his mind of pushing her to the ground and shouting, 'I don't want to do any of this!' right in her face. It was horrendous. It replayed again and again and again until he had to crouch down on the floor and press his knuckles into his temples to try and get it out his mind. Mouthing: *One two three four five. One two three four five. One two three four five.*

'What are you playing at, Elliot? Why are you down there?' He could hear in her tone that she couldn't decide whether to be angry or concerned.

He stood up. 'I'll do it later.'

'Excuse me?'

The energy that led him into the canteen earlier fired up again. 'You don't need to tell me to do those things. I do them anyway. And I'll do them in my own time.'

'Don't get smart with me, Elliot. I'm not asking you, I'm telling you. Helping the household that feeds and waters you is the least you can do.'

He very subtly pushed his right hip forward once, *one*, left once, *two*, right three times, *three four five*. Then reversed it left, *one*, right, *two*, left *three four five*.

'Sorry, Mum, but y'know, sometimes I feel like other parents don't make their children help out as much as me.'

'And how would you know?'

The words burned shame into his cheeks. She went over to take the bin bag out and Elliot was shocked. She wasn't someone who would ever 'let him off' or 'do it herself then'. And so it came into his mind that he really had broken her and his chest cramped with guilt. He rushed over to stop her.

'No, sorry, please, I'll do it.' But as he tried to pull the bag out of her hand she snatched it away and threw it on the ground. The smell of old dairy and bin juice mushroomed out of it. Elliot's mum looked at him, narrowed her eyes and smiled slightly. And then, grabbing her keys from the worktop she said, 'All you do is make my life harder.'

Elliot's mind was completely blank as he cleared up the mess. And it was only after he'd finished that he came back to reality, dazed and regretful. A bud of worry forming in his stomach about the safety of his mum and Willie.

And so he walked slowly towards the stairs, ready to go up them *one two three* forwards, *one two* back, *one two three* forwards, *one two* back, but he needed to crouch down again. He screamed at himself in his head, *What a little idiot you are, stop doing these weird, stupid things, they mean nothing, all they do is make you a little weirdo, just walk up the stairs normally and be normal and people will treat you as if you're normal.* But even before the screaming was over he knew he was going to walk up the stairs in that way. He couldn't help it.

Once he got upstairs he changed his, Willie's and his mum's bedding, tidied Willie's room and then went into his. He reached under his chest of drawers and got his notebook out but something stopped him opening it. He reminded himself that this day was different. He ground his teeth together and put the book back. He took the bedsheets downstairs and put them in the machine. He made Willie his tea and got him settled in front of the TV. But Elliot couldn't get himself to sit down next to him. His muscles were twitching and his mind felt hot and fidgety.

Elliot walked outside. It was pouring. It was freezing. He looked around the (tiny, concrete excuse for a) garden and sat in the centre on the ground. The rain felt good on his face. He pretended he was crying because he wasn't able to do it on his own. And it was nice, to imagine there was a physical expression of his feelings. He made faint sobbing sounds to trick his brain into thinking the water was tears. Elliot tilted his head up to the sky and spoke so the water fell into his mouth.

'Hello, "The One". I, Elliot Wood, make a decision, right here right now, to take control of my life. I will be cool, I will have friends, I will be friends with Fraser, I will have fun, I will have a good life.' He tilted his head back down because the water going in his mouth made his voice sound strange. 'Whatever I have to do, I will do it, mark my words.'

He looked down and his whole arms were shivering but it made him feel good. Like the power of The One was inside him. But he was also getting too cold. So he stood up and ran inside and up to his room, not forgetting to walk up in sets of three up and two back (of course, never forgetting). Elliot sat on his bed, dripping, grinning, waiting for The One.

Elliot was a talented football player. His dad had taken him when he was very young as a bonding activity and it was love at first play. It was the only thing Elliot did other than going to school and looking after Willie and his mum. When he was a child he begged to switch to a team in another town so that he wouldn't know anyone there and had played there ever since. His number one priority at school was being unknown. And this meant hiding every aspect of himself, even the good ones. Whenever it was football in PE, he played the simplest passes and let other people score goals. He was short and skinny enough that people would never assume he'd be good at it anyway. But he was quick on his feet and had watched and played more than enough hours to make smart decisions on the ball. He'd grown a little recently but still played with the same low centre of gravity as when he was shorter.

It was only a few days until the next time football was played in PE. Half an hour of drills went slowly and Elliot's determination to play well waxed and waned with bursts of nerves and desperation. It was the boys laughing together in the end that made him decide to at least try. Anything that meant he might one day be part of a joke was worth doing to him now. Even the risk of rejection or shame.

It was seven-a-side, so one match for all the boys in his class, with a few subs. Usually he put his hand up when Mr Jenson asked anyone if they wanted to be subbed off, but today that wasn't going to happen. They were divided into two teams. Elliot's shoulders tensed when he saw he was on Fraser's. He couldn't wait to start running, the hair on his arms was sticking up almost painfully and his breath came out in visible bursts in front of him. He could hear his heartbeat in his ears as he took his place out on the field but as soon as the whistle blew he allowed himself to relax into the game the same as he did at his Sunday league team.

At the beginning he sat back, playing defensively, but after a couple of good touches early on, he set up Ben with a clever pass, who slotted it in the goal. The team cheered and Elliot expected no response but Joe nodded at him and said, 'Great ball, mate.'

His confidence grew further so he moved forward again. Mike from the other team tried to dribble past but Elliot tackled him, took the ball around Simon and smashed it past the keeper. Walking back to their half, Joe caught up with him and gave him a fist bump.

'That was class.'

Elliot couldn't look at him for long. His gaze was on the ground, focused on keeping his smile turned down.

Fraser tucked another one away and the team celebrated together.

By the time Elliot's team were 3-0 up, the other team started getting frustrated and Elliot heard someone say to the boy marking him, 'You lost your man. This is shit.'

Elliot's goalkeeper rolled him the ball. He dribbled around someone from the other team. But a foot tripped him up and sent him hands down into the mud. As he picked himself up he heard someone run over to the boy that tripped him.

'Fucking hell, that's a foul. Just cos he did you, mate.'

A hand pulled him up. It was Fraser. His square, white teeth revealed in a panting smile. Elliot racked his brain for something someone else might say.

'Cheers.'

Fraser tapped him twice on the back.

The other team managed to bring it back to neck and neck. Elliot was galvanised into action and hungry to win.

Ben passed him the ball in his own half, Elliot did a step over and took the ball past Mike, he put it through Simon's legs, and then was one on one with the goalkeeper. He dummied to shoot so the keeper dived left. Elliot paused for half a second. He could feel everyone's eyes on him and it felt good. He scooped the ball over the goalkeeper. Almost in slow motion he saw it drop into the back of the net.

The whistle blew. His whole body was tingling. Five boys ran over, celebrating – grabbing him, getting him in a headlock, ruffling his hair. Cries of appreciation and joy rung out from them. The feeling of their bodies bashing into his was a rush he'd never known. At his Sunday league team he arrived at the games, played, left. Yes there were celebrations but he wasn't more than an acquaintance with anyone and he didn't want to be. This was different.

All the way back to the changing room people were chatting

through some of the highlights of the game. The atmosphere was electric. Elliot wondered why he'd never done this before.

On the way to their next lesson Fraser walked up beside him, with the rest of the group following, and bashed into his side. 'Oi, Elliot mate. Since when did all this happen, eh? Are you on some kind of drugs? What the fuck, man?'

Elliot shrugged, trying to repress a massive grin. 'I play outside school sometimes' was all he could think to say.

'And what, you've randomly got good?' Elliot could see Fraser was shaking his head in what looked like disbelief at the memory, and Elliot's heart sang with pride but he just shrugged.

Fraser stopped and looked him in the face. 'Who you playing for then?'

The next day as Elliot walked into class, he headed for his table by the front but heard his name being called out from the back.

'Elliot!'

He swallowed. A thousand thoughts of rejection went through his mind. It felt like he was about to get found out but he didn't know what for. He quickly squeezed his bag's left shoulder strap *one two three four five* and then the right *one two three four five*. The thought was neutralised and his brow relaxed as he reached the boys at the back.

Fraser was chewing gum with his mouth open. He kicked the back of the seat in front of him.

'Get out of there a sec, I need to talk to Elliot here.'

The boy sitting in the chair pushed it out with so much force that it wobbled and he had to grab onto the desk to stop himself falling.

Everyone pissed themselves laughing, doing impressions of his 'Whoooaaa.'

The boy didn't look at Elliot but plonked himself into a chair a few seats in front.

Elliot could feel his eyes darting around but he didn't know what to focus on. He wanted to look down but was trying to force himself to seem confident.

Fraser nodded to the seat. Elliot sat in it, not taking his backpack off. He sat side-on and scraped it a couple of centimetres around to face Fraser more.

'So what d'you think? Come try out for the A team and also my Sunday league team?'

'Yeah. Can do.' Elliot ruffled his hair so his face was briefly covered while he smiled.

'Got to tell ya, though, if that was a one-off you'll be back over there.' Fraser nodded to the front of the classroom and everyone around him laughed.

'Right.' Elliot stood up but Fraser kicked the chair leg.

'I said *if*. Sit down.'

Elliot was surprised at how simple it was to slot into a new world. How easy the transition felt. How open the door became once he got his foot in. He sailed into the school football A team and transferred smoothly into Fraser's Sunday league team. He found out he was funny, making short comments here and there, observations, witty one-liners, quick responses. He didn't need to get references or have opinions or speak for extended periods of time to make a joke. Fraser liked these little quips and sitting in the chair in front of him became permanent. Elliot realised there was nothing he liked more in the world than making someone laugh.

Elliot hadn't told his mum about the transfer to the more local team, and so the hour he usually spent travelling out of and back into town was now free to hang about with Fraser. Mostly they talked about football and drank fluorescent blue Powerades that Fraser brought with him. Elliot felt comfortable in this situation, he'd spent his life watching and playing and speaking about football. But in school the conversations were prone to shifting around under his feet and destabilising him, and so he tensed up. It was like he was carrying a secret around but he struggled to pinpoint what it was.

One lunch they were in the canteen sitting at the long table where Elliot had watched them months before. The boys were leaning forward and looking down the table towards the girls who were cracking inside jokes, rolling their eyes, shouting protests against comments thrown at them from the boys' side. Luckily, Elliot was sat on the edge, as far away from them as possible.

The boy sitting opposite him was the boy whose seat Elliot had taken in form time. He was still nice to Elliot though and seemed to have longer standing but equally precarious ties to the group.

He kicked Elliot under the table. 'Hey, Wood. Wanna go get some biscuits from the shop?'

Elliot didn't know what to say. Being part of the group, at this table, was the dream. And yet sitting there in silence was embarrassing and worrying him. Plus, getting to know this boy did appeal to him. When the small bursts of Fraser's sunny attention weren't shining on him the nagging loneliness threatened to reclaim him.

'All right then.'

They snuck out and went to the corner shop a few minutes from the school. They walked in silence for a bit but Elliot didn't feel awkward somehow. Eventually the other boy spoke.

'What shall we get then?'

Elliot looked up at him. His ginger wavy hair made him look kind somehow. 'I thought you said biscuits?'

'Yeah but what type?'

'Urm . . .' Elliot scanned the shelves and then picked up a packet of fig rolls. 'These?'

'Gross.' The boy pretended to stick his finger down his throat.

'I was joking. . .' Elliot shrugged, but then saw the boy's eyes clock and light up.

'What about these then?' He picked up some Fruit Shortcakes. Elliot laughed. The joke was stupid, but they walked around the whole shop picking up different things and suggesting them. Toilet roll, Spam, tampons, pickled garlic. When Elliot picked up the 1 kg bag of rice the shopkeeper told them to buy something or get out.

They spent the rest of lunch in the classroom eating a whole packet of bourbons and talking about easy, simple things that Elliot found natural to contribute to. After lunch was over and Fraser started walking with Elliot to the next lesson, he noticed the boy hang back to walk on his own. The drop from joy to guilt was so large that Elliot felt a physical pressure in his chest. But then the guilt turned into what felt like a premonition. A vision of all this happening to him one day. Something told him that he wouldn't have had this thought if it wasn't likely to happen. It was as if, by thinking it, he had willed it into existence. He felt his mouth go dry and his face start to tingle.

This continued to happen. Bursts of easy fun with the ginger boy, doing silly things to make each other laugh. And then, afterwards, being pulled apart, pushed into their respective positions on the hierarchy, Elliot never able to say 'no, I'll sit with him today.'

Everything the ginger boy, or 'Ginge' as he was now called, said was met with widened or narrowed eyes, inward snorting, parroting impressions, and physical violence masqueraded as a bit of fun. The fear of this happening to him was enough to make Elliot live in a constant state of trepidation.

And so Elliot did whatever his mind told him to do as protection. Tapping on tables, turning door handles, walking up and down stairs, counting ceiling tiles, turning on and off taps, light switches, zipping, buttoning, breathing, walking.

He knew it was strange and stupid. He didn't even really believe that these things did anything. But he felt like a slave to the thoughts. Life became exhausting and stressful. Having to find empty rooms and make excuses that he'd left something behind, or felt ill, or pretend he was daydreaming. It was like he was living on a separate plane to everyone else, with brief moments where the world came into focus and he was allowed to be present. The rest of the time he was in his head, worrying about things or counting things or worrying about counting things.

Mock GCSEs were coming up and Elliot had barely been concentrating in class. At night he could spend half an hour opening and closing a drawer until it felt right to him and he was briefly safe enough to go to sleep.

Mrs Brown was jabbering away about Ox-bow lakes and Elliot's stomach was twisting. He knew he was going to have to count many things before he left this classroom but he was finding it harder to think of excuses to be left alone. He shrugged off his sweater and used the toe of one of his shoes to undo the laces of the other. He practised his lines in his head. He got all the pens out of his pencil case and pretended to test them on the front of his notebook.

The bell rang and everyone jumped into action. Fraser pushing his seat out and throwing his drawstring bag over one shoulder.

He stood for a second over Elliot. Elliot could feel the pulse in his neck. He started packing up his pens as slowly as possible.

'C'mon, prick, let's get out of here.' Fraser kicked the leg of his chair. Elliot put his pencil case in his bag and then reached for his jumper on the back of his chair, pleading with the universe for Fraser to get bored and walk off. But he didn't. He stood there as the rest of the class filed out. Elliot slowly pulled his polo's collar out the neck of his sweater. He didn't want to stand up because he knew he would want to do it at least five times so he turned on his chair and then looked at his shoes.

'Ah, I need to tie this. You head on.'

Fraser leaned on the empty table opposite. 'Nah it's fine. I was gonna say, me and Verity were talking yesterday after school.' There was a pause here that Elliot had learned was there for him to do an impressed expression and nod. 'And she was saying that people have been talking about how quiet you are.'

Elliot felt dizzy. The stress of Fraser not leaving mixed with the idea that people were not only noticing him but making a judgement on him was like a hot hand around his throat. His shoelace had been tied and there was nothing left for him to do except stand and follow Fraser. But the feeling of dread was so intense it was impossible to ignore. He pushed himself off and on the seat in the most micro of movements he could. *One two three four five.* Fraser was listing things girls had said about Elliot but he couldn't focus. His vision was blurred at the sides and his mind felt separate from his body. He knew he needed to reach the door by the number five. *One two three four five, one two* a normal person would have stepped out of the room on the three but he couldn't. The need to comply was overwhelming. He took three mini steps on his tiptoes and then exited the room.

Fraser had turned to look at him precisely as he did the little *three four five.*

'What the fuck are you doing?' Fraser was smirking and looking left to right as if he'd missed something.

'Dunno. Drills, innit.' Elliot shrugged and strode on. His neck was dripping in sweat. He needed to get to the end of the corridor so he could run back and open and close the door properly. Fraser had sped up to fall in step with him. But as soon as they were through the double doors. Elliot pulled one back open.

'Ah, I forgot—'

He left Fraser and then hurried back to the door. He turned the knob in the most subtle movement possible. *One two three four five, one two three four five, one two three four five, one two three four five.* Elliot saw the seat he had been sitting in and a voice told him he should sit back in it. Now that he'd had the thought he had to obey it. What would happen if he didn't? Would everything fall apart? He sat back in his seat and stood up slightly and then sat back down on it *one two three four five.* It didn't feel quite right still so he carried on. Then he saw a face watching him from outside the room. His mouth filled with saliva and he burned red. He didn't know what to do and so sat in the seat as still as possible, hoping that life would somehow end right there. It was unbearably long (a few seconds) until they walked into the light.

Elliot's chest expanded with breath when he saw it was Mrs Brown. She walked in and closed the door behind her. The fear was less now but it had morphed into a worry that he was about to be found out. She didn't come right up to him but rather sat on a chair a few rows forward, clutching her folder in front of her.

'Are you all right, Elliot?'

'Yeah, miss. I am. I forgot—'

But he didn't want to lie for some reason. He just wanted to leave.

She smiled down at the floor and then looked up at him with a serious face. 'Can I ask how you're doing? In yourself?'

'Fine thanks, miss.' He started counting in his head desperate for this to end. *One two three four five. One two three four five.*

'I couldn't help but notice. That I've seen you maybe repeating certain things.' There were pauses between each of the last four words.

'I don't. . .' There was something stopping Elliot from shutting down the conversation. (It was a thin thread of hope that someone would find out and help him.)

They both sat in silence for a minute. Squeals of children running past the corridor both added to and removed some of the tension.

Elliot was tapping one of his fingers under the table in sets of five. He decided it seemed quite normal to do something like this. The feeling that something bad would happen was always lower when he was counting.

'Are you particularly stressed, Elliot?'

'Nah, not really.' He started to worry that she would believe him and end the conversation. A deep tug in him wanted it to carry on.

'Okay.' She pushed the edge of her file into her lap as if to conclude things. Elliot's eyes hurt. But instead of standing up she looked directly at him, her eyes were pleading and her brow was furrowed. 'I won't tell anyone and you're not in troub—'

'Yeah, sometimes I do repeat or like, count things.'

She leaned back into her chair. 'Do you like counting them?'

'No. Not really.' Elliot felt a desire to cry. To let it all out. It was like his eyes were on the brink but they stayed dry and painful. 'I mean, I guess I do in the way that I can't. . . stop.'

'I see. What would happen if you didn't do the counting?'

Elliot shrugged and muttered. 'I dunno. Something bad, I guess.' He looked under the table and saw his hands were shaking. 'I mean, I don't *actually* think something bad will happen.'

'But it might?'

Elliot looked at her face then. She had a round face and was about his mum's age. He liked the way she was looking at him intensely like he was saying something important. He had an embarrassing urge to hug her. 'Yeah, basically. It might. But even if I know it won't, I still just worry. It's hard to explain.'

'I understand. I used to count things too.'

At those words Elliott closed his eyes. He wanted to burn them into his memory so he could replay them whenever he wanted. He opened them and found himself smiling, and saw she was smiling too. He bit his nail to dampen his smile down.

'In the same way?'

'In the same way.'

'But you don't now?'

She shook her head and then looked up. 'Yes and no. I don't count now. But sometimes it's hard.'

His mind was swimming with questions and thoughts but break was nearly over.

She joined him in looking at the clock. 'I can help you, if you like. Learn how to stop. But let's not speak about this right now.'

Elliot pushed his hands on his face and nodded. But as he took them away a dread filled him that she would expect him to leave with her and he could see her watch this thought.

'I'll leave you to. . .' She stood up and walked to the door. 'Come see me in here on Thursday lunchtimes. Tell people I've said you're failing Geography and need help or something. If you like.' She gave an awkward thumbs up and then left and Elliot began his process of standing up.

It was a relief to find out that these strange things he'd been doing for the last year were a diagnosable condition. OCD. He was ashamed of it and decided not to tell anyone, but also glad for the label as it made him part of a group rather than a freak. Mrs Brown told him to take the process gradually. All she wanted him to do at first was wait to count. He was still allowed to count whatever he liked but he should try and wait to do it. After the urge he was supposed to look at the clock and allow himself to count – or do a 'compulsion' as she called them – after two or even five minutes had passed. It was hard but also felt manageable compared to all those times he'd desperately tried to override the feeling entirely.

'Five minutes' turned into 'later that day' and what Elliot started to find was that when he got to his allowed slot, he didn't want to count anymore. The need had gone and if anything it seemed kind of silly to him. Sometimes he would even laugh with Mrs Brown about the things that he'd so desperately wanted to count in case not doing so would have caused something bad to happen.

Then she told him to try and do things only five times. Rather than ten or fifteen or twenty. This was harder but she told him to remind himself that 'it's my OCD who wants me to do it more times, not me'. But if he absolutely had to do it multiple times, then at least end on a number that wasn't five. It was only the OCD which made the number five seem important, she told him. It wasn't long before he was bubbling with confidence. It hadn't gone away but it had reduced and the reduction in itself was enough to make Elliot feel invincible. He could see it in his relationships. Something was forming inside him that was akin to faith that things would be okay. And that he deserved to be there. That he'd earned these friends for a reason. The reason was himself.

The first time Elliot was able to let an urge to do a compulsion dissolve in front of him entirely he put music on and danced with Willie in the living room – he jumped up and down and Willie leaned his body forwards and backwards – and then he lay on the floor listening to the sound of his heart thump, this time for a good reason.

Elliot and Fraser's weekend football team had won an important league game, thanks to solid performances from both of them. Afterwards they sat on the park bench eating jelly worms, talking through the game play by play. Sometimes Elliot would stand up and act out something great that had happened. Sometimes Fraser would stand up and do a silly impression of another boy and they would laugh.

It was warm and Elliot could feel the sun on his cheeks and nose. When people walked past he felt proud to be seen with Fraser. To be seen with a friend, and such a high quality one.

10

Twenty-six years old

Walking home, Noa was in a frenzy. Her mind was trying to analyse the scramble of feelings in her body but before she could land on a coherent thought she would already be feeling something else.

When she arrived home she ran to lie on her bed and think about Elliot, the same as she'd done when she was a teenager. She took out her phone and scrolled down to her contact 'Elliot'. But no, he probably didn't use that number anymore and if he did he'd almost certainly deleted hers. She put her phone back down and closed her eyes. She couldn't help herself picturing the boy she'd loved so hard and then replacing her memories of him with this tall, subtly attractive man he'd turned into. Her hand tingled at the thought of him touching it. She unlocked her phone again and typed out a message.

> Hi. I don't know if this is still your number? This is Noa. It was nice to bump into you! I'm here for another few weeks and have zero to do.
> You free for a drink?

Noa was happy with the message. She went to press send but her finger hovered over the screen. She realised she'd opened her

147

phone without secretly hoping there would be a message from Christopher.

She broke into tears and curled into a ball, thinking of her poor heart, broken so many times. She cried for what Elliot did, for how she'd been feeling ever since, for the fact she still felt for him all these years later. Had she really loved anyone else? Or had it all been some desperate attempt to find that painfully strong love again? But she remembered it was in her control, she was going to choose not to feel like that ever again. Without uncurling her body, Noa patted around the duvet until she found her phone. She deleted the message and threw the phone off the bed. She could almost feel a thick, cold layer forming outside of her. Heavy but protective.

Then it was Christmas day. A day that used to cause Noa to feel like an outsider, but now a day that she was grateful to not participate in. She couldn't imagine how it would feel to sit there, so heartbroken, when she was supposed to feel joy. She slumped on the sofa mindlessly eating a packet of After Eights she bought for herself. All her energy was spent trying not to respond to the inflammatory things her mum was saying.

'A little birdie told me Frankie's gained a lot of weight?'

'Oh right.'

'Is that true?'

'I honestly don't know, Mum. I don't keep track of dad's ex-wife's weight funnily enough.'

'Well, I've got to say it's always the skinny, pretty ones that end up like that.'

'Mhmm.' Noa tried to bite her tongue. She didn't want an argument.

'That's why it's good to be like you. Not ultra-slim but consistent. What are you these days, a size 12?'

'No, a 10 on the bottom, 8 on the— actually y'know what, Mum. I don't really care about sizes. Every shop is different these days anyway. I promise, if I want an opinion on my weight or dress size I'll make sure you're the first person I come to. But can we drop it?' The worst of it was that Noa knew her mum thought she was being kind.

'I'm just saying, sunshine, men might shun people like you but in the long run—'

'Mum, I'm off out.'

As Noa walked into town she thought about her dad leaving a trail of discarded women behind him and realised that she was no different to them. She wanted to say to Frankie, *Was it worth it?* but Noa could now see the answer herself. Frankie had done everything and more, been everyone and more and still ended up on her own. Noa thought about her own relationship with her dad. It was nothing more than a constant striving to be the ideal daughter, to be seen, to be enough. The least imposing but also adding the most value. Trying to have a relationship with her dad had turned out equally unsuccessful for both Noa and Frankie. And yet, this hadn't impacted him. He had *another* daughter, *another* girlfriend. With a visible exhale into the cold, Noa decided if life was going to be nothing but a series of rejections then she might as well pre-reject life. Save herself the middle step.

Walking around the predominantly empty streets of Hanley, Noa's hands became so bitingly cold that she no longer felt the sharpness in her heart. She reached the central square and walked over to sit on a bench to work out how she would be different in the new year. What changes she would make to become less reliant on men. It was going to be hard, returning to her life, exactly the same as before except for a huge hole where something important used to be. She pulled her puffer coat tighter and started to wonder if she should be more ambitious when she saw a figure sitting on the Potteries Shopping Centre steps. It was Elliot. Noa's body stiffened.

No of course it wasn't Elliot. It was one of those things where your subconscious projects the person you're thinking of onto anyone around you. The figure was wearing a jacket rather than a coat and was clearly cold. Noa squinted her eyes to see if she could see him any clearer and (even though it did nothing for her vision) became re-convinced it was him. He stood up briefly to get his phone out of his jeans pocket and there was no doubt about it. The small but sharp nose, thin lips, thick straight eyebrows, it was Elliot.

Noa's stomach contracted and she grabbed her phone out of her pocket and pretended to look at it. It was imperative she wasn't caught looking at him but she didn't want to walk away. Her brain fired up with questions: *Why is he outside, in the freezing cold, alone, on Christmas day? Does this mean something? Is this fate? Should I go over there?*

But as she looked at her phone and remembered the previous night, choosing not to text him, feeling relief as she realised when she awoke from her nap that she really *had* changed, feeling the first bud of positivity she'd had in weeks, feeling like she'd begun a new chapter in her life. Protected from the hurt that pursuing love inevitably ended with. She decided to leave it and walk home. But then her phone screen lit up in her hands. *Elliot.* Heat flushed into Noa's cheeks as she glanced up to give him a smile. But Elliot wasn't looking at Noa. He was still sitting there, staring into the distance now, seemingly unaware of her presence. She shimmied down to the end of the bench, faced away and took a deep breath in before opening the message.

I don't know if I'm messaging the abyss right now or some old man named ron (please block and delete this number if I've reached ron by mistake), but if this is still your number noa, it was nice to see you the other day. lemme know if you wanna come down the pub for a drink.

Noa clicked her phone shut. Her skin tingled with anticipation. Then she unlocked her phone to read it again. And then again. And then the figure walked past her, so she could only see the back of him. But it was the perfect back. His shoulder-to-hip ratio was a narrow triangle and his legs were long and straight in a way that Noa, with her womanly thighs, always envied. Her fingers were so cold they took effort to bend but she returned to the message to read it again and again and again. A flux of repressed feelings soaked through her body: grief, desire, hope. But after the (genuinely) tenth time reading it she started to realise something, it was a blessing in disguise that he had a girlfriend. She couldn't, wouldn't, allow herself to fall in love again, but friendship? With the person she had liked most in this world? This was a chance to change a painful memory into a neutral one. Turn a broken heart into a solid, stable one. And more than anything, a reason to leave the house when her mum started talking about weight.

Now Noa was with Elliot and his girlfriend, trying to form a bond. (Trying not to focus on his prominent Adam's apple or dimples.) 'So yeah, long story short, I did accidentally walk all the way from Kings Cross to Covent Garden looking for a Greggs.'

Elliot laughed but not as much as she hoped. 'Ah, you see, I'm not sure how far apart they are. I've never been to London.'

Beth spoke towards Elliot. 'Yeah, didn't you say that you hate the idea of London?'

Elliot shrugged. 'Probably. But I've never been so it's a pretty pointless opinion.'

'No way!' Noa wanted to suggest he should come, ask to show him around. But she was terrified any overly keen behaviour would be interpreted as her having romantic feelings. 'You should go. Do either of you ever fancy moving away from here?'

Elliot shrugged and swirled around the end of his pint. 'Nah, I don't think so. I quite like it here. All my friends and family are here, y'know?'

Beth was crossing her legs towards Elliot so much by now her back was almost facing Noa. 'Aw. Love that! We're both proud Stokies, aren't we?'

Noa looked at Elliot, waiting to see his answer. Every piece of information about him precious.

But Elliot just nodded and then looked at his watch. He was already shrugging his jacket on by the time he said, 'I need to get going, actually. Was great to see you though.'

Beth reached for her bag from around the side of her chair and slung it over her chest. 'Bye, Noa!'

At first Noa was motionless with shock. But then the realisation that she wasn't here to do anything but offer her friendship soothed her. If he didn't want to be friends then her life would be exactly the same as before. She did not want him. She did not need him. And so she went to the toilet, reapplied her lipstick – for *herself* – and went home. Thinking there was nothing as deeply relaxing as genuinely, fully, wholeheartedly giving up on love.

But to her surprise Elliot texted again and they met up the next evening too. And the day after that. All three of them went to the pub, spoke for a couple of hours and then parted ways. Noa felt surprised at how fulfilled she felt without the extra layer of trying to mould everything into an imagined future she'd created. And so on the fourth night Noa initiated:

> Do you and Beth want to grab
> a drink tonight?

Can we eat?

> We can eat.
> Brunch tomorrow?

Noa booked them a table at a restaurant that described itself as 'grill and contemporary cuisine' because of and despite the fact it sounded almost bafflingly generic.

She got there five minutes early and sat smiling into space thinking about how having Elliot and Beth as friends would be amazing. Having people in Stoke that she actually liked added a whole new dimension to her life. She wouldn't be returning to her identical life minus Christopher, but a new life where she sometimes visited home to meet with her new friends.

By the time they were ten minutes late she was embarrassed and stressed, the whole pull of friendship, after all, being less opportunity for rejection. When they were fifteen minutes late she became offended and started speaking to them in her head. *Well I'm sorry if you were having sex but it's not a good enough reason to—* Noa stood up and scuttled out while the waiter was looking away. But as she opened the door to the restaurant Elliot was standing there.

153

'Oh,' she said, relieved and miffed.

'Shit. Are you. . .?'

Noa stepped back so he could walk inside. 'Am I what? Done with brunch? Maybe I am!'

Elliot walked inside but stood opposite her, his straight eyebrows pushed together. 'Fuck. I'm so sorry.'

Noa rolled her eyes. '*Obviously* I didn't eat brunch on my own but I *could* have and that's the point.'

Elliot glanced at his black plastic watch. 'I suppose you had time for cereal.'

Noa's mouth dropped open. 'How dare you be so cheeky!'

Elliot put his hand out in the air to ask Noa to guide them to the table and said, 'I'll buy you brunch to make up for it.'

Noa faux-moodily shrugged. 'I *suppose* I could be okay with that.'

They sat down opposite each other and Noa pushed her hair off her face. 'When's Beth gonna get here, do you think? You two will be buying me dinner at this rate.'

'Beth's not coming. Is that. . . is that okay?'

Noa's face accidentally cycled through seven different expressions before landing on unfazed. 'Oh, that's a shame. No worries though.'

Elliot's eyes seemed to linger on Noa's face for slightly longer than would be normal and then flicked down to his menu. She took the opportunity to steal a glance at him. He still had the same straight posture, grey intense eyes, pointy ears. She wanted to tell him for some reason.

He changed the subject. 'So what can I get for you then?'

Noa relaxed at the idea that Beth wasn't there simply because it was nice to take a break from worrying about befriending both of them at the same time. She smirked at her old friend and let herself treat him as exactly that.

'I don't want you to *buy* me anything.'

'Well, okay, I was only—'

'I want something else.'

Elliot looked at her in the eyes without saying anything.

'I want to play "Top Joker".'

'Top Joker?' Elliot raised his eyebrows.

Noa could tell she was touching her face in nerves. 'You probably don't reme—'

'I remember.' He looked unimpressed but she could see the subtle things giving his excitement away: twitching lip, a sparkle in the eye, a squeeze of his finger.

'Yeah, well, I embarrassed myself in front of these waiters and I think you should too.'

'Right. Hmm.'

'So, to earn my forgiveness, you need to ask the waiter three questions about the menu before you order.'

Elliot seemed to be pushing down a laugh. 'Absolutely not.'

Noa faux-reached for her coat.

'Okay, okay. Please stay. I'll do it. But. . . well. . . three feels like a lot. Can you do one?'

'Deal.' They studied the menu for a while and then Noa lifted her hand to get the waiters attention.

A boy who can't have been older than eighteen walked over and said in a flat voice, 'What can I get for you?'

Elliot looked up at him. 'Sorry, can I just ask, the twelve-hour brisket, is there any way you could speed that up?'

His face was perfectly dead-pan, Noa gulped from her glass of water to stop the laughing.

'It's pre-made. Will come out same time as the other food.'

'Nice, nice. And here, where it says "generously topped with salsa" – do you know, how is it generous if I'm paying for it?'

'Uh. . .' The boy stuttered and crouched down to look at the menu.

But Elliot swooped in before he could look. 'No worries, mate, the scrambled eggs will do for me, please.'

Noa felt genuinely nervous. Her face went red in advance. 'I'll have the French toast, please. And you know here it says you get a free drink with any burger' – she pointed to the menu – 'is it possible to just get the free drink?'

The boy looked at Elliot and then back at Noa. 'Well, you can get any drink but you have to pay for it. Unless you're getting the—'

Noa interrupted with, 'Makes sense! Sorry, I always misunderstand these things. I'll have a cappuccino, please.'

As the boy walked away she watched Elliot's shoulders shake in silent laughter and felt a nostalgia warming her up. The sadness of a life alone was waning. She kicked him under the table gently and said, 'How you got me to agree to that, I don't know.'

When the food arrived and the conversation turned more general Elliot seemed vaguely uncomfortable. She wondered – was it eating food in front of her? Was it being without Beth? Was it this restaurant? (No.) She didn't know. But she tried to make him feel more comfortable by telling him embarrassing stories and asking him about simple, light-hearted things. Soon he loosened up, asking her question after question in return. He seemed focused on her every word. It made her realise how so often when she spoke to people she could tell they were barely listening or thinking of what they were going to say about themselves in reply.

They paid and went to leave but as they got to the door Elliot said he was going to the toilet and to wait for him outside. Noa said okay but it was freezing and so when he walked off she let go of the door and stood inside instead. She watched his long legs stride off but he stopped at their table and quickly, getting his wallet out, left ten pounds on the table – despite the service charge being included – before heading off to the toilet. As he passed by the young waiter Noa watched Elliot nod at him, saying something and smiling. She walked out and let the cold air cool her reddening skin.

When Elliot came outside and they stood opposite each other, ready to part, Noa felt a strong urge to continue the day. The thought that this would be her last chance to see him without Beth propelled her to say something, but they both spoke at the same time.

'Did you—'

'What are you—'

Noa laughed. 'Oh, I was going to say I'm probs gonna walk that off, if you fancy it? Or do you need to go. . . somewhere?'

'No, I'd like a walk.'

It was bitterly cold and Hanley wasn't the nicest of walking destinations. But Noa stuffed her hands into her puffer coat pockets and tried to act like this walk was a totally normal thing to do.

'How's things with your mum and brother?'

Elliot frowned at the ground and then pushed his eyebrows apart with his thumb and forefinger.

'Yeah, good, cheers. Same as usual. What about your mum?'

'Oh, she's fine. I guess. But I do worry about her. It breaks my heart a little to think of her all alone.'

Elliot looked to his side, directly at Noa. 'I know exactly what

157

you mean. Well, not *exactly*, because my mum still lives with me and Willie, obviously. But that's what makes it hard to leave.'

'Yeah, it's like any enjoyment from independence is tinged with guilt.'

'Exactly.'

Noa led them out of town to the central forest park. The sky was a flat white and her face ached in the cold.

'So how's London? Is it that much better?'

'I do love it. There's so much going on there, everywhere, always. Sometimes it can be a bit much but mostly it's great.'

'Do you think I would like it?'

Noa took two breaths in, cherishing the chance to speak as if she knew him. 'I think you *could* love it. Under the right circumstances.'

'I'm not so sure. It sounds like you have to be good at knowing what you are doing. And I'm not great at. . . knowing what I'm doing.'

'I could show you!'

They had reached the park. It was only 4 p.m. but the sky was already the same colour as the roads. The grass was dead, the only people in there were selling or collecting drugs, except the playground, which was full of teenagers drinking from plastic bottles of spirits and standing intimidatingly in circles.

But Noa walked in as if it were a summers day in Regent's park. She corrected herself, 'You and Beth should visit sometime. I'll show you around. It might not have oatcakes but it has everything else.'

'Sound. We will.'

The word 'we' hurt Noa slightly more than before. But instead of running from it she stepped towards it. 'How long have you and Beth been together then?'

'Not long. Are you. . . do you have a. . .'

'A boyfriend?' After the relief she felt saying Beth's name, Noa found it easy to purposefully close down any possibility of romantic tension with Elliot. 'No, no. I like being single. There's so much going on that I think I would feel a little restricted.'

'Yeah, makes sense. I can see that.'

'So how did you two meet?'

'Just at work.'

'You seem good together. You match well, I think.'

Elliot nodded. 'Thanks. I guess we are quite similar.'

Noa noticed that instead of feeling disappointed she looked back over the day, at how much they'd laughed, how much she felt seen and listened to by him, and felt genuine joy at finally having her friend back.

They stood at the blue railing that edged the olive green lake and looked out onto it. Elliot broke the silence.

'Do you come back here a lot then? It's been really nice to catch up.'

'Well I've still got a week and a half left of holiday here, but yeah, I do come back a lot.' (She did not.)

'Nice.'

The conversation lulled in the way that it does before something important is said. But there was nothing to say (there was). And so Noa said the first thing that came into her mind:

'You're taller.'

Elliot didn't turn to look at her but replied to the lake, 'Than some things, yes.'

'Than before.'

'I'm older than before.'

'So, am I. But I'm not taller.'

Elliot turned to look at her then, 'No, if anything you might be shorter.'

'I'm only more shorter than you than I was before. Since you're taller now.'

'I have no clue what you said, I'm afraid. But your hair is definitely more curly though, I can tell you that for free.'

It felt thrilling to refer to their younger selves. Noa turned to face him fully. 'You look like someone took the teenage Elliot and then underfed him and then put him back on a normal diet until he was back to the same weight again.'

'Are you all right? Nothing you're saying makes sense.'

Noa shrugged. 'Honestly, it sounded very poetic in my head.'

Elliot took a little step back and looked Noa up and down. Her body filled with awareness of itself. 'Well I think it looks like you moved to London.'

She looked at him back, secretly relishing the opportunity. 'It looks like *you* still listen to all the music I showed you.'

For a second he broke into a full smile, like he'd been found out, before dropping back to his typical serious expression. Noa couldn't help a sense of triumph shining on her face.

'Now I think about it, I don't even know if you *are* the Noa I knew because she had big circular cheeks.' Elliot moved as if to touch her face but stopped and made his thumb and forefinger into a circle and squeezed his own cheek with it instead.

Noa felt out of depth, an old feeling tugged at something in her mind. She looked for another thing that had changed but now all she could see was the Elliot of eleven years ago. The brief sparkle of life in his predominately flat eyes, the rarely glimpsed vaguely unstraight teeth, the furrowed brow making every expression look pensive, the upright posture and fidgety hands, the long limbs and narrow hips and the way he sometimes pulled on his earlobe.

She knew it was her turn but felt overwhelmed with thoughts and so let autopilot take over. 'Well you're definitely the Elliot that I knew because no one else has such cute pointy ears.' She stepped closer and reached up to pinch the top of his ear. The skin on her chest grew hot – luckily hidden by thick layers.

Elliot spoke straight away as if to fill the gap. 'Well, the Noa I knew didn't have a mole here.' He touched the small, flat mole at the edge of Noa's lip.

She laughed and said, 'Well you're wrong because I've always had a mole there.'

Elliot smiled and said, 'Nah, I know you have.' And even though it was said lightly, it did not land lightly. Noa smiled back, embarrassed somehow. But Elliot's face turned even more earnest than usual and, for a brief second, he opened his mouth. To say something? To kiss her? His hand went back up to her face and it felt like for a second he might put it on her cheek but it turned into a finger and once again he tapped her mole. 'I like it.'

And then he stepped backwards and turned towards the lake. His face in profile prettier and less masculine than from the front. She turned back too and they stood there in silence for a while until Noa got scared and pulled at his jacket, asking to leave.

Noa and Elliot saw each other almost every day until she had to return to London. But it was like being teenagers again in the way they always had to find places that weren't their own houses.

Together they would spend hours in Costa, nursing hot chocolates, talking about how they struggled to feel like real adults. Or they would find a table in the corner of a pub and play cards until they started yawning, or they would walk around the shops and laugh at the silly things they found. Noa preferred seeing Elliot on his own but not because she was jealous, it was because he was more himself – or at least the 'himself' she knew – when it was just the two of them. But they would do things with Beth too, like go to the cinema and Pizza Express. Noa – never sure what Beth thought of her hanging out alone with Elliot – would make sure to talk about the (fake or exaggerated) men she'd been seeing and ask questions about their relationship in an attempt to secure herself in the friendship.

11

The day before she was due to leave, Noa invited Elliot and Beth round for dinner and drinks, because her mum was away visiting her sister. She had decided that inviting them to London would be a good way to cement the friendship. Making sure this wasn't temporary, but something she could hold on to when she returned to the life that was so broken when she'd left.

She made Spanakopita and 'Limoncello fizz' in a random pan-European theme. She felt quite wired, trying to push down thoughts and feelings and hopes and fears, trying frantically to clean her house to no avail (it was clean, just full of things). She put on a nice blouse and skirt and then changed into jeans and a white T-shirt, then swapped it back to the blouse and threw on a cable-knit jumper.

By the time the doorbell rang Noa was so frazzled she jumped at the noise. At the door, smiling with his mouth but not his eyes, Elliot stood holding a bottle of red wine.

'Oh, hi, hi. Come in.' Noa stood aside and glanced briefly down the street to look for Beth. Elliot handed her the wine.

'Thank you! Very kind. Let me take your jacket.'

It confused Noa that Elliot never wore a coat even on the coldest of days. He was dressed reasonably smart, wearing a navy woollen jumper with his shirt's collar pulled out the neck and smart trousers. Noa went to tell him he looked nice but hung up his jacket on the end of the banister instead. She could barely look at him and led him straight into the kitchen. She felt jittery with nerves, unlike the 'relaxed friend' version of herself she'd been for weeks now.

She spoke looking into the fridge. 'What can I get you to drink? Wine? Juice? Or I made Limoncello spritz? I decided to do this kind of jokey summer—'

'Just a water please.'

Noa tried to respond like that was a neutral answer. 'Sure. Cool.'

As Noa handed him the water her cheeks burned.

She led the way into the living room but in the brief moment they were stood in the hall a sharp-edged memory cut into her brain. Them. Here. Running heavy-footed, like only young people do, straight up the stairs in their socks.

Elliot sat down on the leather sofa and so Noa sat on the textured beige one at the right angle. She watched him as he tapped his thumbs against the glass of water that he held in his lap.

'How have you been?' It had only been two days since they saw each other last but the atmosphere was stilted.

Elliot's eyes darted to hers and then back to the glass. 'Yeah, good, cheers. You?'

Noa almost laughed and asked him outright why he was being like this but it didn't feel like she had the right to ask him about his internal world.

'Yeah, good thanks. Well, I've had enough of this cold, hence the European summer theme.'

'Right, yeah. Good shout.' His voice was low and he left slightly too long between each word.

Noa felt stupid, drinking her stupid alcoholic drink from a stupid stripey straw that was stupidly too long for her glass, while he was there holding a glass which had been emptied of its tap water in two gulps. She filled the lull.

'Oh yeah, I meant to tell you, I've been listening to this song loads recently. And it made me think of you.' She felt herself blush a little. 'As in, I thought you would like it. Shall I put it on?' Noa reminded herself that this is what it was all about. Being his friend, showing, telling, listening, talking to him.

What felt like a beat too long later, Elliot replied, 'Can do.'

Noa bit some skin off her bottom lip trying not to think about his reaction. She stood and connected her phone to the TV and played the song. She tried to find a volume that didn't feel weirdly loud or quiet but there didn't seem to be one. She sat back down and sipped on the sickly drink, feeling like a teenager again listening to a song as if hearing it for the first time but through his ears. *What did he think of that bit? I hadn't thought about that lyric before, will he read too much into it? Maybe this bit's too electronic for him?*

Halfway through the song Elliot said, 'Do you mind if I use your. . .?'

'Oh yeah, of course. It's up the stairs, straight ahead.'

He put his glass on the coffee table and walked out and upstairs. Noa widened her eyes to herself. She reassured herself that things would get less weird when Beth arrived. She went back into the kitchen and started prepping a salad she hadn't planned to make, just for something to do. When Elliot came back down he only walked as far as the kitchen doorway.

'I already cooked the pie but it takes about fifteen mins to reheat. I still need to turn the oven on though. Any idea when Beth will get here?'

He pulled on his earlobe. 'I'm not sure.'

In her head Noa said, *Well can you check?* But in reality she said 'Okay, no worries. Can I get you another drink?'

'No, I'm all right cheers.'

Noa swallowed away a *Really?* She turned the oven on and walked to the fridge to breathe out and get some tomatoes.

After a pause Elliot said, 'I. . . Well. . . Are you. . . How have you found it being back here?'

Noa wanted to say *Amazing, I've loved it* but felt embarrassed of her clearly unrequited enjoyment of their time together, so went with, 'Good, thanks, but really looking forward to getting back.'

Elliot didn't say anything but she saw him nodding in the reflection of the microwave.

She finished the salad and they went back into the living room. Over the last couple of weeks one thing they both steered away from was explicitly reminiscing. For Noa all those memories led to what had happened between them as teenagers. What he had done to her. And so instead she'd only vaguely referenced things, trying to rebuild their closeness in a fresh new way. But tonight Noa could feel him slipping away and felt desperate to form something solid before she went back to London. She skipped songs until she got to one they used to listen to and said, 'I think you once told me you timed everything in songs. Your showers, cleaning your teeth, how long to brew a cup of tea. Is that still true?'

Elliot's eyes seemed to smile briefly but he itched his top lip so she couldn't see his mouth.

'Yeah, I guess so. Do you?'

'Well. . . no. I never did. I like to think in the shower and never know how long I've been in there. Which is why I'm always late.'

She wanted to say *Remember?* But picked at some dried feta on her jeans instead. She felt deflated. Elliot was different to other people because he always remembered things about her, cared about what she thought and did and felt. But maybe that was an old Elliot, or an Elliot she'd only ever created in her mind. Deep in thought, she let the silence go on too long and so this time he broke it.

'What are you looking forward to most about being back in London?' His expression looked normal in a way it hadn't been all evening.

'I guess it really feels like home there now. All my friends and stuff are there. So I feel a little homesick for it in a way.' But this wasn't the time to try and distance herself, she wanted him to know what she actually felt, 'But I've really enjoyed being back home, to be honest. And it's been really nice to catch up with you. I'd love to keep in touch, be friends or whatever.' It sounded silly now she'd said it out loud but also it felt good to tell the truth and lay the groundwork for inviting them to London.

Elliot cleared his throat and replied, 'Yeah, definitely.'

Noa felt her happiness waning. The flame inside her, barely rekindled after Christopher, becoming starved of oxygen again.

She pushed herself to standing. 'Right, well, better put the pie in the oven because she can't be long now.'

Elliot stood up. 'No, wait.'

Noa was shocked in a physical way. His voice was loud and he properly met her gaze for what felt like the first time since he arrived.

'Okay, but we can't wait too long. I know it's European night, but we don't want to be eating at 9 p.m. If she comes a little after it's served that's fine, surely?'

'Beth's not coming.'

Noa didn't know what to do with her face. Things were falling apart again. 'Okay, no worries. Well, I'll still put it in—'

'I think I'm going to leave now too.'

Noa laughed. The oven clicked to 'heated' in the background. Surprisingly Elliot did not look down or away. His jaw was pulsing and his eyes were moving from one of hers to the other.

'Right. Well. I hope you two have a good night or whatever. See ya.' The hurt of what happened all those years ago flooded into her veins and mixed with the frustration of now. Why had she ever let him back into her life? Her house?

Noa walked into the kitchen, shaking her head in disbelief. She got the pie out the fridge (never one to pass over eating in times of stress) and put it in the oven. Her thoughts interrupted each other until a voice made her jump.

'Look, I'm sorry. I don't want to be a dick.'

Noa's heart was still beating fast from the anger, the shock, but she felt herself soften slightly at the apology. 'It's fine. I'm sure my mum can have—'

'But I can't be your friend.'

You're not right for me rang in Noa's head again and she had to turn back towards the oven to shield the blank hurt on her face.

'Okay. Fair enough.' She was indignant but didn't know if she should be. Beth was the priority, of course. Nothing was said for a minute and Noa looked back to see if he had gone but he was still standing there, his eyes closed, thumb and forefinger pinching the top of his nose, mouth twitching lightly. Noa went to say something but she couldn't help taking the opportunity to look at him. His bony hands, narrow hips, mousy nondescript hair, the way his clothes always seemed the perfect ratio of loose and fitted. The way he was a man now; taller, broader, but still delicate in a way. The defined ridge above his lip – painful to look at somehow.

She zoned back into reality, concerned. 'Are you okay?'

He blinked his eyes open as if he were coming out of a trance but kept his gaze on the floor. 'Yeah, I know I should go. But I feel bad.'

Noa couldn't help rolling her eyes. 'Do you want me to give you permission? I've spent a long time not being your friend, Elliot. I think I can do it again. If anything, I'm more upset with Beth. I thought we got on.' A twinge of pain at the loss of a thing which had only just begun.

Elliot's head jerked up to look at Noa. 'Beth? Why Beth?'

Seeing Elliot defend her made Noa boil with irritation (envy).

'Well, because it feels a little two-faced to act like we were all getting on together and then for some reason ban you from seeing me.'

Elliot's eyebrows pushed together. 'It wasn't Beth.'

'Oh. Well, whatever then. I don't need an explan—'

'We broke up. We've broken up.'

The heat from the oven became too hot and so Noa stepped forward, bringing her slightly closer to Elliot. The hurt gave way to concern. 'Oh no. I'm sorry. What happened? Sorry, I don't know why I asked, it's none of my—'

'You happened.'

Noa couldn't open her mouth to speak. So she stood there, looking at him. He started picking paint off her door frame. She saw him take a deep breath in, look at his feet and then begin to speak. 'I can't be your friend because it's impossible to see your face and not get to tell you how beautiful you are. It breaks me to hear about the guys you're dating and pretend I don't wish it was me. It's terrifying to think there's nothing linking us together in any real way and you could easily disappear out my life and that would be totally normal because I'm only your friend and not a guy who loves you and always has and potentially always will. Unless you go back to London and stop being my friend and then I can at least try to forget you even though that's never worked so far.'

Noa watched his Adam's apple bob up and down as he swallowed. But he didn't look up from his shoes.

She felt the blood pulsing around her body. The word 'love' had taken the breath out of her. But she was not feeling what she thought she would. The exact thing she'd dreamed of her whole life was happening and yet she still felt cynical? A thought crossed her mind: *why are men desperate to pretend they love me?*

Elliot rested his forehead on the door frame for a second, glanced at Noa and then walked into the hall to leave.

Noa called out her words dripping with acerbity. 'What do you mean, it's "never worked so far"?'

Elliot stopped and turned around. 'Maybe it's pathetic but I've never found anyone I like as much as you.'

Noa looked at the ceiling and crossed her arms and then stepped into the narrow hallway, closer to him, so she didn't have to raise her voice. 'You didn't like me *that* much though, did you?'

Elliot's eyes darted around the hallway like he was trying to think of something. He scoffed and his voice came out slightly sour which took Noa by surprise.

'As in, after Year 11?'

Noa was struggling to keep calm. 'I don't know, you tell me. When did it stop? Or did you not like me all along?'

Elliot took a breath. She could tell he was angry, but he was not intimidating. 'I know it was a long time ago but surely you can't accuse me of that?' He was close enough now that she could smell him, clean like dish soap and deodorant. He looked down into her eyes, his eyebrows pushed together. 'I know I probably fail the people I care about every day, in every way possible, but you cannot say that I didn't like you.'

'I'm not saying you didn't like me, I'm saying you didn't like me *that much*, did you?'

'I liked you more than anything. Ever.'

Noa started to cry. It was stupid but her brain was feeling too much, too many conflicting things, too many opposing truths and wants. Why did she feel bursting with love and happiness but also hurt and confused. All the memories of everything she'd spent so long trying to forget pushed into her mind. Tears kept appearing one by one. She squeezed her eyes shut and stood still, trying to regain some composure before moving, speaking.

At this, Elliot's hand found her cheek and his thumb pressed the last tears away. She looked up and into his grey, serious eyes and his fingers pushed slightly further up, into her hair and then down to her neck where he brought her face towards his. Noa pushed onto her tiptoes and then he kissed her softly. His lips felt a little chapped. His nose on her face made tingles move down her shoulders.

After he pulled back she saw he was smiling, his little, rare, sunshine of a dimpled smile. She remembered how much she loved that. Being the recipient of that prize.

'Do you still want to go?' Noa asked, genuinely wondering.

'I don't know, am I allowed to tell you you're so beautiful it makes my mind hurt to look at you now?' Elliot said in a kind, straightforward tone as if it wasn't one of the nicest things Noa had ever heard.

'I need to get the pie out' was all she could think to say. But Elliot just nodded and said, 'Yeah.' And then pulled her towards him and kissed her again. It wasn't hard but his fingers pressed more firmly into her this time.

They stayed there for longer than it was normal for Noa to kiss someone in the lead-up to sex. And so Noa went from kissing him thinking, *Oh my God, I'm kissing Elliot Wood. Wow, he's a great kisser. Am I a good kisser? What does this all mean? Are we going to have sex? Are we together now?* To running out of thoughts. To instead being able to focus on the physical sensations, the pressing together of their bodies and then the coming apart to look at each other, smiling, hands moving off the body to clasp by their sides. And then the re-starting. Her lips tingling, bringing even more awareness to the sensation.

But eventually the air became un-ignorably fragrant with burning pie and Noa pulled away, but just barely, to say, 'I need to take the pie out.'

Elliot said, 'Yeah' again but this time she broke away, running – and then embarrassed by her running, walking – to the oven to take out the blackened pie. Noa's cheeks were hot and her lungs were in desperate need of emptying and refilling, but she did not stay for long, she wanted the mind to stay shut off.

Back in the hall Elliot was sitting on the stairs. He had a cheeky, sheepish expression, boyish, that made her heart twist with memories, pain, love, lust. She realised that it was her that needed to be the one who decided. So she decided. Taking him by the hand, she pulled him to standing and then up the stairs and into her – still single-bedded, still baby-pink, still full of memories – bedroom. Elliot looked around briefly, smiling, clearly remembering too, and then moved towards her.

In the past Noa had found passion to mean hurried, hard, grabbing, pulling, pushing. But it wasn't like that with Elliot. The kisses weren't a book to skim through to get to the ending. They were something in their own right. It was only in between these kisses that things progressed, slowly. The way they lay on the bed fully clothed, the way he undid the shell buttons on her blouse, one by one, his fingers delicately pushing them through the holes, the way he stopped to look at her face, not smiling, seemingly just to look, the way they laughed at the clunky moment they had to take their trousers off. But then how quickly it went back to serious. The way all his touches were so purposeful, gentle, firm, the pace unrushed, deliberate. The quietness accentuating the smallest of sounds. The beat of a heart. A sharp inhalation. The sounds of lips parting against an ear.

When the end came it didn't look like the screaming finales Noa often felt the need to perform. Because it wasn't the end they'd been focused on, working towards, it was simply another moment in the pleasure.

And then they lay facing each other, as their bodies became cooler and the dark became darker, skiing his fingers down her nose, pushing her finger into the groove above his lip, or dancing their fingertips on the other's back, arms, through their hair.

Her voice, sounding so loud after the quiet, saying, 'I might still have some of that pie, to be honest.'

12

Fifteen years old

Noa was struggling to find love. She tried to be like Verity, she tried to imitate the other girls but she was no good at it. She couldn't not be herself (and how sad, that for so many years she thought this was a bad thing). Boys might kiss her at a party or they might speak to her on MSN but it was never both, and what is love if it's not kisses *and* getting put in someone else's MSN status?

Eventually she decided to get a job. She needed to take fate into her own hands, shape it into what she wanted. Money seemed like a great way to pull herself out of this stagnation. Buy new clothes to increase her status like they had the first time.

The only place she could get a job was at a pub a bus ride away. Noa spent the journey pretending she was someone travelling to work to provide for her large family while her husband was away at war. The time passed quicker and more enjoyably that way. Once she arrived, and the fantasy had dissipated, the nerves set in and she felt her armpits boil under the cheap white shirt she had been told to buy. She walked in, posture straight, big smiles, picturing briefly that she was a modern version of Snow White, ready to clean away the grime that seemed to coat everything and eradicate the stale smell of beer and oil. She felt the eyes of the customers on her and instinctively crossed her arms.

She was taken into the kitchen by Mr Jennings, a stubbly man who had given her the job.

'Right. You're on tables, you're on washing.'

He nodded his head to someone behind her. She turned to see who it was and then whipped her head back round again, her chest reddening. It was a boy from her class, Elliot Wood. It took her a second to understand that he was working here as well, and that any embarrassment she felt was to be shared by him. She didn't know him well but had thought once that he was the male equivalent to her. He seemed simultaneously unpopular and yet close friends with the most popular boy in their class, Fraser. Elliot was almost joined at the hip to Fraser in a way that made him obscured. She'd never seen him speak to any girl let alone be talked about by one. She thought it was a shame he wasn't the right kind of boy to target as a boyfriend and wished it had been someone else.

As Mr Jennings talked them through some daily procedures in a way that felt haphazard and improvised, Noa felt the presence of Elliot next to her. He seemed significantly taller than she remembered him being. She looked down and saw that his trousers – quite clearly his school ones – were a bit short and she felt happy that for once she wasn't the only one playing catch up. Mr Jennings finished, telling Noa to collect any plates, glasses and cutlery and for Elliot to start washing them.

Elliot seemed laser-focused on his washing job and when Noa tried to apologise every time she brought a pile of plates over he barely responded. The shift passed slowly and finished in an anticlimactic 'You can go now.'

Noa hung around outside while Elliot seemed to take a while to finish up. He hadn't asked her to wait but she wanted to talk through the day and assumed he would too.

He walked out and straight past her. She caught up and fell in step with him.

'I didn't know you were working there.'

Elliot looked at her. His face was serious. Straight eyebrows, straight mouth, something dull about his eyes, hands stuffed into his jacket pockets. 'Why would you?'

'Because I know everything about you?' Noa tried to joke but went red before the words were out.

Surprisingly Elliot's lips widened into the briefest of smiles. Noa took it as encouragement to carry on. 'What did you think of it all then?'

'I washed up. It was what I was expecting really.'

She shrugged and went to ask him about school when he spoke over her. 'What about you?'

'It was okay. I felt pretty bad bringing you all those plates.'

Again, the quick look down at her, the flash of smile. 'You don't need to feel bad. That's what you're supposed to do.'

'It looked pretty gross though. In that sink.'

'Yeah it was gross.' Elliot shuddered. 'I kept thinking about all the spit that was probably on those plates and glasses.'

'If it makes you feel any better, when I was clearing this one table, a man told me I dropped something and then as I looked down he put his hand under my chin and told me to cheer up. But his hand was *sticky*.'

'Sticky?' Elliot exclaimed. 'Sticky with what?'

'I don't know! I assumed food?'

Elliot stopped in the street and so she did, taken aback. He looked at Noa and her body temperature skyrocketed. Seeing him front-on like that she realised how different he looked from last time she'd noticed him at school. His face was less soft, he didn't look like a child anymore.

'What is it?'

'You've got like a brown smudge.' Elliot pointed at her chin. 'I did wonder what that was.'

Noa's eyes bulged. 'What!' She started to slap-wipe at her chin shouting various versions of 'Oh my God.'

Elliot started cracking up, his shoulders moving up and down, and pulled her arm away. 'I'm joking, I'm joking.'

'What the hell! I was going to be sick, Elliot!' His name felt risky to say. She slapped his chest. Elliot squeezed his nose trying to stop laughing and Noa felt a fleeting buzz.

It turned out they took the same bus back into town, but they didn't sit next to each other. They sat on the same row but with the aisle in between them.

When they got off the bus he asked when she was working next. Noa said, 'tomorrow' and he said, 'same.' She was already excited for their next shift. If they could be friends, this job would be a lot more fun.

'Oh yay! Can we get the bus over together?'

Elliot brushed his hand across his nose. 'Okay.'

They swapped phones and entered their details. Noa saved herself as 'Cool Noa'. Elliot had saved himself as 'Elliot'.

Noa (quite literally) skipped home from the bus stop, ran upstairs and flopped on her bed to take everything in. Her mind considered if there was romantic possibility but from her experience these boys were impossible to pursue. Even the promiscuous boys were hard enough to get to look at her. The best bet was to befriend him. At least he might be someone she could speak to in the classroom, get nearer the other boys. She got her phone out of her backpack and texted him.

So cool you were there today! C u 2morrow

She slid the screen down and stood up to go tell her mum how work was but a double vibration came from her bed. She looked down. *Elliot.*

yeh, thank god I didn't have to wash off
all that spit on my own. oh no wait. . .

Noa laughed and text back.

I will clean the spit off before I hand
them to you 2morrow then.

yeh that would be gr8 tnx

At work Noa spoke to Elliot whenever she could. Which usually meant in intermittent bursts. It was inside jokes mainly, repetitions of sarcastic comments they made about enjoying their jobs. Or alluding to funny things they'd bitched about the other workers over text.

Then they started playing silly games to pass the time. Their favourite one – 'Top Joker' – Elliot made up. He described it as 'Like truth or dare but the only option is dare and you're choosing your own.' He told her to watch and learn and then proceeded to ask Mr Jennings if there was a pension plan he could sign up for. Before Noa did her first one Elliot did six; asking if the chef could taste his sandwich and give some feedback, picking up condiment bottles to wash when Mr Jennings was in the room, making up a complex story to the other waiters about the ancient origin of the

178

word 'pot washer'. Noa had to breathe back her hysterics, terrified of getting either of them fired. But at home she would think back on everything he'd done and press her beaming face into her pillow.

It was on the bus to and from work where they got to know each other. They never sat together, but they spoke the whole way, greedily, as if the time was never enough. Noa drank in everything about Elliot. The way he bit his nails when he was listening to her, the way his clothes looked so neat, clean, ironed, the way the tips of his pointy ears went pink when she complimented him, the way he pulled his earlobe when he spoke about himself. She did most of the talking. Elliot would ask her questions and lightly tease her – and she would find herself blushing at the realisation he'd noticed something about her.

At school they didn't speak. They had formed a great friendship at work but when it got to Monday it was like they didn't know each other. No matter how much she tried to catch his attention, he looked away, walked in a different direction, spoke to someone else. It hurt her feelings but at least it confirmed that she was right. He was a boy's boy.

No less desperate for a boyfriend, Noa felt the year slipping away from her. At work one day she was absorbed trying to create a plan for how to get one, racking her brains on how she could utilise her friendship with Elliot. When, carrying a tray of teas to an older couple who were sitting with their extended family, Noa tripped on an uneven carpet tile and spilled boiling water on the elderly woman's lap. The outcome was chaos. A paramedic came, the woman's adult daughter cried, her husband screamed at Noa, Noa cried, the elderly man asked for a full refund. Finally, when the family had left and the mess had been cleaned up, the rest of the shift went on as normal. But it did not feel normal. Noa knew Mr Jennings had something to say by the way he kept raising his eyebrows at her but then telling her to get back to work. She was shaking with nerves which made things even harder to carry. By the end of the shift she was carrying one thing at a time out of fear and getting shouted at by the chefs and the other waitresses. Elliot and Noa barely exchanged a word.

At the end of the day Mr Jennings gathered everyone around.

'As you are aware, there has been a massive incident today. One of our team has let everyone down. She has physically harmed a customer. Worsened the awful situation by making it about herself. And then slacked off for the rest of the day. Noa, what have you learned today which would persuade me that I should keep you on?'

Tears formed and were magically held in the waterline of her eyes. But her arms were shaking so much she pressed them into the side of her body. Her voice broke as she replied.

'I don't know.'

'You don't know? Well. That's not good, is it? Can anyone else tell me what she should have learned?'

Elliot's voice was low and loud. 'It wasn't her fault.'

'Excuse you? Whose fault was it then?' Mr Jennings' face had turned a deeper red and his lips had bunched tightly together.

Elliot's head dropped slightly but he answered confidently. 'It was my fault.'

'How on earth was it your fault? This is not the time to be a Casanova, son. You're going to get yourself fired too.'

Noa started crying at the word fired. She'd lost everything, her job, her money, her independence, her time spent with Elliot, her dignity. She tried to discreetly press the tears away but her breath was irregular and loud. Elliot strolled over and turned Noa to face him.

'It's okay. We don't need this job. Come on.' He took her hand and led them both out as Mr Jennings scoffed and rattled off a bunch of predictions about how their lives would go. In that moment she was too worked up to process the physical touch or the fact that Elliot had stood up for her. When she got outside she burst out into proper inhaling sobs. It was only when Elliot embraced her tightly that she started to realise what was happening. This was it. This was the magical moment, the beginning of her love story. Every laugh, every conversation flashed in front of her mind. It was Elliot all along. Everything was perfect, the clean, masculine smell of his deodorant, the warmth of his chest on her cheek, the way he looked older and almost intimidating in his black uniform cap. As she pulled away, he kept his hands on her shoulders and she looked up at his furrowed brow and pointy ears realising she was the luckiest girl in the world. She stood slightly on her tiptoes and pouted for her first ever sober kiss. But as she neared Elliot's lips he dropped his hands and turned away.

Noa pressed her fingers into her closed eyes as the tears started up again. There was silence for so long that she wondered if Elliot had left. She removed her hands and saw him looking at her.

'Do you like me?' Noa asked, desperate to know.

Elliot's rare smile crept onto his face. 'Of course I like you.' But then he looked down and she noticed the tips of his ears went red before he spoke. 'But I. . . can we just be friends?'

Noa waited for disappointment to rush in but it didn't. She thought of what he'd done in there, how he'd tried to claim responsibility for something that was so clearly not his fault, and then got fired, all to stand up for her. And she still felt like crying, but with happiness, to have a friend who would do that. It dawned on her that he was the best friend she'd ever had. All their conversations, their messages, their joking at work. It was easy and reciprocated and fun.

'Will you actually be my friend for real though? Like talk to me at school?' Noa negotiated, feeling confident now that he actually liked her.

And that confidence continued to grow as the dimpled smile – something that she barely saw him gift to anyone else – once again appeared on his face. 'Definitely.'

Noa was good at accepting things for how they were, especially if it was easy to find a positive spin on the situation. And the positivity of her friendship with Elliot was astronomical. Everything she had ever wanted from a friendship, he gave her. On the days Elliot hung out with her at lunch he let her ramble on about anything and everything, seemingly interested in whatever she had to say. She often asked if she was boring him and he would look down smiling and say, 'No, the opposite.' She didn't have to pretend to be someone else, and it felt amazing, like her mum had said it would all those years ago.

They were both offered their jobs back (more desperately than either of them realised) and this time they sat next to each other on the bus, sharing crisps or sweets. Elliot walked her home after every shift now and one day she asked him to come in.

'Let me play you that album I was talking about.'

He seemed nervous, pulling on his earlobe, but she reassured him. 'I'm not going to try and kiss you, don't worry.'

He laughed and muttered he wasn't worried about that and followed her in. Noa sat on her desk chair and played the album out of her computer. Seeing him, sitting there on her pink duvet, his long slim torso and mousey hair pushed to one side, the length of his limbs, the bones increasingly visible in his face, the subtle muscle to his thighs under his black trousers. He was so masculine Noa felt her cheeks heat up. She pictured him standing up, walking towards her, leaning down, pressing his thin lips onto hers. She shook the feeling away and told herself not to ruin it. She was happy. Happier than she'd ever been. This was the type of friendship she'd wanted her whole life, and now she had it. It didn't harm that it was with a boy, in fact it felt very mature. (After everything blew up, and she was alone again at a new sixth form, friendless and empty, she painfully reflected on these moments, wishing more than anything for her friend back.)

'I'm so glad you got a job at the same time as me.' She was swivelling back and forth from left to right on her desk chair. She liked seeing the way he smiled when she said nice things. 'We probably wouldn't have ever spoken otherwise. What a horrible thought.'

'I don't speak to most people,' Elliot said onto his thumbnail.

'What did "most people" ever do to you?'

Noa liked when Elliot looked down – which was often – because she could study the ways his expression changed when he thought about certain things. This time he flicked his gaze up to catch hers.

'I dunno. It's tiring.' Noa saw his Adam's apple bob up and down as he swallowed.

'Is it tiring to speak to me?'

'No. Is it tiring to speak to me?'

'No. But I don't get tired speaking to people. If anything I wish I could speak more! People get tired of *listening* to me. I can see it on their faces.'

Elliot pushed himself further on her bed so his back was against the wall. His face was back to blank, unreadable, serious. 'That's not true. Everyone likes listening to you.' (They did, but how was she to know, they never showed it.)

'Yeah, right. People are only friends with me out of pity.' Noa sharply exhaled, the statement sounded less light than she'd hoped.

'Why d'you say that?'

'Because it's true. Maybe people like me because I'm a bit silly, and I'm pretty nice. But the main reason is because I make people feel better about themselves. They're glad they're not me.'

'Why would anyone be glad they're not you?'

'Because I've got a big nose and big, wide feet and frizzy hair and I'm probably a bit clingy or desperate or whatever. People don't like that.' Noa always felt a relief when she presented her flaws and faults to people. It was nice to come clean, to not feel like she was hiding behind something. No one could hurt her about something she'd already accepted. But she could also tell that most people thought it was strange, being that open.

Elliot pushed himself off the bed. 'Stand up.'

Noa stood. Elliot walked towards her. Her heart started beating so loud that she was worried he could hear. She tried to have a casual expression but she couldn't take her eyes off him.

'Let me see.' Elliot, facing Noa, put his socked foot next to hers, so their arches were touching. They weren't that different in length or width.

'See!' Noa put her face in her hands and mumbled. 'They're weirdly big.'

Elliot carried on studying her, running his finger down the bridge of her nose, running the palms of his hands down the hair that sat over her ears. Then for one brief second he looked her in the eyes. Their faces were so close that she could see how long his eyelashes were. Noa's whole body was vibrating. But she knew they wouldn't kiss, they were just friends. Elliot turned and took his place back on the bed. Noa sat back on her chair. She didn't know what to say. The tension had built up so much she burst out laughing. He laughed too. It was hilarious but she didn't know exactly why.

She started to worry that they were laughing at her when he said, 'What's wrong with big feet anyways? They don't look bad to me. They make you look. . . more sturdy.'

'Sturdy!' Noa burst out laughing and went to hit him playfully. Elliot put his hands over his face to protect himself. Eventually she stopped and sat next to him. 'Sturdy doesn't make me feel better.'

'It's not meant to make you feel better. Because I disagree there's anything to feel sad about in the first place. All the things you described, they're not bad or good. You might as well have said you look bad because you have a nose, feet and hair.'

'What are you on about?' Noa couldn't look at him anymore. She felt her throat close up and her tear ducts prepare themselves.

'Having a big nose, big feet, frizzy hair. They're just descriptions. You could have a lovely big nose or a rubbish one. A "big nose" is neutral. So if anyone was glad they weren't you because they didn't have a big nose, they'd be stupid. That's like being glad you weren't someone because they owned clothes or had a voice.'

Noa stood up and walked over to her desk slyly itching away a tear that had made its way down her cheek.

'I think my mum will be back soon. But I'll see you tomorrow at work?' She knew it was weird to say all this facing away from him but she could feel her eyes were bloodshot.

'Cool. See you tomorrow.'

A moment later Noa heard her bedroom door close and she blinked free the few tears that had collected in her eyes. She felt strange. A thought agitated her and she tried to turn away from it but it was there. *You* like *like him*, is what it said. Usually Noa was more than happy to admit these thoughts to herself, inflate memories she had with boys to make them better, more exciting, more romantic, but she didn't want to. The thought of being rejected by Elliot wasn't disappointing it was distressing. She would lose the best friend she'd ever had. But this feeling was getting harder to ignore.

After Elliot came round that first time, Noa's mum offered to French braid her hair. Noa sat on the floor in between her legs and her mum began a conversation in that sickly voice that meant she was going to impart wisdom.

'Noa, sunshine, I didn't say you could have boys over, did I?'

Noa had prepared for this. 'You said you would be pleased if I had a friend over for once.'

'A boy is not a friend.'

Noa closed her eyes as her mum started to wind the sections of hair around each other, happy for the undivided attention. 'He is a friend. Believe me. He said specifically he only wants to be friends. And anyhoo, I like having him as a friend. Sometimes it's better to have a friend than a boyfriend, d'ya know what I mean?'

'No. I don't know what you mean. Boys and girls cannot be friends. That's biology, Noa.'

'If he wants to be more than friends, I'll tell you.'

'Oh, don't get me wrong, I don't think he wants to be more than friends. If a boy wants you, you'll know about it. If he's always telling you that he'll do things in the future or he wants something

186

from you first, then cut him off right there and then. Those boys don't want you, they want something else.'

Noa knew the answer but she had to ask. 'What do they want?'

She felt her mum tie the bobble around the hair and gently push at Noa's back to get her to turn around. Her face was deadly serious. 'They want to use you. Use your body. Use your generosity, your kindness. Use it all up until you have nothing left to give, nothing left for yourself.' Noa's mum stood up and smiled warmly at her. 'But you won't be silly like me, will you? None of that will happen if you don't let it. Promise?'

Noa looked up at her. She didn't want to believe what her mum had said but she couldn't help herself nodding. 'Promise.'

Noa stretched out on the sofa and looked at her body in front of her. She didn't hate it but she also couldn't imagine someone wanting to use it and that was like a kind of safety blanket. She felt confident that the person she would lose her virginity to would have chosen her. Specifically. Out of everyone. And she would have chosen him back.

13

Twenty-seven years old

Elliot was falling into love, the rest of his life blurring at the edges as he cascaded further into the world of Noa. Everything he normally found hard came naturally. Understanding his feelings was straightforward when all he felt was love. Having a conversation was easy when he had endless questions to ask her. Trying to find an identity was no longer necessary, he was simply half of a two, a couple made to experience things together.

His purpose was to make her happy, to show her how amazing she was when she couldn't see it herself, to protect and support and comfort her. They'd spend every weekend at Noa's in London – since there was nowhere to stay in Stoke – and they would wander around laughing at the world, at the Tube advert puns that didn't work both ways, at the things people said and did which seemed too sincere, at the pretentious cafes and £90 glass teaspoons that her local shop sold as 'gifts for the girl who has everything'. They would eat fruit on a park bench or a full English at the local cafe or a pizza in bed and it would all taste equally delicious and flavourless – their minds locked on each other rather than the taste. Elliot would book 6 p.m. trains back to Stoke but then get the 11 p.m. one, needing those extra hours to absorb every last drop of her being.

Elliot cared for Noa so keenly he found his mind entirely

connected to her, primed and ready for any action required. He learned the specific things that would make her life better: when to listen to her, hold her hand, give advice. Or when to distract, offer to learn how to paint her nails, help organise her room. He learned what her body needed to feel pleasure and how her mind needed to feel to let the body follow. He found out the difference between purely physical sex and sex as a way of saying something when there were no more words.

And then there were the days apart. Time when life would move in and out of the light. Work and responsibilities and eating and drinking and sleeping and breathing when the person he was doing it all for wasn't there. Elliot would try anything to drag those days into the glow he felt when he was with Noa. Hiding a note in her wardrobe for her to find when he was away that said *You are beautiful, I love you.* Making stupid PowerPoints at work to send her:

10 reasons my week has been awful.
Slide one: Grey ham = bad ham, a story.
Slide two: Things that were not available today:
Noa; Kit Kats in the vending machine; The cubicle someone walked into when I was having a poo.

Noa knew of Willie. Elliot spoke about him in brief soundbites: 'He's good, thanks', 'Same as ever, thanks', 'Ups and downs, but that's life.' He wouldn't tell her about specifics because he didn't think she would understand and he didn't want the sting of her saying something wrong, offering misplaced advice, using outdated words. He was sensitive about it because the topic was like a fresh layer of skin, never touched before. (Subconsciously, he didn't want the two parts of his life mixing because that would raise questions.

How would these two parts of his life combine? Were Noa and Willie competing for a place in his future?)

Eight heady months passed, quickly tumbling from one storey of commitment to the next. They didn't take it slowly (both unashamed of their love for each other) and it felt like the only thing keeping them apart was the distance. One night, on the phone, Noa suggested they go away. Spend longer than the brutally short forty-eight hours in each other's arms.

'Imagine. Spending a day without the looming departure.'

Elliot smiled at the cheese sandwich he was making. 'As in like, abroad?'

'I dunno, maybe like Brighton?'

A breath expanded in Elliot's chest. He was never quite sure when Noa was going to suggest or talk about something that was out of his depth. 'Brighton sounds good. They probably do fish and chips there.'

'That's right!' Noa said as if she were talking to a child, and they both laughed, but Elliot closed his eyes and shook his head in embarrassment.

They talked about the sea and sun and sugary doughnuts and spent a minute saying how much they loved each other and then hung up.

Elliot took the sandwich in for Willie and sat down next to him. Bolstered by the still-new feeling of possibility, Elliot felt inspired to connect with Willie in a way he hadn't for a while.

Taking advantage of a reasonably unscheduled time, Elliot said, 'Remember when we used to do "dance class", Willie?' (That was what Elliot called dancing but he named it that because Willie liked the structure of something being a 'class'.)

'Yes. I remember.' Willie nodded and chewed.

Elliot waited for Willie to finish his sandwich and then said, 'Right, let's do a dance class for *adults*.'

'What's a dance class for adults?'

'Kind of like what we. . .' Elliot stood up and gestured for Willie to join him. 'Right. I do a move, you copy and do the same.'

Elliot moved his leg out to the side and Willie copied. Elliot lifted his opposite arm up and Willie copied. He shimmied his chest and bent forward, and then stood up straight and carefully, quietly, clapped his hands above his head. Willie reflected his move at each step. It was fun and silly and they did it until Willie was out of breath and they were both giggling. A guilt tickled Elliot's brain – why didn't he do this more often? (Because in between caring for his family, working, and nourishing a relationship with Noa, he had no energy left to simply be a brother, a friend.)

Of course it had dawned on Elliot that going on holiday was not something someone with his kind of responsibilities just 'does', but for a few hours he let himself play the role of a carefree person who lived like that. Then he would explain to Noa that he wouldn't be able to find the time and placate her with promises of nice things they could do without going on holiday.

Elliot was preparing shepherd's pie for himself and his mum. It was summer and although their dark house kept reasonably cool, it was still hot enough that a warm winter's dish wasn't what he wanted, but he had the ingredients and needed to use them up. As he spooned the mashed potato onto the mince, a picture came into his mind. That wasn't unusual (as we know) but the phone call had seemingly diverted his mind from the well-worn images into a new one. Noa's heart-shaped face, beaming as her hair flew around in the wind, the sea lapping gently behind her. He put the dish in the oven, sat down at the kitchen table and closed his eyes, pictured himself kissing every inch of her face, and let the playlist he had on – created by Noa – accompany the scene.

By now the worries he'd had most of his life had dampened down into a background buzz. The same distressing images would come into his mind but would be pushed out by stronger, calmer thoughts. They weren't dreams, just simple thoughts of Noa, what she was doing, what she would think of something he'd seen, a compliment he'd figured out how to express. But, sitting at the kitchen table, Elliot used his imagination, fantasised about the holiday they could have, and his muscles relaxed in a way that was so unprecedented, he found himself drifting off.

The front door opened and clicked shut and Elliot opened his eyes and mind to reality.

'Evening.' Elliot's mum dropped her bag and keys onto the table and lowered herself into one of the wooden chairs with a loud sigh.

Elliot yawned and then smiled at her. 'Good day?'

She scoffed. 'I'd be so lucky.'

'Well things are all good here and tea's nearly ready.' The image he'd dreamed up was slipping away and it hurt. He wanted to snatch it back.

She nodded and stood up. 'I'm gonna change out of these.' She pulled at her uniform and walked towards the doorway. Elliot felt a propulsion of energy.

'I have something to tell you first.'

'Can't it wait?'

'I'm going to go on holiday. With Noa.' (His mum knew about Noa of course, but her name created a bitter and uneasy atmosphere whenever it was said.)

His mum walked out of the kitchen without saying anything and with each dull thud of the stairs Elliot's dream was crushed.

By the time she was walking down them again Elliot was sitting at the table with the plates of food, a smile prepped on his face, and was ready to ignore what he'd said and skip all the consequences.

'Any rude customers today?' he said when she was barely in the room.

She took her time to sit down and push the mashed potato around, letting out steam, before replying. 'Isn't there always?'

Elliot spooned some mince into his mouth, his tongue stripped of a layer, a bead of sweat dropped down his neck. The physical sensations were so uncomfortable he didn't manage to reply before she spoke again.

'I can take a couple of days off and you can go on your holidays.'

Elliot's mouth opened and then closed and then opened again. But, not wanting to fall into a trap, he couldn't get any words out.

She didn't look up from her plate as she continued, 'I was planning to anyway.'

'Yeah, but surely you don't want to use up—'

'I've got things to do.'

The unknown, the uncertainty (Elliot's worst feeling) pricked the skin all over his limbs and he found himself rearranging and readjusting his position on the chair.

'What kind of. . .' His words trailed off as his mind lost focus on the room.

'Me and Will are looking round a couple of different acco-mmodations.'

Elliot tried to respond but his mind was moving far away.

She continued, 'He needs to move – gradually, of course – into

supported-living accommodation. I have to work and you have. . .
your own things going on. We can't rely on you like we used to.'

It was never a good thing when his mum referred to her and
Willie as 'we'. It usually meant he'd let them down, severed himself
from the unit. But supported-living accommodation? This was a
threat he'd never heard before. His mind grasped around looking
for clues as to what he'd done that was so bad. All he could say was,
'But. . .'

'It will take six months to properly get him settled, living there
full-time, approved by the council. Those types of things. But
anyhow, you got what you wanted.' Her eyebrows shot briefly up
her forehead as her lips pressed downwards.

Elliot truly had no idea how to respond. It was surreal and
shocking and he couldn't work out what she wanted him to say,
sacrifice, promise, atone for. He tried to find the right words and
facial expressions but instead found himself repeating, 'right' and
'okay', struggling to find more than that. Eventually he coughed and
said, 'Tell me more', and sat listening to details and names and to-do
lists and processes. Elliot braced himself for guilt to overwhelm and
destabilise him but it didn't arrive. Instead a sense he had never
experienced before – possibility – tingled the synapses in his brain.

Elliot and Noa rented a studio in the centre of Brighton for four
nights. The weather was vast, relentless sunshine.

After dropping their bags and making the room into a temporary
home by having sex and leaving make-up, deodorant, worn clothes
and charging devices scattered around (as if marking their territory)
they headed into the centre to get a drink.

Elliot had never been somewhere like Brighton before. It was
not the quaint seaside town he thought it would be. It was bright

and fizzy and full of young people. London was hard enough to get his head around, but he tried to view each borough as individual towns and it felt more manageable that way. Brighton was more like central London – a place he did not feel comfortable. The one thing that London offered as a coping mechanism was the facelessness of it all, in Brighton however, he felt boring and noticed. (He was not boring or noticed.) At first he felt his body tense, as if to protect himself from all this that was going on outside him, all this difference from him. And worried that this holiday was a bad idea, not something someone like him would do. But seeing Noa point to quirky antique shops or cafes in glee he managed to persuade himself that he was part of this too. She was his ticket into this world.

'Where should we take our aperitifs this afternoon?' Noa said in a chic accent.

Elliot looked at her, confused. His muscles seizing up as he was thrown into the 'other' category again. 'Huh?'

'Sorry, I've been reading *Bonjour Tristesse* and thought I was in a French novella for a second there. Where should we get a drink?'

Elliot tried to let the unknown reference trickle away and took her small damp hand in his to remind himself that they were together. He went to say 'You choose' but at the last minute he changed his mind.

As someone with minimal experience in the world and even less opinions on it, Elliot always 'let' Noa make decisions on things. But an anxiety had gradually been spreading through the core of him. This idea that she wouldn't want to be with someone who had no personality and nothing to offer, when she could easily be with countless other men who would surprise her with restaurant reservations, suggest unusual films, make food from world cuisines, take her to art exhibitions. Usually the idea of this alternative man made him squeeze his eyes shut. But this time Elliot remembered about Willie moving out and realised he had stumbled into a new, unexpected part of his life. He was free to become someone like that himself. And so he decided to step into the shoes of one of these imaginary men.

'How about there?' Elliot pointed to a 'cocktails and wine' bar. Wooden tables were filled with sunglassed people sipping on golden drinks and eating small foods on small plates.

'Perfecto!' Noa's eyes lit up and Elliot swallowed the sharp feeling that this confirmed it was what she'd wanted all along.

They sat down and ordered their drinks. Quickly the conversation moved on to the holiday itself. Noa was holding Elliot's hand across the table. She squeezed it. Elliot felt his body relax again.

She started stroking his palm and spoke with her eyes cast down, 'I know this is pathetic but I'm already sad for the holiday to be over.'

'Why is that pathetic? Aren't holidays supposed to be something you don't want to end?'

'Yeah, I guess you're right. I just hate that leaving is always on the horizon.'

'But so is arriving?'

Noa let go and leaned back and even though it was a neutral movement Elliot's heart crumpled a bit.

'I know, I know. I'm being silly.'

'You're not being silly.' (Reassuring Noa always Elliot's passion.) 'It is shit. I wish it was endless arrivings.'

Noa's mouth curved into a shy smile. 'Well. . .'

Elliot looked at her dewy olive skin and inhaled with love. 'Well?'

'Well why don't we do endless arrivings? Or at least less time between the leavings? Eight-hour leavings, to be precise. . .'

'What d'ya mean?'

'As in, don't you want to move to London one day anyway? Why not get a job there now and move. . . in with me?'

Elliot tried hard to keep his smile as he let that sink in. He didn't want to move to London. He found it intimidating and overwhelming and like he didn't fit in. And yet – what was he hoping for? That she would move back to Stoke? He knew she hated it there. But what then? He certainly didn't see their relationship as fleeting. The idea of being without her terrified him.

'I mean, I hadn't really thought about it. And I don't think I'd get a job there anyway,' he said, to fill time.

'Course you will. Anyone can. There's a million jobs and you're a hardworking lad. It'll be easy.'

Elliot tried to think about it, picture it, let the dream play out like he had done with the holiday. But the sun felt hot on the crown of his head and other people's conversations sounded exaggeratedly loud and no matter how many times he tried he didn't like the feeling of alcohol in his blood. But he was used to this, he reminded himself, this putting off for later, this leaving the plans and hopes and dreams for Noa to decide. Absorbing them pleasantly but absent-mindedly, as you would a horoscope that promised success and felt vaguely specific enough to hope for.

'You're right, it would be pretty great. I guess I'm moving to London then!' But it didn't feel great or even neutral. Detachment wasn't working. These weren't nice ideas anymore; these were real decisions that he was free to make now.

She started talking about rent and batch cooking and cinema subscriptions and meeting for lunch and his neck felt itchy from the sun. He realised how important all these things were to her; this was what she expected from life. The thing that was different with Noa than with anyone else he'd ever met was that he felt no expectations from her. He felt able to be nothing (which allowed him the space to become something). But that familiar feeling of expectation became hot in his chest. He didn't want to run away though, he loved Noa and wanted, more than anything, to be with her. Stumbling around in his mind he came across something that helped him handle the situation. A principle he'd used so often and yet hadn't felt the need to use with Noa before: to earn a place in someone's life first you need to work out what they require, what they expect, and then you simply do those things. Elliot had already spent far too many hours wondering what kind of man Noa deserved to be with, what desirable traits and attributes he would have.

And so he forced himself to sit back on his chair like that man would and pick up his beer like that man would and order food and make suggestions and talk about living in London like that man would.

The holiday passed quickly even though they did nothing except eat and drink and talk. Elliot spent a lot of time and effort trying to act how he should act, say the right things, live up to the mark. The peace started to slip away from moments he would usually enjoy, replaced by exhaustion. He couldn't wait to get home, sit alone in the comfort of being nobody.

The day before they were leaving they sat on the beach, legs stretched out in front of them. Elliot was turned inwards slightly, watching Noa watch the sea, her sharp, pink tongue jabbing a pastel green scoop of ice cream.

'Elliot can I ask you something?'

'Depends what it is.'

'I know you don't like to talk about your brother much. But I know you do a lot for him, and your mum. And I just, y'know, wondered if that's what was keeping you from moving?'

'I've said I want to move?'

'Yeah but, I can tell that there was some reservations.'

'Nah, honestly. There's no problem there.' Elliot bit his nails. 'He's going to be fine without me. I actually won't have to care for him so often anymore.' He let his eyes close for a second thinking about something he'd been trying not to think about.

'Do you want to talk about him more? I know he's so important to you. I'd love to hear about him. I'd love to meet him.'

'He's the best. He's everything. You'll definitely meet him one day. Sorry I haven't introduced you sooner, it's only—'

'No need to ex—'

'I know, but I do want you to. I actually want that more than anything in the world but also can't ever imagine it happening, to be honest.'

'Oh.'

Elliot could tell Noa was waiting to eat the last little bit of cone but was choosing not to because the conversation had turned serious and he ached with how lovely she was. He forced himself to say more.

'But I think that's more because I can't imagine *anything* happening. Ever. Well, actually, that's not true. I imagine a lot but it's never anything good. So usually I try not to.' Elliot laughed nervously.

'What kind of bad stuff do you imagine?'

His heart was racing and he was worried he wouldn't be able

to express himself, worried this was the wrong setting to tell her everything, worried this was the beginning of the end. The awareness of the irony of these thoughts made him laugh. But he could see out the corner of his eye that Noa was not laughing or smiling with him and his throat felt dry. Elliot made himself think of the man he was supposed to be evolving into. Someone independent and normal.

'Nothing. I'm exaggerating. Let's paddle.'

'Really? I didn't think you'd want to!' He didn't, but then again, he thought, do I really *want* to do anything?

After they had sex that night Elliot found himself homesick and clingy. He wished he could stay inside Noa, climb into her fully and live there. Make her his home. He felt her slipping away. A vision of Noa finding out who he really was and leaving made his body stiffen. But no, she was right there. Her head was on his chest and he watched it lift up and down with his breath, letting the repetitive sight soothe him. She brought his hand to her lips and kissed it. The sensation gave him goosebumps and he wished he could ask her to touch him until he fell asleep. Her voice vibrated his skin.

'The other day, when I asked if your plan was to move to London, you said you'd not thought about it. Well what kind of thing *have* you thought about?'

He felt himself swallow. 'What d'you mean?'

'Just like, how do you see the future? Either short-term or long term. I know we joke about things but like actually real stuff.'

The word future made his hands tingle. For the majority of his life it had been something both empty and set in stone. With vague but heavy responsibilities and no plush, colourful details to fill in the gaps. But Noa had a way of imagining things that allowed Elliot to feel wanted in the fantasy, not a figurine needed to complete it. She would offer him options: 'Do you think you'd rather have three children in the chance that one of them would be good or one to minimise the chances of having a bad one?' And make suggestions tailored to what she knew about him: 'You know, Elliot, everyone respects you without you even trying, maybe you should be a teacher or something?' Or present a vision of them as a couple that made him believe in a joint future: 'I can see us moving to somewhere like Manchester one day because I think we would be bored in a town but I think we both prefer the friendliness of up north?'

But to do this he had to suspend disbelief. And over these past few days, he'd realised this time was up, he was going to have to begin one of these lives, make a decision to become someone. But there was a growing certainty in him, one that said these futures didn't exist. He wasn't sure what that meant yet, only that these different choices and paths were fruitless; all roads lead to a sudden dropping off. Yes, he could go to work, visit Noa, think about what to have for dinner or what series he should watch next. But as soon as the thoughts went further than that and involved a new era, the sight of himself in the picture disappeared.

'I don't know, I guess I try not to think about it.'

Elliot could tell Noa was getting frustrated because she was drawing out her words like a child. 'Oh come on, Elliot. It's fun to think about. The world is your oyster!'

Elliot kept pressing his thumb into the palm of his hand but making himself do it in random sets of numbers rather than fives. He was trying to slow his heart rate, the thought of Noa feeling that it was speeding up only made things worse. Noa shuffled off him, put the ends of her fingers on the top of Elliot's head and then splayed them downwards in a soft massage. His heart crumpled up and a desperation to please her overcame him.

'I know I want my future with you.'

Noa continued with the strokes. 'Someone asked me this thing at work a few weeks ago. I'm gonna do it on you. Okay, close your eyes. Oh right, you already are. Well, keep them closed.

'Imagine you're at your eightieth birthday party and you look around at the people there. Some are family, some are from work, could be a romantic partner' – she coughed jokingly – 'or people from your community. This isn't people who you think *will* be there but people you would *want* to be there. In your dream life.'

Elliot felt his leg start to twitch. He shimmied around, trying to shake off the feeling. Noa pressed his shoulders.

'Stay as still as possible. Right, have you pictured that?'

Elliot had not pictured that. The thought made him clammy. He tried to block the idea out but he couldn't. It was in there now. The room was there but it was empty. He started to feel trapped, on this bed, in this room, with this image. He wanted to stand up and leave but he knew he couldn't. So instead he tried to do what she said. He tried to put an elderly version of himself into a room. A generic old man appeared in an armchair.

'Right. Have you done that?'

Elliot inhaled and nodded.

'Okay, so. Next picture one of these people standing up to give a speech about you. What would you want – not what you think is *likely* – but what would you *want* them to say? So it could be something you've done in your job, or community or a family member or anything really.'

Elliot tried to fill the imaginary room with these conceptual people but he couldn't. He couldn't dream of doing any other job or living in another city or having a family or doing anything worthwhile and he didn't want to. It felt like hoping for good test results after a terminal illness diagnosis. It was impossible and hurtful. It dawned on him that he'd been biding time. But when he tried to think what he'd been biding his time until, his mind went blank, and his body twinged.

Noa started to say something but Elliot spoke over her. He let his body be taken over by the man he'd been playing the role of all holiday and answered as him.

'I definitely would want loads of people from different places. Not just from Stoke or London or whatever. I want it to be that I've travelled around, lived different places maybe, and so I wouldn't know just one type of person.'

'Ooo. That's a good one.' She kissed his shoulder and it felt like his ribs compressed. 'Carry on.'

'And then I would like a family member.' Willie popped into his mind and it sent a shock through his body. He bit down hard on his cheek to send the image away. *This is not reality*, he said to himself. 'Maybe a child of mine or grandchild saying how I've been really present in their life. Like a parent who's actually hung out with them and been their friend. Like a family who is close and does a lot of things together out of choice. Holidays, celebrations, Sunday roasts, anything really.'

Noa was gripping onto Elliot's hand now. It both spurred him on and made the chest pain worse.

'And it would be cool if someone spoke from the place I work doing something creative.' He nearly laughed saying the word, it was so at odds with anything he'd ever done or been but he thought it would be desirable for someone like Noa so he swallowed and continued. 'Yeah, something like... a job creating something I would be proud of.' He tensed his jaw and made himself say something more specific. 'Like, maybe something in TV or writing or. . .' He trailed off hoping that was enough. He felt disgusted with himself but was waiting for the relief that he'd get from finally giving her what she wanted.

He opened his eyes and turned to look at her and saw her deep brown eyes were shiny and glowing with tears. She looked away.

'Wow. I didn't expect you to say all that. I loved hearing it.' She was shaking her head, fiddling with her hands. 'I didn't know you wanted all that.'

Elliot couldn't bring himself to say any more and after a moment she looked at him again, a pretty, almost coy, smile on her face. 'I would love that to be your life. . . Our life?'

Elliot forced out an, 'Of course, our life.' And then an idea expanded in his mind. *Did I just manipulate someone into loving me? Did I just lie to the woman I love because I'm so pathetic I know she won't love the real me? Am I some kind of psychopath man who gets a woman to love him under false pretences? I have no personality and so pull the wool over her eyes and pretend to have one. I must be one of these men that people are warned against. That keeps a woman locked into a dead-end relationship to stave off his own loneliness. I'm an awful person. I don't deserve Noa. I will never give her the life she wants.*

The thoughts felt hot in Elliot's head. He felt dizzy. His heart skipped a beat and then the beats became irregular. He pushed himself up, an energy compelling him to escape from something. He tried to speak but his throat was dry.

'You okay, El?'

He managed to choke out a, 'Be right back just going to buy cigarettes—' And strode around the room throwing on his clothes.

Noa bolted up. 'What the hell? Since when do you smoke?'

'Ah, since people at work… I don't usually…' He was struggling to get sentences out. 'I'm just gonna…' He grabbed his phone and wallet and the keys and flashed a smile.

Noa stood up, 'Well at least let me—'

'No, no. I won't be long.' Running out the flat, almost tripping down the stairs on his way down. He pushed into the fresh air and mentally checked the feelings in his body. Racing heart, tingling skin, shaking hands, dry mouth, a sense that he was about to die. No matter how often he had these feelings, he never got used to them. He never trusted himself to survive it.

He crouched down to try and catch his breath. At the other end of the street he saw a woman walking towards him. He wondered if it would be scary for her, to see a lone man crouched down like this. The thought made him nauseous. *Do I want her to be scared? I must want it or why would such a sick thought come into my mind in the first place? Normal people don't wonder if they are intimidating women.* He forced himself to stand up and walk in the opposite direction. He needed to get away. He was a danger to women. A disgusting creep who got joy from their pain. (The irony of this thought he could not see yet.)

He couldn't reattach to his body for some reason. He couldn't remember who he was. He couldn't feel that he was a person alive in the world. *Who am I?* throttled through his head. He tried not to care but the physical feelings kept coming. It was unbearable. Unsustainable. He couldn't think of a single thing that made him a person. Not a thought or feeling or opinion or desire that differentiated him from a robot. Or corpse. Then an image popped in. Willie. In the chair in that imaginary room. *But it won't be an imaginary room soon,* he thought, *because Willie is being taken away to a place that isn't his own home.* Bile tickled the top of his throat.

Elliot was on the main road then. People drinking tins of G+T and Pimms pushed past him. Or did they? Was he just standing in the middle of the pavement? Regardless, he hated seeing them. Their stupid laughs and flowing conversations and the spontaneous night ahead of them, another step in the open road which was their lives. Out of nowhere thunder rattled the air and people squealed. But there was no rain and so Elliot pressed on, trying to burn the energy or thoughts away. After a while he got to the beach front and the sky turned white with lightning and emitted the loudest crack of thunder he'd ever heard. He inhaled twice without exhaling. The sky let out a blanket of rain.

His mind emptied for one moment. A loud voice, different from his own, spoke in his mind, telling him that he had failed at the one thing he was supposed to do. The one thing that gave him an identity. His life's purpose, gone. His lovely, vulnerable brother chucked out of his own house just so that Elliot could move to London and pretend to be someone he was not. His real life was finished and a new, fake one had begun. But Elliot had built his whole life, his whole *self*, around looking after Willie. There wasn't another version of himself he could be. This was it. The mess of thoughts settled into one and it coursed through his body: *without Willie you are no one.* He wondered if he would be able to physically bear it. Then his phone buzzed.

> You've been ages
> I'm scared.
> Where are you?

Elliot tried to reply but the screen wouldn't work in the rain so he started to run back. He let himself be nothing more than a body until he got there. Before he went in he stayed in the rain for one moment longer. Leaning his forehead on the brick wall he decided that if he loved Noa he had to let her go. He could see it so clearly now, the false pretences he would be offering her a life based upon. She deserved to be with someone who wasn't pretending to want all the things he'd told her earlier. A real, fully formed person. It was a relief to come to this conclusion.

He trudged up the stairs, his shoes comically squelchy, but the door to the studio was opened before he could put the key in. Noa didn't say anything. She stood and looked at him. Her hair was even fluffier from lying down and her cheeks were blotchy and her brow was quivering slightly. Elliot felt his throat close with guilt. He opened his mouth to try and end things, set her free, but a burning heat rose up inside him. All he ever wanted was for her to be happy, to know how much she was loved. He felt his mind being pulled in two opposing directions but seeing her there, wiping her nose with the back of her hand, the desire to protect won out.

'I'm sorry I should never have left you here. I wasn't feeling quite. . . I didn't know what to. . . I love you so much. Do you know that?'

Noa nodded and sat on the edge of the bed and held her hands in her lap, looking at them. 'Sorry I said that stuff about "our life". It was weird. Way too soon. I probably forced you into this holiday a little, didn't I? It's fine if you don't see us as. . .' She trailed off.

Elliot's heart cracked at the thought that she might not believe in his feelings anymore. He felt his eyes darting around the room trying to think of something to prove to her how he felt. He didn't want to be like one of those men, all words no action, but all he had left was words. What could he do, sit on the floor and say 'I love you' until she believed him? An idea popped into his mind and

207

he immediately started talking himself out of it. But seeing Noa pressing away the tears that were escaping from her eyes, her chest inflating with deep breaths, Elliot scrunched his face up to stop the thoughts and shimmied his phone out of his pocket. 'I didn't write this with the intention of sharing it with you but I wrote down some of the reasons why I love you.'

Noa looked up. She looked tired and confused. 'What do you mean? Right now? What for?'

'No, not now. It's complicated. It's. . . silly. Sometimes I have to write stuff down. It's hard to explain but. . . I guess I like seeing things all written down. To help me understand.'

'Okay. . .' Noa's tone was bewildered but her eyes were glued to him now.

Elliot shook his head, swallowed, wiped off the rain that had been dripping from his hair onto his face, and then began to read out the note on his phone.

'1. *She makes me feel positive even though it's a feeling that scares me.*
2. *She has a beautiful smile that makes everyone else feel happy to look at.*
3. *She's the only person who I've ever felt comfortable enough with to even consider telling things about myself, and that's because I can tell she understands. She's the only person that understands somehow.*
4. *In a way I wish it was something between us but I can see she makes everyone feel comfortable and happy in themselves.*
5. *She's the only person that has made me feel like I'm someone worth getting to know.'*

He cleared his throat, pushed his wet hair off his forehead and continued.

> '6. *She is fun. There's not much more to say on that. She's hilarious. She makes boring things more enjoyable. She pushes me to be more fun. Which I need because I'm such a boring miserable guy.*
>
> 7. *She's really cool. The way she absorbs films and music and books and creates opinions on these things and builds up a taste and knowledge without even having to try.*
>
> 8. *I love when she touches me, even the briefest physical contact with her is the best feeling I've ever had.*
>
> 9. *I don't feel like I'm trudging through the days when she's in my life. Like I'm just getting by. Both times I've known her it's like she's a drug which makes me present in the world. Without her I'm just floating above it all, watching it like the most depressing TV programme ever made.*
>
> *And lastly, 10. Even when I'm not with her, even all those years apart, even if I never admitted it to myself, she is what I hold on to in my darkest moments. Because, to me, she is pure hope that good things are possible. Even on the most boring, dull, repetitive days, there is a possibility for happiness. Because I have felt it with her.'*

He had never shown someone something he'd written and it felt surprisingly alleviating, the heavy feeling lifted off his chest. He clicked his phone to black and looked up at her. At first she seemed unchanged but then Noa started to cry again, into her hand. Elliot rushed to her side and stroked the back of her hair until the crying subsided and she leaned into him.

After they made up Noa fell asleep twitching and clinging to the side of his body as he lay on his back. The relief of mending their relationship was quickly poisoned by the thoughts, *But should I have saved it? There wouldn't have been anything to 'mend' if this was healthy? Have I forced her into staying in a toxic relationship?* He tried to think back over everything that was said in the conversation. *Did I tell her how I feel or did I say the things I needed to in order to convince her to trust me? Was that burning feeling in my chest enjoyment at seeing her upset or was it sadness? Surely I wouldn't be having these weird thoughts if there wasn't something to them?* As soon as the thoughts stopped Elliot's eyelids became heavy, but like a shock the fear would return and the thoughts began again.

14

Fifteen years old

Noa began to feel her mood swaying wildly. She still enjoyed working with Elliot but every time she got home she would feel a heat rise in her veins and pace around her room, her thoughts barely coherent to herself, tears sporadically spilling out her eyes. And then the feeling would peter out and exhaustion would replace it.

One day the gloominess carried on overnight and all throughout work the next day. It was hard to interact with Elliot. Every attempt at an inside joke felt like a jolt, every sight of his dimples, prominent Adam's apple or deeply-thinking smoky eyes gave her a sore throat. By the end of the shift all Noa wanted was to get home and cry, but she knew they had to travel back together. She chit-chatted about Mr Jennings and the chefs on the way to the bus stop, but once they got on she sat back in her old place – across the aisle – and put her earphones in. When they stepped off the bus Noa lifted her hand up to wave goodbye but Elliot mimed for her to take the earphones out. She took a deep breath in and pulled one out.

'Do you want me to walk you home?'

'I'm feeling a little bleugh today, so I think I'll go on my own.'

'Or, maybe, do you want to come to my house?'

Noa felt like her heart was being pulled in the opposite direction to her mind. (With Noa the heart always won.)

'Really? I thought you didn't have people round?'

'Ah well, I don't care. Come on.'

At Elliot's house they ran straight up to the bedroom as they did at hers. His room was very neat and clean but the stuff looked childish: trains on his bedsheets, various figurines lined on his chest of drawers, felt-tips on his desk. It was the first time she'd been in a boy's room and she felt mature and exhilarated. But there was still the muddy feeling in her mind. Everything was tinged with the reality of the situation. She could feel a part of her slipping into fantasy mode, exaggerating the meaning behind her being there, the potential of what was to come. But the difference with Elliot compared to everyone else was that she'd rather a disappointing reality with him than a perfect fabricated dream.

They usually spent their time listening to music but Elliot didn't have a computer. So Noa sat next to him on his bed and gave him an earphone. As the music played Noa realised she had spent her whole life pretending with everyone else, and so made a promise to never do that with him. (Do we only make promises that we'll one day break or does it just feel like that?)

Elliot lay down and his earphone pulled out so Noa lay down next to him and pushed it back in. The presence of him so close to her, but not touching, made the hair on her arms stand up. She tried to absorb the moment, the almost bleachy smell of his room, the feel of his sheets on her arm, his moving chest in her periphery. When Noa realised that she was purposefully committing something painful to memory she understood that this was love. All those other love-like feelings she'd had for boys were like getting a good mark for homework you'd copied. It felt good and simple but it was empty, hollow, false. This felt like drowning.

As the song faded out she felt Elliot's hand, cold and bony, softly move onto hers. It didn't squeeze or intertwine with hers, it just lay there, gently, ever so slightly on top. Noa's hand quivered but she tried to stay completely still.

Finally Noa found the energy and stood up. Elliot pushed himself to seated. She looked directly at him and spoke as if they had already been in conversation and this was a continuation.

'I guess, what I've been trying to say, I mean, what I want to say, is that I find it hard to be your friend these days.'

'Right.'

'I get it, you don't like me in that way. *Boys* don't like me in that way. And why would you be an exception? Of course you wouldn't. I think it's something to do with the way I'm a bit over keen or I dunno, I can't quite work it out. But basically, I'm finding it harder to be "friends" when I. . . well I. . . I massively like you. As. . . more than a friend.' She pressed her hands flat over her face as it flushed.

Noa peered through her fingers to gauge his expression. But he was fidgeting with his fingers, blank-faced. She could see his jaw pulsing. She dropped her hands and sighed wondering how long to wait for a response before leaving.

Elliot raked his fingers through his hair and then looked directly at Noa.

'You know I told you the other week, that those things you say don't look good are actually neutral things. Like, frizzy hair and a big nose?'

Hearing those cruel words in his mouth made her want to walk out of his eyeline. She was ultra-aware that she was standing right in front of him.

'Well you know that I came and looked at them.' Elliot stood then and came so close to her she had to tilt her head slightly up to see his face. He tucked the wisp of frizz that stuck out near her temple behind her ear. It felt as if all the electricity in her body was drawn to where his finger touched her skin, like the plasma ball she'd seen at the Science Museum.

'Yeah?'

'Well, that was because I was looking at you, specifically. To see what *your* feet, *your* nose, *your* hair were like.'

'Oh.'

'And well, they're perfect for you.'

'For me?'

Elliot wasn't looking her in the eyes anymore. He was still close, but his gaze had wandered over to the window.

'Nothing about you is small or bland or the same as everyone else. It's big and beautiful and in a group of people I always end up looking at you. And I like that you're keen, or whatever you want to call it. Who wants to be around someone who doesn't want to be there? All the things you don't like about yourself are the things I like about you.'

Noa's lip was quivering, just slightly. For once, she was too scared to believe what was being said. The stakes felt unbearably high. She couldn't say anything.

Elliot, as if he had suddenly awoken, widened his eyes and then looked directly at Noa, smiling broadly in a way Noa had never seen before. 'You're my favourite person.'

Elliot leaned down and pressed his lips onto Noa's, kissing her with his arms by his side, she was too overwhelmed to use her arms either. Then after a second he seemed to realise and softly held her head with one hand and her waist with the other. Noa took note and lay her forearms over his shoulders. (The kiss was a kiss for novices, the lips a little stiff, the tongues not quite in sync, the pauses not quite enough to take breath. But to them it was as perfect as every kiss they'd seen on films or conjured up in their minds.) Eventually they pulled apart and rested their foreheads on each other's for a moment, faces still close, smiles still wide.

The weeks that followed the kiss with Elliot were the best that Noa had ever experienced. Things went from good to better. It was nearly the end of Year 11 and Noa's hope for the future felt less like hope and more like inevitability. Noa and Elliot hung out constantly. They worked together, kicked about in town getting McDonalds or walking around the shopping centre laughing at anything and everything. And even at school he wasn't ashamed of her. They didn't kiss, but they spent the whole time together; listening to music, talking more openly about their lives, secretly linking and unlinking their hands under the canteen table. The best moments were ones where she felt picked out, special. Those seconds when he walked across the classroom towards her or took something out of his backpack to give her. The centre of his attention.

Noa and Elliot's noses were the only things separating their faces. They were lying down, facing each other, their mouths kissing softly, briefly every few minutes. Sometimes they were in silence. Sometimes Noa was whispering whatever came into her mind. But then he kissed her, a kiss that was different to how it had been so far. Noa felt their bodies were involved more, pressing into each other, their hands moving over each other's clothes. And then his hand effortlessly moved underneath her work shirt, but it wasn't grabbing and groping her like other boys in dark rooms had done at parties. His hands stayed on her back, her waist, her stomach. His touch was soft and natural. Noa mirrored him, her hand gently gliding over the skin of his back. She felt physically and emotionally overwhelmed. Usually every step of progression in their relationship felt like an accomplishment but now it felt as if she were on the edge of a precipice. She had loved him for a while. But now, now that their bodies and minds and hearts were interweaving, Noa realised all this was terrifying. She pulled away, feeling a new sense of emotional self-preservation. Her mum's warning rang in her mind. If they were to do this, what would that mean? Did she feel confident he felt the same way? Is it possible he didn't feel what she did? How would she be able to deal with it if he had her heart, her virginity, her whole life and then it all ended?

'Sorry. . . uhh. . .' Elliot pushed himself to seated. 'Sorry.'

'No. Don't be.' Noa stood up, her mind was overflowing, she wanted to tell him what she was feeling but she didn't know how to express it so blurted out, 'I just like you. . . loads.'

'I like you loads too.'

She looked, expecting to see a small smile but his face was blank.

'Are we just friends or. . .?' Noa laughed when she said it because she knew it was stupid. Obviously they were not just friends, and yet, nothing had ever been said. No emotions, no labels, no declarations of love. Exactly like her mum had predicted. A moment passed and she filled the gap between them with her words. Pleading with the universe for him to give her what she needed.

'If we're going to be. . . properly together like that, then you need to show me I'm different from everyone else. . . In some way.'

'I'm not. . . urm.' He was staring at his knees, furrowed brow, and Noa was about to confess she loved him when a (rare) instinct to hold back a thought kicked in and she blurted out that she needed to go.

15

Fifteen years old

Fraser was rocking back and forth on his seat, chewing gum, laughing at something a boy – Dean – was telling him. Dean was standing in front of Fraser's desk, looking down at him, JD sports bag still slung over his back. He had been moved down a year to repeat his GCSEs. Elliot was aware that Dean had started buying weed and MKAT for Fraser. It was only a couple of months into Year 11 and a friendship between them was already forming. Elliot, watching this from the doorway, couldn't bring himself to go fully into the classroom. But someone barged past him and told him to stop standing in the fucking way. Elliot took a deep breath and walked towards the desk.

'All right.' Elliot grunted to Fraser as he slid into the seat next to him. The teacher walked in and Fraser nudged Elliot in the waist. 'Oi, move somewhere else, yeah? I'm talking to Dean.'

Elliot felt his legs twitch. It was like his body was saying *You're going to run away now, using these.* He bit down hard on his cheek and found an empty seat at the front.

At lunch the football team met on the field for training. The grass was crunchy with frost but that wouldn't stop them. The cold hitting Elliot's skin felt like an ointment for the internal heat that had been building all morning. Football was still Elliot's favourite. He didn't need to speak, he didn't need to keep up to date with anything and he couldn't be left behind, made to feel immature or embarrassed. Dean, who didn't usually play, was coming with them and Elliot felt an uneasiness in his stomach but he tried to concentrate on the ball and not look at him. Unrelenting voices popped into his head telling him that this was the beginning of the end. Football was how Elliot got into the group and now it was going to help Dean take his place. He swallowed a gulp of cold air and focused on the game.

As the boys walked down the corridor towards their classroom Fraser kicked the heel of the boy in front of him. 'Oi, Ginge.'

The boy turned around.

'What the fuck are those shoes? Are they Velcro?' Fraser turned to look at Elliot and shot him a one-sided smile, his eyes sparkling with laughter. Elliot let his face mirror it despite the painful feeling of guilt in his chest. The ginger boy, who Elliot hung around with less and less, shrugged and said the sole was coming off his other shoes. Elliot wanted to turn the subject to something else but his mind was filled with white noise. Fraser punched the boy in the arm so he turned around again.

'How long did your dad save up for those then?'

The boy rolled his eyes but his whole face bloomed with patches of red and Elliot had to avert his eyes to the ground.

Fraser fell into step with the boy and spoke half to him and half to the group. 'Saw your dad in Woolworths the other day didn't we, Wood?'

They hadn't. But Elliot knew that the boy's dad worked there. He didn't want to reply but he didn't know what else to do, he couldn't exactly say no to Fraser. Elliot swallowed so hard he could feel his Adam's apple bob up and down. And then he nodded.

Fraser curved his shoulders into a low bend, miming walking with a stick. It was a massively exaggerated version of the boy's dad's reasonably hunched posture. Elliot's ears were tingling with the sounds of laughter around him and every second that passed without him joining in felt like a huge, risky defiance that he wasn't willing to take. He squinted his eyes and moved his shoulders up and down but it was fake and he felt (wrongly) like everyone's eyes were scanning him, checking him for legitimacy.

'Help me out, son, I struggle to get to the bog sometimes, which explains the smell,' Fraser said in a crumbly, old man voice and held his hand out to Elliot to be guided past the boy. Elliot saw the boy's eyes drift blankly to meet his. They weren't pleading or pre-emptively angry. It was worse. He was just waiting. Waiting to see what would happen. And the fact that Elliot had to make a decision and see it reflected in this boy's changing expression made him nauseous. (Of course all this happened in the briefest of moments.)

Elliot let his mouth turn up into the required faux-repressed laugh and took Fraser's arm while leading him down the last bit of corridor and into the classroom. Fraser made farting noises, 'whoops's and 'pardon me's'. It would have been easy not to look at the boy's face and keep his gaze, cowardly, averted. But Elliot would rather deal with reality, however hard it may be to take. (Truth and certainty were what he valued over everything.) The boy's eyes were not looking at Elliot anymore. And they were not looking at the ground or at anyone else. They were glazed over, deep in thought, looking into a far unknown distance. Elliot's body turned cold.

Eventually the boy's voice came out loud, directed to the rest of the group which were continuing with the probing questions. 'Fuck off now.'

Elliot felt a desire to go over and help, say something, tell everyone to leave it. He felt sick and out of his depth. The image popped into his mind of him and this boy being pointed and laughed at by the hyena noise he knew they could make, them giving him a cruel nickname that would never leave him. He slowly backed away, out of the classroom and then, when he was far enough, he turned and power-walked back through the double doors and a few steps around the corner. But he couldn't shake a sense of impending doom. His body was pulsing, begging him to leave, and so he snuck out the back and ran home. Ready to spend the rest of the night thinking incessantly (as he did every night) that his family were safe and everything was going to be okay.

Elliot made sure to get into school early the next day. If he could avoid seeing Fraser in the hallway, where he had humiliated the ginger boy, then that would surely protect him from humiliation. But before he could get to his classroom door, two flat palms pushed into his shoulder blades.

'Oi, boner boy.' It was a nickname only Dean had used so far, seemingly an extension of when he'd once called him 'Morning Wood'.

The whole of Elliot's body tensed and froze like he could turn invisible if he tried. But then, as if it realised it couldn't, his body flooded with the familiar tingling energy and urge to run away.

'What's your fucking problem?' The body moved around to face him. Fraser.

He needed to get out of the hall fast. As soon as he was in the classroom he would be safe. The hall was where the bad thing had happened.

Elliot tried to make his voice sound casual but it cracked a little. 'What do you mean?'

'Why did you fuck off yesterday?'

'Just felt a bit shitty. Headache.'

Fraser raised his eyebrow in a way that made Elliot's throat turn hot. He walked towards what he assumed was his new desk at the front but Fraser yanked his jacket and they walked to their desk at the back. He glanced at the clock. They were there twenty minutes early. Twenty minutes to fill with talking.

'I'm gonna get some people round this weekend.'

Elliot tried to do a normal expression but it felt too shocked. His brain was stodgy, like he'd lost any of the small ability he had to converse. 'Yeah?'

He thought he noticed Fraser double take at his face. He looked down and started to pick his cuticles. (He would think over this conversation many times in the following days, weeks, months even. As he did with all of the conversations he had.)

'Yeah. But I was thinking boys round first. Have some cans, play some FIFA, have some pizza or whatever and then get the girls over.'

Elliot tried to work out if that was a question or not. And if not, how do you respond to a statement without sounding boring? He bent down to get a water bottle out of his bag and took the time to think. But he'd already forgotten what had been said.

'Yeah.' Elliot did a weird stuttery laugh. His fingers started to twitch. But before the silence could build three other boys walked in.

Dean had walked into school with other people from the group.

Elliot felt himself close his eyes for slightly longer than what would look normal. He pushed his eyelids open with his index fingers but then realised that was weirder.

'All right, mate.' Fraser fist-bumped Dean. Chairs were pulled around and conversations ebbed and flowed but it was white noise in Elliot's ears. It wasn't that he was too shy or couldn't get a word in edgeways, but that he didn't have anything to say. Watching everyone else's mouths open and close like it was as easy as breathing hurt him in the guts. He wondered what was wrong with him. Why he was so empty inside.

Fraser was wheezing with laughter at a story Dean was telling about this guy he knew who put peanut butter on his balls and got his dog to lick it off. The ginger boy, who rarely spoke up these days, said something to Fraser.

'So *that's* why they call you butter balls.'

A few people started to laugh but Fraser's face was stone. Then it morphed into the face that Elliot dreaded more than anything. The eyebrows slightly pressed in and the nose wrinkled up a bit, either squinted or widened eyes. It was the face that got you less access to the group.

'What are you on about, Ginge,' Fraser said, without it being a question.

The ginger boy shrugged and Fraser continued the conversation. Elliot found his mind straining to think of things he might contribute to it but the physical feeling of trying to create thoughts felt strange and uncomfortable. He didn't like 'feeling' his brain work.

When the teacher strolled in, Fraser turned around so his back wasn't facing Elliot anymore.

'What you reckon for drinks on Saturday then? I've got someone who will buy us it if we give him an extra fiver. I'd want cans but maybe spirits would be good for the long game. What d'you reckon?'

Elliot tried to think what the right answer was. Did Fraser seem leaning to one side already? Would either answer be acceptable? He was definitely out of 'I dunnos', that's for sure.

'Yeah, I think beer.' He tried to muster a reasoning, taking a second to clear his throat. 'Just tastes way nicer.'

Elliot felt Fraser's eyes inspect his features and panic rose in his throat like bile. It seemed like Fraser had seen into his mind and therefore witnessed the emptiness and the strange way he came up with fake opinions. He quickly re-thought the thought as genuinely as he could, *I think beer would be good because it tastes nicer than spirits* trying to mentally 'say' it in the most believable way he could. As authentically as someone having the real thought might think it. Fraser said something in reply but Elliot barely heard it because he was repeating the thought again.

At school he couldn't avoid Fraser, and therefore it was imperative he made sure everything was set up to ensure he didn't get humiliated or rejected from the group. He persuaded himself that it was right around the corner. Unless. Unless he was charming enough, interesting, funny, talented, loyal. All things that felt impossibly heavy and weighed on him. He spent his time practising witty phrases, writing lists of conversation starters, preparing opinions, cataloguing facial expressions, analysing previous interactions and closely watching others; those who got eye rolls and punches and those who got fist bumps and nods of approval.

Eventually Elliot got so tired of socialising and preparing to socialise that he decided to get a job. It was the perfect excuse to turn down events without isolating himself. He caught the bus to anywhere outside town, anywhere people couldn't visit him, and applied for jobs. Unfortunately a girl from his school, Noa, had also got a job there. All day at work he tried to set a precedent that they wouldn't be friendly simply because they went to school together but he couldn't help being amused by her silly demeanour and overly worried comments, and so it wasn't long until a friendship formed.

The trouble was at school he felt he had to ignore her. He wasn't sure what befriending a girl at school would do to his status. Elliot had a feeling that Fraser liked his lack of attention from the girls as he sometimes seemed icy to other boys who were becoming popular with them. Plus, he had to make sure to be at Fraser's beck and call, standing on the sidelines waiting for the right times to laugh or do as he was told.

After one particular time when he had to be blunt to Noa, he noticed in form that she was looking particularly forlorn. A thought popped into his head; maybe she was feeling unwell because he was rude to her? Maybe she would start to get really ill if he continued to ignore her like this? It didn't seem too far-fetched. And it dawned on him that he really cared about Noa. All he wanted was for her to be happy and healthy and therefore if he wasn't careful he could jinx it and she wouldn't be.

Back at home Elliot made sure to incorporate Noa into his protective rituals for his family. After picturing Willie and his mum safe and happy, he would picture Noa at school beaming and laughing like she did sometimes at work. He would sift through memories of his family and Noa, looking for moments that they seemed to be acting unusually or showing any signs of distress, and then he would mentally replace them with normal and safe alternative versions. Only after these were done could he relax. Until the next time a worrying thought appeared and then he would restart the process.

One day at work, when his mind had been on Fraser, Elliot had barely thought protective things about Noa and as soon as he heard the screams he knew it was his fault. His heart felt like it was collapsing and his chest squeezed.

After they both got fired for the terrible thing he made happen, Elliot looked at Noa's usually golden skin, now red with blotches and matte with tear stains, and realised he felt strongly for this girl. He wanted her to be safe and happy but he also wanted some kind of tie between them. He couldn't be sure why but he didn't like the idea of them as separate entities anymore. But that thought was terrifying. He wanted to push it away. Keep her safe from the gravitational pull in towards his peril.

At work Elliot was lost in a big pile of dirty plates. Leftover chunks of meat and soggy chips sludged between his fingers. Something slapped over his shoulder and he jumped. He turned – dripping hands kept over the sink – to see Noa holding some bright yellow plastic gloves.

'What are those?' Elliot's shoulders tensed up, waiting to hear something that he stupidly hadn't realised or had accidentally ruined.

'They're all the rage, that's what they are.'

Elliot flicked the water off his fingers, dried them on a rag and turned fully to Noa. 'What d'you mean?'

'They're gloves. Little clothes for your hands.'

Elliot wondered if he'd been doing everything wrong. 'Am I supposed to wear them?'

'Well. . .' The round apples of Noa's cheeks were reddening and he wanted to press the back of his hands on them. 'You don't have to. . . I just thought. . . you always say how gross the water is and stuff.'

'Where did you get them from?' Elliot felt a kind of fear build in him, but not the usual type, it was a fear that something good was going to happen, and he didn't feel capable of dealing with that emotion internally or externally.

'Down the shop. On my road. Don't worry, you don't have to—'

Elliot took the gloves from her and tried to sound normal but he stumbled over his words. 'That's so. . . thank you. That will change everything. Thanks so much.' His expression felt out of control, too smiley, too over the top, she would think he was strange and overacting. And so he turned back around and let himself grin at his hands while he put them on.

Later that evening as Elliot lay on his bed, ready to perform his mental rituals, he thought about something else instead. He replayed the scene with the gloves again and again. Not checking for anything or trying to reassure himself about something. But because there were so many joyful layers to peel: The fact she'd been thinking about him outside work, the fact she'd wanted to make his life better, the fact she'd listened to and retained the information about him hating the water on his hands, the fact she'd spent money on him, the fact she went red when she told him about the gloves. He couldn't think of another example where someone had done something like this. Even his mum. It was the feeling that you existed in someone else's mind even when you weren't with them. And as an individual rather than a featureless son, a nameless student, a generic employee. It made him realise how conditional his relationship with the boys was. How much they required from him and how little they gave back.

★

226

After PE one day, as they were changing, Elliot felt aware of the ginger boy's presence on the bench behind him. So when Fraser gestured with his eyebrows behind Elliot, he already knew who it was aimed at. Elliot turned to see the boy in his boxers and turned back shrugging, trying to avoid eye contact with Fraser. But it was impossible not to see him miming pulling down the boxers. Elliot tried mentally repeating to himself, *I didn't see it,* in an attempt to reassure himself that he wasn't disobeying Fraser. Then, in a flash, someone behind him did it anyway and there was swearing and shouting and roaring laughter.

Elliot was frozen to the spot. It felt like if he stood still then maybe the thing didn't happen to the ginger boy. And if this particular thing didn't happen then maybe things like this didn't happen in general. And if things like this didn't happen in general then things like this couldn't happen to him. But shoving caused him to fall into the wooden bench in front of him and so he grabbed his drawstring bag and sped out of the changing rooms. As he left he heard 'Calm down, baby dick' and 'Grow some pubes' being called out by one and then multiple people.

Elliot power-walked home, trying desperately to neutralise the bad thoughts breaking into his mind. Predictions of bad things happening to his brother or mum, of humiliation happening to him, of the loneliness that was destined to follow. He replaced them with new, positive ones. Again and again.

Elliot was late the next day. And so the classroom was full when he finally got into school. Fraser sat at the back with an empty seat next to him. Elliot swallowed.

'All right,' he grunted as he sat down.

But Fraser didn't reply. The hot blood pulsed around Elliot's body. He wondered if he should get up, run, never come back, but then the teacher came in.

As the names were being called Fraser muttered without turning to Elliot.

'Where the fuck do you keep running off to then?'

'What d'you mean?' Elliot was squeezing the tips of his fingers to stop them shaking.

'Yesterday. You fucked off. Did you have a problem or did you think you're better than us?'

Elliot felt his eyes look everywhere other than at Fraser. The words stuck to his windpipe. 'What. . .do you mean?'

'"What do you mean" "what do you mean",' Fraser repeated in an impression of his choked voice.

'Quiet, please,' the teacher called frustratedly before Elliot was forced to retry and speak.

The register passed so slowly it was almost amusing (it took the normal amount of time). Every pause, every name that was called, every minute he had to keep his body still, felt too much, too long, too impossible to surmount. Each moment that passed where Elliot stayed in his seat, still and not convulsing, felt like a miracle to him. He told himself to wait, but as the time drew closer, and the promise of freedom was becoming more realistic, the wait felt more unbearable somehow. It was like he was desperately running towards a toilet, his bladder bursting as he opened the cubicle door. But in this case it was when Fred Young's name was being called, Elliot couldn't wait any longer, his body propelled itself off the chair and stumbled out of the classroom before anyone else. He gasped for air like his head had been held under water for slightly too long. It felt as if his consciousness left his body, like he was somehow being pulled out of himself and into a dangerous place. A place that if he fully let go, he would never come back from.

He burst out of the canteen doors, onto the school field and found a bay where industrial bins were stored. People were pouring out now, finding their way to lessons but it was imperative that he wasn't seen, so he squeezed himself behind a large, blue metal bin and managed to crouch into a squat. He held his head in his hands. What was happening? His chest was thrumming and his vision blurred and he realised he was going to die. This was a heart attack or a stroke or an aneurysm. He could feel his heart stuttering and crunching, struggling to work in these last few moments of life. His toes were pulsing up and down in his shoes and every fibre of his body was telling him to stand up and move. And so he did. He paced back and forth and back and forth and back and forth frantically squeezing his fingers with his other hand and wondering if he should run out, scream for help, go to hospital, or just force himself to lie down and die.

It wasn't long until Elliot felt himself come to. As if he had awoken from a dream. His consciousness returned to his body, the air was now cold against his cheeks and he could no longer feel his heart beating. He sputtered out a giggle and then came out from the bin area. Everyone had gone to their lessons. There was a kind of euphoria that flowed through his body then. He couldn't help grinning to himself. He'd survived. But this only lasted a couple of minutes. Because what came next was exhaustion. A tiredness that soaked into the bones and stung the eye sockets and hurt something deeper than any organ.

★

Elliot's fear of humiliation didn't go away, but it was reduced once he realised that Fraser hadn't been the great friend he'd thought he was. Hanging out with Noa had taught him that friends should make you feel good, happy, confident. Not scared, awkward, embarrassed. But the fear of rejection had followed him for so long it wasn't easy to shrug off. He still slunk around next to Fraser, laughing at jokes he wasn't even listening to. Playing football after school. Nodding along to Fraser planning his end–of–Year–11 party, saying 'yeah maybe' and 'yeah definitely' and 'sounds sick', whenever required.

When Elliot finally told Noa how he felt life became brighter than he'd ever known it. Weeks passed where he thought of nothing else but her. The next time he could kiss her, the song he had to show her, the silly thing he'd thought during History. The change was so large that feelings he'd never had before started to blossom: hope, optimism, contentment. He even began to think she might understand if he told her everything weird about him. But towards the end of the year she started to pull away. It was impossible to satisfy both Noa and Fraser. It seemed like pleasing one would be the exact thing to upset the other. He could see Fraser watching him from across the canteen when he was sitting with Noa, their knees gently touching under the table. And then, every time Elliot went to speak to her, Fraser started asking him to do something or start up a conversation or would make a cruel joke at his expense. But it was easier not to care now.

16

Fifteen years old

Fraser's party was in one week. Noa was seeing and talking to Elliot less, but not never. It was like their relationship had rewound a few weeks and this was equal parts relieving and distressing. Noa was desperate to claw back the intensity she had left behind but didn't know how. She felt ashamed of herself for stopping what was going to happen in his bedroom. She felt ready to have sex. She loved Elliot. So what was the problem? The problem was the image of Elliot walking away that kept popping into her mind, leaving her emptier than she'd ever felt before. (But Noa had a passion for love that gave her bravery where others may have shied away, and that is why for Elliot, she would have, and did, do anything.)

Turning over her mum's words in her head again and again she stumbled across a loophole. It didn't have to be the boy to initiate the conversation. To suggest a relationship. Noa sent a message to Elliot saying she had something to tell him at the party, and he replied saying he did too. She hugged herself with nerves and excitement.

Fraser's house was in a new estate outside of town. Walking inside with the group of girls was almost surreal. She truly felt she had it all. Inside the boys were standing with boys and the girls were standing with girls, but the night had only just begun and Noa knew from experience now that it wouldn't be long until this binary broke down.

She was nodding along to the girls chatting, sipping the WKD Verity had kindly given her, but really she was looking around for Elliot. There was a serene positivity in her, she felt sure this was going to be one of the best nights of her life (Poor Noa. Her optimism always punished.) It was like her senses had been turned up past full; the sweet, bubbly, blue taste of the drink, Get Low blasting out from a speaker somewhere, the strands of the distressed denim hem on her skirt tickling her bare legs, the sight of boys chugging cans of beer in her periphery. And then, Elliot walking in the back door with Fraser. She loved seeing him outside of school and work. It was a whole new layer of real to see him in his own clothes. A whole new compliment to herself to see this well-dressed person give her attention. He wore a black Harrington, a white polo shirt and black skinny jeans. Fraser was saying something to him but he was looking down, his hand in his hair sweeping it to one side. Noa felt her fingers and lips twitch.

Time dragged on and they still didn't interact. But his mere presence took up the whole of her awareness. It felt like some kind of scientific phenomenon. Wherever she moved, he would be in her eyeline. No matter how many people spoke around her, Noa's ears were attuned to the sound of his voice. Eventually she excused herself and found an empty conservatory. She sat down on a soft, floral sofa and went over what she wanted to say to Elliot, if she could ever get him on his own. She wanted to tell him she loved him. She wanted to ask him to be her boyfriend. She wanted to explain to him that if he felt the same, if he could give her the assurance that they were together, properly together, boyfriend and girlfriend, then she was ready to lose her virginity to him. A silhouette appeared in the doorway and she jumped.

'Oh my God. You scared me.'

Elliot walked into the light. Noa decided he was full of paradoxes. He seemed like his posture was upright and proud, but when she focused on him she noticed a kind of folding in on himself, everything pushed towards the centre. He seemed strikingly attractive in a way that gave Noa a shock whenever she looked at him, and yet she struggled to pick out anything specific about him that was particularly unusual or better than anyone else. He gave off an air of confidence and yet often was fidgeting or shifting his weight, jigging his leg, chewing his nails. She loved him.

He nodded his head and sat down next to her. 'All right.'

'Hey.' Noa replied, looking up at him and then realising they were so close that she whipped her head back round to the front, nervously. 'How's it going?'

'Okay thanks. You?'

'Yeah, good thanks.'

The conversation felt stilted. Noa couldn't work out why and the fear started to creep in that she'd been wrong this whole time. He didn't like her, he actually liked someone else, or he felt she was too immature or clingy or he was bored of her. Noa pulled her hair into a fake ponytail to disguise her deep inhale.

She tried to say something, anything. 'Are you excited for summer?'

'Yeah, I dunno. Sometimes, I find it hard to be excited about stuff.'

'Oh. How come?' Noa tried to shake off the urge to search for hidden meanings in that.

'Never mind.'

'Elliot, I—'

'The thing is—'.

Nervous laughter bubbled out of them. Elliot got in first.

'Sorry, actually, hold on, be right back.' He stood up and hurried through the glass doors. She stood and paced the room telling herself that he'd just gone to the toilet. *Because he'd said 'back', right? Which clearly implies, no* states, *that he will be returning.* But seconds turned into minutes and minutes turned into slightly more minutes and Noa, twirling her hair round and round her fingers, staring at the floor, walking in circles, was struggling to think what could be taking so long.

'What are you doing?'

Noa didn't notice him standing in the doorway. She swivelled to face him. But it wasn't Elliot. His eyebrow was raised and his one-sided smile was in full force.

'Oh, sorry.' Noa laughed nervously. 'I'm waiting for Elliot.'

Fraser walked over to a reclining armchair and sat down in it, flinging both legs up onto the woven coffee table. 'What are you sorry for?'

'Oh, I don't know. Sorry.' Noa felt awkward. She could feel herself bumbling. She forced herself to sit back on the sofa.

Fraser didn't take his gaze off her or smile. She could only look at him in brief glimpses. His confidence was stronger than an adult's. He seemed to feel at ease no matter what the situation, and this was a situation where he naturally had the upper hand anyway. In his house, at his party, with a girl who should count herself lucky to be there.

'You know what, Noa, you're a strange one.'

'How come?' Noa was pushing her bottom lip together and

folding the condensed lip inwards and then pushing it outwards. She knew it was this kind of thing that made her look geeky but she couldn't help it. Despite her relationship with not only a boy, but a cool and attractive one, she still found Fraser unbelievably intimidating. He was shorter than Elliot but broader and had a way of moving and speaking that made him seem years older than her.

'Who are you actually mates with?'

The question knocked her back. She tried to have a neutral expression but felt her cheeks burn. She looked down at her nails and exhaled a laugh, hoping that was enough of a response. But then she saw his trainers move off the coffee table and his calves walk towards her. The sofa jolted as he fell down onto it beside her. He nudged her with his elbow but she still didn't look at him.

'I'm only fucking with you.'

He smelt strongly of aftershave and Noa worried he heard her inhaling. She could feel him staring at her.

'I mean, you popped up outta nowhere.' Fraser made a popping sound with his mouth in Noa's ear.

She turned to look at him, giggling. Their faces were close and she saw his eyes linger on her lips. A smile made its way onto Noa's face. The attention was becoming comfortable and enjoyable. She saw herself through Verity and the rest of the girls' eyes. Someone worthy of attention, someone worthy of Fraser's attention.

Noa tried to think of something to say. 'Are you having a good party?'

Fraser pushed the corners of his lips down as if laughing at her. 'I am now. Are you?'

Noa realised that Elliot had been gone a while. She looked at the door to check if he was standing there, worrying he might have got the wrong impression. Then she felt all ten of Fraser's fingers around the circumference of her head. They swivelled it back round to facing him.

'Oh, sorry.' Noa instinctively looked forward but he turned her head back to facing him again.

'Am I minging or summat?' Fraser folded his arms as if to pose.

'No, no. Sorry I just. . .'

'So what am I then?'

'What do you mean?'

'If I'm not ugly. What am I?'

Noa looked at him then, at his diamanté earring and square teeth and shiny blue eyes. 'You're. . . cool.'

Fraser leaned his head back and laughed a breathy laugh. He looked at her with a raised eyebrow. 'What's cool about me then?'

'Urm, I dunno, you're like, confident and look. . . good.' Noa was struggling to answer his questions.

'You're pretty cool yourself, Farina.' He shuffled forward slightly. His hand brushed her neck as he popped the collar on her checked shirt. 'See.'

But Fraser didn't pull completely back. Noa could smell the wheaty beer on his breath. She pictured herself walking into school, hand in hand with Fraser, everyone's mouths dropped open. The way her whole life would change. But then she thought of Elliot and her heart ached. She shimmied subtly away from Fraser and turned to look at the door.

'Why are you so obsessed with Elliot anyway?'

Noa couldn't help grinning at 'you' and 'Elliot' being said in the same sentence.

'I just like him.'

'Do you think he likes you?' Fraser was looking at the ceiling and making a clucking sound by creating a suction between his tongue and bottom lip.

'Yeah. . .' Noa tried to sound confident but the word came out choked so she had to say it twice. 'Yeah, I think he does.'

'You might be right.'

Noa checked Fraser's expression to see if he meant it. The blankness of it seemed to suggest he was sincere. But then his lip started to extend on one side into a smile. Noa looked between his eyes and mouth desperately trying to work out what he was implying.

But then Fraser pushed himself to standing and wriggled out a packet of gum from his jean pocket. He pulled a piece of gum up and out of the packet with his teeth and then put it away without offering Noa one.

'Anyways, this convo has zapped the fucking life out of me.' He slapped himself playfully on the cheek. 'I need to get me sen a beer.'

Noa was turning her collar down so she had something to do. She nodded politely at him and he strode out. Noa put her face in her hands and blew out a sigh. But before she could get her thoughts together a voice made her jump.

'You've got to ask yoursen though, why is he not here?' Fraser gestured around the room. 'If he likes you so much.'

The question made Noa touch her face nervously as she pretended to think. 'Urm. . .'

Fraser walked back into the room and started a heel-toe heel-toe dance. (People liked Fraser because he had the extremely rare trait of being able to successfully pass off silly or strange things as charismatic quirks and funny jokes.)

'I can tell you why.' He was chewing the gum open-mouthed with his back molars.

Noa started flattening down her hair with her palms like she did when she was nervous. She didn't want to know the answer. She wanted to live in her mind where her and Elliot were boyfriend and girlfriend at the beginning of their love story. But the thing with Elliot was that, when it came down to it, she didn't *really* want to live in her mind with him. A totally neutral, platonic moment with him meant a thousand times more to her than any daydream where they confessed their love to one another.

'Why?' Noa was pinching her lip again, she was struggling not to let all her thoughts pour out or her desperation show.

Fraser sat down next to Noa again and linked his fingers behind his head, leaning back into his palms and sighing. 'I dunno if I should tell ya. It's none of my business.'

'I don't mind. It can be your business too.'

Frasers eyes lingered on Noa's lap so much that she felt the urge to pull at the hem on her denim skirt.

'You're a virgin, right?'

Noa's palms had started to sweat. She wasn't ashamed as such, just shy. She'd never spoken about losing her virginity to anyone before and it had only very recently stopped becoming something that would happen in a far-off fairy-tale future. It seemed strange that the world had started talking about it as soon as she'd started considering it. Noa shrugged and nodded at the same time.

'Yeah, well, that's fine. No one is saying that's a bad thing.'

'What's this got to do with Elliot?' She felt impatient for some kind of good news. The hope that things would all work out perfectly was becoming painful.

'It's that taking a girl's V card. . .' Fraser spoke over his left shoulder, away from Noa. 'It's not. . . no one wants to do that.'

Noa was squeezing her thighs together hard, trying not to cry. She couldn't trust her voice to speak.

Fraser, turning fully towards her now, pushed his back against the armrest and twisted his right thigh onto the sofa. He laid a gentle hand on her shoulder. 'Noa, look.' Her name in his loud voice managed to stop her spiralling. She tried to focus on the positive. Yes, Elliot had been gone for ages and didn't want her but look, Fraser was choosing to spend time with her, at his own party, when he could be with anyone.

'Honest, he does like you. Believe me.' He moved his head in front of hers to catch her gaze. 'Why wouldn't he, eh?' He gave Noa a wink and she started squeezing her hair.

Abruptly he removed all contact and stood up. Her shoulder felt cold where his hand had been.

'He's said to me that he wants to be with you. But *after*, if you get me?' Fraser turned and walked out the room.

She realised that he was walking away, leaving her in this room where Elliot had not returned, would not return. She looked up to the glass roof and saw the sky had turned a lilac grey now. A long time had passed. She didn't want to believe it but all the facts were pointing to this being true: Elliot not returning, his mood seeming off, Fraser knowing that they had been considering having sex.

'Wait!' She followed him into the hall and he turned around. He was more intimidating in his full stance, seemed more like the boy she'd watched command the classroom all those years. He didn't acknowledge her with words.

'How am I supposed to. . . If I want to be with Elliot?'

Noa could hear the pumping R&B and the shrieking of girls and the booming voices of boys from the living room. She felt drawn to look for Elliot but the thought hurt.

Fraser leaned down and clamped his lips onto Noa's. Her mind flooded with Elliot, the soft pressure of his lips against hers, his cold fingers on her neck. This kiss felt hard and clammy. She couldn't make her lips move against his. When he pulled back she assumed he would leave. But he didn't. He took hold of her wrist and guided her, up the stairs and into a square, white bedroom with a double bed in the centre. She didn't have much time to take things in because Fraser closed the door, spit his gum on the floor, and took Noa by the waist, mashing his lips against hers again. This time he slid his wet tongue deep into her mouth. It jabbed in and out and Noa didn't know when and how she was expected to use hers. It didn't feel natural or instinctual like it had with Elliot.

Fraser's hands were clasped tight around her hips. Without removing his mouth he guided them to the bed and sat them down on the edge. His hand pushed its way under her shirt and it made her jump. She stood up, gasping for breath. She felt light-headed, almost dizzy. Elliot and Verity popped in and out of her mind like bubbles but she couldn't quite grasp a coherent thought.

'I. . .' Out came a long, nervous laugh and she started to wring her hands trying to regain some composure. 'I don't think. . .' She struggled to form words to describe what she wanted to say. How could she turn down something that hadn't been explicitly offered? It felt silly.

'Noa, it's fine, you don't need to stay here.' Fraser leaned back on his forearms. 'Leave. I was only passing on a message from Elliot. Why d'you think I came to find you in the conservatory? I was just doing what I was told.'

Noa was facing the door, ready to leave. Except she couldn't leave. Her body was fixed to the spot. Her mind muddy from alcohol and half-thoughts. Had Elliot really wanted her to be here? Suddenly Fraser was next to her again. A hand was placed on her waist and then moved slowly around onto her stomach and then even slower it moved downwards, into her waistband. As his hand moved underneath the elastic of her underwear Noa felt her stomach muscles tense and her left eye squeeze shut. Things progressed rapidly and soon she was lying on his bed, naked except for her white M&S T-shirt bra. Things didn't seem to be going well. It wasn't like films where men would slide effortlessly into women as if their genitals were magnets. Fraser was trying to jam his penis inside Noa using one hand to push it in and the other hand's fingers to locate the entrance. Noa kept picturing herself rolling over into a foetal position or saying 'let's just leave it' but she couldn't. She felt frozen and it was as if the conscious part of her had left her body and was floating above, looking down, watching. She focused her efforts on getting her consciousness to look away, avert her eyes, concentrate on the windowpane check of the bedsheets or the floating dust illuminated by the setting sun. There was a sharp pain and a tear collected in the corner of Noa's eye. She tried to see this moment as another scene in the story of her life. A stepping stone towards her future with Elliot. And then it was over. Fraser was standing up and whipping on his jeans one leg at a time, muttering something that Noa was struggling to hear. She shuffled the duvet down and got underneath it, not wanting to dress until he was out of the room.

Minutes passed and she couldn't get herself to stand up. Her body was still constricted by something abstract. Noa put her hands between her legs and then looked at her fingers. No blood. She chewed on her lip wondering why Elliot was so reluctant to do this. But it didn't matter now, she'd done it and she wanted to reap the rewards for her task. Her cotton pants were lying open on the floor and it made her feel silly, like a child had been undressing rather than the adults she'd seen stripping off their lacy lingerie before they had sex on TV. She dressed herself and walked downstairs but she couldn't find Elliot. So she stood in random groups trying to involve herself in the conversation but she couldn't concentrate. She had a cramping feeling in her stomach and the inside of her thighs hurt. But worst of all her heart was breaking. She tried to tell herself that this was good, that her world was about to open up to new highs, but something deep inside her didn't believe it.

17

Sixteen years old

At school, on a day that the sun was finally felt on people's faces, the boys and girls were sat out on the field, some sunbathing, some chatting about exams or Fraser's upcoming end-of-Year-11 party, some stealthily smoking Sterling cigarettes. Elliot was trying not to look at Noa, who was sitting on the other side of the group. He was trying to keep a neutral expression so no one looped him into the conversation. He was trying to look interested enough that he still came across as someone with a personality, someone with thoughts and feelings about the topics being discussed.

It was impossible not to be attuned to the aura of Fraser, as that is what Elliot had trained himself to do. And in that moment Elliot noticed a shift in his attention. Fraser's eyes fixed somewhere behind Elliot and then glanced upwards as if considering something. Elliot knew who Fraser would be looking at. He knew that smile; the smile of someone enjoying themselves before the real enjoyment had begun. A pulsating internal burn began in Elliot. He tried to look down at the grass in front of him, picking at it one by one, as if this were a task that would excuse him from having to participate.

'Oi.' A pincer of fingers gripped the pressure points on his knee. He tried to take his time to look up. All he could manage as a reply was his eye contact.

Fraser nodded his head towards something. 'Come with me over there and crouch behind baby dick and I'm gonna push him over you.'

Elliot tried to laugh as if it were funny and then shrugged. 'Nah, you're all right.'

'I'm not asking, mate.'

Fraser stood up and tugged so sharply at Elliot's sleeve the material dug into his armpit. He managed to stay focused on the grass and tried to keep his mind blank. He didn't see how Dean was beckoned, but a second later he was standing up and following Fraser instead. Images of humiliation for himself and the ginger boy flashed into his mind and he squeezed his eyes shut to try and delete the images but that only made them stronger. He knew he was going to have to leave before his face and hands started to do weird things because of the bubbling urgency inside. But after he mumbled some excuse, stood up and started to stride back to the canteen doors, the energy inside him felt propulsive rather than evasive. His body turned and he started to run towards where Fraser and Dean were headed. Just as Dean had taken his crouched position and Fraser had walked around the front, Elliot called out.

'Dom! Watch it mate.' And gestured to look on the floor behind him. Dom hopped to the side and looked all around him as if to check for other traps. Then looked at Elliot and nodded. (They would never mention this moment again, but it was always there, underpinning their friendship).

Dean stood up and walked towards Elliot. 'What's your fucking problem? Can't take a joke?' He pushed Elliot's chest.

Elliot stumbled backwards a couple of steps. 'No. Sorry. I—' But he couldn't think of words to explain himself.

Fraser just scowled at him, spat his gum on the grass and walked away.

Dean blew out a laugh and added, 'You're such a freak sometimes, boner boy.'

Fraser and Dean headed off on their own. Elliot didn't want to but he couldn't help a quick glance back at the group. Most people's eyes were directed at him. Noa was standing up but she hadn't moved from where she sat. He tried to walk slowly but his legs were pushing him faster than that. Out of the field, through the school and then out the foyer into the car park and down the road. He walked into the housing estate nearby and collapsed onto a grassy verge, shuffling himself as far into a bush as he could go. He could feel his heart pumping in his chest, throat, temples, palms. Elliot turned onto his knees as bile came into his throat and dug what remained of his fingernails into the dirt. After spitting out a dribble of saliva he sat back on his heels, reached into his bag and grabbed a pen and his Geography book. Flipping to the back page he started to write.

Please keep Noa and my family safe. Please keep Noa and my family safe. Please keep Noa and my family safe. Please keep Noa and my family safe. Please keep Noa and my family safe.

Please let things be okay with Fraser. Please let things be okay with Fraser. Please let things be okay with Fraser. Please let things be okay with Fraser. Please let things be okay with Fraser.

He looked down at the page and realised his chest had stopped hurting. He pressed the book to his face, smelling the biro and thanking The One for his help. Then he breathed out an embarrassed laugh and shut the book. But as he pressed his fists into his eyes in frustration, an idea came to him.

Noa had said to him a few weeks earlier, 'If we're going to be. . . properly together like that, then you need to show me I'm different from everyone else. . . In some way.' He hadn't known what that meant, but now it made sense. Showing her his notebook would be the perfect way to show Noa who he was. To give her the chance to know him like nobody else did, just like she asked. Then they could be together.

Elliot thought it would be easy to keep a low profile at Fraser's end-of-year party because there would be so many people vying for attention. But things were taking a while to kick off, and it was mainly people standing around chatting.

He was pretending to drink, keeping his lip pressed against the hole on his beer can when he put it to his mouth. It was hard to seem normal and he could feel Dean's eyes on him. He heard him muttering something, laughing, to the boy next to him. Then he could hear the other boy laughing. Then he could feel that one of his ears was burning hot.

'Elliot. Why the fuck are you wearing a backpack, mate?'

The other boy laughed. 'We're not at fucking school.'

Now it was other people's gaze he could feel, as more laughs picked up.

Dean continued. 'Honestly mate, take it off, it's so weird. It's making me feel like we're about to go into fucking English or summat.'

Elliot shrugged and tried to wait out the digs but it didn't work. Fraser came over from another group.

'What's in the bag, Wood?'

'What d'you mean? Just leave it. It's just a bag. I don't want to lose it is all.'

'Let's have a look then?' Fraser grabbed at the strap and tried to pull it off but Elliot stepped away.

Elliot thought this could be the end, it could be the humiliation he'd been dreading. If they were to find the book, with all his weird thoughts written out again and again. Thoughts like, *Please let Fraser be my friend*. He would have to run away and kill himself. He was certain that would have to be the course of action and the thought calmed him surprisingly. It was verging on a win-win situation. Everything being fine or death. With this clarity of mind he realised that the book was harmless looking. A plain notebook mixed in with his planner and textbooks. If he confidently showed them the contents of his bag, they wouldn't think to go through each of the book's pages. Probably.

'Right, if I take it off and show you lot what's inside, will you leave it out?'

'Go on then.' Fraser tugged on the strap adjuster cords so it sat higher on his back and people laughed.

Elliot pulled it off himself and, after taking in a sharp breath, pulled the front flap so it unzipped and the bag's mouth opened. Dean walked over and picked his way through the books, loose pens, crisp packets. Elliot couldn't stop staring at the book even though he tried not to. Fraser yanked open the small front pocket and took out the random rubbish in there.

'See.' Elliot wished he didn't sound so childish but he felt like a child. Victorious.

Fraser threw the bag into the corner of the room. 'Don't be putting it back on, you fucking freak.'

And so it sat there. It was still in his sight, if his eyes moved as far left as they could. He allowed himself a few sips of the savoury-tasting bubbles. Things were going well, all he had to do was somehow get the notebook and then go and find Noa. He'd seen her out the corner of his eye, gesticulating madly while recounting an anecdote and found it impossible not to smile. Her energy always absorbed into him somehow, like just by being near her he was part of something good, fun, light.

The conversation moved on (and drinks got drunk by shy mouths that had nothing else to do). Elliot felt his thoughts soften into the present – not the usual impact he felt from alcohol which was an ultra awareness, a feeling of seeing himself from a thousand other perspectives.

By the time he heard a girl say, 'Where's Noa?' He'd actually forgotten his plan for a second. He was enjoying himself, cracking the odd joke and even responding easily to the few things directed at him.

One of the boys shouted back, 'Probs taking a shit.'

Elliot realised this meant she taken herself away on purpose so he could go and find her. He felt his heart squeeze with nerves and excitement. The window he had to find her would probably be short. He glanced at the backpack and felt his armpits heat. He didn't know how to get it without drawing attention to himself. He couldn't risk everyone becoming interested again. And so he made a split-second decision to find Noa, tell her to wait for him, and then return to find a way to extract the backpack.

When he saw her, sitting on the floral sofa, staring off into a distance further than the wall opposite her, twiddling an earring around in her ear, he thought how beautiful she looked in profile. Her sharp nose and pouty lips and dark eyebrows made her so striking. He decided he should tell her right then. That he loved her, that he wanted them to be together officially, that he'd never felt so alive and happy and full as when he was with her and that, he knew they were young and people said stuff like this when they didn't understand life properly yet, but that he couldn't imagine his life without her now, because there had never been a future that existed without her in it.

But as he opened his mouth she turned and said, 'Oh my God. You scared me.'

Now, walking into the intensely intimate room, he felt his confidence to say all that drain away. Her big emotive eyes, her irises as black as pupils in this light, stalled him a little.

All he could mutter was 'All right' as he sat down beside her. Their thighs touched as the cushions deflated under his weight and he wanted to reach out and run his fingers over the bones of her knee.

'Hey.' She looked at him and he thought about how he loved seeing her this close, the lilac underneath her eyes and the soft fuzz on her cheeks. He was so distracted he forgot what he was supposed to say and so she ended up filling the silence.

'How's it going?'

'Okay thanks. You?'

'Yeah, good thanks.'

Elliot decided to plan his first sentence and then let the rest come naturally. He was thinking whether to start with a compliment when Noa said, 'Are you excited for summer?'

Elliot was beginning to feel stressed. The conversation was getting away from him. It was time to force it back on track, 'Yeah, I dunno. Sometimes, I find it hard to be excited about stuff.'

'Oh. How come?'

Because I'm a freak. Because I have no personality. Because I ruin everything around me. It was too hard to express it without the prop of his book. 'Never mind.' He hated himself for not being able to say the way he felt when she deserved to know. Deserved to be told all the amazing things about her. He tried again. 'The thing is—' But it was no use. He needed the book.

'Sorry, actually, hold on, be right back.' Elliot stood up and gave her a quick smile before running out to retrieve his backpack.

He wanted to enter the kitchen as casually as possible. The thought that something bad would happen crossed his mind so he mentally repeated 'something good' to himself to neutralise it. He decided to walk to the fridge to 'look for a drink' and then get it on his way back. But the bag was not there. The shock winded him and he couldn't keep it together. He didn't have the self-control to act calm. Elliot looked wildly around the room, in every corner, on all the surfaces. No one seemed to notice him. He stood to the side and replayed where it was thrown and confirmed it was definitely in that corner. The fear was becoming stronger. Elliot walked over to the group of people, unable to hide his distress.

'Have you seen my bag?'

The girls shrugged and said no. The boys looked at each other with badly concealed smiles and said no but that he needed to chill the fuck out.

An urgency propelled Elliot out the room and into the other rooms on the ground floor looking for it. In the lounge he found Dean posing for a picture downing a WKD.

'Where's my bag?'

'What are you on about?'

Elliot was immediately pretty certain that Dean didn't know. His expression was genuinely confused for a second and then morphed into amusement.

'For fuck's sake, Elliot. Who gives a shit about that bag? Someone's probably chucked it away for your sake.'

'It's got my stuff in it. Do you actually think they've thrown it away?' Elliot didn't care that his face was desperate. He was desperate and happy to convey it.

Dean's expression changed again to a narrow-eyed suspicion. 'What the fuck is in that bag, mate? Have you got drugs?'

Elliot felt dizzy. Images started to pour into his mind. He stumbled out of the room, almost delirious. The heart attack feeling was brewing. Looking for somewhere to hide he found a cupboard in the hall with coats in. It was full to the brim and not tall enough to fit his body in standing up. But he bent over and pushed himself in, through the coats, and crouched on his tiptoes, on top of the floor of shoes. His cheeks and palms were tingling. He held out his hands in front of him, they were shaking so much it felt like he was putting it on, but he couldn't still them. His body flushed with heat and he pulled off his jacket. The pain in his chest was radiating and he gripped at his heart but the feel of it beating rapidly onto his hand terrified him so he ripped it away. Once again he had the strong feeling that he was dying. His consciousness seemed to be leaving his body and his heart felt like it was petering out. One thing was for sure, there was no more air.

He decided he needed to get to Noa, tell her his weird secrets before someone else did or before he died of a heart attack. He opened the door, his shaking hands rattling the doorknob as he turned it. He closed his eyes and pictured Noa's glassy black ones, using it as motivation to fight through the pain. If anything, he told himself, showing her this, this secret, defective part of him would be the ultimate proof she was different to everyone else. All he needed to do was hold it together until he found her. But it didn't take long to find her. As Elliot exited the cupboard door he saw her on the staircase directly in front of him stepping out of sight. As he took one step towards the stairs and craned his head to look up, he saw Noa again, holding on to Fraser's hand. It took a few seconds for his brain to catch up with what he saw and it only sank in when he leaned further forward over the banister to see Fraser's door clicking closed behind them. The sound made his stomach turn solid.

'What are you doing muthafuckaaaa?'

Elliot turned to see a boy from his class, his eyes bleary with drink. 'Urm, nothing.'

'"Urm, nothing."' The boy mimicked in a silly high voice.

But Elliot didn't care. His body was cold and hard now. He could no longer feel his heart or feel his skin or feel that he was alive. He walked through the house. People were now dancing or paired off or shouting at each other or swaying on their own. The music was being skipped before the song had finished. The floor was sticky. The rooms smelt of cigarettes and strong alcohol that belonged to parents. Elliot felt serene. He walked out the front door, leaving it open. It would take an hour to walk to his house but he didn't care. He didn't care about anything. And that felt nice.

But half an hour into the journey, as he turned off the main road and into the town he came back to life. It was so sudden he had to crouch down and let out a noise somewhere between a grunt and a scream. Staying in his squat, he pulled on his hair hard with both hands and it felt like water collected in the corner of his squeezed-shut eyes. He pushed into them with clenched fists and muttered to himself to grow up. But as he continued his journey the feeling only expanded inside him and he found himself kicking every bin he went past. When the bins ran out he started kicking walls, so hard until his toes felt mangled and the taste of beer in the back of his throat made him stop to choke out bile. It was turning night-time dark when Elliot arrived home, but he didn't want to go inside. He felt depleted and not able to fulfil the duties that could fall on him if he opened that door. So he sat down outside on the dirty pavement and then slowly tipped over into lying down. His stomach contracted as if he were sobbing but no tears came out. He didn't understand. He was certain that Noa liked him. It was the only thing in his life he didn't doubt or worry about, so how could this happen? He knew that Fraser was charismatic and attractive and popular and an endless amount of things that girls liked. But it still didn't make sense. He replayed what he saw again and again and there was no other way to interpret it.

Someone turned onto his road and Elliot instinctively pushed himself to standing and got his key out. His house was cold and dark and quiet and no one called out to him. Fear seeped into his mind and body and he sat down crossed legged on the doormat. He mumbled to himself.

It's past 11 p.m., Elliot. Of course no one is awake. Why are you scared? Of course no one is awake. Why are you always scared? You know everything's fine. It's past eleven. Of course no one is awake. But the fear was painful and not something that he could talk himself out of. When he got upstairs he pictured that everything was fine with Willie and his mum and choked out under his breath, 'everything is fine, everything is fine, everything is fine, everything is fine, everything is fine.' And then crept into their rooms checking to see if they were still breathing by staring at their duvets, looking for movement. After he felt confident they were alive Elliot dragged his body through the motions and he felt a new feeling, *I'm so glad I never told anyone about this.*

Elliot didn't have the luxury of wallowing. He had a routine to follow. A brother to care for. A house to keep running. And so in the morning he looked in his scratched-up bathroom mirror and said to himself, 'Nothing has changed. Your life is the same as before. The same as it will always be.' He tried to force himself to find comfort in that and then physically swallowed down his feelings.

By the evening things had settled back to normal. Elliot was watching *Dr Who*, Willie's latest obsession. His eyelids were heavy in the heat of the day-long warmed living room. There was a knock at the door. His mum was at work and it was rare for someone to come round unexpectedly at any time let alone the evening. Elliot's body tensed and he whipped around to look at Willie, whose face was scrunching up in distress.

'I'm sorry, Willie. I will get that, be right back. Try to focus on the telly.'

Elliot walked out and closed the living room door softly and then opened the front one. He didn't know what to expect but it certainly wasn't Fraser. Elliot immediately clocked his bag held in Fraser's hand by the top handle. His cheeks burnt with fury and shame.

'All right, mate.'

Elliot couldn't bring himself to reply. His mind had short-circuited.

'Everything okay, mate?'

Elliot nodded and struggled to maintain eye contact. He held his hand out for the bag and then found some words. 'Where'd'ya find it then?'

'Was shoved somewhere, don't remember.'

Elliot found Fraser's eyes then. He scanned his face and found nothing.

'Right. Well.'

He was trying to work out if Fraser had read the book. If Noa had read it.

'Doubt anyone's took anything, but you can have a check yoursen.'

Fraser had got his phone out of his pocket and was clicking away, looking up every now and again to check if Elliot wanted to say anything else. There was something about his behaviour that completely convinced Elliot that he'd never read or heard about what was in the book. Elliot held up his rucksack, said cheers and closed the door to Fraser who was picking up a phone call.

He took a seat on the bottom step of the staircase and rubbed his fingers along his hairline. Elliot took the numbness he felt (sometimes, if you feel low enough, finding out bad news trickles off you like rain on a car window) as opportunity to open his bag, look for clues as to what had happened. As he looked inside a hard ball formed in his throat. He didn't want to be sad, he wanted to feel nothing. But something was pushing itself through the emptiness. Despondency, self-loathing, regret. On first glance the contents of the bag looked normal because nothing was new and everything was there. But as he slowly slid out his notebook he could tell immediately it had been read. He didn't know how he was so sure, but he was certain.

Elliot placed the notebook back in the bag, zipped it up and put it on the floor underneath the coats. But as he walked towards the living room the well-known image of Willie, lifeless on the settee as the TV flickered on, presented itself to him. He wanted to burst through the door, prove to himself that it was stupid to

255

be worried about something so unlikely and that his stupid rituals offered nothing in the way of protection. But the oppressive voice in his head said, *But isn't it better to be safe than sorry?* and *How can you be 100 per cent certain?* and *Why would you be thinking things like this if there were no truth in it?*

With misery, Elliot replaced the terrifying image of Willie with a nicer, normal one and then, now that it was safe to do so, he entered the room.

Elliot was not one to hope, but more from a lack of understanding he spent the next two weeks waiting for Noa to message him. Some kind of explanation or reassurance or rejection. But there was nothing. It was unbearable, the not knowing.

Images filled the gaps soon enough. Noa, out the back of Fraser's house, leafing through his book, frozen with shock at what she saw, and then the shock turning into cringe, her reading the words through her fingers because she was so embarrassed for him, and then bursting out laughing once it'd sunk in, maybe by herself, maybe with others, and then shoving the book back in the bag, full of disgust and ready to move on to something better, someone better. It was the only explanation that made sense.

On the day when Elliot went to collect his GCSE results he saw Noa from across the school car park. She didn't wave or come to speak to him, but did she smile? (Yes, painfully.) He would replay the moment thousands of times, each new version of the memory becoming less likely to be true and more likely to be distorted. A memory of a memory. But he couldn't help himself. At least one thing was for certain, it was her who had read his book and now she found him disgusting. He relaxed into this certainty, learning from it. He couldn't go back in time but he could say *Never again.*

18

Twenty-seven years old

Noa had revelled in her new position as Elliot's girlfriend. There was no need to seek constant reassurance or try her utmost to be a certain way, her eyes locked on a prize, because she had already won the prize. Elliot had offered her everything she wanted on a plate. She didn't need to infer that he saw it as a serious relationship because he had said it explicitly. She didn't have to look for clues that he loved her because he told her all the time. She didn't have to act in ways she thought would please him best, or navigate the relationship in a certain direction because she'd already arrived at the destination; someone loved her for who she was. And so she let herself enjoy it, she put aside all dreams of weddings and babies and houses and fairy-tale endings and luxuriated in the day-to-day. Confident that was all to come.

But as time moved on Noa craved something, anything more than a brief weekend together. A taster of their future, proof of their commitment to each other. So they went on holiday and it was perfect. And then suddenly, it was not. Noa had asked Elliot to move to London and he had acted strangely. And that was that. The seed of doubt had been sowed. Noa went on with life but she wasn't able to get that faith back. Instead of letting it drop and hoping it would be forgotten, Noa doubled down and asked him often if he'd thought about it anymore. But he would only ever say something evasive or make an excuse to leave. Noa would seize up and sit there alone massaging the muscles on her chest, her shoulder, her jaw, waiting for the feeling to dissipate.

Elliot seemed altered somehow. He would smile at her with his mouth but not his eyes. He was quieter than usual and even when they were together, he seemed to be on his own. His grey eyes flickering over the walls every time they sat or lay down. But his response to her constant 'What are you thinking about?' was always 'Not much.' She vowed never to ask him again, finding the blatant lie of it verging on unbearable. But she couldn't help herself, desperate for information, she would always ask again.

One night in bed – mindlessly scrolling through other people's photos and her own thoughts – Noa wondered what had changed. She clicked onto her own grid of photos and chose one of Elliot holding a bottle of 'Daddies' brown sauce. She'd taken the photo when she'd been helping him do the weekly shop for his mum in those magical weeks before they'd got together. Elliot had taken it off the shelf and said, 'I guess we both need one of these?' And Noa had snorted and begged him to pose for a photo which she'd proudly uploaded. No concern as to whether that would be too clingy because they were just friends. Noa clicked the side of her phone so it turned black. Her eyes adjusted to the dark and her thoughts took shape. Maybe Elliot wasn't as different to other men as she thought. Both times he'd fallen in love with her when she hadn't been romantically pursuing him. He only wanted her when he thought she just wanted to be friends. It was like she finally understood the mind games she saw other girls playing. All the times her mum had told her to withhold herself flashed before her eyes. They were all right. Instantly she felt not only the desire to be elusive, but that she had the willpower to do it. If it would be the thing to bring her relationship back from the edge then she was going to play hard to get.

Elliot and Noa only saw each other on weekends as it was, and so in the week, she made sure to wait at least an hour to reply to every text. She stopped asking him about moving to London, she stopped referring to their future. She made more plans with her friends and when she spoke to him she alluded to fun things she was doing, while maintaining some intrigue. In her texts she spoke about people that Elliot wouldn't have heard of, and made out that she was close with them. It enlivened her. It gave her power where she felt helpless. (But it crushed her as much as it helped her. To Noa, power was loneliness. An island for one.)

One Friday, Elliot arrived at Noa's flat a few minutes before midnight. She had told him to come late because she was trying to seem like she had other things on. In reality, she had sat on the edge of her bed working herself up into a frenzy. Playing out scenarios and conversations, unable to work out if they were great or terrible ideas.

Elliot dropped his backpack down and flopped his back onto the bed, his feet still on the ground.

'I'm knackered.'

'Well, if you. . .' Noa went to remind him about moving to London but remembered she didn't do things like that anymore. 'You didn't have to come here if you didn't want to.'

Elliot said nothing and Noa felt frustration building monologues inside of her. But she doubled down. 'I could have been doing something else tonight, rather than hanging out with an asleep person.' The cruelty hurt her stomach. But she felt terrified without its protection.

Elliot didn't open his eyes, he just said, 'I've been up since 6 a.m., worked all day, sorted out loads of stuff and then travelled nearly three hours to get here.'

Noa was desperate to ask why he refused to close up the gulf between them but instead stood there, silent, watching his body turn slack with fatigue.

'Elliot, you can't go to sleep. You're still wearing your shoes.'

'I'll get up in a second, I need a chance to recoup some energy.'

She needed something out of him. 'Well maybe you should have stayed at home if it was such a drag to get here. I don't know why you always pretend that you want to see me. I'm not forcing you.'

Elliot sat upright like he'd been shocked with energy. 'What?'

Noa was trying to sound irritated rather than hurt. 'If you don't want me then come out and say it so I can get on with my life.' The skin on her chest was flushing. She barely knew what she was saying, she hated what was coming out, but she couldn't stop herself.

Elliot leaned forward and put his head in his hands. His voice was uncertain. 'Why do you think I don't want you?'

Noa opened her mouth and then closed it again. She wasn't allowed to say that it was because he refused to move to London, that she was worried he was falling out of love with her. So she made herself say something else. A bigger, deeper truth came out by accident.

'You say you want one thing and then act completely different. History is clearly repeating itself.'

'What do you mean "history"?' Elliot squinted up at Noa.

The hurt was safer now, more distant. 'You know full well what happened. What you did. Cutting me off like that, after everything. I thought you—'

Noa closed her eyes and pressed her thumbs and forefingers into them to slow the inevitable filling with tears. Over the years she'd spent so much effort not thinking about this, her whole body couldn't handle the fact it was being allowed to. She felt herself wobble and sat down on the floor in one movement.

Elliot looked both concerned and angry. He clicked the joints in each of his fingers and then spoke. 'I lost my friend and the girl that I loved in one single second. Sorry if I didn't want to speak to you.'

Noa's words came out choked as the memories poured in. 'I don't know what you wanted from me. I don't understand even to this day. You made me feel worthless. Not good enough. And I don't think I've ever felt good—' Noa was sobbing in a breathy, struggling to speak way. Elliot came over and crouched down. He put his hand on Noa's arm, stroking it, but stayed a little distance away, as if there were two competing parts of him and he had settled on a compromise.

Noa focused on slowing her breath and then decided to ask him the question she'd never wanted to truly know the answer to, until now. 'Why wasn't I good enough for you as I was?'

'In what way did I make you feel not good enough? All I tried... All I ever wanted...'

'God, it feels so silly to say now. But why did you not want to be with me because I was a virgin? And why... afterwards... did you not speak to me ever again?'

Elliot stopped crouching and sat down next to Noa on the floor. 'What do you mean, didn't want to be with you?'

'Fraser said...'

Elliot's voice was coarse. 'Fraser said what?'

Noa was blushing as she spoke. 'Well, that you'd only want to be with me after I'd. . . I assumed you knew? That I—'

'Slept with my best friend? Yeah, I saw you go off together.'

'I didn't want to.' Saying those words made Noa's stomach turn solid. Shaking her head at her lap, she went on, 'It sounds absolutely crazy to say but I didn't know what I was doing. It's hard to explain. As an adult saying this out loud it doesn't make sense but I thought that's what you wanted. Fraser told me you wanted that and I would have done anything to be with you. I thought. . .'

Elliot laid a hand on Noa's shoulder, his fingertips touching her neck. 'You didn't want to?'

Noa could only speak with her eyes closed. 'I didn't want to. You didn't want me to?'

'Why would I wa— Of course I didn't want you to. I loved you. It broke me seeing you and Fraser walking off like that. Maybe it's stupid, but I've never been the same.'

Noa opened her eyes and looked at Elliot. He was looking at her so tenderly her heart squeezed painfully.

When they had spoken through it all, how all the pain that followed had been for nothing, they lay down and hugged tightly for a long time. Noa's arm underneath his body went numb, but not for a second did she want to pull it out and let the blood rush back. Eventually, as they pulled apart, she looked at Elliot's charming dimpled smile and felt an unwelcome wave of concern. 'I feel like you haven't smiled like this in a while.'

She said it hoping for an explanation but Elliot coyly nuzzled his face into her neck and so she let it go. She fell asleep for an hour before waking up in the night to properly get ready for bed.

At first Noa felt physically lighter after that conversation. The knowledge that Elliot hadn't rejected her so cruelly strengthened her trust for him. She smiled every time she looked in the mirror. She felt more attached to her body, aware of her senses, her mind emptier than usual. But then a murkiness began to lightly coat the world around her. Her concentration was worse, her back ached, and when she was on her own she spent the time tossing and turning in bed, almost muttering out loud with resentment. She found herself thinking about all the things men had taken from her. The brightness with which she used to see the world had been plastered over bit by bit and now was nothing more than a faint glow. And for what? What did they get from it which was so worth it?

But Elliot was different. Noa loved him so much by now it was painful and beautiful at the same time. And now, she thought, it surely wouldn't be long until the grand finale happened. An ending that erupted into a new beginning. Elliot just needed to move to London and she could finally step into the life that she'd dreamed of for so long.

But slowly, and no matter how much she ignored it, she noticed Elliot withdraw from her even further than before. Life became a limbo. A liminal space somewhere between her previous world and the world Elliot had promised her. So she waited. But time moved almost impossibly slowly, the second hand on the clock tantalisingly taking what felt like ten minutes to bridge the gulf of a single moment. She didn't beg, she didn't cling to him, she didn't try to make him love her. She used a strength she didn't know she had until now to act as a sort of anti-person. A person who requires nothing and feels nothing. But over time the stagnation brewed inside her and caused a sour taste in her mouth. Interacting with Elliot became hard but she swallowed the bitterness and waited some more.

Elza was unaware of all this because Noa didn't tell her anything. She kept it hidden inside, hoping to hide it from even herself. That is why it was hard to know how to react when Elza told her the news. Instead of sitting next to Noa on the sofa Elza grabbed a cushion and sat cross-legged on the other side of the coffee table. Noa tried to look for signs of nervousness but there didn't seem to be any so she relaxed a little. Adjusted her neck to try and ease the ache, and listened to the announcement.

'I'm moving away for six to nine months. But don't worry, I will still pay rent, and I'll be keeping my stuff here. It's only temporary.'

Noa's first thought was that she was grateful Elza didn't pull her punches. Her second thought was that she didn't believe it was temporary. Whatever it turned out to be, it would almost certainly set Elza on a path that didn't lead back to her living in a box room in a shared flat.

Elza filled the silence while Noa rubbed the sore tendon or muscle or whatever it was at the base of her skull.

'I'll leave in about a month. And there won't be anything for you to do. It will be life as normal.'

Noa forced herself not to laugh by biting on the miscellaneous gristle that was inside the flesh below her lip. While she pressed each ear to each shoulder in a stretch she made herself say, 'Where you off to then?'

Elza said something about living somewhere while her girlfriend did something – maybe a secondment? – in Europe? Was it Italy or were they travelling around Italy before they. . . Noa nodded enthusiastically but didn't manage eye contact. If she let the news wash over her maybe she could bypass the pain of Elza leaving and feel nothing at all.

Immediately after, lying on her bed, in her clothes, with her hands lightly on her stomach, Noa tenderly looked at the thought, *This is the perfect opportunity for Elliot to move in.* She didn't let herself picture it or hope for it or plan for it. She let the thought hang there, suspended by itself. A concept. She wondered whether to tell him, if she would be able to present it as a casual suggestion. Barely an extension of the simple fact that Elza was leaving. But a physical aversion to the idea overwhelmed her. (It was fear. Fear of losing it all, of losing Elliot). She grabbed the duvet on both sides of her and ground her teeth. *Why?* Why? Why? The question reverberated around her mind and then quietly added, *Why won't he do what he told me he wanted?* The terrifying thought followed. The worst one of all, about her spending her life alone, not *theoretically* alone but alone because she was without Elza, alone because she was without Elliot. She rolled onto her side and pressed her knees up to her eyes to try and blot it out.

After waking up from an unplanned nap Noa wiped the drool from the corner of her mouth and sat on the edge of the bed. She couldn't tell Elliot about Elza because the best-case scenario would be her manipulating him to move in. The victory would feel hollow. She wouldn't be able to believe in the relationship, she would be waiting around for it to end. She needed him to bring up moving in and then she could present the news of Elza leaving like a present.

While she'd been napping a plan had seemingly formed in her mind. Being cold and distant could only get her so far. A serious committed relationship could not blossom out of nothing. Yet, being clingy, showering him with love was certain to drive him away. Those were both facts. And so she fell back on an old way she would have dealt with this situation. Leading her life with the sole purpose of enhancing Elliot's in the hopes to become indispensable to him. Any action, device, system, measure she could think of would be put in place. If she couldn't be wanted then she would make herself needed.

Over the following weekends Noa carried out the plan. It came easy to her, she had done it many times before.

Noa was stuffing Elliot's dirty clothes into a plastic basket. He came back from the toilet.

'What are you up to?'

'I'm gonna do you a wash. If I wash and dry these here then you can take them back clean and it saves you a task.'

Noa walked to the kitchen and Elliot followed her. 'Ah, you don't need to do that, honest—'

'It's fine! It will be nice to have them—'

'Okay, well at least let me do—'

'No! No. I'm doing it. I won't be long.' She nudged him out the way and bent down to load the machine. The satisfaction of doing something for him started to relax Noa. But she felt his presence behind her still. She spoke without turning this time, just a push of his shin. 'Go choose a film. I'll be right in.' But, again, she could hear that he didn't leave.

'You don't need to do this for me, y'know?'

She looked up at him and tried to smile in a relaxed way but her lips felt taut. 'I know I don't *need* to but I want to. Is there a problem?'

'No, no. Not a problem. But I'm wondering if I've done or said anything to make you think you need to do that for me? Because you don't. You really don't.'

Noa turned back to the machine to hide the slapped shock on her face.

She tried to sound placid. 'Okay. Well I'm already doing it, so. . .' Noa held up the fabric conditioner she'd bought recently. 'I'll put this in, so your clothes will smell nice.'

'Don't worry about that. It'll be wasted on me, I don't actually like fabric conditioner. Thank you though.'

Noa had to clench her jaw to stop the flood of thoughts and feelings pouring into her. She loved using fabric conditioner. She loved the luxury of her clothes smelling like lavender. She loved the way the soft clothes caressed her skin and associated it with when her mum was feeling less frugal than usual. Noa had gone back into her overdraft to buy this bottle of Lenor with the intention of doing Elliot's washing better than he'd ever done it himself and therefore adding value to her role as girlfriend.

She tried to sound placid. 'Okay.'

She stood up and struggled to remove the plastic detergent drawer to wash out the pastel liquid she'd already poured in.

'Ah sorry, I hadn't noticed you put it in. Don't worry. Honestly, Noa—'

She kept tugging and tilting it until there was a snap and it ejected itself, spilling on her top and the floor. She whipped around to look at him to check if this was, for some reason, his last straw and he would finally shout at her. Would admit that he'd had enough and end things.

But he didn't. He mumbled, looking anywhere except at Noa.

'God, sorry. I feel bad. I guess it's just I don't like it when my clothes are soft. I associate *dirty* clothes with being all. . . flexible like that.' For the briefest moment he scrunched up his nose and another piece broke away from Noa's heart. 'And I guess I associate *clean* clothes with being kind of crisp and. . . hard?'

Noa placed (slammed) the broken drawer into the sink and moved towards the kettle.

'Tea?'

'Uh. . . okay, thank you. I'll just. . . finish putting this on then. Is that all right?'

She could see Elliot tentatively move towards the machine but he stopped and waited for a response. Noa didn't respond though. She couldn't speak without betraying her emotion.

'Noa?'

'Sorry, did you say something? I was filling up the kettle and didn't hear.'

'Noa, I'm standing right next to you.'

She clicked the kettle on and then stood facing it, both hands resting on the worktop. 'Honestly, don't worry. I'll put it on in a second. You go in the living room and I'll bring you a tea.'

Noa was feeling sorry for herself. The waste of time and money given to this trivial offering that she intended to have the opposite effect. But the self-pity quickly bubbled into frustration. She wanted to roll her eyes back into her head. She wanted to press her fingers into her temples. She wanted to scream.

'Noa.' She felt his hands gently on her waist. 'I didn't mean to offend you. I'm so sorry.'

She spun around. 'Offend me? You didn't offend me. Why would you say that?'

'Well, you seem upset.'

She wanted her voice to be soft and apologetic but it came out tight. 'I'm not upset. Not at all.'

'But I can tell. . . you're quiet and like, stiff.'

'I'm not! What would I even be upset about? Not your fault you didn't want me to do this small thing.' She was struggling to mask her bitterness.

Elliot's eyes dropped to the ground and she wanted to push him and tell him to look up. He sighed. 'Sorry, you *can* do it. I don't know why—'

'Oh, I can do it? You're letting me wash your clothes? Thank you so much!'

Elliot's lips were parted slightly as he looked into each of her eyes. 'God. I'm such a dick. I don't know what the fuck's—'

'No you're not.' Noa's voice turned back to treacle. She ran the tips of her fingers through the side of his hair. She looped her arms around his neck and kissed him. 'See. I love you.'

Elliot pushed his lips into a flat smile and Noa wanted to say in her soft voice, *If my well-being concerns you so much, then why are you pretending to love me?*

But it dawned on her that she had failed. She was doing the opposite of what she needed to do. An impatience for the relief that being the perfect girlfriend would give her made her stand on her tiptoes and kiss him again. She pulled away and his smile, still small, was at least turning up now. And so she pulled him into a deeper kiss, bringing his hips close to hers. He kissed back but she couldn't tell if he was liking it. And so she dragged him to her bedroom and pushed him onto the bed. She stripped in front of him, revealing the lingerie she bought for Christopher. It made her feel a hot shame but she was willing to try anything to compete with the girls she assumed were in his imagination or on his laptop.

'Uh, you look—'

But she didn't want to hear what she looked like described

back to her. And so she straddled him and started making out with him in the most sensual way she could think of. Biting his lip, moaning, grinding herself on him, maintaining strong eye contact. She tried not to analyse his expressions but she couldn't help it. She couldn't tell if he was confused, shocked, aroused or concerned. The question was unbearable and so she undid his jeans and gave him the best blow job she could. Implementing any techniques she could remember from porn. Big, innocent eyes, softly playing with his balls, spitting on his penis and then licking it off.

By the time it was all over and Noa had rebuffed all Elliot's advances on returning the favour, they lay side by side in silence. Noa contemplated what he would want to have for dinner. Elliot said he was going for a cigarette and didn't look back before leaving the room.

19

Noa was washing up the dishes in the kitchen, her shoulders were aching, she had a headache, she felt like the day was dragging on even though she didn't want it to end. Because she had decided that this was the night she would tell Elliot about Elza. Get down on the floor, press her forehead to his feet and beg him to move in.

Noa had gradually felt herself unravel. The day Elza was moving out had crept up on her. The day she would be left on her own. Because no matter what she had done, Elliot was no closer to moving in. In fact, he had started going back to Stoke on Saturday nights, or sometimes skipping weekends altogether. A slimy suspicion began to coat the lens she saw the relationship through.

Elliot was sat facing the TV, the insteps of his feet resting on the edge of the coffee table, and Noa stood watching him for a second. His eyes were glazed over and he was biting his lip looking forward to an invisible place beyond the TV. Noa knew how this interaction would play out.

'Hey.'

He glanced at her before returning to the wall. 'Hi.'

'What you thinking about?'

'What am I thinking about? Uh, nothing really, was watching the news.'

She sat down next to him and kept her voice light. 'But it seemed like you were deep in thought?'

'Just thinking about the news, I guess. It's pretty bleak, eh? When is there ever good news?'

'Maybe there is but they don't want to brag.'

Elliot laughed and looked into her eyes. His full attention like this still made her body tense. 'I think I'm gonna head home tonight. But I'll be back next Friday.'

The words felt dry in her mouth. 'Why do you keep doing that?'

'Doing what?'

'Going back on a Saturday? We see each other less now than we did when we got together. I thought you were going to get a job here? You said that months ago but I haven't seen you do anything about it. I thought—'

Tears fell through the air and landed on her lap making splashes of true black on her washed-out jeans. But it wasn't a big deal, she cried all the time now.

'No one's going to hire me.'

Noa's stomach ached with feeling and she wanted to go to bed. She always wanted to go to bed these days. 'You didn't even try. You don't want to move here. Just say you don't.'

She could tell he was exasperated because he was inhaling deeply. 'Have you ever thought that maybe I'm not the right guy for you?'

What she said came out as a scream. 'Just break up with me already!'

'I don't. . . I can't. . . I don't want to.'

She'd always intensely hated it when men called her crazy, but now it seemed a fitting label. She felt like her eyes had doubled in size and black animated lines were coming out of her head. She was hysterical.

'Why do you always want to be back in Stoke now? I don't understand. What are you doing there?'

His voice turned quieter and deeper whenever hers turned loud and high. 'Please. Can we not speak about this. I'm begging you.'

She mumbled now. 'You're just like the rest of them.'

'What?'

'I said you're just like the rest of them. Why do you all want to be with someone you don't like? What am I not understanding? Surely you're not all sociopaths. Am I pressuring you all into a relationship against your will and you're struggling to get out? It doesn't make sense. Who wants to spend their days in misery? Or are all of you right and I'm actually insane – imagining things are bad when they're actually perfect? I'm too weak. I'm never going to break...'

Noa looked up. His head was in his hands. She could see his back rise and fall with exasperated breath. She took her weak, nauseous body to sit on the bathroom floor even though she knew she wasn't going to throw up. Half an hour later when the front door closed she flinched and then dragged herself to bed, ignoring Elza's quiet concerned voice coming from her doorway.

But he hadn't left. He had gone for a cigarette. And he did stay the night, though they didn't speak another word to each other. His presence in the bed still comforted Noa, even if she didn't want it to.

In the morning Elliot brought her a cup of tea and sat by her side. He started to gently stroke her forearms.

'Can we talk about last night?'

Fear shot into Noa's stomach. Regret spiralled in her mind.

'Okay. Well, I guess I want to say sor—'

'You don't need to say sorry, Noa. I just thought maybe we should check if we still think we're. . . good together?'

Noa tried to wait for Elliot to stop fidgeting and look at her but he wouldn't.

'What do you mean "good together"?' Noa could tell her skin was going blotchy red with anxiety. Why had she mentioned breaking up? This was her own doing.

Elliot stood up and started pacing. 'Just like, maybe we're not right for each other? I don't know. What do you think? Maybe you want to be with someone less negative or. . .'

He trailed off. The worst part was he didn't sound angry or bitter. The light-hearted questioning tone of what he was saying seemed to imply he was encouraging her to agree with these statements.

'No. No, not at all. You're not negative? It was an argument. Everyone has arguments.' Noa tried to move into his eyeline by standing up. 'Do *you* think we're good together?'

Elliot wouldn't look at Noa but she could see his ears were red and his hands were trembling again. Tears stung her eyes because she knew this dance well. This trying to persuade someone it's a mutual ending.

His voice was shaky. 'I don't know. Sometimes I worry that we're not. I've been wanting to tell you.'

'Sometimes?' Even though she'd been expecting this it did not mean she was prepared for it. After all the times he'd told her she was worrying for nothing. *Sometimes.* It felt like she'd been pranked. Noa lost touch with reality for a second until what felt like an electric shock went through her body.

She spoke from the heart because she had nothing to lose. It felt like a life-or-death moment. 'I never think we're not good together. In fact, the only goodness I can imagine feeling is with you. It physically hurts my heart to hear you say that because I'm so, so, *so* happy to be with you. Even if it might not always seem like it. Every day I wake up and feel lucky like I'm in some kind of fairy tale because I'm with someone who I love so deeply, who I hoped...' She couldn't help tears spilling out and felt like a dramatic child but there was nothing she could do about it. 'Sorry.' And with that she sat on the floor. A place she found herself surprisingly often these days.

Elliot came and sat in front of her then, he rested his forehead on her bent knees. 'No, I'm sorry. I don't know why I said all that. Just ignore what I said. Just forget it. I didn't even mean it.'

Noa could see Elliot was shuddering now. She pushed him up to see if he was sobbing but his eyes were dry. He moved to sit next to her and put his forehead on his own bent knees. She could see his chest was moving rapidly.

'Elliot, are you okay? What's happening?'

Noa tried to bend to look at his face but he said bluntly, 'Please. Just leave it.'

And so she sat next to him in silence, not touching or talking. And then, to remove any pressure, she got out her phone and aimlessly scrolled on it, eventually hearing the sound of his breath return to normal.

When Elliot left that afternoon and Noa was alone in the flat, she took herself to bed and squirmed around. (Desperation and hopelessness are opposites and so feeling them at the same time is uncomfortable. It is a fight and only one can win.) The only crisp feeling she had was love. Love for Elliot. All the others were complex and contradictory. And so she decided to let love win out. She thought of when, travelling back to Stoke nearly a year ago,

275

she had decided to be alone, had accepted being alone, and felt a longing for that peace.

She got up and walked around the empty flat, letting the silence ring in her ears, tensed her body and withstood the feeling. She lay down on the sofa but didn't turn the TV on. Instead she thought about Elliot, his cold hands and sarcastic comments and the way he touched her so gently as if she were precious. And she smiled to herself. Inhaling and exhaling the feeling. She would tolerate being alone to have him. With him and yet, without him. That was better than without him entirely. When she was allowed, she would rest her head on his chest and drink in the smell of him and then she would tolerate being alone. For as long as he made her. Forever, maybe.

The relationship had changed shape again. Noa no longer made plans like she normally would. She didn't try to orchestrate their lives or her actions or what he was feeling. No matter what things she put in place in her life, nothing had worked out in the way she had hoped or expected. And so now she was free-falling. Living on instinct. She said and did whatever came to mind.

Every day Noa asked Elliot if he loved her. She would ask him if he thought she was ugly. She would beg him to tell her what he was thinking. (The quality of the answers varied but they were always irrelevant, she was barely taking in what he said.) She would send him short sharp messages if he didn't text back quickly enough. She would ring him and keep him on the phone for hours, her voice swinging from sickly sweet to thinly disguised desperation. She would shout and cry and then beg for forgiveness.

She still had fantasises but they were different now. They all carried a sense of foreboding. When Elliot was back in Stoke she would lie in bed and picture him cheating on her with a selection of beautiful (invented) girls. She would play out any future that seemed possible but they all ended up the same – her alone. And then she would tell herself there was no other choice and get on with her day.

Then there were the rare times that the relationship was fine. The days where they would chat for hours about funny things they'd seen or heard or thought. Or walk for miles until their legs hurt and then stop for a sandwich. Or not be able to keep their hands off each other, hugging whenever they passed in the flat, holding hands on the sofa, and at night tenderly cherishing each other's bodies as if they remembered how lucky they were to behold it. No one could say why these days came and went. Noa was never able to fabricate a day like this and she didn't want to anymore.

But the mental instability that she felt when things were going well between them was worse than the times that they had fallen out. It felt like her sanity was deteriorating and caused a kind of physical ache in her mind. Waiting for something bad to happen became worse than the bad thing itself. And so she forced things into a comfortable state of constant turmoil. Getting ready to the bare minimum standard, spending whole evenings lying in bed, constantly enquiring who he was texting and what he was thinking, barely wanting to touch him, picking at his behaviour, having huge reactions to the smallest things; the look in his eyes, the tone of his voice, anything that might bring her closer to the bittersweet relief of finding out the truth.

Noa knew what he was going to say before he said it. The way he stood in the doorway. Lingered.

'Right, so yeah, I am gonna head back tonight. And then I'll let you know about next weekend.'

Noa was staring into the Bolognese she was making, feeling like she'd rather die than eat the leftovers on her own tomorrow. She stirred the red mush and spoke softly.

'Do you know what it's like? To be the person abandoned? It's a different feeling for the person who leaves, because they are in control. *You* are in control.'

'I miss you as much as you miss me. Believe me.' Elliot came to stand behind Noa. He squeezed her, kissed the top of her head and guided her around to face him. 'I promise you. It kills me every time I have to say goodbye.' His eyebrows were pushed together to show that he meant it.

She hated how much she loved him. She hated that he looked perfect without trying. She hated the way it felt when he looked at her. And so she turned back around.

Elliot left to pack and, as Noa fantasised about what he would do back in Stoke, an energy built in her. She decided to go and ask (again) Elliot's plans for the days he was home, but on her way out of the kitchen she realised they were using his phone to follow the recipe. She always asked him who he was texting but she never looked. Partially because she didn't want to know, partially because it was the last shred of trust she awarded him. But it had been two weeks since Elza had left and Elliot hadn't even noticed. She felt the heaviness of the upcoming time; that evening, the rest of the weekend, the next week, maybe even two weeks. All alone. It triggered an almost hysterical mental spasm. Noa let herself be guided by the destructive autopilot which had gained so much control of her these days. Her heart was racing as she picked up the phone. She stood facing the doorway in a casual stance, and decided she could easily click back onto the recipe if he came in. She didn't know where to start and had to force herself to press on the bright green soft-edged square. She blushed looking at the screen, feeling acutely the invasion of privacy she was committing. She squinted her eyes to blur out his messages to neutral people like his mum and Dom and focused on the names. There was nothing untoward that she could see. Propelled by the win she tapped on his texts app. Her eyes lightly scanned the messages but the latest one was from weeks ago. The relief that was softening her stomach made her realise how much she'd suspected something was going on. While she had the chance she clicked on his social media – a place she'd been stung by others before – but his inbox was virtually empty. For no particular reason she clicked on the search bar and one 'recently searched' result came up.

Beth Wills

She felt her body temperature rise instantly. She clicked on the profile to confirm what she already knew. It was his ex-girlfriend. A nausea rose in her throat, the meaty smell of the Bolognese somehow suddenly unbearable. She clicked on the Reddit app, unsure as to why he even had it and looked at the search history.

how do you know if you're in love
what is attraction
what are signs of a good relationship

No tears or words formed. There was a palpable lack of thoughts and emotions. She became very aware of everything: the sound of the food spitting on the hob, the narrow, airless kitchen, the sense of being alive and inside a body. The heat had completely left her and now she was cold. Instinct took back over. She placed the phone down and positioned herself how she thought a normal human might stand.

They ate dinner on their laps and this time the instinct was to pretend to smile and talk. But the more breezy she acted the more unhinged she felt inside. It was like two parts of her – physical and mental – were being pulled apart, the rope that was holding them together fraying and thinning. By the time Elliot was about to leave, Noa wasn't even acting. Her internal self and external self so practised at being out of sync it was easy to treat them like two separate entities. She was pressing herself against him and asking him to stay, telling him to ring her when he got in and saying how much she'd miss him. She kissed him and ran her fingers through his hair. But as he was about to put his jacket on he stopped and handed it to her instead.

'I'm gonna have a quick piss, actually, rather than be caught in an "out of order" train toilet situ again.'

Noa stood in the hallway waiting for him, the jacket draped over her arms. She brought it to her face and inhaled deeply. She loved his smell, clean and basic, the same after all these years. An image of them lying on his single bed as teenagers flashed into her mind and she physically felt the length of time she'd loved him. The toll of it. Her thoughts crashed back down inside her body. The bowl where keys and wallets were kept caught her eye and she saw her AirPods. Without a second thought she picked them up and slipped them into the inside pocket of his jacket, zipping it back up. A few minutes later he was wearing it on his way out.

★

At first Noa told herself that she wasn't going to track the device. It was just nice to have the option if he did something suspicious. Simply knowing it was there simmered her hysteria into a calmer state of heightened agitation. There were no tears anymore because answers were coming. The unknown was ending.

But it didn't take long for something to flag itself to her. After work Elliot rang her but seemed eager to get off the phone. She asked him if he had any plans and he said no, except helping his mum out. But he didn't text her for hours. And why wouldn't you text someone back for hours if you were only doing housework?

Noa sat cross-legged on her bed, logged on to her laptop and opened the tracking app. She was smiling. It felt weird. But that's what her face naturally did. After a deep breath she decided it didn't feel right and guided the laptop screen down to close. But then she realised, either he had nothing to hide or he did. Was it that outrageous to find out the answer to such a simple question?

It surprised her anyway, seeing the circle hovering over a different, unknown, house on the other side of town to his mum's. She placed the open laptop down on her bed and lay next to it. Watching the screen refresh itself every now and again, the circle not moving. Only the 'Last Seen Today' time was updating.

By the time Noa woke up the circle had moved back to his mum's. She softly closed the screen and text him a loving message goodnight. He replied straight away in a similarly affectionate tone and she immediately turned her phone off, storing it in a box under her bed and then falling back to sleep fully clothed.

She didn't go to work for four days — impulsively emailing in that she had a serious stomach bug — and wasted the hours eating biscuits, drinking squash and watching YouTube videos of beautiful girls doing their make-up and running errands. She made sure to respond normally to Elliot, keeping her phone in shoes or old bags in between responses. Every day after work she watched his location move to the unknown house for hours. She lay there, devoid of feeling, except maybe a distant alarm, a tightness you might get from watching a thriller.

Noa couldn't bring herself to use this information as she would have in previous relationships. No fantasies formed of her confronting Elliot and him reassuring her, begging for forgiveness and demanding she gave him one last chance. She thought about all the things she'd put up with from boys beginning with what happened when she was a teenager. All with the expectation that – if she did this or that, became a certain person, acted a particular way, inflated the lives and egos of those around her, bent over backwards, asked for nothing, gave everything – then *surely* it would turn into a beautiful, solid, easy, joyful relationship. But it didn't work. It was all for nothing.

She paced around the flat in an old ripped T-shirt and period-stained pants, music blaring, all the lights on, her face cycling through the expressions of someone speaking out loud. But she was just thinking. How she did not want Elliot anymore. She did not want to lie in this empty flat waiting to find out the next time she might, if she was lucky, get to see the man who said he wanted to move in with her five months ago. What she wanted was to see the look on Elliot's face as she described to him how he'd been making her feel recently, she wanted to explain in great detail how what he'd done was beyond cruel and then she wanted to tell him to leave her alone forever.

★

Friday morning Noa returned to work, rebuffing probing questions about her illness with graphic insinuations. At lunch time she opened her phone to write some fake platitude about being excited to see him but he had already text.

gonna go out tonight but will come
to yours first thing tomorrow xx

She sputtered out a laugh and found herself staring blankly at her screen.

'You okay, Noa? You look very pale.'

'Yeah, sorry. I mean. . . I guess I'm still feeling pretty ill. Just feel physically and mentally drained.'

Tears sprung to her eyes and her voice broke at the end of the sentence.

'Oh, Noa. You go on home then.' Her boss stood as if to go to her side but then sat down. 'You go home and have a restful weekend.'

'No, I'm fine. I'm fine,' she said, fully sobbing now, struggling for air.

'Oh dear. You get yourself home. Do you need a taxi? What can we—' Her boss's lips were pushing nervously from side to side.

Noa, sniffling, packed up her stuff and grumbled her goodbyes. She left the office and when the cold air hit her wet face she couldn't help but grunt in frustration, pressing her fists to her eyes.

'What am I supposed to do now?' she said to her feet as people walking by moved around her.

'Excuse me.' A man in a trench coat frustratedly said as he pushed past her.

'You're excused!' Noa shouted at him so loudly he turned back to look at her again. Noa did not look away in embarrassment because she did not feel any. Any complexity of emotion that carried her as a normal person through a day-to-day life had dwindled away. And now she felt one, clear, crisp emotion: rage.

Her hair whipped in front of and behind her face in the strong winds as she walked to the station and she liked it. She pictured it getting tangled and frizzy and smiled. She rubbed at her eyes knowing full well her mascara would be making black smudges under them. She couldn't wait to see Elliot's shocked, innocent face as he saw her in the doorway of his lover's house.

20

Twenty-eight years old

(As we age, endless possibilities narrow into one reality and 'could have beens' fill in the gaps. We can feel relief or loss for missing out on these unknown timelines we paint in our mind, but either way we are only guessing. It is nothing more than an exercise of the imagination. And so it is not these fake scenarios that cause us to suffer, but our relationship to them.)

Elliot looked at the large, red-bricked house on the opposite side of the road. He couldn't get too close to it because the windows were low and uncovered and he worried someone would see him. He was concerned enough as it was, coming here every few days, that someone would call the police for loitering. There was nothing that he was planning to do, no decision that he was reckoning with. He wasn't contemplating whether to knock. He just wanted to be near his brother. Missing Willie felt like a constant numbness periodically disturbed with sharp electric shocks. But he couldn't go in because then he would see what he had done to him. The thought of Willie looking bored or uncomfortable or lonely or scared or anything other than relaxed made Elliot bend in half with pain. The reason he came to the house was because it was the only place he felt like himself. Everywhere else he was either pretending to be someone else or an empty vessel, a lack of a person.

It was raining and he'd been standing there for so long his shirt was like a second skin. He needed to get to London. He was late. But in London he had to be more than this person standing in the rain, a person who fit easily into the role of a London-living boyfriend. Someone with prospects, ambitions, opinions. And so Elliot stood there for another minute or so letting his eyes trace the sides of the individual bricks.

Elliot's eyelids were heavy and his head kept falling forward as he momentarily fell asleep. His neck snapped back and he glanced around the train carriage looking to see if anyone saw the lapse in consciousness. But however much it embarrassed him, he couldn't stop it from happening. It was still an hour until he arrived at Euston.

As he dragged himself through the Tube journey – that he finally understood how to do without looking at Maps – he realised there was an ache in his bones which felt permanent. He stood in the busy Tube, his back curved to fit flush against the convex doors, and felt an urgent need to rest. To rest by sitting down, and sleeping, and not going into work, and not speaking to another human being, and not thinking. He got out his phone and opened his chat with Noa. Holding the screen close to his face so no one could read it, he drafted a message.

Nearly there. I'm so tired.

He deleted 'tired' and wrote 'exhausted' instead. Then he deleted it all and tried again.

I'm so exhausted. I can't do it anymore.

He highlighted the whole sentence and deleted it, locking his phone and returning it to his pocket.

Elliot put the spare key Noa had given him in the door and was tempted to unlock and re-lock it but he took a deep breath and reminded himself that it never helped and waited a moment for the urge to pass. He opened the door in one and felt proud that he'd overcome it. Things might not be perfect but at least they were better than that.

He wanted to walk straight into the bedroom, to fall face-down on the pillow and press the sides up to his ears. Or walk into the bathroom and stand under a boiling shower until his skin felt new. Or walk into the kitchen and stand by the open fridge, pushing bits of leftover food into his mouth until his stomach didn't ache. What he didn't want to do was what he had to do. Find Noa in the living room and chat to her about his day.

She was sitting on the sofa sharing a blanket with Elza watching some kind of documentary. His chest inflated with relief.

'Hey!'

'Hi. I'm just gonna go get changed. Don't get up.'

He didn't wait for her reply and walked straight into the bedroom. A few seconds later Noa was standing behind him, hugging his waist. His body relaxed at her touch and he turned around to kiss her, taking a second to look at her brightly smiling face.

She nuzzled into his neck. 'I missed you.'

'Me too.' He squeezed her into him

She pulled away, 'Are you damp?'

Elliot turned to change out his smart clothes and into some joggers. 'It was raining a bit.'

'So, what do you want to do?'

He zipped up his hoodie and pressed his hands into the pockets. 'Just chill, I guess. Whatever. What are you watching? I'll come watch that.'

'But you haven't seen the first half?'

'I don't mind.' His stomach tightened, worrying where the conversation was going.

Noa didn't reply for a second and Elliot looked in the mirror so he didn't have to see her expression. But his face seemed hollow and grey. His eyes were deeper set than they used to be. He noticed two soft lines forming between his eyebrows and wondered if that was normal for a twenty-eight-year-old.

'I'll make you a cup of tea and we can catch up. I feel like I hardly have a chance to speak to you these days.'

Elliot's eyes felt extremely heavy and dry and he wondered if he would be physically able to keep them open. But he smiled and followed Noa into the kitchen.

He asked her how her day had been and she pressed her thumb and finger into her eyebrows.

'Oh God, I did something so embarrassing.'

Elliot struggled to concentrate on the anecdote. It felt like his brain paused and re-started again during a sentence he didn't hear the beginning of. Then thoughts burst into focus rebuking him for his lack of engagement. By the time she had finished speaking Elliot tried to have the expression of someone who had been listening while he said, 'Nah, that's not embarrassing.'

He could see Noa looking in each of his eyes as if one of them would hold a truth.

He looked at the floor, heat rising to his cheeks.

She handed him his tea and he replied as if it were a comment. 'Sorry, I'm just so tired.'

Noa pushed the hair on his forehead back and he closed his eyes.

'I know. It must be so tiring. I can't even imagine.'

He wanted to kneel down and thank her for understanding. Rest his head against her stomach until he drifted off. But instead he thanked her for the tea.

'Are you too tired to look for jobs right now?'

'Yeah, I think so, sorry.' He tried to make his voice sound normal but it didn't. It was hoarse and weak.

What he couldn't tell her was that quitting was not an option. He couldn't admit that he'd casually tried browsing for jobs and that the results stared back at him as if they were mocking him. With average A-levels at best and his whole CV consisting of working in shops, a call centre and one entry-level job in Logistics, who would want him? What would he even want to do anyway? Biting what he could find left of his nails a thought had popped into his head fully formed. *To get a job you have to be someone and I am no one; I have no skills but I also have no desires, no dreams, no passions.* His cheeks had burned hot at the thought and he'd slammed down his laptop screen. Weeks passed and he wanted to look again but even the thought of it brought him straight back to that burning shame.

Noa started stroking his arm. 'Totally understand. It's just that you'll always be tired after these long days and the only way to get out of them is to get another job. Here.'

He found her hand and squeezed it. 'I'm just run down. Usually I don't mind the journey. Promise.'

'But surely you can't do it forever? We barely get any time together. And I thought the whole point was that you wanted to move to London?'

His eyes were almost closed but he tried to speak as energetically as he could manage. 'Yeah, I still do. Definitely.'

But it wasn't only the job that was stopping him. Since Brighton he didn't believe that he would enjoy spending long amounts of time with Noa. On the one hand, that is what he wanted more than anything, to be surrounded by the light-hearted walls of her world, but on the other hand there was a pressure that built in the centre of his chest. A type of exhaustion that stemmed from the extra effort that went into all his interactions by then. The filter through which he scrutinised everything he said and did before he said and did it: is this what the man Noa would want to spend her life with do? The thought of moving permanently to London, where he would have to become this man full-time seemed so unlikely it was almost absurd to him.

It wasn't long until Noa started acting strange. She seemed more focused on the areas of her life that didn't involve Elliot. It did not come as a surprise to him. And so the pain was pre-packaged and ready to serve. It did not shock him or worry him. He had resigned himself to it.

One Friday as he was travelling down to London, he knew that this would be the end of their relationship and for once he did not sleep. His body and brain felt light and free. The uncertainty of when they would break up was coming to an end and in that moment the relief was more potent than the pain.

But when he got there something happened which changed his

whole life. He found out that Noa had not wanted to sleep with Fraser. She had loved Elliot all along. She had wanted him. They held each other and he breathed in the scent of her warm neck, feeling a deep serenity. And from what he could tell, it seemed like she hadn't read his notebook. He considered telling her about everything he'd kept from her, but as the relaxation was so rare Elliot let himself save that for later. Then, Noa told him that he was smiling and thoughts rushed into his head, *Why do you feel happy that Noa had sex with someone she didn't want to?* He immediately countered it, *I don't feel happy, I feel awful and sick and furious that I can't do anything about it.* But the voice replied, *Well then why were you smiling?* He answered, *I'm not sure, I was happy I found out the truth.* The voice replied, *If it wasn't an inappropriate reaction then why did she mention it? A normal, loving boyfriend wouldn't have smiled.* The questioning and answering went on like this for an hour while Noa drifted off.

From then on Elliot started to revisit every interaction they had, scanning it for signs of him being a terrible boyfriend. In bed at night he stayed up sifting through memories wondering if he had said certain things on purpose, to upset her. Was he being controlling? Rude? Misogynistic? Sometimes when he spoke to Elza he would get a shock of panic wondering if he thought she was attractive. Or if he laughed at something another girl said he would spend hours debating whether he should confess to Noa. The thought of keeping it a secret gave him the prickly feeling down his shoulders and arms that he knew could so easily turn into a breathless catastrophe.

His whole journey to and from London was now taken up

trying to mentally prove to himself that he was a good boyfriend and that their relationship was successful and working. He tested theories in his mind. Thinking of something he'd done and then checking to see if he thought that was the behaviour of a good boyfriend. Sometimes, in the night, Elliot would sit up in a cold sweat, the worry that he was doing something wrong by staying with her pressing down on his chest.

Elliot dragged his body through the days. Exhaustively asking himself, *Am I with Noa for selfish reasons or because I love her?* One day he looked at her, chopping an onion and chatting away to him about work, and a new answer occurred to him. *Maybe I am being a bad boyfriend because I don't love her.* The idea made him nauseous. He tried to replace it with a calming, nicer, truer one. *I love her. I love her. I love her. I love her. I love her.* But the original thought came back stronger. He could physically feel the thought in his mind. *It's not true*, he tried to reassure himself but the voice replied, *You wouldn't have had the thought in the first place if you loved her.*

Sometimes he was so inside his own head, trying to deal with the thoughts, trying to keep breathing, that he struggled to concentrate on what she was saying. And so would cough some excuse about needing a cigarette, grab his coat, stumble downstairs and outside. The voice would ask him, *Did you enjoy that? Interrupting her? Leaving so rudely? Is that because deep down you wanted to make her feel shit? Is that because you don't love her?* He would walk down the street, flipping through his thoughts, looking for proof that this was wrong. Eventually he would find an image, something like watching Noa asleep, mouth open, hair spread about the pillow, and he would squeeze his teeth together trying to absorb the love he felt in that moment. It calmed him. He would sit on the wall outside, enjoying watching the cigarette – that he wasn't smoking – reduce in size. Knowing that he had the time it took to finish before he had to go back in.

Elliot continued with his life but a feeling that things weren't sustainable started to grow. It was like he knew life was going to end soon but he didn't know how or why or when. It was as if all this had been a fun little game, but actually, as soon as Willie had moved out, there had been a countdown until some kind of end. It wasn't based on literal time though, but more of a feeling. A barometer that told him when the time to pretend was up.

One day, in a daze, Elliot walked from outside Willie's accommodation the three miles to Dom's bungalow. He'd only been there a few times even though Dom and Sarah moved in nearly a year ago. The thought of going to London was unbearable and so instead of going to the station, he went there.

As he knocked on the white uPVC door he wondered what he was going to say. He seriously considered saying everything in his mind. Everything he had felt since he was a child. Every weird thing he'd done and all the horrible thoughts that had come into his mind. He wanted someone to tell him that he was not awful or strange or dangerous. (Elliot, you're not awful or strange or dangerous!) But he knew they wouldn't be able to say that once they heard the truth.

Dom opened the door and then his mouth. He looked back over his shoulder, into his own house, as if to look for some kind of explanation.

'What the hell, mate?' He pulled Elliot in for a hug. Elliot felt his body relax in Dom's arms and he had to pull away to keep himself together.

'Sorry, I was in the area, I thought—'

'Don't be daft. You dunna need to explain yoursen. Get in here.'

They chatted about bills, putting up shelves, and gardens and Elliot noticed himself calming down. There was no right or wrong answer with Dom and the conversation felt more like paint by numbers than improvisation. But when Sarah brought them in teas and sat on the sofa's arm, an uneasiness started to build in his chest. *Do I look at Noa like Dom looks at Sarah? Does it mean I don't love Noa if I don't choose to sit as close to her? Do they seem to know each other better than me and Noa do? Is Dom thinking that I don't love Noa because of how I speak about her? Do I love Noa? If I do, then why am I thinking like this?*

His heart rate increased and instinct took over. 'Do you think me and Noa are a good couple?'

He knew it sounded weird but he felt his consciousness start to detach and would have tried anything to make it go away.

'Course I do, mate. You guys have always been a great couple.' He turned to Sarah. 'They were school sweethearts in a way. I always remember seeing them together like they were joined at the hip.'

She smiled at Elliot. 'Dom's told me before. It's so cute. I love it.'

Elliot smiled back. So strongly that he worried it might look weird. He swallowed it away. 'Do you think it's good then? If you like the same person as you did at school?'

Sarah looked up as if she were considering it. Elliot tried not to watch her hand in Dom's hair. 'I don't see why not? Why wouldn't it be?'

He wished he could go back, not ask the second question but he got greedy.

'Urm. I guess maybe it could seem like two people are together just because it's the only person they know?'

She nodded and his chest contracted. 'Yeah, but you had a gap or whatever. So it's like you never found anyone you liked as much as each other. It wasn't settling or whatever.'

Elliot breathed out.

It became addictive. This method of checking with other people if his relationship was good. He knew it sounded weird, especially if he'd been doing it too much or in quick succession. But the relief it gave him to hear people confirm that his relationship was normal and healthy and looked loving was unparalleled.

He started to analyse other people's relationships and compare them to his own. Watched to see if they held hands when they walked or spoke with the same enthusiasm or talked about their futures together. He even checked relationships on TV. But this often made him feel worse. *Do I love Noa as much as this character loves their partner? Do I feel that she is my soulmate in the way that character did? Do we have sex as much as this programme says is normal? Did I 'know' about wanting to be with her the way that this character knew instantly about their love?*

Even worse was when the characters seemed happy and in love but it turned out to be false. It made him panic and he often had to leave abruptly to 'smoke' or 'sleep'. He worried that these storylines were 'signs' that he should be looking closely at his relationship for clues that things were breaking down.

Every time they had sex he checked to see if he felt sexually attracted to her, looking at each part of her body and wondering if it turned him on. Sometimes, among all the checking, he couldn't sustain an erection and so he would spend an hour outside in the cold, his heart beating at such a speed that he typed out '999' on his phone to be ready, just in case.

The best days were when he had moments of clarity – sometimes they lasted seconds, sometimes they lasted a whole day – where he could see how much he loved Noa. How much he enjoyed her company and found her funny and kind and interesting and attractive. In those moments he tried to save up the feelings to reassure himself with later when he inevitably wasn't sure again. But when he presented himself with the evidence the voice questioned its reliability. *If you do love her then why do you spend so much time worrying about it? Someone in love gets on with their happy life. They don't do this. You wouldn't do this if things were fine.*

One day on the Tube he smelt the scent of a woman's perfume next to him and fear hit him. *Did I like that smell? Did I want to like it because I want to cheat on Noa? Do I find this woman attractive? Should I tell Noa when I arrive and put her out of her misery? Let her be with someone who doesn't do awful things like this?*

And so he started to do it on purpose. Looking at other girls' pictures on Instagram or people at work and tested to see if he found them attractive. If he didn't the relief was magnificent. But sometimes he would see something like a woman in a bikini and test to see if he felt anything. A twitch in his crotch sent him outside, breathless. And so he started to spend hours online looking for answers searching on Google and Reddit and Quora and chat rooms he'd never heard of.

What does love feel like?
Is it a bad sign to wonder if you are in love?
Didn't get an erection does that mean I don't find her attractive

Didn't laugh at her joke does that mean I don't love my girlfriend

How to know if you don't find your girlfriend attractive

What to do if you don't find your girlfriend attractive

Thought another woman was pretty should I break up with girlfriend

Is it cruel to be in a relationship if you're unsure about it

When to call it quits on a relationship?

I love my girlfriend so why don't I want to be with her

Sometimes he would find something that made him feel better. Someone posting online saying that feelings of love fluctuate in a normal relationship and he would realise with great relief that he was allowed to stay with Noa. Stay with the person he loved. But that reprieve was only temporary.

Eventually the desperation to prevent the thoughts and heart attack feelings led him to avoid anything that could spark them. He avoided seeing Noa naked. He avoided looking up in public so he couldn't see other women. He avoided watching TV in case something he saw concerned him. It became harder to interact with Noa on any level. He wanted to avoid her at all times. He wanted, desperately, to feel stable. To not have the shock of adrenaline when she said she loved him and he worried that he didn't get a fuzzy or warm enough feeling. He even avoided going to places that he'd previously had the hot, tingly feelings, in case the location alone triggered it.

And then one day something magical happened. Dom told Elliot he could use his house if he ever needed his own space because him and Sarah had both started working night shifts at the warehouse.

At first, the offer sent a whirlwind of thoughts into his mind. *Why is he offering that? I know he can tell something is wrong. I know he can tell I'm acting weird. But does he think that's because of my relationship? Does he think it's failing? Is he trying to tell me to end it? Should I?*

But then his mind flipped it into a new light. A place all to himself. Where no one would look at him or expect anything of him. A place he wouldn't have to pretend to be someone or wonder how he was coming across or making other people feel. He tried to seem chilled about it and accepted, saying it might come in handy.

The first time Elliot spent the evening alone at Dom's he sat neatly on the black faux-leather sofa and watched TV, checking his phone constantly, worrying that they would come back before he left.

The second time he put the TV on and then turned it off. He walked around the house and looked at everything without touching it. Trying to look for clues that his relationship was as good as theirs. He was concerned by the fact they had a framed photo of themselves because he and Noa did not. It hurt his stomach. He tried to picture if he would be embarrassed by Noa asking a stranger to take a photo of them. She had done it before and he thought it was nice. But would he still think that? He worried that he wouldn't and suddenly he couldn't stay still. He paced around the house and found his mind going to thoughts even he knew were ridiculous. He could almost laugh at them. But the part of him that took them seriously was stronger. *Does the fact they only have one cereal between them mean they're more suited to each other? Does their bedroom look more used sexually than ours? Does the fact I looked at Sarah's toiletries mean I want to have sex with her?* Standing in Dom and Sarah's bathroom he closed his eyes and pulled at the roots of his hair. He wanted to scream. He wanted to fall to the floor. He wanted to stab a knife into his brain to get it to stop.

Then something occurred to him. He didn't have to keep it all in here. Yes, maybe he couldn't scream or stab himself but he could do something to try and get it all out. Like encouraging yourself to throw up when you're sick, maybe he could coax it out of himself. He knelt down, right there on the bathroom floor, and started speaking out loud. As loud as he could manage without feeling embarrassed.

'I don't know what to say. I want to say please help me. I want to say I hate my life. I want to say I know I shouldn't be but I'm so. . .' his voice broke '. . . unhappy.'

For the first time in many years water came into his eyes. Just a thin layer. It felt weird and silly and he rubbed at them hard. He sat back against the wall and put his head on his knees and continued, now unable to speak louder than a mumble. 'Everyone's life would be better off without me. I'm such a freak. But I can't help it. I just' – the words came out in a sob – 'want to die.'

Tears streamed out of his eyes directly onto his knees and he started to struggle to breathe. He moved onto all fours to try and catch his breath but he could only breathe inwards. It was not like all the other times he couldn't breathe though. There was no panic now.

The crying was guttural. He was gasping. He was making sounds he didn't recognise. They came from deep within. His throat contracted like he might throw up but all that came out was cries and tears. There were no thoughts in his mind. Just a radiating pain. A desperation so strong it was animal. Snot and saliva combined on his face and dropped onto the floor. He moved into a crouch and leaned back on one hand desperate for air but his breath was quick and shallow. He leaned forward again, pummelling his fists into the ground. And then fell onto the floor. He sobbed out some more words. 'I don't know what to do. I can't do it. I can't do it. Please. I can't.'

Eventually the tears subsided and an embarrassed smile flickered onto his face and back off again. He pushed himself to sitting but his bones felt hollow and his body floppy with exhaustion. He tried to take a deep breath but his throat was sore and scratchy and he had to cough to clear it. Dragging his sleeve across his face he was amazed at how wet it felt just from crying. He pulled himself to standing using the sink and kept his weight up by holding onto the rim. He glanced in the mirror for a second and then instinctively looked away. But he forced himself to look again. His face looked gaunt and swollen at the same time. His eyes were bloodshot. His facial expression was flat and empty in a way that scared him at first. But then he clenched his jaw and stared harder. A positive feeling somewhere between relief and pride trickled from his shoulders down his arms. This is the real you, he thought. He dragged his body to the sofa and lay down on his side, knees bent with his head on the low, flat arm rest. He set an alarm for 11.45 p.m., fifteen minutes before Dom and Sarah's shift finished.

The beeping rang for a while before it dragged him out of a deep sleep. The deepest sleep he could remember having for a long time. He shoved on his shoes, jacket and backpack and quickly checked that the house looked normal before heading off.

Sitting on his bed at home he got out his phone and opened his chat with Noa. She had sent him a few normal messages and then a moody goodnight one. Fear jumped into his chest but he pushed it down repeating, *it is fine*, five times. And then twice more. He forced himself to text her goodnight, barely looking at the screen.

Elliot took up Dom's offer as often as he could. If anything freaked him out when he was watching TV or spending time with Noa or speaking to people at work, he saved it all up to think through at Dom's. He would sit, hands in lap, awkward at first, but then he would bring to life all the thoughts and feelings he'd been repressing. He even had notes on his phone of things he wanted to think about. And he would trawl the forums and check photos of Noa to see how he still felt about her.

At first these things reassured him, he felt the knot in his chest loosen. But as he clicked his phone shut or leaned back on the sofa the thoughts came streaming back. *There's no way I would be doing all this if there wasn't some truth to it. If I don't love Noa then why is it so hard to break up with her? Wouldn't it be easy to break up with someone you don't love? Am I a psychopath that gets enjoyment from ruining her life? Am I waiting for someone better?* The thoughts never seemed right but they didn't seem wrong either. They looped round and round until he could physically feel his brain inside his head and he started getting spacey. A sense that he was in a different dimension somehow.

Within an hour the feeling would subside and the exhaustion would return. He would fall onto the sofa and sob loudly. Holding his face and shaking his head. Muttering how he didn't know what to do. Eventually he would drift off and wake up to the alarm he had set for him to leave before Dom came back.

It became addictive, this release. This space to think freely. But it seemed to make things worse somehow. The rest of his days became blurs, intermediary spaces between his real life at Dom's. He could barely concentrate. He couldn't eat or think or speak without extreme effort.

Eventually the thoughts became more abstract. *Why do I bother doing this anyway? What do I bring to the world? How do I enrich anyone's life? They would all be better off without me. Without this fake person who pretends to bring them love but actually brings them nothing.*

It was clear to him that he was coming up to the end. He saw his life stretching in front of him and winced with the relentlessness of it. He didn't understand what made him like this but there was no way his life was sustainable.

The thought of suicide finally dropped into his mind like a clean, medical light. An energy propelled him out of the foetal position he was lying in on the sofa and into Dom's kitchen for a glass of water. As he was filling up his glass he noticed his hand was violently shaking. He left the glass and went to look into the bathroom mirror. His lower lip was trembling. He looked away embarrassed but he knew what he saw: sorrow and resignation.

In the end the thing that kept him convinced of this course of action was that he didn't feel alive anyway. He felt separate to what was going on around him, and separate from his own body, like he was floating above himself watching from a spectator's role rather than an active member of the world. Much like he imagined being dead might be like.

It was achingly hard to interact with others. He dragged the shell of himself around, going through the motions. His voice sounded alien and so fake it hurt to hear.

Pretending things were fine with Noa gave him a physical pain in his heart. Once, he saw her big, loving eyes dance around the floor in worry after he said something, and he almost broke down, telling her everything, about the constant misery. But then the spacey feeling enveloped him and the thoughts of doubt piped up.

He lay, sleepless, next to her in bed and remembered, with a laugh, that time years ago with the rope. How half-hearted that was compared to this now. That feeling was an emptiness, a lack. Whereas this. This now was an energy. It felt like a strong force propelling him towards the surface of the water, where once he broke it, he could gasp for breath. Funny, he thought, how he saw dying as breathing.

21

Elliot lies on Dom's sofa staring at the papered ceiling and decides that he will kill himself when there is a sign to do so. Both the thought of waiting for the sign and the thought of seeing the sign are equally frightening. His chest heaves with sobs but barely any tears come now. They have been drained.

Then there is a knock at the door. Fear goes to his stomach and he instantly regains control. He runs to the bathroom to look at his face. It's red and puffy but he thinks it could pass as a cold. He tries to think of what to say, but it takes him a second to realise the truth is probably fine. Dom and Sarah are not in but he's their friend. There is another knock and he feels scared. Maybe he should leave it. But what does he have to be scared of? He won't be alive soon.

He walks to the door and looks through the crescent of translucent glass. It is a woman. He opens the door and steps back, mouth open with surprise.

'Noa?'

'Who does it look like?'

Her face is scrunched up and red with cold. His instinct is to bring her into a hug but he reminds himself of the bad thoughts that will come from that.

'What. . . how did you know I was here?'

'So, where is she then?' Noa moves her head to the side to look past him into the hall. Then she looks him up and down. 'Ew, have I actually interrupted?'

It pains him to see her this upset but he's also confused and ashamed. How does she know? Why is she being so cruel?

'How. . . do you know?'

'It doesn't matter how I know. You are a sick bastard. Disgusting. Why didn't you just break up with me?'

His heart starts racing and his mouth goes dry. Can she see into his mind? Does she know all the sick thoughts he's been having? It's his worst nightmare. Something that he's spent so many years persuading himself was impossible.

'So you have nothing to say for yourself?'

He really doesn't. But he still wants to make her feel better. 'I'm sorry. I'm so sorry.'

She shouts now. 'Where is she? I want to see her. Beth! Beth!'

'Beth?' He moves into the house, hoping she will follow. He can see she is cold.

She walks in and looks him dead in the eyes. 'Well, who is the lucky girl? Let me see once and for all what I don't have.'

Noa peers into the four rooms and then turns to Elliot in the hall. She doesn't speak this time but he can tell she is asking for an explanation.

'This is Dom and Sarah's house. They're at work. I don't know who you're looking for. There isn't another girl, obviously.' The last words get caught in his throat a bit as he worries about the legitimacy of the statement. *Does it count as 'another girl' if I've thought about her? Did it count as cheating when I spoke to Beth at work?*

'Why "obviously"?' Noa still looks furious, but her body

language has changed. She's clasping one hand with the other and her gaze is less direct.

'Because why would I. . . there is no other girl.' He repeats the statement because he can't think of anything else to say. Her eyes close in what looks like exasperation but he hopes there is an element of relief.

'Why would you? I don't know. How about because you've been lying to me? How about this has happened to me countless times before? So go on then, if it's not cheating, what brand of lying have you done?'

Elliot doesn't know what to say. He doesn't want to lie or tell the truth. And so like a child he says nothing. He pinches his earlobe. *One two three four five.* Trying not to feel anything, he can't help but focus on counting. He can't help the relief that the number five gives him. In this moment it's too hard to override.

Her voice is flat. 'Elliot. If I walk out of here without an explanation you will have ruined me.'

The counting isn't enough. He tries to focus on the numbness. The fact that this is the end. This is the sign. But then something unexpected happens. He realises that he is free now from all the lying and pretending. He has nothing to lose. He will tell her what she deserves to know and then he will put everyone out of their misery.

'Noa.' Tears form in his eyes instantly. But he doesn't rub them away or speak differently, he lets them stream down his face. 'I don't know what to say. Or where to begin. You're right I've been lying. I've been lying to everyone for as long as I can remember.'

His knees are shaking but he tries to stay still, stay standing. Noa comes to him then, she takes him by the arm and peers through the doors again until she finds the living room. She drags him to the sofa.

'Here sit down, you look awful.'

They both let out a breathy laugh. Noa's voice is normal for a second and it hurts him to hear somehow. 'Where are Dom and Sarah then? Are they coming back?'

'No, they're on the late shift. That's why I'm here.' He sounds bunged up.

Noa doesn't touch him and he appreciates it. 'I still don't understand why you're here. If you want to break up, just break up. It's happened to me before, I'm a big girl.'

Elliot stands up, his heart flutters and the spaciness returns. He can feel his hands tingle. He doesn't want this to happen in front of Noa.

'Uh. . . I think I need to. . . leave.' He can feel his breath become shallow. He walks out the room.

'Elliot? What the hell? Do you hate me or something?'

Every painful thought he's had over the last few months flicks through his mind. The world around him loses focus and an overwhelming dread hits him. He feels the urge to run away, but to where? He wants to be home but where is home? He wants to feel safe but where is safe and from what?

He rushes back to the sofa and sits down. He can't breathe. He thinks this is it, this is how he will die. Noa is asking him if he's okay but he can't speak. He can feel his lips, his hands, his mind, vibrating. He can't look her in the eye. He is standing and sitting and standing. Noa is telling him to breathe but it's making him feel worse because he can't breathe. He wonders if he should ask her to call an ambulance but then he remembers he wants to die and a wave of some unknown emotion hits him. Noa brings him a glass of water and he drinks it in gulps and then asks for another. The act of drinking it helps him. He drinks the second glass.

Time passes and the feeling filters away slowly at first and then entirely. He can't look at Noa. She is sitting next to him in silence. He can't remember what she has been saying or doing and he feels humiliated. But it doesn't matter, he tells himself, it will all be over soon.

He starts speaking before he can chicken out. 'I don't know if I hate you. I don't know if I love you. I don't know what I feel about you. But it's not because I don't love you. Of course I love you. So much it hurts. I wish I didn't love you because then I would be certain.'

'Oh.'

'But you don't understand.' He turns to her now, motivated to try and convey what he means. 'Maybe the best way to explain is to start by saying there's always been something wrong with me. This is nothing to do with you, but, I guess, now, it is. I don't know how all these things are connected but I have a strange, broken mind.'

There is a silence that Noa doesn't fill so he continues. 'How can I explain. It's like I'm constantly terrified that something bad will happen and it will be my fault. So I either have to work things out or I have to prevent things in the first place. I do know most of it's stupid though. I know I probably have no control over these things. But I have to do something. Just in case.'

'In case what? What are you worried will happen?'

Elliot laughs. It's funny. In case what? The reasons all sound so silly now he has to say them out loud.

'Christ, it's a million things. But I guess, with you, it's in case we're not meant to be together. Or in case I'm keeping you from living your life. Or in case there's better people for us out there. In case you'll regret it or I'll regret it. But it's also that I have to say in

308

my head that my brother is safe just in case *not* doing it will make him die.' Elliot looks down, embarrassed.

Noa takes his hand and squeezes it. 'Oh. I can't even imagine. . . That must be very. . . hard.'

He wants to say it *is* hard but the tears are back now and he knows he can't speak normally. He nods at his lap as the tears drop through the air. His sniffs back some snot and wipes his face on his sleeve. 'I wanted to tell you when we were younger but I had OCD for a bit. I think there's something badly wrong with me.'

'You should have told me. We could have got you help. We will get you help.'

Help. The word had barely occurred to him because it didn't feel possible. The OCD had gone and yet things were still awful. You can't 'help' someone out of their personality. Out of the person they are at their core. But the word undoes him slightly anyway and a pinhole of hope breaks through the heavy wall in his chest. He starts sobbing again and Noa puts her arm around him. He cries into her shoulder as she strokes his hair.

'I'm sorry.' He feels pathetic and forces himself to sit up and look at her. 'I'm genuinely so sorry, Noa. For putting you through all this just because I'm a freak. You deserve so much more.' Elliot hurts but a relief is spreading through him like a drug. Saying everything he's said, even though it's only the tiny tip of the iceberg, creates a gap, just large enough for him to reassess how resigned he is to the darkness.

She is shaking her head and jigging her leg wondering if she should tell him that it's fine. Earlier, when she was on the train, she'd felt anger rather than sorrow. It was a new feeling. Now that has reduced down. But as she sits, looking into Elliot's eyes she is not overwrought trying to work out what he's thinking. She is thinking about herself. And how to convey the fact that it isn't fine, what he's been doing, even though she is also heartbreakingly sad and worried for him.

'Please, Noa, say what you're thinking.'

She takes a breath. She is still. She says what she's thinking. 'The whole way here, when I thought you were cheating, I kept feeling such a fury that my whole body was tensed. It was like everything came crashing down and I'd been so stupid to let this happen *again*. And then I had this clear thought: *I need to accept, I will never be able to get anyone to love me.* It made me uncomfortable because it sounded weird but I'd already thought it. So I had to ask myself: *what do I mean "get" someone to love me?*'

Noa is not speaking emotionally because it doesn't feel emotional. It feels euphorically logical, like she's noticed a word in the crossword and she can't believe she hadn't seen it all along.

'But I realised that is genuinely how I see life. I see it as a quest to "get someone to love me". And I was thinking how sad that is. Why can't I be one of these girls who lives life just for themselves? Is happy and fulfilled on their own and doesn't need a relationship. So for a moment I decided I was going to become one of them, but then I realised it was as hopeless as trying to get someone to love me.'

Noa takes a long sip of water. She briefly wonders if she should stop speaking but for once she doesn't care if she's boring Elliot or freaking him out or putting him off. She wants to speak, and feels herself slowing down, as if there is no rush to get the words out.

'So then I asked myself, why is it so wrong to want people to love me when I love so easily? And it clicked. That actually I love so easily because I'm desperate for it. And it's not that my love is fake. I love you so much.' Noa takes Elliot's hands in hers, never wanting

310

to hurt him, but now equally not wanting to stray away from the hard truths.

'But I'm getting into all these relationships that don't work out because I'm not looking for one that *fits*. I know I should probably be ashamed to say this, and Elza would chastise me, but yes, I want to get married. I want to have children. I want to get my own little family unit and to experience life from within that. But I kind of realised that I shouldn't jump into that with literally anyone who will have me. I want to be with someone who will melt their life into mine fully and completely. Someone that enjoys telling me everything they think and feel.' She squeezes his hand gently to say sorry but he smiles and nods, as if to tell her to carry on.

'It's crazy but I started to think about what *I* want and the ideas poured out as if I'd been plugging them away behind a hole. I want someone that's basically a bit clingy and over the top and doesn't want to play it cool. Someone who doesn't think it's silly to celebrate Valentine's day. Someone who would rather go to the supermarket together than alone. . . Sorry. I'm getting carried away. The point is when I started to think of it like that, the thoughts kept coming and coming, and instead of feeling unlovable *myself* I started to see the men I'd been with as people who weren't right for me. And with you. . .'

She doesn't want to hurt Elliot but swallows to psych herself up. She will tell the truth.

'With you, Elliot. I was having all these thoughts with the knowledge that you were having a literal affair, writing you off with the other men. But you're not like those.'

The sentence sounded final but he found himself saying. 'And yet?'

'And yet. . .'

It doesn't feel right to kiss her, even though a large part of Elliot wants to; she feels separate to him now. But in a way it is a relief. He looks at his watch.

'What time is it?'

'Half eight.'

'What time are they back?'

'Midnight.'

'I'll stay until midnight then.'

'Well, quarter to. I don't like to cross paths.'

Noa guides them to lie down on the sofa. It is wide enough for them to lie on it pressed together, but narrow enough that changing positions every now and again is necessary to prevent pain. For a few hours they nap and then they wake with awkward giggles and a growing feeling of grief. Once they are fully awake and sitting up with a tea, Noa blurts out, 'What do we do then?'

Elliot hangs his head slightly. 'I want you to have everything you described. But I just. . . I can't give that—'

Noa still carries the respect she found for herself from earlier, but now, the man she loves, the man who hasn't actually done anything wrong, is slipping through her fingers and she can't believe it is the right resolution to all this. 'But I would wait. I'd do anything to be with you.'

'I know you would, but that would be your loss. We need to be strong. Who knows when or if I'd ever be able to give you all that. Right now I can't think of one thing I want in life, let alone. . .'

Noa is crying now. Speaking desperately and fast.

'Please, Elliot. I know what I said but it doesn't mean I want to. . . What I want is *you*. Yes, I want all that other stuff as well but right now we need to focus on getting you better. I don't want you to be on your own when you need supporting the most. I love you so much and always have and there is no one else I want except you.'

It hurts him badly, because everything in him wants to accept this, stay together, be in love. But he knows he can't give her what she has described. And what he wants, most of all, like he always has, is for Noa to be happy and safe.

'I love you too, but I think the right thing to do is to. . . not be together anymore.' He tries to look her in the eyes but his body aches with sadness.

Noa is nodding and biting her lip and crying silently. It was too hard not to fight for him one last time. But she knows he is right. She moves to sit close to him and burrows her head in his neck.

The subtle floral smell of her is too much for Elliot. It immediately brings to life all the mornings he has lain next to her, watching her sleep, a fleeting moment of feeling blissfully happy. And instead of pushing this pain away, he tries to keep hold of it, he will need it for motivation to get help, the promise that good feelings are possible. Happiness is possible. His faith in this thought feels wobbly but, as if Noa heard it, she says, 'We will be all right.'

He wants her to believe in it too so he says, 'I know we will.'

He kisses the top of her head and they let themselves cry for the loss of this happiness they have briefly brought to each other's lives. Twice.

By the time his 11.45 alarm goes off they have been cuddling in silence for a while. They gather their things and decide they will go back to their respective mum's houses. As they stand in the doorway and Noa looks up at him and remembers all the times she'd looked at him as a teenager, longing for their lives to intertwine indefinitely, she feels happy that they have got to live more life together.

Elliot doesn't know if this is the right thing to do but he doesn't care. He leans down and gives her a soft kiss on the lips and then pulls her in for a tight hug.

'Are we going to stay friends then?'

Noa reaches up and ruffles her fingers through his hair as if to sort it out. For now there is a calmness in her. The hope is back but this time it is herself she is fantasising about.

'Please don't make me be your friend again. I can't do it a third time. . .'

22

Twenty-nine years old

Noa does find unconditional love. As soon as Kevin comes into her life she cannot imagine it without him. She loves him so entirely she can't help telling him every single time she lays eyes on him. And he loves her back just as much, jumping with excitement to see her every morning, following her from room to room desperate to spend every second together. Even when she is on the loo he tries to join her.

Noa – aside from Kevin the miniature schnauzer – now lives by herself. It turns out that she doesn't hate it. When she thought about it, some of her happiest memories were when she was on her own. It was the concept of 'being alone'. The label. She hadn't thought about the ways it actually manifested in her day-to-day life, such as 'going to get a cup of coffee' or 'reading and eating chocolate yoghurt in bed'. She thought of it as something large and distasteful, something that was an identity, a state of being, an absence. The *thought* of being alone was terrifying. But thoughts were just thoughts, she had realised. A thought cannot be scary.

Noa works from home a couple of days a week and leaves Kev at her friend Jenny's when she goes into the office. She sees her friends, and her colleagues, and goes on dates and then she goes home and luxuriates in the pleasure she's found in getting to do whatever her heart desires.

On weekends Noa and Jenny take Kevin for long walks and get coffees and pastries. Kevin never gets put off by all the lovely things Noa does for him; in fact, he is so grateful every single time she gives him a treat that he goes through the whole roster of tricks he knows – sitting, lying down, rolling over, standing – without her having to say anything. Equally, Kev's love never waxes or wanes, she is his main priority, and always will be.

Noa allows herself to grieve for the loss of Elliot rather than jumping into something new. She has to let go of a lifelong narrative she told herself about romance and soulmates and the journey of life. It is a bumpy ride. She tries not to contact Elliot but sometimes it feels impossible. And so there are the odd calls of 'Did we do the right thing?' and 'I can't live without you.' They are met by Elliot with compassion and love but reassurance that they have done the right thing. Soon it becomes longer in between these moments of weakness and Noa only contacts him with words of encouragement and support rather than desperation. Even if she can't have him, she wants him to know how great he is and how proud she is of him.

During this time she doesn't swear off men completely. If someone asks her out or she gets lonely and succumbs to the apps, she tries to go in with a new frame of mind. Simultaneously showcasing her true self to the best of her ability, and light-heartedly scrutinising these people in a way she's never done before. It's hard but not undoable because she has her friends, she has Kevin, and more than anything she has a desire to enjoy her life as it is in that moment, rather than planning or working towards a particular dreamed-up future. Things never turned out in the way she expected, and so why not, she thinks now, try and at least make the current moment as pleasurable as it can be. It turns out that 'the future' became more enjoyable when she stopped setting her expectations in stone anyway.

But it isn't until a year has passed that she feels a spark of pure hope. A feeling of being completely – romantically – alone but neither fighting against that idea nor succumbing to it. Instead, simultaneously holding that desire for romantic love without feeling broken by the lack of it, without feeling like she *needs* it, without collaring the nearest man and trying to squeeze him into her life, pushing herself out of shape in the process.

Noa was enjoying listening to Ewen talk about his job as a teacher. It was appealing to see someone have a passion for something that wasn't money or status.

'So the parent asked me if I had a favourite child, in my class.'

'Do you?'

'Well, I said to them, do *you* have a favourite child – you see, they had three kids themselves. And they said, "Well, to be honest with you, no of course not but also. . . one of them is a lot easier than the others." And I was like, "Exactly the same here." And I think they were so refreshed with the honesty that they let the whole thing go.'

'So you *do* have a favourite then?'

'Well, there's a boy called River who is clever, kind, quiet and yet, when he wants to be, also cheeky as hell. It's a great combo. How could I not have a slight *slight* preference for him compared to this little girl who once told me I looked "so ugly" that she "can't concentrate"? It's more that the preference shouldn't change my behaviour as a teacher.'

317

Noa laughs. The little girl is wrong, he isn't ugly, but he also isn't making her nervous in the way Elliot did. She often finds her mind making these comparisons, but instead of struggling against them she learns to accept their presence and let them float away. Letting go of what she can't control is the best thing she's ever learned to do.

She reminds herself that either her opinion will change, and she *will* fall in love with this man, or she won't, and once again, will be out there looking for someone better suited. Neither of these options are bad. In fact, having regained her positivity and hopefulness in a whole new way, Noa feels that both options seem exciting; either she will get a slow-burn romance with someone like Ewen or however many days, months, years in the future she will find someone instantly compatible. Both are lovely because they end with Noa having a boyfriend who loves her and is right for her. It's not that she's given up on love, or become less romantic, because Noa loves romance, it would be a sad world where she feels she has to shake that away. It's more that she knows what she wants in a partner, knows who she wants to be in a relationship. So by relinquishing control there is no other ending possible for her because she won't settle for less.

Ewen gestures to Noa's glass of wine and offers to top it up. She declines, deciding that she'd rather keep a level head. She'd rather a sober her decide whether to go back to his or not. She's also found a new relationship to sex, only sleeping with men when she wants to. When she realised this hadn't always been the case, she felt embarrassed, but working this out has had a huge impact. She never finds herself flitting around nervously after leaving a man's house, trying to persuade herself that she doesn't regret it, because now she makes that decision herself. *What do I want?* A new question but one she asks herself often now.

Ewen picks up his wine and smells it but in an almost childish-curiosity way that endears Noa to him. He takes a sip and then asks, 'Do you like children then?'

Noa leans forward and speaks in a hushed tone. 'Why, what have you heard?'

Ewen snorts and covers his mouth to stop wine coming out.

Noa pushes her lips together, laughing. 'Sorry, I shouldn't be making paedophile jokes on a second date.'

'Or ever, maybe?'

'Yeah' – Noa points to him as if to say *you're right* – 'or ever.'

She looks at his full cheeks scrunching up with what seems like enjoyment and smiles back. 'My actual answer is that yes, I do like children, but in a kind of theoretical way as I've barely spent any time with any and know nothing about them.'

Ewen leans back slightly. 'I see. Well, let me tell you they're not like how they're portrayed in *Mary Poppins* if that's what you're going off.'

'Shit, really? I guess I really should stop using *Mary Poppins* as my most up to-date reference point then.'

Ewen laughs again and Noa laughs with him.

As she walks home Noa feels proud. She hasn't tried to force him to like her, or herself to like him. She has let the interaction play out as neutrally as possible and now she can ask herself, *yes, no or maybe?* The future is the perfect balance of known and unknown.

On her twenty-ninth birthday Noa wakes up and looks at the other side of her bed. She expects to feel sad but it is not empty, Kevin is there of course. And as soon as he sees she's awake his tail starts beating on the bed. And when she says, 'Morning, Kev,' he jumps straight over and licks her face until she has to gently push him away.

As she strokes him she takes a moment to reflect. Twenty-nine and single. It's not what she had expected or wanted. But things she *had* expected and *had* wanted haven't always turned out how she'd imagined, so maybe this isn't a bad thing. There is fear in the unknown but there is also magic. What if she never finds someone? But equally, what if something amazing she can't even imagine happening happens? If we could shape our lives the way we wanted that second question would close off. So right now, on her twenty-ninth birthday, Noa tries to focus on the thrill of the unknown.

The day is lovely, some of her friends take her to go wild swimming at Hampstead Heath and she thinks of nothing other than the cold water on her skin and the laughter of her friends as she shows them her 'butterfly stroke'. Afterwards they sit on the grass, drip-drying, drinking warm Prosecco and passing the Bechdel test, for the first half hour at least.

When Noa gets home she is tired from being out in the elements for so long. She climbs into bed with Kevin. Her hair is crunchy and her eyelids are heavy.

She wakes up at 9 p.m. from an accidental sleep, boiling and confused. The silence of the flat destabilises her, and she speaks to Kevin to break it. But her brain can't stop focusing on the discomfort, like the throbbing of a paper cut, and she can't let it go somehow. Making dinner for herself to eat on her own feels sad but there is no other option. Her mind slips into fantasy mode for a second, what she could have in a dream world; a man to take her out for pasta and cocktails. But she doesn't take it further than that. She won't make herself jealous of a fake reality that isn't filled out with all the complexities of a real life; she might as well be jealous of Cinderella, and she had been, but not anymore.

But however much she tries to get herself out of bed, she can't. The warm air sedates her like a duvet. Just as she is drifting off again she hears the sharp doorbell and then Kevin barking. She sits up bleary-eyed and stumbles out of her flat door and down the stairs in her dressing gown. She peers through the tiny circle of glass. Backlit by the orange light she can't see who it is in detail, but the small frame and messy short hair make her gasp. She swings the door open.

Noa's voice is surprisingly devoid of emotion. 'I thought you weren't going to be back for three weeks?'

'I wasn't.' Elza pulls Noa in for a tight hug. Elza's smell, warm and sweet and familiar, makes Noa take in a long, deep breath. They traipse up the stairs and sit on the sofa. Kevin runs in circles and licks Elza's ear until she's in a fit of laughter and says, 'Not gonna lie, that is what I expected *your* reaction to be. But I'll take it from him.'

Noa shakes her head in bemusement. 'So, what the hell happened?'

Elza gets out a cardboard box of cupcakes, gives one to Noa and takes one for herself. 'You tell *me* what happened. You said you had stuff to do tonight?'

'No, I mean why are you back early?'

Elza stops peeling the case off her cupcake and raises an eyebrow. 'When I realised you lied to me, I booked earlier flights. Obviously.'

'But *why?*' Noa feels like she should stop eating her cake like Elza has, but it's sweet and lemony and she is enjoying it so she decides to let herself continue.

'Because I asked Jenny what you were doing and she said that she wasn't free but you didn't seem to have any plans. I'm not going to leave you on your birthday, No. Even if you want me to sit outside your door for the night, I'll do it.'

Noa can't look at Elza because her bottom lip is trembling and she worries it is an overreaction. She tries to keep a steady voice. 'So you've come back? Just for me?'

'No, I'm actually busy in Berlin right now. This is a very sophisticated hologram. Of course I came back for you.'

They laugh and eat their cakes and talk about Berlin and techno and Noa's new chequered dressing gown and Kevin.

There is brief silence where Elza texts her girlfriend and then she claps her hands. 'Right. Shall I order some Thai? I'll just get a bunch of sides – that's your perfect takeaway, right? And then we can watch *Sex and the City* but I'm afraid I will be commenting on how problematic it is the whole way through.'

Noa smiles broadly. She wants to tell Elza this is the best birthday she could wish for. But she know it will seem hyperbolic. So instead she nods at her lap and says, 'Thank you, that sounds perfect.' It isn't what she had wanted, and yet, it *is* perfect.

23

Elliot has bitten his fingernail until it's bleeding by the time the therapist calls for him to come inside. They sit in silence for a moment after exchanging pleasantries and Elliot wonders if they will have enough to talk about to fill up the time. Eventually, after five long seconds, Elliot decides to say something, anything, to this lightly smiling man rather than sitting in silence.

'I guess I'm here because. . . basically I've always been a bit fucked up. Like, I could never just live my life like a normal person. And then I had OCD when I was a teenager. And then I got rid of that but then it's like, I can never just get on with life normally. I always have to make it a struggle. I don't know what I'm saying. Sorry. I don't know why I can't just be normal. Basically.' He knows he is babbling and starts to wonder if he isn't quite right for therapy.

'In what way are you struggling, Elliot?'

'It's silly.' Elliot can feel himself grinning with embarrassment but he forces himself to continue. 'It's like I know I've got so much good going on but there's something eating away at me that tells me it's all wrong or all going to break down or something awful is going to happen.' He hates how much he keeps doing short breathy laughs because the man never laughs with him.

'Can you give me an example?'

'Well, I had a girlfriend recently – we broke up—' His voice cracks a little and he wishes he wasn't so pathetic. All the people that come in here with real problems and here he is crying about a break-up. 'But the thing is, I knew I *did* love her but I also had these endless doubts.'

'You say you broke up? Maybe your doubts were right?'

'No, no, no.' Elliot is muttering, already frustrated with his lack of ability to express himself.

'How so?'

'Because I did love her, *really* love her. And things were good. And I ruined it. And I know that people won't understand. They will think there must have been something wrong but what was wrong was *me.*'

'What was "wrong" about you?'

'So, it's like I get in my own head. I was so worried that I was wrong for her or she was wrong for me or our relationship was wrong. And I made myself sick trying to work it out. I could barely look at her or be with her in the end because I was so scared of realising that I didn't love her. But I did love her. I can't explain it. I'm sorry.'

'So you were *scared of* realising you weren't right for each other rather than *sad by* realising that you weren't right for each other?'

'Yeah. Exactly. Because I could never know for sure what I really felt. Sometimes it would be so clear to me and then it would fall through my fingers. Still now it haunts me in a way, the uncertainty. I had this desperation to know the truth. But I guess if we *were* right for each other then I wouldn't have had the doubts.'

'Hmm.' The man nods.

Elliot feels an urge to ask him for reassurance that this theory is right but gets a feeling that he shouldn't and so waits for him to speak. Eventually the man leans back in his chair, cradling his chin with his thumb and forefinger, and Elliot wonders if he knows how cliché he is being.

'Have you ever had feelings like this before? Where the uncertainty about something is a major stressor for you?'

'Yes. Definitely. I think it's a core personality trait of mine, really. I'm always worrying about things that might happen but it's like I *know* they won't, but it's also the small chance that they *might* happen. That's what kills me. The never being sure. It's like I have a low tolerance for the world or something.' Elliot scoffs at himself, wondering if he is a weirdo or exactly the same as everyone else.

'And you mentioned you had OCD? Are you okay to tell me more about that?'

'Yeah, well, when I was younger, like a teenager, I used to do these weird things like write down things incessantly to stop bad things happening. Or I would have to do these stupid things like touching doorknobs while counting otherwise I was worried that if I didn't, well. . . something bad would. . .' Elliot trails off wondering what the man is about to say.

'Yes. Are you familiar with the term "compulsions"?'

'Right, yeah. The things I did were compulsions. I remember her saying that.'

'Her?'

'Ah, my teacher – Mrs Brown. The woman that helped me with the OCD.'

'And how did she help?'

'She helped me with techniques to push through the desire to do the. . . compulsions. Because after I waited out the urge I could see that they were silly. If that makes sense. I could see they didn't help.'

'Have you ever heard of the term "Pure O" OCD?'

'No.'

'It's a bit misleading, as it suggests that the person has only the "O" or "obsessions" and not the "C" or "compulsions". But what it actually refers to is a type of OCD where the compulsions mainly take an internal or invisible form. So rather than doing something physical like touching doorknobs or writing things down, it would be an action that takes place in the mind. Like mentally repeating a phrase or ruminating over an idea or psychologically testing theories in an attempt to reassure oneself. And often these come with other compulsions which are technically external but are more invisible, such as avoiding places or people.'

'Right.'

'Does any of that ring true with you?'

Elliot racks his brain but all he can hear is the blood pumping in his ears. 'I'm not sure.'

'It's really tough. Because people who have this feel such a huge weight on them. This responsibility to find out the truth and protect themselves and others. Anxiety is often the price we pay for caring about something. It's exhausting. Carrying that around.'

Elliot nods but can't find any words. They sit in silence for a while.

'I don't know if it's as simple as all that.' Elliot is looking at his therapist's black shiny shoes while he speaks. 'Because I don't know if it would be possible to get rid of these things that I think. Like how I did with the doorknob touching. These thoughts are just my personality. Because that's the crazy thing, this is my only identity. I like nothing, I do nothing, I am nothing. There's no reason for people to like me or want to be my friend or hire me or hang out with me unless I pretend to be someone else. I've spent a lot of time being lonely but it's because I have no personality and I've tried to force one but it doesn't work like that. And what I've come to realise is that *this* is my personality. Just obsess— just being focused on really weird things and thinking about them all the time. That's me.'

Elliot wipes a bit of spit that has formed by the side of his mouth.

'What if I told you that it wasn't your personality. At all. And, in fact, over time we could lessen this need to think about things all the time. Then, what was left, *that* would be you.'

Elliot's leg is jigging on the spot viciously. 'Without that I am nothing. I told you.'

'Consider this then: maybe you haven't had the space to form what you call a "personality" but what we might distil as: interests, hobbies, opinions, relationships, etc. Maybe you have been filled up with this anxiety and all your energy has been spent on what you've felt the need to think and to do in the interests of yourself and others. And maybe there's been no room left for you, Elliot. For you to grow and form.'

Elliot shudders out sobs. He's never considered this before but he is now seeing his life through another lens. A more compassionate one. A more hopeful one.

It is hard to let go of his mental compulsions. OCD is his worst enemy but it is also his best friend; it offers to keep him and everyone he loves safe, but eventually he understands it is also the thing that makes him scared in the first place. He learns that his thoughts are not magical. That thinking or saying something doesn't make it more or less likely to come true. And that they are not scary. Thoughts are nothing more than things in your mind. *Life* on the other hand can be terrifying, because he cannot control it but, also, it is giving up the urge to control it that allows him to break the endless cycle and live his life.

Elliot's whole arms are shaking the first time he goes to visit Willie in his accommodation. Willie's support worker, Anya, brings Elliot into his living space. Elliot is already crying before he sits down. But it is good crying. It is letting out the swirling of emotions. It is beginning something, and beginnings can be just as hard to process as endings. Anya and Willie show Elliot around his room. He has decorated it how he likes. There is a timetable on the wall, and posters of 'wild mammals' and 'British wildlife' and a storage unit for all his favourite DVDs. Anya talks about them incorporating more movement into his routine and how they've been going to Whitfield nature reserve, and how they're now considering visiting a local allotment.

It is shocking to Elliot to see the increase in Willie's world. He realises that Willie needs independence as much as he does and that him and his mum probably did more for Willie than they needed to. They never gave him a chance to grow because they didn't think it was possible. It hurts Elliot to have that thought, but he tries to focus on the good. The fact that Willie is here now, flourishing.

At the end of the meeting Elliot asks if he could maybe get put on the schedule sometime and Willie invites him to the communal Sunday lunch. Elliot cries again and tells Willie how much he's missed him and they part ways, for now.

What Elliot finds out over time is that their relationship is stronger, not weaker, now that Willie is less dependent on him. Because he can be his best friend again. He can be his younger brother. And so he tries to apply this revelation to his relationship with his mum. He detaches himself and then reconnects in new ways. They go to Willie's for a roast every Sunday. Sometimes he brings her a big shop. Sometimes she makes them tea. Naturally it takes a while for things to get like this, there are bumps in the road. But Elliot sees them as just that, bumps.

There is still grief to come. He mourns losing those formative years to the overbearing, relentless voice of OCD, and this is as hard to overcome as the illness itself. The intrusive voice asking to know something for sure would always be there in times of stress and sadness. But Elliot would learn to sit with the uncertainty rather than fight against it. And as this ability grew, so did the space for an identity.

It's funny to Elliot, when he realises that the small things you take for granted about yourself are what makes up your personality. When he takes up playing football again – because his therapist advises him to do exercise – he finds himself thinking, 'ah, I love playing' after every match. And then it clicks, that's what it means to be a person. Frivolous things like enjoying playing football and being a morning person and getting a fry-up with your friend every week, and feeling proud of your collection of jackets. These are the things that make a person. Playing football is something Elliot does for himself, and so he treasures it. Sees it, finally, for how special that is. And sometimes, he lets himself think about it, thinking over matches he's played, thinking about ones to come, contemplating the different ways he can incorporate it further into his life, and feels excited.

But after his first therapy session, Elliot trudges through snow back to Dom's, where he is staying on the sofa. He can't help but feel a warm glow as he thinks about his friend. Dom has never expected anything of him, and yet is always willing to give. Their relationship was never transactional. He decides to tell him when he gets back what he has thought for a long time, that he is his best friend.

His mind whirls with thoughts and feelings, and for a second his own future feels unknown in a good way. For a brief moment he can see how, it is possible, probable even, that he will feel whole all by himself.

Epilogue

It will be a day hot enough that Elliot can't find anything he likes to wear because his style does not thrive in hot temperatures. He will try not to care because he won't want to focus on such petty things, but he will fail. He will want to be in the moment, rather than in his own mind, because he has spent so long learning to do so.

Or it might be a day in the depths of winter. A coat that embarrasses him but he has finally bought simply to keep warm. Essentially it is going to be a day that Elliot is aware of the weather because of how it impacts him. And everything will impact him, on this day. Every detail will be over-thought despite his best efforts. Because it's the day when he sees Noa.

And this day will come, it doesn't matter how or when. It might be nine months or two years later but it is inevitable.

At first Elliot will hope that he'll bump into Noa. Or that they will be thrown together somehow, like the world had done to them twice before. He will even practise his expression for this eventuality; the perfect balance between nonchalant and pleased. But he will remind himself that there is no need to practise such things anymore, because whatever comes naturally is fine, is *best*.

But after a while Elliot will realise that it isn't necessary to meet Noa in such a serendipitous way. In fact, asking to see her would be the most accurate way to convey his feelings. Because he will *want* to see her, after all.

He will message her something like:

Hey Noa

Want to meet up for a catch-up?

And he will probably cringe at something, his double use of the word 'up' or a typo, for instance. Noa will reply something like:

Does the pope wear a pointy hat?

And Elliot will smile so brightly at his phone that Dom will ask him who the lucky woman is. Elliot, grateful for his smiles by then, will reply, 'Noa.'

And Dom will fold his arms and raise his eyebrows and say, 'Oh yeah?'

And Elliot will say, 'It's not like that.' And he will be right.

Elliot will just want to see her large smile and bouncy energy and listen to her talk at speed about all the things she's thought and felt and done but also – and newly – tell her what *he* has done.

When he eventually sees Noa – with her hair, even bigger than usual and shorter, chin-length or maybe even over the ears – his own ears will become hot as she strolls towards him and squeezes him into a hug. But as soon as she says something like, 'Oh my God, someone on the Tube just sneezed on my neck and I said sorry to *them*!' Elliot will laugh and relax.

Noa will ask what Elliot has been up to and wait with a sense of excited trepidation, like she is about to find out results for an exam. She will have almost no idea of the answer and her heart will hurt at the breadth of possibility. Has he been okay? Is he doing better? Is he doing worse? Has he asked her here to tell of a fiancée or serious illness?

Elliot will seem shy and confident, like he always did, but the proportions will be different by then. He will seem keen to talk about himself in a way she's never seen before, something in the way he will be enriching his stories with details or the eye contact or the unusually big smile on his face.

He will tell her, 'I've been getting my coaching badges. For football. I'm loving it.'

She will respond, 'Wow! What does a coaching badge let you do? Or is that a stupid question? Really cool though.'

'Cheers. It means I can coach any age group in football – once I get the badges. Right now I'm coaching a group of teenagers and I deffo want to stay with them. I've had this idea—'

Noa might notice Elliot's face drop or a quick bite of the nails or a look into the distance and she will take the opportunity to encourage him, in a subtle way. It doesn't matter how much time has passed, she still knows that pushing him only makes him want to retreat further into himself.

'Sounds great. Are you at a point where you can talk about the idea? Or is it still a work in progress?'

'It's barely even that. It's just football has always been one of the best things for my mentality… mental *health*, sorry' – it's taken him a while to get used to the vocabulary – 'but at the same time all it did was distract me. Rather than addressing or even acknowledging the problems.'

'That's such a good point!' Noa will be overwhelmed to hear him speak like this, pride not being a strong enough word; awe, maybe, elation. 'I never know which one is right. Like, should I be thinking things through or trying not to think at all?'

'Exactly. Well, I was thinking. . . it's probably a bit of both.' Elliot is going to look into Noa's shiny black eyes and feel the interest and encouragement in them. He won't doubt for a second the genuineness of her feelings. 'So the idea is to get young lads talking about their feelings. And also teaching them what kind of things they can do if they have problems. And then go and forget all about it on the pitch!'

'*Such* a good idea, Elliot.'

He will feel himself smiling broadly but won't push it away. In that moment he will want to tell her more but it is always hard for him to have complete faith that what he has to say is interesting. Noa might encourage him again or maybe he won't need that. Either way he is going to find the confidence to carry on. 'The younger generations are better than us lot already. But essentially I start by saying something I've felt that week and then they all go around saying something too. It can be good or bad or anything really, and anyone can respond. It doesn't have to be too deep. It's just about getting in the habit. And then I tell them, "Right, let's go think about nothing except football for two hours."'

'Are they reluctant to do it?'

Elliot might pinch his nose, worried about looking too pleased with himself, or he might not – life is a process, after all. 'Well, we're the best team in the league so they can go somewhere else and be beaten by us or they can win trophies and learn that it's fine to say, "It felt great to pass my German test this week."'

Noa will laugh and grin at her coffee or beer or ice cream and say what she's thinking: 'That's absolutely amazing. I'm so proud of you. You're going to make such a difference.'

Tears are going to threaten Elliot's eyes – ever since he's started crying again, they appear unexpectedly and easily at any emotion – but he will try not to be embarrassed.

334

Whenever Noa receives the message from Elliot, asking to see her, she will let herself be carried away, with the love she has for him, for the sparkling potential of their reunion, and then she will let the thoughts dissipate. Let them be just that – thoughts. Things that have come into her mind but are not to do with reality, are not predictions or objectives, not a perfect image that she should hold up and compare her own life to. And so when she meets Elliot she is present, ready to experience their meeting as it comes. No stakes. No preconceptions.

Elliot will ask her, 'What about you? Any news?' He will do a coach-like voice: 'Tell me something you've *felt* recently.'

Without the weight of moving towards a preconceived destiny she will be able to laugh and answer questions without thinking of the implications. 'Well, I've got Kevin, who makes me feel amazing every darn day. He's my whole world.'

For less than a second his name will hang in the air until Noa will clarify or Elliot will remember she is talking about her dog.

'What's so good about Kevin? Sell him to me.'

'Never!'

'I mean *verbally*.'

'I know, I know.' Noa is going to speak while scrolling through her phone trying to find the best picture and easily finding 'an amazing one' as, to Noa, they are all amazing. 'Well first of all, look at him!' Her phone will show a picture of a small grey dog with a long face, big eyebrows, moustache and a pompous attitude.

'Okay he *looks* 10/10 but I'm not a shallow guy. What else can he offer?'

'He can't *offer* anything. His life's purpose isn't to make our lives amazing. He just gives and receives unconditional love like it's easy.'

'Sounds like he takes after you.'

Noa will blush, Elliot's ears will probably go red, but mainly they will smile knowing it is true.

'The great thing about having a dog is that I do more wholesome things. Like often I'll go and get a pain au chocolat and walk down the canal, but I'm not on my own cos I'm with Kev.'

'Do you and Kev chat?'

'Just in the same way I chat with everyone, me speaking for an hour and them zoning in and out.'

'That's not true! People love speaking to you. *I* love speaking to you.'

'I know, I know.' And she will know.

Over this meeting Elliot is going to see proof of this new self-esteem; in the relaxed way she will take his compliments and how she will talk about the positive things in her life as much as the negative and neutral things, the way she will request something without a nervous glint in her eye.

Noa and Elliot will finish catching up and naturally move onto lighter and more current topics. The way a woman near them is telling her husband about a 'me me' that her grandchild showed her on the computer. The way a man is making a chip butty with three layers of bread. The large, mysterious red stain on the rug of the pub they are in. It could be anything.

It might be that Noa will say, '*Please* ask if you can have a free puppucino and then start eating it yourself near the counter.'

And Elliot might say, 'Only if you say to that man "You can go to the toilet if you like, I'll watch your laptop for you."'

Whatever it is, they will laugh.

(Look at these two, enjoying each other's company with such ease you'd think joy was a simple thing to come by. We could watch them chat for hours, because that is what's going to happen, of course. But there's no need. We know them by now, the kind of things they will talk about, the way they effortlessly interact as if it's an instinct in them; the desire they have to glean everything they can about each other's lives, the earnest passion for the other's well-being, the amusement of exploring and analysing the world around them together. They are going to stay in each other's lives, you'll be glad to know. How could they not? And there are many ways for this to play out, slight variations that feel so important to these people at the time, but are only coloured dots that make up a beautiful painting we can only see by standing back. These two are beginning to understand that to live a life rather than to watch it they have to focus on the flecks of paint, forget about their bigger picture, let their eyes blur, accept the chaos and uncertainty of where life will take them. And so the least we can do is join them, in this unknown.)

Acknowledgements

Thank you to my amazing agent Rachel Neely. An official Rising Star in the industry and a fully fledged superstar in my life! I don't know what I'd do without your endless support and talent. And thank you to the whole team at Mushens Entertainment.

Thank you to my brilliant editor, Clare Gordon, for being an absolute pleasure to work with. I'm extremely grateful that you instantly understood exactly what I was trying to do with this book and helped shape it to be the best version of itself. Thank you to everyone at HQ for all the hard work you put into my books behind the scenes: Becci Mansell, Francesca von Krauland, Grace Marshall, Caroline Oestergaard, Caroline Lakeman, Angie Dobbs, Halema Begum, Brogan Furey, Emily Scorer, Lauren Trabucchi and everyone else who has helped!

Thank you to Orly Greenberg, Katie Seaman, Chloe Michelle Howarth, Elvin James Mensah and Joe Gibson.

Thank you to my family: my mum, Suzanne, and sisters, Hannah and Charlotte, for being my first readers, constant cheerleaders and best friends.

Thank you to my husband Ben. I could fill a whole other book with all the things you have done for me while writing this novel.

But if I had to choose two, it would be for all the cups of teas and the laughs.

Thank you to the rest of my friends, family and pets for the myriad ways you inspire and encourage me.

Thank you to all the booksellers and bloggers who so passionately supported my debut. Thank you to all the readers who took a chance and spent their valuable time and money reading an author they'd never heard of. And to everyone who wrote to me saying the book meant something to you, those messages have been the highlight of this whole journey.

And lastly, thank you to Radiohead for providing the soundtrack to my life and more specifically for writing *In Rainbows* which is (unofficially) the soundtrack to this book.

ONE PLACE. MANY STORIES

Bold, innovative and
empowering publishing.

FOLLOW US ON:

@HQStories